KeALOHA
The Keeper

by

M. L. Kamahele

For my young editors, ages 7 - 12, who grounded me.
Mahalo Nui Loa.

[1. Fantasy – Fiction. 2. Witches – Fiction. 3. Wizards – Fiction. 4. Romance –
Fiction. 5. Historical – Hawaii. 6. Hawaii – Fiction. 7. Mythology – Hawaiian.
8. Hawaii Island (Hawaii) – Social life and customs. 9. Brothers / sisters – Fiction.]
ISBN 1-59971-328-4

Parental Note: This novel is based on true Hawaiian rituals and beliefs.
Therefore, some sections may require parental guidance
for children under the age of ten.

Summary: Neglected by a mysteriously dysfunctional family, a young girl with a
great destiny is hurled into the dark, exciting world of Hawaii's gods.

First Edition, January 2006

Hawaiian Pronunciation

Names

Kealoha	:	kay – ah – low – ha
Moho	:	mow – ho (as in "mow the lawn")
Anna	:	ah – nuh
Momi	:	mow – me
Pu-pele	:	pooh – pay – lay
Ailani	:	eye – lawn – ee
Manna	:	ma – nuh
Mano	:	ma – no
Tutu	:	too – too
Ku-hai	:	coo – high
Aikoa	:	eye – ko – uh
Kau	:	cow
Iki	:	ee – key
Waka	:	vah – kah
Moku	:	mow – coo
Kokala	:	ko – kah – lah
Hi'u	:	hee – ooh
Pahau	:	pa – how
Sanjiro	:	san – jeer – oh
Taro	:	tar – oh
Shoda	:	show – dah
Tadashi	:	tah – dah – she
Keawe	:	key – ah – vay
Kane	:	kah – neigh
Ku	:	coo
Lono	:	low – no
Kanaloa	:	kah – nah – low – uh
Wakea	:	vah – kay – uh
Haumea	:	how – may – uh
Pele	:	pay – lay
Hina	:	hee – nah

Hawaiian Pronunciation

Expressions

maile	:	my – lee	(perfumed dark green vine)
brah	:	bra	(local Hawaiian boy)
hoi hoi	:	hoy hoy	(glad, brisk)
ai	:	eye	(the, relative particle)
aloha	:	ah – low – ha	(hello, good-bye, love)
i'iwi	:	ee – ee – wee	(small red bird)
puka	:	pooh – kah	(hole)
shaka	:	shaw – kah	("How's it going?" hand signal)
mana	:	ma – nah	(power)
auwe	:	ow – way	(surprised exclamation)
tita	:	tee – dah	(local Hawaiian girl)
wahine	:	vah – hee – neigh	(woman)
baboose	:	bah – boose	(dummy)
bolo	:	bo – low	(bald)
hemo	:	hem – oh	(separated, peeling off)
ete	:	eh – tay	(misfit, no manners)
ho'o maka	:	ho – oh – ma – kah	(begin)
pau	:	pow	(finished)
tahuna	:	tah – who – nah	(expert practitioner)
akua	:	ah – coo – uh	(Hawaiian god)
mo'olelo	:	mow – oh – lay – low	(Hawaiian history)
ne'epu	:	nay – eh – pooh	(cross-legged sitting position)
noho	:	no – ho	(sit)
mai	:	my	(come)
keiki	:	kay – key	(children)
nui-akea	:	new – ee – ah – kay – uh	(power supreme)
loco-moco	:	low – ko – mow – ko	(local breakfast)
mimi	:	me – me	(urine)
haole	:	how – lee	(foreigner)
i'o	:	ee – oh	(flesh)
ho'opa'i	:	ho – oh – pa – ee	(punish, revenge)
ohana	:	oh – ha – nah	(family)
mahalo	:	ma – ha – low	(thank you)
heiau	:	hay – ow	(altar)
aumakua	:	ow – mah – coo – uh	(guardian spirits)
piko	:	pee – ko	(navel, belly button)
ehu	:	eh – who	(red haired Hawaiian)
lolo	:	low – low	(not right in the head)
kino	:	key – no	(body)
mo'o	:	mow – oh	(lizard)
kikiki	:	key – key – key	(to cheat)
hapa	:	ha – pah	(half)

Contents

One

The PAIRING , page 1

Two

The HOT DOG , page 21

Three

The BURNING GIFT, page 33

Four

The BREATHER in the CLOSET, page 52

Five

DON'T MOVE , page 74

Six

The LESSON , page 119

Seven

The RED HANDS , page 132

Eight

In the BEGINNING , page 147

Nine

KILLER , page 164

* Contents *

Ten

PELE'S HAIR , page 186

Eleven

The SHARK'S BITE , page 215

Twelve

The LAST ONE , page 232

Thirteen

LOLO , page 275

Fourteen

OHANA KeALOHA , page 287

Fifteen

TRAPPED , page 300

Sixteen

The FETCHER , page 313

Seventeen

MISPERCEPTIONS , page 334

KeALOHA
The Keeper

Chapter One

The PAIRING

Moho streaked down the autobahn – spraying fountains of grey water past his towering truck – shoving sluggish little cars out of his way. Some of the frightened drivers swerved and honked. Braver souls flashed their lights and hollered – but they only incited Moho more as he floored his vibrating, whining machine.

Today was the day! This one was for him!

White lightning bolts flashed beyond his hood and burst into brilliant scattered fray. Freezing rain pelted and smeared his windshield, and a hazy fog blurred what was left of his view. Driving conditions were dangerous for everyone – except Moho. He was in his element. Through gleaming mirrored shades, he peered at the fuzzy masses that hurled towards him and swam through them with ease.

Hawaiian drums and chants pounded through his massive body as he slid to a stop at the turnoff. He drummed the thick brown fingers of his right hand on the top of his steering wheel and nodded his dark, curly head in time with the beat. His enormous left hand gripped his hip, bunching the bottom of his tank top around his surfing shorts and forcing the bulging muscles in his arm to stand solid. His bare elbow pressed hard against the door, while his hairless left knee bounced up and down furiously. Looking at him, you'd never guess that three pretty little girls called him "Daddy" – and you certainly wouldn't guess that he belonged to a secret world, deep under the Hawaiian sea. But easily, you'd guess he was impatient.

Hurry up, he growled.

The sopping light changed. Quickly, he punched the gas and barreled down the center of the slick two-way street. But out of nowhere, something zigzagged in front of him and purposely blocked his path. It was a long, black BMW.

Moho couldn't believe it. Someone was foolish enough to block him!

Reacting with speed, he pushed his hunched back deep into the seat, bracing for probable impact, and jutted into the oncoming lane. Blaring cars streamed out of his way and sloshed onto the left shoulder. In no time, he was alongside the sedan. Feeling curious, he slowed down and looked in.

Inside was a swollen, red-faced man with a lit cigarette in his steering hand. His greasy brown hair poofed up in front, and his fat, wet lips mouthed widely what was most certainly profanity, while his left hand waved madly, punctuating each word. His fleshy cheeks puffed in and out as he swore, blasting the window with gusts of hot steam. He looked like a huge tooting blowfish – and Moho couldn't resist. He flashed his wild, toothy smile and jerked his wheel to the right, pretending to ram the sedan.

Immediately, the man started, and the BMW swerved – to the right, to the left, back to the right – and then spun out in a slippery orbit, grinding to a stop against a drenched brick building. Moho whizzed by laughing, *If you wanna play with the big dogs, you better learn to bite!*

As he approached the next dripping light, it turned red. He stiffened and sped through it, unscathed.

At the next light, a long line stood waiting. Without thinking, he

2

veered right, splashed down the shoulder and sliced a sharp, fishtailing turn. A metal-crunching crash sounded, but he couldn't stop to check the damage. If he did, the cops would realize that, at age twenty-seven, he'd never owned a license. Besides, he *needed* to be there – NOW!

He made a hard left and slammed on the brakes. A red and white guard rail blocked the hospital entrance. Annoyed, he frowned at it ... and then noticed. It wasn't raining here. He looked into his rearview mirror, back at the cross street. It *was* raining there.

Growing suspicious, he looked at the sky. It was grey and scattered with lazy, dark clouds that drifted slowly to the east. Below the clouds, a light German mist drooped carelessly to the ground. It seemed as though nothing was there, even though a rainless storm always marked the Demon's coming.

He began to look away – but suddenly, as if by command, all the dark clouds rushed together and whirled in an excited circle. Then, one by one, they jumped out of the circle and spiraled upwards – forming a tremendous spinning cone that stretched through the sky.

Immediately, anger burned Moho's chest. The Demon wasn't welcome!

The cone stopped traveling upwards and hung in the air for a moment. Then slowly, it descended. As it drilled toward the ground, it tilted and pointed at the hospital building – like a twisted black finger. At once, the sky boomed a horrible threat, and the finger jabbed at its prey.

The Demon's thunder vibrated hate through Moho's chest. He clenched his wheel and snarled, "Back off, Brah. This one is *mine.*"

Snapping his head down and to the left, he scowled at the parking ticket vendor. It reached into the street, insisting that he ask for a ticket. Seething, he slapped its protruding red button with his open palm – but nothing happened.

Quickly, rage boiled up his neck. The stupid thing wasn't working.

He slapped the button harder. Nothing!

Furious pressure shot to his head. That gate was still in his way!

He made a fist and pounded on it. Still – NOTHING!

His head exploded.

"ARRRRRRRR!" he roared, then floored the truck and plowed through the candy-striped barrier.

The loud, wrenching crunch and jarring force of annihilating his obstacle instantly relieved Moho's anger, and immediacy surged back into his brain. He'd been here three times before, and he knew exactly how to get there – FAST!

He gassed the truck, blasted through the crowded parking structure, careened around the doctors' stalls and hit the curb without braking. Expectedly, the truck caught air. Moho liked that. Mid-flight, he jammed the brakes, then slammed to the ground and skidded to a stop between two dark green Dumpsters. To the left was his destination – the blue double doors of the hospital's back entrance.

Happy to be there, Moho felt a surge of jitters. He couldn't wait! He swung open his door and dented the metal Dumpster with a loud, *Clang!*

Grunting in disgust, he squeezed out the door and whipped it shut behind him. He didn't lock it, though, nor did he take the keys. He didn't have to. No one would dare climb into his truck.

Facing the truck door, he leaned back a bit, his left hand squeezing his hip, and squinted at it, searching for damage. Luckily, there was none. His eyes skimmed down the side of his ominous four by four, and he admired it for a moment.

Its silver paint shimmered mysterious wet, and its huge deep-grooved tires shined wicked black. The front wheel suspension gaped much higher than the back, causing the truck to tilt up, open-mouthed. A fierce, beady shark eye glared on the front fender – and below it, a horrible jagged frown ripped down and around the wheel. Four long gill-like gashes cut through each door.

Moho smirked, thinking, *She's killer.*

He started to head round the Dumpster, but something inside, or maybe behind the truck, caught his eye. He leaned his head to the right and looked in from the back.

A yellowed shark jawbone, razor-sharp teeth intact, hung open from the rearview mirror. A twisted, dried clump of maile lei vines hung behind it. The ends of the vines reached up and spread through the mouth like shriveled, groping fingers. The long back window was splattered and smeared with blood-red stains. Two huge stickers were plastered on either side – they read, "Big Island" and "No Fear."

Moho smiled. When wet, the glass looked like glistening, red-spattered shark kill.

Turning abruptly, he tramped around and past the Dumpster, his huge flip-flops slapping loudly against the ground, and then hurried towards the hospital doors. But right before he got there, the evil stench of dead squid rotting in a pool of warm, runny feces swarmed in his nose. Knowing who came with that stench, he stopped cold and cursed in his head, *Man, I don't have time for you.*

With a wet sucking sound, like that of a stuck toilet plunger being pulled from a commode, a lanky blonde man popped out of the ground and stood casually on the stoop – his shoulder-length curls tumbling in his face. Despite the winter cold, he wore nothing except a boarskin loincloth – and oddly, his pasty white body glistened with sweat.

He jerked his chin up and greeted Moho with fierce blue eyes. His long, crooked, down-turned nose and sharp, jutting jaw seemed to intentionally point at his victim. He glared at Moho for a moment, the corners of his pouty pink mouth oozing with bluish-grey drool. Then slowly, his mouth curled up around sheared yellow teeth to reveal a childlike, devilish grin. His eyes crinkled with the smile and almost looked friendly. Holding out a clawed, bony hand, he said, "Brah."

Moho locked thumbs with the man, then wrapped his other fingers around the thumb's base, gripping it roughly as they shook hands.

"What's up?"

Without waiting for a response, Moho let go and breathed out to avoid the stink.

"Their time, Brah," sneered the man, bluish-grey saliva bubbling through his teeth. "It's almost up."

"Naah," corrected Moho, still refusing to breathe in as he watched the hateful spit foam. "This one's for me."

"You never when see the clouds?" the man said, peering at the darkened sky. "He's come for His Child ... and soon ... very soon ..." He trailed off into a greedy, open-mouthed cackle, his horrible teeth fully exposed. Bluish-grey spit stretched between the top and bottom fangs and blew in and out with each high-pitched wheeze. Then the man lunged forward, shoving his face into Moho's, and hissed, "We will have His supreme power!"

Spittle sprayed into Moho's face, stabbing through his cheeks and blinding him with hatred. By instinct, he grabbed the man by the throat and squeezed hard.

The child belonged to him and no one else!

Suddenly, a tawny, medium-sized dog came out from behind the man and interrupted with a short yelp. Her fur was steaming, and her brown eyes glittered with fiery flecks. Her tail swished slowly – back and forth, back and forth.

Moho looked down at the dog, and his anger floated out and away from him, just like the vapor off her fur. Then, her fiery eyes penetrated and massaged his brain. His entire body relaxed and his hand fell back down to his side. Willingly, he followed her tail with his eyes, knowing that it would soon hypnotize and enslave him in a seductive trance.

The dog pawed Moho's left foot timidly, and he smiled hazily at her in return. Anticipating what would come next, he closed his eyes to enjoy it.

Slowly and softly, she climbed up his legs with her front paws, until they rested on his stomach. Then, she threw back her head and stretched, longer and longer. As she stretched, she slowly transformed into a woman.

First, her paws spread into small, tanned hands, and then arms, that slid up and around his neck. At the same time, her pointed snout pulled in and flattened into a round, broad nose – then puckered below into a plump, heart-shaped mouth above a soft, chubby chin. Her shimmering cheek pushed gently against his chest as her face reached for and then nuzzled his neck. She murmured quietly as she wiggled against him, her upright ears melting into her nape. Then there was a loud, *Bang!* and at once, huge orange-red flames burst out of her head and a long beige fur coat whipped out behind her, caught in a sudden wind. Slowly, the flames settled into long, wavy golden-red hair that glimmered and flowed in its own gentle breeze – and the fur coat wrapped itself loosely around her. She squeezed Moho tight and squealed, "Brother, it's so good to see you!"

Moho wrapped his strong hands snugly around his sister and sighed. Then, gingerly, he lifted her off her feet and breathed in deep. He savored the sweet smell of lehua blossoms and ohia wood that floated through him, and snuggled into the softness and warmth of her body as it engulfed and smothered his cares. He took her in slowly, squeezing her supple, hot flesh through his fingers and burying his face in her tingly hair. It had been three years since they had last meet, and the feel of her was like home. He missed that more than anything and wanted to hold on to her ... forever.

Slowly, she pulled back, brushing her cheek up and against his.

Then, with downcast eyes, she touched her nose to his chin. Knowing what that meant, he reluctantly loosened his grip and placed her back on the ground. Her gleaming eyes looked up and locked onto him.

"How's my little girl?"

"Nothin' but trouble," he snorted, despite the pleasure he found in her hypnotic stare.

She threw her head far back and burst into a deep, throaty laugh. Moho felt like laughing with her, but she stopped before he could. She looked at him playfully and twinkled. He gazed back at her, a captive audience.

"Like mother, like daughter," she giggled.

As she spoke, a cold wind blew through them, whipping her fur coat up and away from her body. A cloud of vapor burst out of the coat before she could snatch it back down and around her.

"Brrrrrrrr," she shivered, her large round breasts jiggling under her folded arms. "Maybe if you get her outta this cold she'd be more ... da kine ..." She paused, searching for a word, then smiled, "Pleasing."

Moho was still transfixed on her, snug under her spell.

"Like you?"

She beamed, and then remembered why she came.

"Isn't it strange – this pairing?"

Moho didn't answer. She made him want to hold her again. So, frantically, he tried to think of ways to get her back.

Maybe if he ripped her coat off, she'd cower from the cold and jump into his arms. Naah, more likely, she'd scorch his face with a vengeful smack.

She seemed to read his mind and smiled up at him, coyly. He grinned back, hesitating, unsure if that was an invitation. She bent her knees slightly, as though ready to jump – and then flowed backwards a few steps, hips swaying.

Moho leaned forward to grab her – to keep her from getting away –

but she stopped and stood up, then pointed her straightened arms to the sky. Her coat shrunk down, fusing to her skin from her small wrists down to her broad, round hips. Then it flapped open at the thigh and exposed one long, curvy leg, bent at the knee. Her chubby toes pointed down to and touched the cold, hard ground.

Lightly, steam sizzled up from her toe tips and crawled over and around her knee. Then it puffed into a small white cloud that floated up and through her stiffened arms. She touched her hands together and formed a steamy arrow to the sky.

"Ai Kane – Ai Ku – Ai Lono – Ai Kanaloa," she began.

As she spoke, Moho heard the vibrating whine of a conch shell demand his motionless respect. Then vaguely, he heard heavy wooden gourds pound while deep masculine voices chanted, *Hoi Hoi ... Hoi, Ai ... Hoi Hoi ...*

The beat and chant grew louder and louder, till it shook his mind.

Suddenly, she began her fiery dance – and Moho stood mesmerized.

Her hips swayed widely, side to side, to and fro, as though ebbing waters pulled her in their whimsical direction. Her fingers waved over her swelling chest, spraying orange-red vapor from their tips as they passed. Her fluid arms flowed around her body, her golden-red hair splashing against them from all sides. She twirled to one side, and then the other, reaching out to him with open arms, pulling him closer and closer to her orange pool of fire.

Moho braced himself as the words that escaped her lips swam around and through his body.

She sang of home, and the pairing of opposites that defined their land. The cold, rigid mountain that stood in the middle and the warm, gentle ocean that flowed all around; the rising sun in the east and the setting sun of the west; the time of the gods in the night and that of man in the day; the erect male who stands high and the leaning female who stoops low. She sang of Ku and Hina – Kane and Kanaloa – Moho

9

and ....

Anna, Moho snapped out of his trance. *I need to go to Anna!*

Immediately, his sister stopped dancing and snatched her coat closed. She glared at him, angry that he'd taken away his attention.

The man, whom Moho had completely forgotten about, came from behind her, clapping and hooting loudly.

"Beautiful song, my child." His eyes ran up and down her figure greedily as he licked his dripping lips. "Breathtakingly beautiful."

Ignoring him, Moho grunted, "I've gotta go, Sis."

Now pouting, hands on her hips, she demanded, "Promise you'll come visit – soon."

Knowing better than to look her in the eye, lest she hypnotize him again, he looked at her bare feet and promised. Satisfied, she pressed her red, open lips against his cheek and licked him with her fiery tongue – a small punishment for baby brother's rudeness. Then, she whispered lovingly, "Aloha."

His singed face and feelings stung as he pushed through his two visitors and swung open the blue double doors. But as soon as he tromped over the step, the warm, sterile air of the hospital rushed over him, and his excitement returned.

This was it!

Moho knew the maternity ward sat on the fifth floor, but he wouldn't take the elevator. It was too slow, and the people on it always scattered and gawked, bulgy-eyed and trembling in the knees. It was like being trapped in a jar of live jellyfish! So, he bolted past the elevator and ripped open the stairwell door.

Taking the stairs four at a time, he dashed up five flights and burst through the hall door. He heard a short gasp, then a human thud and glass shatter, but he didn't stop – no one was yelling, and he had gotten used to this. Seemed like everywhere he went something broke. Either he was too big, or everything else was too small. He shoved his way through the swarming, white-clad shrimps, peering through the large birthing room windows as he passed.

In one, a skinny brunette with a sharp nose jabbed a long pointy bottle at a howling baby. Nope, that wasn't his.

In the next, a corpulent blonde sat sucking bon-bons, dripping white cream on a heavy pink bundle. That one wasn't his either.

In the next, a curly redhead sat with her knees up, pale and panting, her strained, white fingers buried in a screaming man's face.

Moho snorted. Good thing that one wasn't his!

Then suddenly, he was at the end of the row, and he hadn't seen her. Alarmed, he swung around to search again, and there she was, directly across the hall – his sweet little baby. She was propped up in her bed by a mountain of fluffy white pillows, her fine blonde hair smoothed across her forehead and tucked behind one dainty ear. Her clear blue eyes twinkled angelically, and her fresh white skin glowed.

Moho shivered. They'd been married for over five years, but to look at her still made him nervous.

He pushed his shades up on top of his head and tucked his shirt into his shorts, smoothing down the scratchy decal in front. Then he puffed out his vast chest – she seemed to like that – crossed the hall stiffly and pushed the door open with a shaking hand. He hoped she wasn't angry that he took so long.

She looked up and bit her pink bottom lip with her cute, perfectly straight, white teeth. She did this when she was upset – but she also did it when she was confused or had made a mistake ... and sometimes, when she wanted a kiss.

Worried, but hoping for the best, Moho swooped down and pressed his lips hard against her forehead. She was warm and tasted of sweet salty sweat. Moho really loved that.

She pulled away and tilted her head up, raising her thin arched eyebrows and lowering her tired lids. Her hair fell out of her face, exposing high, pink cheeks that shined with soft blonde fuzz.

"Hi, Baby," he grinned, still not sure if he was in trouble.

She smiled and opened her eyes.

Instantly, his heart skipped. This was a good sign!

"I'm glad you're finally here," she sighed.

Relieved, Moho chuckled inside. It was funny that a man of his size and demeanor was so afraid of such a small, sweet thing.

She lifted up a blue bundle and said proudly, "It's a boy."

Moho couldn't believe it. A boy – just what he wanted!

He ripped off the blankets and held him up high.

He was perfect, a bit scrawny, but perfect nonetheless! His black, ruffled hair was still wet, and his bright brown eyes were scrunchy. He held both tiny fists up in the air and yawned a little, round 'O' – and to Moho's delight, he had six teeny white teeth.

Moho flipped the baby into his open right palm, balancing the boy by the tummy. The cute little thing liked it and wiggled, happily.

Grinning, Moho lifted his right elbow way over his shoulder, so that it pointed at the ceiling, and brought his son up under the crook of his arm. He looked at the boy's little face, which was now just inches from his, and his chest tickled with pride. Quickly, he muttered, "Hele mana o Ka-moho-ali'i i ka keiki o mano kumupa'a."

"Her eyes are black," Pu-pele complained from the other end of the bed.

Moho snapped around and sure enough, there lay another baby. She was on her back, with her head pointing to the foot of the bed. Her dark, empty eyes rolled away from her three sisters, all of whom sat above her.

Moho's skin crawled as he stared in disbelief.

Four-year-old Pu-pele sat directly above the baby, straight-backed

12

and cross-legged, with both brown hands tucked under her left shin. She was leaning far forward (to get the best view of the baby, no doubt) causing her long, light brown curls to form a mobile of glimmering ringlets above the motionless baby's head.

Momi, the eldest at five-years-old, sat on Pu-pele's right, leaning back on her large hands, legs straight out in front of her, ankles crossed. She tapped her big right foot vigorously against her left, causing the bottom of the bed to vibrate. The wooden chopstick that was stuck through her tight blonde bun rapped noisily against the steel bedpost.

The littlest, three-year-old Ailani, sat curled up in a ball on Pu-pele's left. Her feet were tucked snugly under her bottom, and her white chin was shoved deep into the bed. Her straight black hair hung down the side of the sheet as she gently, but methodically, stroked the baby's fingers, mouthing, "One, two, three, four, five. Hmm. One, two, three, four, five ..."

"They're always that color, dummy," answered Momi.

Fear crawled off Moho's skin and into his stomach. There it churned, his stomach refusing to digest it.

This couldn't be true. This wasn't how it was supposed to happen!

"She looks weird – like dead," insisted Pu-pele.

"She's just new ... and tired. They all look like that," quavered Anna.

"No. Ailani was purple and wiggly – and she screamed the whole time," corrected Momi.

"I can make her scream," grinned Pu-pele. Her numerous curls barely concealed the devious gleam in her dark green eyes.

Moho flexed his stomach muscles and squeezed away denial, allowing the truth to smack him in the face.

He had been tricked!

Momi arched both of her wide brown eyebrows, squinted her blue eyes from the bottom only, and took her first look at the baby. Quickly, she announced, "Nothing's wrong with her. She's just ugly." Then she

13

jumped off the bed with the loudest thud she could conjure with her big, clumsy feet and stomped through the bathroom door, slamming it hard behind her. The baby girl didn't move, and Pu-pele noticed. She leaned in close, her lips almost touching the baby's ear, and hollered, "Are you deaf?"

"Pu-pele!" cried Anna.

"Look! She didn't move. She's deaf – and blind."

Moho's face stung with anger. There weren't supposed to be two – only one ... for him – and then panic gripped him. Which one was his?

"Who came first?" he blurted.

"The boy," whispered Anna.

Whew, he thought. Then he looked back at the other one with disgust. He didn't want it – now or ever – and he most certainly wouldn't keep it.

"I know you only wanted four ..." quivered Anna.

Moho looked down at her. She was biting her lip again, but this time tears pooled in her eyes. His heart and chest sank. He couldn't stand it when this happened. Nothing stung more than seeing his baby cry. Quickly, he sat next to her and lied.

"Oh Baby ... four ... five ... what's the difference? I like her, *really*. I just was surprised, you know ... no one said anything ..."

He groped for the right thing to say, because he knew – if he didn't get it right early on, she'd never recover – or forget. Running a blank, he defaulted to a proven complement.

"She's beautiful ... like you."

Anna smiled a little, so he knew he was off to a good start. Looking hopeful, she asked, "Really?"

He always felt guilty about lying to her, even though he did it often, but she meant everything to him, and he *had* to keep her ... happy.

So, he hid what he was ... and how he felt – and he hid it very well.

"Really, Baby," he breathed through curled lips. "She's perfect ... and

I'm so glad we've got her."

Anna's eyes looked dull, so he knew he had to come up with something better – more adamant. Buying time, he leaned forward to kiss her, and it came to him.

"Already, I can't imagine being without her."

That did the trick. Anna lit up and hugged him tightly. Thankful, Moho squeezed her back and thought, *This is the nicest place in the world.*

"Tante Theresa!" Pu-pele squealed.

Pu-pele hopped into her aunt's arms, knocking an armful of presents to the floor. Momi bolted out of the bathroom, without wiping, flushing or washing, and stood right next to the fallen gifts. Ailani slid off the bed and began separating the packages by name. They were all, of course, for the girls.

Moho tried not to groan as he let go of Anna and stood to greet his sister-in-law. The rest of her family had disowned Anna the day they eloped – because she was fourteen and he wasn't white – so it was always difficult for him to meet her sister, Theresa, even though he liked her a lot.

Theresa was twenty-eight years older than Anna, and from her fancy clothes and impeccable style, you could tell she had lots of money and time. Her pink Chanel hat matched her pink Chanel shoes, that went perfectly with her pink Chanel suit. And her pink Chanel bag matched the pink, curly bows that wrapped prettily around her shiny, pink wrappings. Of course, her lips, cheeks and chin were pink, too. But her short, curly hair was silver, and at times, Moho would swear it was blue.

"I hope you like it," said Theresa, as she handed a flat, pink package to Anna. Anna smiled and opened it carefully. Inside was a wooden picture of an angel hovering over two children – a girl and a boy – as

15

they walked across a broken bridge. The different colors of the picture were not painted. Instead, they were different-colored pieces of wood that were cut to fit snugly against one another, like a puzzle. Moho thought it was beautiful – the way Catholics thought of the world.

"Thank you," beamed Anna. "It's beautiful."

"Ooooh, and so is she," cooed Theresa, as she picked up and cuddled the baby girl. "Her eyes are so deep and round, like Einstein's, and her hair is wonderful – red on black."

Theresa rocked and adored the baby for a moment, and then gushed, "Oh, Anna, she looks like the wisest of autumn's angels!"

Anna beamed brighter, but that's what Moho expected. She always beamed the brightest when Theresa was around.

"And we've another – a boy!" bragged Anna.

She looked up at Moho, very proudly – and then frowned, her eyes darting around him. Moho looked back at her, stumped for a second, and then it hit him.

He dropped the baby!

Frantic, he fell to his knees and looked under the bed. It wasn't there. He grabbed at the sheets. It wasn't there either. He rifled through the mountain of pillows. It wasn't there either.

"Look Tante, I've got a brother," grinned Pu-pele, bouncing the little bundle that slept safely in her arms.

Moho glared at her. The little thief stole the baby when he wasn't looking.

"He's beautiful, Pu-pu," smiled Theresa. Then she tapped Pu-pele's nose with one finger saying, "You take good care of him."

Looking back at Anna, she asked, "What's his name?"

"Mano!" boomed Moho.

Theresa jumped, but she didn't blink. She had grown accustomed to the strange Hawaiian names, and one would have thought Moho said something German, like "Wolfgang!" instead.

"And the girl?"

Moho didn't respond, even though Anna looked up at him for the answer. He had named all the other children, but he wasn't going to name that one.

"We haven't decided," Anna recovered sweetly.

"How about Manna – for Anna with an M?" smiled Theresa.

Moho hated it – apparently she didn't know what that word meant. But Anna giggled and looked back at him.

"Yes, Anna with an M – for Moho."

Moho felt himself smile back. It was nice to think about he and Anna together, even if it was because of that ... thing.

Moho sat up, awake in bed again. He was always full of energy and bouncing – his knee, or his leg, or his foot – so he never needed to sleep. But Anna slept all the time. It hadn't taken him long to figure out that if he wanted to maximize his time with her, he had to stay in bed. It seemed to work well for them both, anyhow. He liked holding her relaxed, breathing body and stroking her sweet-smelling hair. And she liked the way that he and the bed vibrated. She said it lulled her to sleep.

The clock above the bed ticked off the seconds with a faint, steady rhythm, while the breath of his children filled the spaces in between. It was almost like being at the beach, with gentle waves patting the shore and an ocean breeze kissing his ears. Completely at ease, he leaned his head back against the wall, and thought.

It wasn't so bad ... about the baby. After all, she wasn't the *real* problem – it was the next that would wreak havoc. Perhaps she would just keep to herself. But he'd have to find a way to get Anna to separate the two. With the matching name thing, she had gotten the idea that they would be a matching pair – inseparable. So, to his dismay and her delight, Pu-pele had put the twins in a crib together.

Moho glanced at the crib, which stood to the left of the bed. His son lay right next to that thing, with barely an inch between them. He didn't want it to touch his boy, but he hated to let go of his wife. He wondered.

If he kicked the crib, would they roll apart?

He lifted his foot to take aim, but froze.

Mixed with his family's breathing was a soft rustling sound – that made the hairs on the back of his neck stand tall and shiver.

Moho looked down, and there it was – a shapeless black shadow that glided across the floor and spread wide, fluttering at the ends like a dark cloak. It slid past his sleeping daughters and crept up the side of the crib. Once at the top, it slowly rose and rippled in the air, like a shadowy flag marking its territory. Then, it curled and spun around itself ... slowly at first, then faster and faster. Suddenly, it expanded into a large twisting cone that thrust forward and stabbed at the baby girl.

"MOHOOOOOO!" shrieked Anna, as she lunged for the crib.

Moho snatched her back into the bed and pinned her down. At the same time, the cone vanished.

"It's not real," breathed Moho.

"It killed her!" cried Anna, as she struggled helplessly against his weight.

"It was a dream, Baby. Nothing's there. Look," he jerked his head towards the crib. "Nothing."

Shaking, she looked over.

"I'll check her," he whispered. "Don't get out of the bed."

Moho got up, and naturally, she obeyed. She had these kinds of nightmares often, and always, nothing was there – because Moho could get rid of anything.

Blocking Anna's view, he stood above the crib and peered at the baby. His stomach flipped when he saw her.

She was covered with quivering white maggots that slimed over her body and squirmed in her face. Her eyes were wide open, staring up as if mortified – and her lips were pressed tightly together, almost as if she knew they would slither down her throat if she let them. Some of the worms slipped down her sides and formed a wet, wiggly pool around her.

Moho looked at the pool and didn't like it – the worms were much too close to his son. He wrapped both hands around the girl's chest and lifted her up, being careful not to slop any worms on his boy. Then he pressed her to his chest and covered her back with her wet blanket. Turning to Anna, he groaned, "She's okay. She just spit up. I'll wash her."

Anna bit her lip again. She looked embarrassed about her mistake, and it made him want to kiss her, but he couldn't – some of the worms might fall out. Abruptly, he turned, tramped into the bathroom, and flicked on the light.

He dropped the baby into the basin and turned on the cold water. The blanket clogged the drain, and the sink began to fill – but strangely, the baby didn't budge as the frigid water splashed over, and then consumed her.

First her legs, then her tummy, then her face went under. As the water rose, so did the maggots. They floated and wiggled to the top, then quickly skimmed down the upper drain.

Awed by the baby's serenity, Moho looked closely at her submersed face.

Her large sullen eyes stared quietly behind long black lashes that fanned up and touched her dark arched brows – and her round chubby cheeks flushed bright red, but her small pudgy nose stayed tan. Her reddish-black hair floated gently around her face, and her hands bobbed, limp, to the surface – and Moho thought it peculiar that she didn't struggle for air. Even a kitten would claw its way to the top.

How come something so powerful lay still?

19

Then slowly, her dark red lips parted. A tiny bubble escaped and swam to the top. It popped – and that's when he knew.

He would drown her.

"MOHO!"

It was Anna. Panicking, Moho grabbed the baby and dragged her out of the water.

Did she see? Did she know what he was doing? Oh Kane, what was she going to do?

Anna's shoulders sagged with exasperation.

"That's not how you wash a baby – it'll drown, or catch a cold! Look at her ... she's shivering!"

Moho exhaled loudly, his heart still racing. Without thinking, he shoved the baby towards Anna and let go. Luckily, Anna caught her before she hit the ground.

Anna held her up awkwardly and instructed, "Use a towel."

Moho grabbed a white towel off the rack and began dabbing it hard on top of the baby's head.

"I can do it," offered Pu-pele, from outside the bathroom door. Her green eyes glinted in the bright bathroom light, and her round face shone with mischief.

Looking grateful, Anna handed her the baby – and Moho wondered, *How long has she been there?*

Pu-pele plucked the towel from his hand, plopped down on the toilet seat, and laid the baby in her lap. Then rubbing it firmly, she puckered out her lips and baby talked, "Bad baby. If you spit, you won't be fed."

Moho knew she meant it – and he had a burning feeling that she knew *he* meant it, too.

Chapter Two

The HOT DOG

Manna's heart was racing. She had to move fast. If she got caught sneaking out of school, she surely would be punished. And it wouldn't be something quick and easy, like spankings with paddles or rulers on hands. No, Momi was much crueler. She'd torture you slowly with something insipid that would agonize any kid – like making you go to school, all day long, five times in a week!

Manna's quick blue shoes crunched hard against the grey, packed snow as she tore through the playground and towards the hill that guarded the wrought iron fence. Gasps of freezing air pierced her bursting lungs and stabbed needle-sharp icicles through her flittering heart, but she was determined to escape. She gritted her teeth, clenched her flying fists and dug in with her heels.

Over the hill, she caught sight of her fleeing sisters. They were already scaling the fifteen-foot gate, leaving her far behind. Panic shot through her heart.

She had to go faster! She had to catch up!

She put her face down and focused on the blur of her pounding tan knees.

Go, go, go! she willed them. *Faster, faster!*

CLANG-G-G-G!

She hit the icy black gate at full speed. Her head jammed through its rungs, and her body smashed, vibrating and pinned, against them.

"Stop it," snapped Momi, from up in the air.

Manna froze. Nothing hurt, except her hungry lungs. She gulped air and guessed.

Her heavy coat must have buffered her body, and her stiff shoes clanged that sound. Relieved, she exhaled completely, turned to the side, and slipped through the cold slat prison.

On the other side, she twirled around instinctively, to check on her brother. As usual, he was stuck between bars – but he wasn't scared. He never got punished.

"Move it, fatty," barked Momi, now on the ground.

Manna looked up and there was Pu-pele, tottering on top of the arched gate. Her arms were on one side, her legs on the other, and her wide bottom smiled at the sky. Bouncy corkscrews tumbled off her red, upside-down face, as she wiggled and piped, "Stuff it, chimney."

Manna looked back at her brother. Pu-pele could take care of herself, but this one was practically useless. His head and one arm dangled through the rungs, on her side of the fence, while his feet stay planted on the other – and he was flopping about like a fish in a net, trying to set himself free. She scrunched her nose at his wild hair. It stood on end, except in the front, where it stuck to his forehead, all sweaty.

Hurrying, lest Momi blame *her* for *his* delay, she grabbed his slimy hair in one hand and his bony arm in the other, and pulled with all her might.

Blam! - "Oof!"

Mano landed on her, and Pu-pele on him – and they both thought it was funny. Pu-pele jiggled, spread-eagle on her back, and gurgled her thick throaty laugh, as Mano jerked wildly in Manna's face, spewing his high-pitched guffaw.

Manna lay squished and squinting, shocked to be under the pile. Her brother's huge bobbing head sprinkled cold sweat in her eyes, and his round, flared nose blew gusts of mirth onto her lips. His only crooked, stick-out tooth jabbed at her chin and tickled her in the tummy. Quickly, she popped into giggles.

"Shut up, stupid, or we'll get caught," growled Momi. Her long blonde head loomed way above them.

"Oh, loosen your bun, bunchy," quipped Pu-pele, scrambling up with a toss of her golden-brown curls.

Manna grinned silently. Pu-pele was right. Momi's waist-length hair *was* screwed on too tight, in a double-twisted knot that tugged hard on her face. It stretched her long brown brows past her pale forehead, and slanted her flashing blue eyes way up. Manna liked to pretend ... and Momi was usually the sea witch.

"Let's go – NOW!" hissed Sea Witch.

Manna shoved off her brother and jumped to her feet. This was the best part of her day, and she wanted to get started.

Following Sea Witch, she skipped along the cold, grey concrete, throwing her feet up high. Biting winter winds sheared her naked legs, and her stiff leather shoes jabbed her frozen bare feet – but she didn't care. Kindergarten was full of white meanies that called her names and yanked her hair, so it was fun to be free. Sea Witch didn't bother her, either. She was the one that always made them leave school three hours early, and Manna knew – no one else's mom would let them do that.

Manna gazed at the shiny silver buildings that guarded the path, and the shimmery grey sky that misted the air. Together, they formed a glimmering maze, and she was the fearless red I'iwi bird that darted through it, searching for the stolen treasure that belonged at the rainbow's end – a dazzling ruby-studded egg filled with magical, colored candies that tasted of love and happiness ... forever.

She flapped her arms up and down, and jumped into the air.

"Ow-w."

It was Mano. He was standing too close again, and she bonked him on the head. But that was okay – he was the hungry, spitting caterpillar that was trying to beat her and horde the sweetest egg. He raised one hand to his head, and the other to the air, then spit at the birds on the wire. Three fell down, dead.

"Take one," said Pu-pele, suddenly in front of them and opening her magic black bag.

Manna stopped flying and peered inside. At the bottom were two white wursts dripping with sauerkraut and mustard. She wished she could have one.

Caterpillar grabbed the biggest one and crunched it down. Pickled grass sprung from his huge mouth, and yellow bug juice dripped down his chin.

Manna pouted, her short reddish-black bob blowing off her neck. He always got more than her, because he was the boy ... but not this time. She put both hands up to her shoulders and fluttered them – fast.

She would get to the egg first!

"Hurry up!" hollered Momi.

Manna glanced back, still flitting her wings.

As usual, Ailani was a block behind, playing her game, "Don't Step on a Crack or You Have to Go Back ... All the Way to the Beginning."

Manna didn't like that game. Only perfect people could finish.

Caterpillar spit again and knocked the antennas off two passing cars.

"This is it," said Momi, sucking on her cigarette. She flicked the butt to the ground and blew a sharp trail of smoke out of her mouth, stabbing her short Turkish boyfriend in the face. He smiled hazily and stared at her neck with wide glassy eyes.

Manna wondered why boys liked to watch Momi smoke. It made her look like a curd-snorting bull, and it coated her square buckteeth with a yellowing stench that spumed forth whenever she screamed. Why would anyone want to play "How Many Cigarettes Can You Die on Today?"

Ailani caught up and Momi clipped, "Get lost."

The boy looked hurt and confused, so Manna tried to help out.

"Give her the pack," she chirped, her little wings buzzing.

"Shut up!" snarled Momi. Then she snatched the boy's cigarettes out of his hand and tromped across the tracks. Her short pleated skirt flipped up in her wind and exposed worn grey panties.

Quickly, Ailani crossed the tracks close to Momi, careful not to touch them or lose count of her steps.

"Three-hundred-seventy-four, three-hundred-seventy-five ..."

The boy's face and shoulders sagged for a moment. Then, he shoved his fists into his pockets, turned, and shuffled away.

Manna knew how he felt ... to be treated so cruelly by someone you wanted to please. No matter how hard she tried, her father treated her like a roach, avoiding her and yelling whenever she got near.

Manna smiled. The boy was lucky. He got away.

Looking both ways, she hummed over the tracks and flew to the trolley platform. Then she noticed – Caterpillar was gone. She turned around, and sure enough, he was putting rocks on the tracks again, hoping to see some sparks.

In school, Caterpillar spent recess stuffing rocks in his clothes – that's why he always got stuck in the fence – and on the way home, he would throw them at cars, and people, and birds. His aim was amazing (pinpoint precision). He could knock down three birds with a single shot, right out of the air, and he could trip Momi's boys by shooting round stones, quietly, under their heels.

Knowing better than to leave him behind, she fluttered back and pulled him up by the sleeve.

"Come on."

RUH!

A tall yellow train whizzed by, an inch from Caterpillar's back. The ground trembled and steamy wind blasted Manna's face. Hot white sparks exploded at her feet and crackled up to her ears. She gasped, her heart in her throat.

"Did you see that?" beamed Caterpillar, his eyes sparkling.

"No, and neither did you," she breathed back.

Ever since she could remember, everyone said she had to take care of "the boy" – and he made it hard. He was clumsy, and reckless, and didn't always follow ... and never ... never was he serious.

She frowned. He was too much trouble.

Immediately, Caterpillar's innocent brown face dulled and his flashy smile fell.

Oh well, she thought, *at least he always listens.*

Grabbing his rough hand, she dragged him over the tracks and onto the wooden trolley platform.

"Ta da!" gleamed Pu-pele, suddenly in front of them, her bag wide open.

Pu-pele's game was "Now You See It, Now You Don't," and she was really good at it. Anything she wanted would mysteriously vanish, then pop, show up in her bag.

Manna peeked in. The bag was stuffed with candies – rainbow-colored, square ones with chocolate swirled inside – and each one had a different picture, of a girl, or a boy, or a baby animal, painted and baked in the middle. Manna leaned forward and breathed in their fragrant syrupy smell. She could almost taste them, but knew she wasn't allowed.

Smiling greedily, Caterpillar grabbed a bursting handful and stuffed it in his huge gaping mouth. His bloated cheeks bumped out as he chomped them down. Then licking his stained, wet lips, he grabbed for more.

Manna's nose stung. Caterpillar got to the egg first ... again. She put her little wings over her head, squinched her eyes, and promised herself, *One day, I'iwi Bird will win.*

Swinging her bag, Pu-pele flowed past Ailani, who was squatting on her feet in the middle of the stop, rocking back and forth, humming. Pu-pele dropped a few candies in front of her sister, but they went unnoticed.

"Move it!" bellowed Momi.

Quickly, Manna grabbed her brother's shirt and dragged him onto the trolley.

This was the funnest part – and she wanted to get to it!

Manna had to time it just right. You could only slip out at the stops, and you had to do it when no one was looking. She stretched taller in front of the emergency exit and held her coat open wider, hoping no one would see what Mano was doing.

With a soft clank, he unlatched the door. Then slowly, he creaked down its handle until it snapped. Holding her breath, Manna listened to her pattering heart and waited.

At once, straining metal brakes screeched and the trolley shuddered to a stop. Most of the passengers stood up and hurried off the train.

Manna spun around and breathed, "Now!"

Quickly, they shoved out the door, jumped onto the narrow car coupling, and clanged the door shut behind them. Then giggling with excitement, they scurried up the back of the tall front car and lay facedown on the roof.

Manna's heart was pounding. She clutched the electric trolley pole with both hands, right above Mano's, and pressed her chin against the slick steel roof.

Suddenly, the car jerked, and they were off.

Titillating wind raged past Manna's face, howled over her ears, and whipped through her scattering hair. Rapid, it shivered down her neck, splashed over her body, and swiped between her wiggling heels. Rattling, the roof vibrated excitement through her chest and tickled her bouncing brain.

Dizzy from the thrill, Manna squeezed the frosty pole tighter and it showered white fairies around her in response. The tingly fairies shocked her wet face, and then fizzled into shimmery sparks of blue.

"Wee-ee!" she squealed into the wind.

"Woo-hoo!" Mano hooted back.

Manna laughed. Nothing, no nothing, was better than this.

"Save me!" a little voice cried from behind.

Manna glanced back. Nothing was there. She looked at Mano. He grinned back at her with red, wind-stripped eyes.

Facing forward, Manna squinted stubbornly at the wind. Sometimes she heard voices, telling her to do things, but they weren't real and she didn't have to listen.

"Help me," the tiny voice whimpered. "I'm scared."

Dread clutched Manna's heart and it stopped.

What if this voice *was* real? What if someone was hurt ... or falling ... under the train? Maybe she should check the couplings. It sounded like it was coming from there.

"Manna, pleeease," the voice pleaded. "I need you."

A howling wind suddenly whipped around Manna, chilling her taut insides. She shivered. It must be real. It called her by name ... and it needed her – now!

She loosened her grip on the pole, trembling from fingers to toes. The wind whirled furiously, but didn't pull her away.

"Hurry," urged the voice.

Panting with fear, she squeezed her eyes shut and let go of the pole. Frigid air sliced under her body and the trolley jolted from side-to-side, but she stayed put.

Trying not to think, she flattened her palms against the roof of the train and shimmied backwards to the end of the car. Then, biting her bottom lip, she got up on her knees and peeked over the edge.

BAM!

Something hit her from behind and knocked her off the car. With a wrenching thud, she hit the cold, hard ground and everything went black. Then, with a lurch, the ground opened up and swallowed her!

Black sheet rock bulleted past her face, blasting hot steam over her cheeks and pricking pins through her nose. Scorching air seared past her body and slammed her back into jagged darkness. At once, the earth moaned and closed tightly around her, hurtling her deeper and deeper down its throat.

Dazed and confused, Manna slid down the dark tunnel without struggling – until she noticed ... her feet were burning. She jerked her knees up and looked down.

Two orange-red eyes, burning with hate, were coming at her from below.

A goblin! cried Manna. *It's a goblin! And it's going to eat me – ALIVE!*

Panicking, she tried to scramble away, but the horrible thing reached up, clawed her in the gut, and pulled her down to its hungry mouth.

"NOOOOOOOO!" she shrieked, as she tore at its bony fingers and kicked its evil eyes. "DON'T ... EAT ... ME!"

Suddenly, the lights went on. Train tracks hammered past Manna's contorted face, less than an inch from her nose. Stiffening, she grasped the rigid fingers that clutched her tummy.

It wasn't a goblin. It was Mano.

He had tumbled off the trolley, knocking her down to the coupling, and then clung to her, scared, through the tunnel.

Recovering quickly, Manna wondered, *What were those eyes?*

Careful not to touch the slashing ground, she squirmed up and looked past her brother. Just below his feet hung a darling brindled pup, clinging to the coupling with fuzzy speckled paws. Its big brown eyes blinked, helpless, and its pink, wet nose twitched, scared – but when it saw Manna it smiled and stuck out a cute red tongue – then it wagged its short bushy tail. Manna tingled with instant love and cried, "A puppy! For me!"

She reached down to get it, but at that moment, Mano slipped and shoved his clumsy boot into the pup's face. Startled, the pup lunged forward and tried to grab Manna's hand with its teeth, but fell. With a sickening yelp and curdling boom, it slipped under the train and exploded. Red steam sprayed out from under the car, and the train screeched to a halt.

Manna gasped in horror, but Mano didn't care. He grabbed her hand and bolted. This was their stop and he needed to keep up with the others.

Manna wanted to cry. She trudged down the cobblestone street, clinching her little fists and fighting back tears.

He ruined everything – because he was the boy. The special boy ... that got everything. All the attention. All the praise. All the happy things.

She sucked on her bottom lip.

It was all his fault. He was the reason she was nothing but an extra girl.

Snuffles quivered in her throat.

He was the reason that no one needed her – except that puppy, and he had to ruin that, too.

Tears burned her nose.

It just wasn't fair. Why didn't his tummy ache because no one wanted him? Why didn't his chest burn because nobody loved him?

Mano bumped into her and mumbled, "Sorry."

Manna frowned at him. There wasn't anything special about an awkward, skinny boy. Bitter, she squeezed back a tear and wished she wasn't there.

They were home.

Momi threw her bag onto the concrete step and growled, "Do it." Then grunting, she rolled down her skirt, buttoned up her blouse and tightened her jacket around it.

Manna frowned deeper. The problem with going to the best school in town was ... you had to wear uniforms. That way, all the children were equal – uncomfortable, hot and grumpy.

Manna knew her woolen, blue-plaid suit was thoughtfully planned for Germany's mushy weather, because it fit like a tight, itchy sock and when it got wet, it shrunk down two sizes too small, squeezing and trapping you in it. Certainly, an evil boa woman had designed them to smother small children – but that was okay. Momi said they didn't have to wear them, except when they left for ... and came home from ... school.

Pu-pele worked quickly. She dumped out Momi's bag, sorted the clothes and passed the piles to the children.

Manna picked up her woolen hose and kicked off her shoes. Carefully, she stretched the hose over her legs, trying to keep its prickly needles off her skin as long as possible.

Mano grunted and squirmed next to her. Pu-pele, who was already dressed, had tightened his thick woolen tie and was wresting his shrunken cap onto his head. Roughly, she pinched both of his cheeks to give him a little color. His eyes popped out and he howled, close-mouthed.

Manna almost felt sorry for him – but couldn't. She was next.

31

Pu-pele smashed a woolen beret over Manna's head. It squeezed every thought out of her brain. Then, she choked on a wide bow tie. Manna sat up straight and tried to get air. Next, she buttoned the stifling jacket and Manna exhaled hard, trying to ignore Pu-pele's blistering pinches.

That was it. They were all dressed and matching. Now no one could tell – how very different Manna would be.

Following Momi, with Manna in the rear, the children clambered up the five flights of metal stairs to their small apartment. Manna usually thought their clomping shoes sounded like inmates walking death row, but this time she didn't. She could only think of the puppy.

Everyone stopped at their door. Surprised, Manna looked up, directly into the face of her sister, Ailani – and gasped.

Ailani was breathtaking ... beautiful. Her flawless porcelain skin shone translucent, and her long shiny black hair glossed straight down the sides of her sweet, colored cheeks. Her round Hawaiian nose tilted gently to the sky and her full pink lips shimmered, calm with patience. A soft white light danced hypnotically above her head, and Manna wondered if she was an angel.

Ailani stared tenderly at Manna, her light brown eyes pooling with pity – and suddenly, Manna felt hopeful.

Maybe, one day, someone will notice – I'm special, too.

Brrrring.

The sound made Manna jump. She looked around. Everyone was staring at her. Quickly, she looked down and held her breath, hoping it would go away – but it didn't.

Brrrring ... Brrrring.

Oh no, she thought, *not again.*

Chapter Three

The BURNING GIFT

Manna didn't want to go in, but she didn't have a choice. It was either get it in there, or have her chase you down and do it in the street. It seemed better to just have family stare instead of the whole jeering neighborhood – so, mustering up her courage, she straightened her back and walked stiff-legged through the door.

Instantly, Momi banged the door shut in time with the last telephone, "Brrring."

Anna leapt out of the kitchen and grabbed Manna's biceps, gouging her with sharp white nails. Her slanted blue eyes glowed wild, like a cat caught in headlights, and her lips paled white with fear. She arched over Manna and hissed, "Stop it! Stop it!"

Weird things happened around Manna, but that didn't mean it was her fault.

Who knows why her teacher flipped headfirst into the trash can – just as she was about to rap Manna's hand? And how could Manna have pushed her classmates down the sewer that day? She was stuck in the big black Dumpster ... where they'd thrown her. And this time, there was no way Manna could be the one haunting Anna with chilling prank calls, tearfully begging for help. She didn't know their phone number!

"How many times do I have to tell you ... STO-O-O-OP IT?" wailed Anna, shaking Manna briefly, but hard.

Manna didn't know the right answer, so she looked away, respectfully.

"I can't help you!" cried Anna.

Manna thought she was right. No one could.

"Look at me!" screamed Anna.

Manna looked up at her trembling mother and felt sorry. Sorry that she was hurting her. Sorry that she couldn't help her.

"I said look at me!" Anna exasperated.

Manna tried harder to look at her mother, but to no avail.

"You're the devil. That's why you can't look at me," spat Anna. Then she put her face very close to Manna's and hissed through cold, dry lips, "I see you ... hiding in there ... and God help me ..."

She shook Manna furiously.

"I'LL ... SHAKE ... YOU ... O-O-OUT!"

The shaking was terrible. Manna's brain felt like it would hammer through her skull. She held her breath and clamped her teeth down, trying to stay steady.

It c-c-can't last forever-r-r, she promised herself.

Suddenly, Anna let out an exhausted cry and threw Manna to the floor. Then she scurried to the kitchen and slammed the door shut. The sound of running water and Anna mumbling in German seeped under the door, so Manna knew – it was over. Slowly, she teetered to her feet, her dizzy head throbbing.

"Change clothes," barked Momi, at the three little kids, then looking at Pu-pele she ordered, "You! Make snack!" – but Momi didn't have to say that. It was a given.

Pu-pele was the only one allowed in the kitchen. Anna was in there all day, mumbling and washing ... something, and only Pu-pele could sneak in and out, unnoticed.

No one ever talked about what Anna washed or said. They only reminded, "Never go in there!" – so Manna only saw her mother on Sundays and special occasions (like when there was trouble) ... and sometimes when Moho came home.

It seemed Anna always knew exactly when he would arrive. Five minutes before, she'd sprint to her room, fix her hair, squeeze into a dress, and don a single strand of pearls – then she'd emerge, fresh and beautiful, and run for the closed front door. Just when you'd think she'd smash into it, Moho would jerk it open and catch her with a sloppy kiss.

Sometimes Manna hid under the dining room table to catch a glimpse of her parents ... happy – but she always slipped away during the kiss.

If Moho caught her, he'd kill her.

Pu-pele leaned close to Manna (twinkling the playful half smile that usually adorned her face) and wagged her finger.

"Bad baby. No snack for you."

"She's looking in the wrong eye," whispered Ailani. "The one that stares away ..." Ailani humphed twice, as if clearing her throat, then continued. "Make her look in the other."

Manna had no idea what she was talking about.

"What? Which one?" she asked, but Ailani didn't answer. She just looked at the ground, tapped each foot twice, then shuffled to her room.

Oh great, cried Manna, finally upset. *I'm cross-eyed!*

Pressing her palms over her sockets, she bolted to the bathroom and locked the door behind her. Then she crawled onto the sink, tottered onto her knees, and crammed her face into the mirror.

The worried little girl that peered out of the mirror had a cute round face with a matching round nose. A flat black spot dotted the right side of her nose, just below her huge watery eyes. Her dark red lips lolled open with curiosity, and her long pointed tongue wrapped snugly over her small front teeth.

Manna looked at her left eye. Nothing wrong there. Then she looked at her right. It wasn't *exactly* in the middle, but it wasn't crossed either. Thankful, she leaned back, comparing her dark eyes, and decided they were even enough ... but looked sad. She knew how to fix that.

Sticking her pinkies into her eyelids, she stretched them up until all the whites showed. Then she stuck her thumbs in her mouth and stretched it into a gaping clown smile. Sticking her tongue out, she blew a messy raspberry and rolled her bulging eyes. Quickly, the little girl in the mirror popped into giggles and everything brightened.

Manna really liked that girl – she always made her feel better.

Buzzzz! Buzzzz!

Excitement bubbled through Manna, like soda pop pouring into a glass.

It was the door ... and only one person ever rang that bell!

Manna hopped off the sink, bolted to her bedroom, and rifled through Mano's toys.

"Got it!" she said, holding a pirate patch over her head. With a snap, she plastered the patch over her crooked eye and scampered to the dining room table.

A large postal package dwarfed the already small oak table. Anna smiled prettily as she sliced through its brown paper wrapping and bright colored stamps – with a long, jagged knife – and all Manna's siblings sat, leaning over the table, hungry smiles spread across their twinkly-eyed faces.

Manna's chest swelled with Christmas joy.

Tante Theresa's presents made everyone happy!

Quietly, she slid into the chair furthest from Anna and cocked her head to the right, letting only the good eye show. Mano shook next to her, bouncing both legs with anticipation. Who could blame him? He always got more.

The package ripped open. Anna slipped her small hands inside and lifted out ten exquisite German candles. They were tall hand-decorated ones that stood three inches thick, with wax grooved and swirled in delicate patterns that dripped down their sides like shimmery icing. Manna loved to run her fingers through the smooth wax grooves ... and over the carved metallic flowers that bloomed on top.

Next, four glass jars of candy emerged – powdery peppermint softs, frosty lemon drops, color-sprinkled nonpareils, and molasses-covered caramel. Manna's mouth watered.

Five wheels of brie (Manna's favorite) and ten bars of liquor-filled chocolates came out next. Then, Anna put both hands deep into the box and shook out a long, pink-flowered shoe box that was labeled, "Mutti." Anna looked at the box for a moment, gripping it so tight that the pinks of her nails turned white. Then she looked down at Manna and shivered.

Manna shivered back. Something was wrong.

With glassy eyes, Anna leaned forward, closer and closer to Manna, wielding her pointy, shaking knife.

Manna held her breath and concentrated on looking sideways at her mother.

Biting her lip, Anna jabbed the knife between Manna's brows and sliced up to her forehead. With a rubbery pop, the eye patch snapped off Manna's face. Thinking fast, Manna winked her crooked eye shut.

"Did you take her?" Anna's voice was soft and hoarse.

Not knowing the right answer, Manna guessed.

"No."

Anna winced, dropped the knife, and scurried to her room with Mutti's box.

Manna breathed out and smiled, *Right answer!*

As though nothing unusual had happened, Pu-pele held up the peppermint jar and said, "How many?"

Ailani glanced up quickly, then stared back down at the table.

"Forty. Eight each."

"Manna only gets one. How many?"

Manna's heart skipped a beat. Pu-pele would let her have snack after all!

"Nine each. Three left over."

Manna knew that Pu-pele, Momi and Mano would get the three extra, but she didn't care. Pu-pele parceled the mints and tossed a chipped one at Manna. It looked yummy.

Pu-pele held up the lemon drops, and Ailani immediately said, "Fifty-two. Twelve each. Three left over." For the nonpareils she said, "Thirty-three. Eight each," and for the caramel, "Forty-two. Ten each. One left over."

Pu-pele passed the candy out quickly.

Huffing, Momi stood up, swiped her share into one large hand, snatched a liquor-filled bar with the other, and tromped to her room.

Manna and her siblings sat far forward, drooling over their candies.

Manna decided the best way to go was sour to sweet. She picked up the lemon drop and put it close to her eyes. It was coated with white, glimmering sugar frosting, speckled with crystalized granules. She rolled the gem between her fingers, then sucked it into her mouth.

What a surprise! The frosting was so sweet that it stung her cheeks and drilled through her teeth. Quickly, she flipped it from cheek to cheek, sucking the opposite cheek in to slurp away the sweetness.

Suddenly, the frosting vanished and a flood of sour rushed over her tongue, swelled up her nose and surged through her contracting brain. Squinting out tart tears, she swallowed fast and hard.

Light-headed and jittery, Manna blinked to regain her vision.

Cool, she grinned.

Next, she chose the peppermint. Its pink, powdery coating came off on her fingers, so she put them in her mouth with the candy and licked. Mint powder puffed down her throat and prickled up her nose. She sneezed and accidentally swallowed.

The peppermint zinged down her throat and zapped cold gas into her tummy. Immediately, she burped – out loud.

Manna looked around, embarrassed, but no one heard her belch. They were too busy wolfing down their stash.

She picked up the caramel and put it between her teeth, so it didn't slip down her throat like the mint. The sticky molasses melted slowly, coating her teeth with spicy syrup that glooped over her gums and oozed out her lips. She sucked the syrup back in and realized – her teeth were stuck together. Making lots of saliva, she swished it between them until they loosened with a jolting – Crack!

Instinctively, Manna slid her tongue along her teeth and thought, *Good, they're all still there.*

Last, she picked up the nonpareil and nibbled off a bright colored dot. Instantly, it sparked in her mouth and fizzled on her tongue.

Manna giggled. The popping dot tickled.

Wondering how a mouthful felt, she scraped all the dots off with her bottom teeth (as though they were Oreo cream) and quickly shut her mouth. At once, the dots exploded and sizzled up her nose, like turbo-charged soda pop – then crackling loud, they shot to the back of her head. With a snap, everything turned into flecks of white, and Manna thought she would faint – but instead, her whole body started to tingle, as if it was a fallen-asleep foot. Then, with one body-twitching spasm, she shuddered and the flecks disappeared.

Manna opened her eyes wide – *How weird ...*

Stretching her lower jaw down, she stuck the bittersweet chocolate wafer onto the roof of her mouth. The wafer melted slowly, dripping chalky heaven off her palette and coating her rubbing tongue. Comforting, rich happiness soaked through Manna's being – and she felt certain.

Tante Theresa was related to Santa.

She had his friendly pink face, his curly white hair ... and she always sent presents.

Pu-pele gobbled down her last candy with a snuffling sound and pouted at Anna's stack of bars. Her chubby fingers rapped the table for a moment, then shot out and snatched one off the top. Working together, her deft hands slid the bar out of its paper, unwrapped its foil (without a rip) and flattened it, silver, against the table.

Manna had a funny feeling that something bad was about to happen, but shrugged it off. There was a chance Pu-pele would share.

The dark brown chocolate bar was sectioned into square, fluffy pillows arranged in five rows and eight columns. Manna hoped they would each get a whole row, but Pu-pele snapped off one column instead and rewrapped the bar.

Manna was impressed. The bar looked as good as new.

Quickly, Pu-pele did the same to the other bars, and Manna watched her, thinking of Momi. She always said Pu-pele was stupid, but Manna thought her clever. Pu-pele always figured out how to get what she wanted, without getting caught.

Biting her lip, Pu-pele snapped off one of the squares, popped it into her mouth – and choked. Brown, bubbly liquid spurted out her nose and spattered Mano, who was sitting directly across the table.

"Ya-ah!" she laughed, wagging her red tongue. "That's hot."

Manna chuckled. Sometimes Pu-pele was funny.

Mano wiped his splotched face on his sleeve and grabbed one of Pu-pele's bars. He broke off a square, cracked off the corner, poured out the brandy, and shoved it in his mouth. His eyes turned red and watered, but he didn't choke.

Manna was surprised. He took without asking.

Pu-pele's emerald eyes narrowed like dragon slits, but she copied Mano without a word. Again she choked, but nothing spewed out.

The race was on!

Snorting and slurping, Pu-pele and Mano ripped through the caustic pillows, spilling brandy all over the table.

In the end, Mano got three more pillows than Pu-pele, and she acknowledged her loss with a hot glare. Mano smirked back at her, his chin dripping with golden-brown liquid.

Manna couldn't believe he would be so bold – and felt jealous no one shared.

Licking her lips with a singed tongue, Pu-pele grabbed one of the German candles and flowed into the kitchen. When she returned, the candle was lit. She stood it on the table, in front of Mano, her eyes flickering red in its light.

"Bet you can't do this."

Slowly, she ran her finger through the dancing flame and her fingernail caught fire – but she didn't flinch. She just smirked and playfully tapped it on Mano's nose. Instantly, the flame jumped off her nail and onto his nose, flickered, then vanished with a snap.

Manna's mouth hung open with awe. Pu-pele was neat.

Mano growled through curled lips, and of course, tried to do the same. He would counter any challenge.

"Ow!" he yelped, jerking back and sticking his blistered finger in his mouth.

Manna wondered what Pu-pele's trick was ... or was she really magic?

Triumphant, Pu-pele giggled and leaned over the table, her face almost touching the candle.

"Ha!" she breathed.

Tongues of fire shot out of her mouth and licked Mano's face. Barely blinking, he pushed his face up to the candle, opened his mouth wider than hers, baring all his pointy white teeth, and tried to blow flames back at her with a resounding, breath-filled, "HAAAAH!"

Nothing happened ... but Manna knew – something would happen now.

Mano tried to hurt Pu-pele, and she *always* got even.

The veins in Pu-pele's eyes swelled blood-red and her face glowered yellow, like an eerie summer moon. She dug her top teeth deep into her bottom lip and gingerly moved her fingers, one by one, through the leaping flame. As each finger passed through the flame, its tip glowed bright orange as though it were an ember.

With a devilish grin, she raised her fingers above Mano's head and flinked them, as if to sprinkle water. Little balls of fire showered onto his hair and singed his crown. Jerking, he batted the tiny orange meteors away with his hands, but Pu-pele just chortled and flinked more.

Manna breathed in the thin putrid smell of Mano's burning hair and hoped Momi couldn't smell it. If she could, they'd *all* get in trouble.

At once, Mano snarled, grabbed the candle, and swung at Pu-pele's hands – but it passed through them ... without hurting her.

Pu-pele threw her head far back, hands still raised, and laughed heartily. A deep, throaty sound gurgled in her chest, emitted through her plump, jiggling skin and sprayed through the air with the sparks off her fingers.

Manna's heart froze ... and waited for disaster.

Pu-pele quieted, then stood straight and tall, and squinted down at Mano. Her wavy hair shone orange and flowed electric around her body. Two trails of smoke curled out the corners of her mouth and passed over her glimmering red-bordered eyes. Her outstretched hands flickered and cracked.

Manna's skin crawled over her back and hid.

Pu-pele had turned into a fire witch!

Glinting a wicked half-smile, Pu-pele spread her fingers wide and touched them to the table.

SHROOM!

The tabletop burst into flames and blasted Mano's face. He jumped backwards out of his chair, yelling, "Whoa!" and slammed against the window – but standing up quickly, he held his shaking candle up with both hands and growled, "Back off."

Manna was shocked. The children never fought.

With a quick swirling motion, Pu-pele ran her open palms over the crackling table and gathered two fireballs in her hands. Raising both balls above her head, she sneered, "Batter up!" and fast pitched them both.

One fireball exploded on the window curtain and burst into flames. The other tore straight for Mano's face, but he swung the candle and batted it back at Pu-pele. She ducked, and it exploded against the wall, spreading orange-blue fire over the paint.

Furious, Pu-pele jerked up and snatched fireball after fireball off the table and pelted them at Mano. Rapid-fire, he returned them. Some exploded on the ceiling, others on the walls, but most of them smattered a retardant Pu-pele, inciting her more. Faster and faster, she flung her fireballs, and even faster, he whacked them back, splattering flames everywhere.

Manna started to panic. Someone was going to get hurt!

BANG!

With a crackling bang, the room burst into a red-hot swirling inferno.

Terrified, Manna jumped to her feet and tried to run, but a sudden broiling wind pressed her backwards, scorching her face and gorging the angry firestorm. Sharp red flames lashed around her and engulfed her with stifling pangs, just as an orange-red, smoky shroud whipped over her cheeks.

Manna cried out in fear. The world had turned into a child-devouring, hellish haze!

All that she saw – and felt – and breathed was heat. Intense, sweltering heat.

They had to get out of there – FAST!

Without thinking, she lunged at Mano to drag him out of the room, but a flying chair barreled through her legs and flipped her to the floor. Coming down hard, her head slammed against the tiled floor with a splitting – Crack!

Dizzy and blinded, she tottered to her knees and began clawing across the floor, searching for her brother – but the sizzling wind screamed against her back, seared her groping hands and flattened her, stiff, to the ground.

Instantly, dread pulled Manna's insides into her throat. She couldn't see or breathe – and now she could barely move. Surely, this was it. Her last hour had come.

"Mother Mary, help me!" she wheezed, as she struggled up to her trembling knees.

WHOMP!

Something large and black whapped her to the ground and vomited white foam in her face. Squinting and groaning, she tried to scramble back up.

WHOOSH! WHOMP!

The dark, shapeless thing sailed through the orange fog, whomped her on the head and buried her tear-filled nose in its bubbly puke.

Manna gasped and choked on the acidic froth – and understood.

The horrid thing would kill her.

"Stay still!" screamed Momi, as she beat Manna with her heavy coat.

Manna jerked, then curled into a ball and covered her head with her burning arms. Her clothes raged with blackish-red fire and Momi was putting it out.

44

WHOMP!

Momi clobbered her with the coat again, but it felt like she was using a red-hot iron frying pan. Manna squeezed her eyes shut and tried to ignore the searing pain – and the thick, bitter lather that splattered her face.

WHOMP! WHOOOOOSH!

Manna gulped air between beatings and opened her eyes.

Ailani was dragging the fire extinguisher around the room, spraying down the fire. Pu-pele was glaring at Mano, white and wet, as he stood over Manna, gawking – and two large black boots stood behind them ... waiting.

WHOMP!

Manna winced.

"What's wrong with you?" demanded Momi, throwing her coat at Pu-pele.

Manna was glad the beating had stopped – but knew it would start again.

Those big ugly boots belonged to Moho.

"ARRRRGH!" growled Moho, grabbing Pu-pele by the throat and slamming her hard on top the blackened table.

Manna froze, forgetting what she was supposed to do.

The table collapsed with terrific force. Moho slipped and lost his grip. Quickly, Pu-pele escaped into the living room and snatched at the vacuum cleaner hose. Stomping so hard the whole apartment shook, Moho rushed over, picked her up, and threw her across the room.

CLA-A-AM! - "OOF!"

Pu-pele smashed against the wall and sunk, brandishing one steel vacuum pole like a sword.

"Move it!" ordered Momi, kicking Manna to her feet.

Moho lunged at Pu-pele, who was now standing. Before he reached her, she swiped at him with her weapon and slashed his face. Unfazed, he squeezed his hands around her shoulders and pounded her repeatedly against the wall, grunting, "You good-for-nothing little ..."

Pu-pele shrieked and kicked back.

"NOW!" hollered Momi, shoving Manna out of the room.

Shaking uncontrollably, Manna sailed down the hall, into her room and over her trundle bed, landing neatly under Mano's top bunk. He and Ailani were already hiding there, balancing a sawed-off two-by-four board. Manna slipped into her designated spot, snugly in between them.

The trundle bed made the strongest barricade. It stood in the back corner of the room, one side facing the door, the other against the wall, and the footboard solid to the floor. The lower bed rolled on wheels and slid under the top bunk, just like a giant drawer.

If you were fast enough, you could slip under the top bunk and roll the lower bed in a bit – then you wouldn't be seen. And if you were quicker, you could strap the upper bunk legs to the lower bunk legs, so the lower bed wouldn't roll out and expose you. And if you were even faster, you could wedge a thick piece of wood between the lower bunk and back wall, and the bed wouldn't roll in and squish you. At least, that was Momi's plan.

Grumbling, Momi struggled with the leather belts, knotting them as best as she could around the bed legs. Ailani rocked back and forth, humming softly, her right arm hugging the wooden wedge. Mano sat cross-legged, knees bouncing, peering through the thin crack between the lower mattress and upper bed.

Manna folded her hands in her lap, as though she was praying, and wished it would end. Pu-pele's shrieks were slicing through her heart and bleeding a hole in her chest – while Moho's punches throbbed in her head and bruised her battered mind.

Manna wondered why things had to be so bad. Why couldn't Pu-pele just give up?

Scared, Mano slipped one blistered hand between Manna's and squeezed.

"She's so stupid," muttered Momi, from her vigil by the door.

There was a loud thud, one pain-filled scream, and then a sickening silence.

TROMP! - TROMP! - TROMP!

Manna's heart pounded as loud as Moho's charging buffalo steps.

Here he comes.

Moho whipped open the door and grabbed the first thing he saw – Momi.

"Where were you?" he growled, lifting her off of her feet and shoving his flared nostrils in her face.

"In the bathroom," she lied.

"Useless," snorted Moho, throwing her to the floor. Her head slammed against the lower bed, and it jerked in – but Ailani's wedge kept it from going far.

Manna wished there was something she could do.

"I'm sorry, Father," Momi gurgled from the ground. "I'll try harder."

Moho squinted and leaned over the rolled-out bed.

Manna shivered. He seemed to be looking at her.

Suddenly, he shoved his long, ugly fingers into the mattress crack and yanked. The belts around the legs creaked, but didn't give, so the top bunk scraped forward. All the frightened children jerked back.

"Moho," squeaked Anna, from inside the door.

Moho spun around. Anna's sad eyes were swollen pink, and her face was streaked with tears.

"My mother died," she quivered.

Manna's stomach hurt.

"Oh, Baby," Moho breathed, gently scooping his wife up and

cradling her in his huge arms. "I'm so sorry."

He kissed her softly on the forehead and carried her down the hall to their room.

Momi stood up and glared at the children. Thick red blood streamed out of her nose and dripped off her chin. That's what always happened.

"Do your homework," she ordered. Then she tramped out of the room, muttering to herself.

Looking down at her wringing hands, Ailani leaned past Manna and muttered, "Only take what she offers."

Mano snorted, then grunted back, "Tell her – Offer what I take."

Manna was the only one who would check, so she always made sure to do it. On her tiptoes, she crept down the hall and peeked around the corner into the dark living room. Pu-pele was crying, hunched over her bent, twisted vacuum pole, cross-legged on the edge of an easy chair. Her beautiful brown hair bounced around her soft, shaking shoulders – and yellow-green snot stretched from her nose to the floor. With each sob, the snot stretched longer – and with each gasp, it pulled back in.

Noticing Manna, Pu-pele quieted and frowned. Then, she twirled the gooey nose strand around her index finger and popped it into her mouth.

Manna felt sick.

Pu-pele would never learn to give up ... even if it killed her.

Through the pitch dark, Manna could hear it.

Rap, rap.

She pulled the blankets over her head, but that didn't help.

Rap, rap.

Why did he have to do that?

Rap, rap.

She couldn't take it anymore. She jumped out of bed and stormed through the dark hall to the kitchen – and there he was, batting at roaches with a candle.

Manna shuddered. Mano was afraid of the dark. So when Momi ordered, "Lights out!" he would sneak into the kitchen, open the oven door (to turn on its dim light) and play golf with the little brown roaches that coated the kitchen floor.

Roach golf was gross. Some of the roaches would squish and smear over the tile, and others would explode into yellow-brown goo – but most of them would birdie under the cupboard and then frantically run out, pieces dragging.

Manna hated roaches, especially when they climbed over her with their poky, nervous legs.

"Why don't you use it the way you're supposed to?" she asked.

Mano looked up at her, small, and admitted, "I don't know how to light it."

Manna frowned. Neither did she – but she couldn't stand any more of that rapping. She flicked the kitchen light on and all the wounded roaches scurried away.

Determined, she strode over to the stove and turned one of its white knobs.

Click ... click ... click.

Nothing seemed to be happening. Manna put her face close to the burner and peered through the cracks.

Click ... click ... click.

There was a silver dish thing in the middle, and it smelled sort of funny, like gasoline.

Click ... click ... click.

"Is it working?" asked Mano, his face next to hers.

Manna turned to look at him, her nose touching his, and feigned, "Yeah."

WHOOSH!

Wide blue flames shot out in a huge circle and sizzled over their cheeks.

"Cool!" beamed Mano.

Manna smiled back at him with pride.

She did something he couldn't!

A soft rustling sound woke Manna up. She squeezed her eyes shut and held her breath.

"In the Name of the Father, and the Son, and the Holy Spirit."

It was Anna. She was putting a cross on a sleeping Mano's forehead.

Anna kissed her finger and tapped it on the tip of her son's nose.

"Boops. God's gonna watch over you."

Manna held her breath and laid perfectly still. Maybe this time she would get a cross, too.

"I know you're awake," whispered Anna.

Manna didn't answer.

"You watch out for him. He follows you everywhere."

Manna's heart sank. She wasn't going to get a cross.

Anna turned around and walked to the door. Right before she got there, she stopped and said dryly, "Don't call me. I can't help you."

Manna's chest hurt.

Why was he so special, and she nothing at all?

Hearing Anna leave, Manna opened her stinging eyes and stared at the wooden picture on the wall. In Mano's candlelight, the Guardian Angel shone bright and tall, hovering over a girl and a boy as they crossed a broken bridge. The sister, who was bigger, hugged her arm protectively around her brother as she guided the way – and the angel floated above her with open arms, ready to catch her if they fall.

The angel made Manna feel better.

Things weren't so bad. She would watch out for her brother, and the angel would watch out for her.

Manna closed her eyes and smiled.

She could feel the angel now, watching ... and waiting.

Then something soft rustled under her bed.

Chapter Four

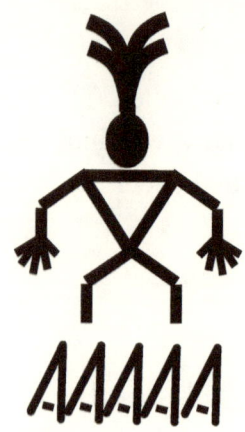

The BREATHER in the CLOSET

"MOHOOOOOO!"

Manna sat straight up in bed. Something was wrong – with Anna.

"It's not real," hissed Moho, his stern voice seeping through the walls. "You're dreaming."

Mano slid down to Manna's bed and accidentally sat on her feet.

"I can hear breathing ..." Anna's whisper quivered with the candlelight. "Something's in the closet."

Creepies crawled off Manna's neck and scurried down her chest. Instantly, she shuddered.

The monster that hid under her bed had crept into Anna's closet!

"I'll check," barked Moho. "Stay in bed."

Manna heard Moho's heavy steps cross the floor. She looked at Mano, who was staring wide-eyed at her, bouncing both legs and painfully crunching her toes. Tense, cold air hung silently between them.

"See, Baby. Nothing," announced Moho.

Relieved, Manna breathed out and Mano quit bouncing.

"Pu-pele – make milk!" roared Moho.

Always hungry, Mano jammed a clammy hand into Manna's and headed for the dining room table.

Manna wrapped both hands around her warm mug and peered inside.

Sticky white bubbles clung to the sides of the cup and large chalky lumps floated in the middle. It seemed like Pu-pele never mixed the powdered milk enough, but that was okay. She always warmed it up.

Using her teeth as a filter, Manna took a sip and swallowed. Comforting warmth passed through her chest, massaged her tummy, and made her feel safe and cozy. Keeping her nose in her cup, she peeked up at Anna, who was sitting across the table, very close to Moho, looking sad and embarrassed.

Moho leaned over with a frothy white mustache and smooched her on the cheek.

"It's okay, Baby. You've still got me," he grinned.

Anna smiled weakly and took a sip of her milk. Then, she smiled a little bigger – at Pu-pele.

"And I've still got my little girl."

Gleaming, Pu-pele hopped into Anna's lap and smacked a wetter kiss than Moho's across her cheek. Anna giggled, and Moho's whole face frowned. Slapping his left knee hard, he growled, "Come here, Boy."

Grasping his piping hot cup, Mano slid out of his chair and walked around the table to his father.

Manna started when he sat down. Half of his milk poured onto Moho's knee – but luckily, Moho didn't notice. He was busy glaring at Pu-pele.

"And my little angel," said Anna, raising her left hand as an invitation.

Smiling happily, Ailani cleared her throat twice, tapped her cup on the table thrice and touched the back of her hand to her teeth. Then, rising slowly, she tapped her left foot on the floor, then her right, and shuffled around the table to Anna.

Anna smiled and hugged her tight.

"Momi," barked Moho, without looking at her. Instead, he aimed his glare at Ailani, looking as though he might eat her.

Momi huffed up, smirking at Pu-pele, and slid onto her father's lap. Then resting her head on his shoulder, she stuck her tongue out at Pu-pele – but nobody noticed.

Anna beamed at Moho as she squeezed her kids.

"Thank you for giving me a family," she cooed. "They mean everything to me ... and so do you."

Moho's hard face melted, at the same time as Manna's heart.

He was glad to be part of Anna's family, and she was sad that she was not.

Manna squinted at Moho through watery eyes and noticed Mano staring at her. She looked at him as if to say, "What?" and he gazed back with pity-filled eyes.

Manna's chest burned.

How could he, of all people, feel sorry for me?

She gripped her cup tightly and gulped down her milk. Choking heat seared her throat and singed her eyes, filling her chest with pain.

"Drink fast and it'll burn ya," jibed Pu-pele.

Manna put her cup down and scuffled back to bed.

"In the closet, Moho," whispered Anna. "They're in the closet!"

Manna sat up and peered through the darkness. Anna was at it again.

"I can't see," squeaked Mano.

Hurrying, Manna stumbled across the room and flicked on the light.

"What am I looking for?" asked Moho.

"The pictures," quavered Anna. "She said to get rid of the pictures."

Manna could hear Moho grunt as he rifled through the closet.

"Where are they?" he asked.

"In the envelope, in the box," whimpered Anna. "The ones of my mother – in her coffin."

Moho continued to grunt, then said, "Got 'em."

Anna's voice was hollow.

"Burn them."

"Okay, Baby. Stay in bed."

Manna heard Moho tramp to the kitchen and slam some drawers. Then, the fire alarm went off. Quickly, a chair splintered and crashed to the floor, and soon after, the alarm stopped with a pounding – CRUNCH!

Muttering complaints, Moho tromped back to his room.

"Done, Baby," he breathed. "Go back to sleep."

Manna heard her mother's muffled sobs, and it made her stomach ache.

"Could you light it?" asked Mano, holding out his candle.

Manna looked at the candle and felt dizzily overwhelmed. There was always so much to deal with – and now this. Someone had to help her.

"You have to come scare the roaches," she said, but she was more worried about seeing the pictures. Dead people scared her.

"Okay," Mano nodded, his stick-up bangs bouncing up and down.

Holding hands, they crept past their parents' room to the brightly lit kitchen.

Immediately, Manna felt better. Moho left the light on, so all the roaches were gone. Biting her lip, she looked around.

In the sink, a small fire smoldered, and under the punched-in fire alarm wobbled a cracked wooden chair, teetering lopsided on top of a crushed one.

Mano squeezed his sister's hand and giggled.

It must have looked funny when the chair buckled and Moho flopped to the ground!

Manna squeezed his hand back and tiptoed to the sink. Inside, a pile of curled, blackened pictures smoked in a putrid, nose-stinging heap, while thin orange lines flickered hot across their edges.

Manna let go of Mano's hand and plugged her nose, glad that she couldn't see her dead grandmother through the black char. Carefully, she touched the candlewick to one flaming edge, and it lit with a loud – CRACK!

Manna jumped back.

Grey smoke whirled around her and pins pricked her spine.

Manna shuddered. Something was still wrong.

"We're going to the Kris Kringle Mart!" squealed Pu-pele.

"It's Christ-kindl-markt, dummy," scowled Momi, from the back of the freezing, wet line.

Manna thought Kris Kringle sounded better, and even though she was only four the year before, she remembered all the excitement well. There was no happier place than the Kris Kringle fair ... but for now, there was no unhappier place than where she stood, waiting in line for the shower.

Manna hated to bathe, but Momi said they had to – and to speed things up, she said they had to do it together. So there they all stood, shivering in the tub, waiting their turn to get clean. Luckily, they only had to bathe on Sundays.

"You're done," announced Pu-pele, from the front of the line where she had been scrubbing Mano, mercilessly. Mano climbed out of the tub, slipped (again) and cracked his head against the toilet. Before Manna could check if he was okay, Pu-pele grabbed her and dunked her under the ice cold stream.

Every one of Manna's pores screamed and tried to escape, bulging out into stiff, pointed pimples. Yelping, she flung her chicken-skin arms around her twitching chest and pretended to be a pirate, braving an arctic storm.

Briskly, Pu-pele glooped dish soap on Manna's head and scrubbed it hard with a washcloth. Rubbed off hair and blumps of lather dripped down her face, seeped into her eyes, and burned its way round her pupils.

Manna squeezed her eyes shut and remembered – Pu-pele said the soap would make your eyes shine. Manna wished it would straighten them, too.

"You're done," grinned Pu-pele.

Manna jumped out of the tub and snatched the towel from Mano. Pu-pele said the three little ones had to share (so she would have less laundry) and Mano always got it sopping wet.

"I *said* – Just use the corner," complained Manna, as she quickly wrung the towel.

"I did," mumbled Mano, looking at his feet, his head and body still dripping.

Manna looked at the soaked towel ... and the smeared puddle that pooled around his feet.

Oh brother, she thought. *He dropped it.*

"You're done," whiffed Pu-pele.

Manna spun around. Ailani was out already.

Panicking, Manna started to dab the towel over her body, but stopped.

Ailani was frozen solid. Her splotchy blue skin shriveled around her purple-grey lips, and her stiff, goose-pimpled arms twitched furiously beside her sunk-in, trembling chest. Wet-eyed and spooky, she stared at Manna, silently begging for help.

Manna tossed Ailani the towel and frowned back at Mano.

"Next time – Keep it on the rack."

Ailani wrapped the towel snugly around her shoulders, tapped each foot to the floor twice, and tiptoed sideways out the door.

Manna looked at the hot steam that spilled over the shower and shivered.

You could always tell when Pu-pele got in. The fire witch turned ice to steam.

This was, by far, the most brilliant Christmas tree, and Manna was glad Momi let them touch it – as long as they stood hidden behind it. It loomed taller than a building, shone brighter than a torch, and twinkled white with glimmering lit candles (instead of electric lights). Manna thought it looked like a sparkling fairy wand, waving "Hi!" to heaven. She stroked one of its long branches, and the candles winked and bowed.

"Every year, the Christkindlmarkt is held here, in the Marienplatz – the city's center – and to mark the beginning of the fair, Lord Mayor lights this tree," murmured Ailani. "It stands ninety-eight point four-two-five feet tall and boasts two-thousand-five-hundred candles."

"Two-thousand-four-hundred-eighty," smiled Pu-pele, swinging her magic black bag.

"She's here," barked Momi. "Line up."

Manna felt excitement swell up in her chest, like bouncy helium blowing up a balloon.

Santa was coming!

Jumping high, Manna landed in her designated spot, second in line after Mano.

"Grützi!" exclaimed Tante Theresa, hugging Anna with a broad smile. Anna gushed and rattled off something in German. The sisters hugged again, then holding hands, they smiled at the children.

"They're so big!" gushed Tante Theresa. "And beautiful!"

Anna beamed gratefully at Pu-pele, knowing she was the one who groomed them.

Tante Theresa rushed over to the two littlest ones and swooped them up in her arms.

"Have you been good?" she asked playfully.

Mano jerked his head up and down, flashing his bright, toothy grin.

Manna's eyebrows shot up in surprise.

Didn't Santa know?

In church this morning, he knocked off the bishop's hat – with a flying marble – and tripped two elderly wine servers with a rock.

Tante Theresa looked at Manna.

"And you?"

Well, if he wasn't in trouble then neither was she ... for only *pretending* to pray. Smiling eagerly, she nodded her head.

Tante Theresa squeezed them tight, and for a moment, Manna felt safe. But suddenly, Theresa plopped them down and pressed a crisp paper into Manna's hand.

"Just like a Hummel angel ..." Theresa smiled at a glowing Ailani.

Manna opened her hand and gasped.

One-hundred Marks! Santa gave her one-hundred Marks – enough money to buy anything she wanted!

Manna looked bug-eyed at her brother, and he stared back, his mouth hanging open ... and a hundred Mark bill crumpled in his bony left hand.

Recovering first, Manna slid her money into her shoe, to make it hard for Pu-pele to steal – and copying as always, Mano did the same.

"... and my big girl, Momi," chortled Theresa.

Momi smiled wide with a long outstretched hand and (of course) Theresa filled it – with one bill and five silver coins.

"Keep a good eye on the children," cooed Theresa. "And warm them with a glass of Gluehwein."

"We'll be back at three-thirty," chirped Anna. Then she grabbed Theresa's hand and skipped towards the fair, chattering something.

Momi came back running, gripping five large wine glasses between her fingers. Her face was glistening red, as though she'd run the whole way.

"Get 'em, they're hot!" she huffed.

Pu-pele's hand shot out and wrapped around the top of one glass.

"Yow-w!" she yelled, jerking her hand back.

"From the bottom, lead head," sneered Momi.

Pu-pele reached out slowly and fingered the wine glass stem.

"Watch out or it'll spill," she grinned, tipping the glass as she spoke. Reddish-brown liquid sizzled over Momi's arm, but she refused to show pain.

Carefully, Manna wrapped both hands around the bottom of one steaming glass and pulled it away. She had never tasted wine, but knew that adults thought it was special. Feeling grown-up, she huddled over her glass and breathed in.

The light smell of cinnamon and cloves sprinkled on top of a tangy orange muffin warmed her nose. She closed her eyes and savored the smell. It was almost like standing in a bakery – sampling frosted fruit-filled cakes! Anxious, her tummy grumbled out loud.

Breathing out first, Manna pressed her lips to the hot glass and took one long inhaling sip.

Instantly, spicy vapor stung her tongue and rushed into her head. She swallowed fast, and tingling, the warm liquid soaked through her chest, over her tummy and quickly back to her head. Delightfully light-headed, she took another huge sip and giggled.

The warmth tickled her ribs!

Suddenly, everything turned a brilliant spinning orange and Manna nearly lost her balance. She closed her eyes to steady herself and tried to focus on the orange flecks that danced in her head – but without warning, her heart fluttered like a hummingbird's, and something heavy clubbed her behind the knees. She sat down hard, panting – the wine glass gripped in her reddened hand.

After a minute, the orange flecks in her head shrank to dust and her heart slackened its speed. Dazed, she opened her eyes and stared at a teetering Mano, thinking, *Boy, this stuff isn't for kids.*

"GLUP. GLUP. AHHH!"

Momi enjoyed her glass noisily and didn't look dizzy at all. Licking her lips through an oddly contented smile, she pointed at a tall building and said, "The clock's there. No matter where you are in the fair, you can see the clock and this gaudy tinsel torch."

"Taunenbaum," hiccuped a bright red Ailani. The wine was too strong for her, too.

Momi rolled her eyes and faced Pu-pele.

"Have them here at a quarter past three."

Pu-pele's face flushed blank, like a pink pig caught in a drunken stupor.

"Got it?" asked Momi, her blue eyes drilling through Pu-pele.

Pu-pele narrowed her shiny eyes in defense. This was the first time Momi told her to watch the kids – and she didn't want to.

"Yeah," she glinted, turning her round face towards the fair, her black bag swinging at her side. "I get it ... all."

Momi bounded off to the fair, and a second later Pu-pele followed, throwing her head back to call out, "You heard her – quarter past three!"

Manna couldn't tell time, but it seemed like they stood there an hour, holding their wine, while Ailani circled the tree, getting perfect count of the candles.

"One-thousand-six-hundred-forty-five,   one-thousand-six-hundred-forty-six ..."

Mano was bouncing from foot to foot, almost as if one hurt. Manna remembered one of the neighbors said, "Money burns a hole in your pocket." She wondered if it would burn a hole in your shoe.

"One-thousand-six-hundred-fifty-two ..."

Manna looked at the clock. Must be the arrows tell you what time it is. They could just come back when one of them pointed at three.

"One-thousand-six-hundred-sixty-one ..."

"Let's go," Manna said, knowing Ailani couldn't watch Mano.

"Can we dump it?" asked Mano, raising his glass.

Manna wasn't sure. The wine in church wasn't supposed to touch the ground. Maybe this stuff wasn't supposed to either. It was easy enough to keep it for Momi to drink, so they might as well ... to be safe.

"No, and don't spill it," she answered, looking towards the bustling fair where hundreds of flapping white peddler tents shone in long perfect rows.

Streams of merry people milled through the tent rows, hauling shopping bags and steaming treats, like food-gathering ants in underground tunnels. To the right, a green-striped Umpa band blasted horns to a loud beat, and on the left, a puffy, rectangular beer tent swayed sideways in time. Bright yellow light streamed out of the closest row of tents, and grey smoke curled over the furthest.

A cold wind flurried up Manna's skirt, and she squealed.

For once, she was free ... to do – and have – *anything* she wanted!

Brimming with excitement, she ran towards the first row of tents and cut a sharp left down the aisle – but froze, blinded in her tracks.

The bright winter sun bounced off mirrored hanging ornaments and pierced her pupils shut. Squinting, she spun around and skipped backwards down the aisle to avoid the sun's burning glare.

Jerking her head up and down, and from side to side, Manna tried to see every ornament. The highest hung ones shone striking gold, and the lowest ones glowed coppery brass, but the middle handmade, silver ones spurt the most dazzling diamond-white light as they swiveled and chimed in the wind.

Amazed, Manna couldn't decide which ornaments she liked best ...

the rotating stars and planets, or the praying Mary and Jesus, or the fluttering birds with red streamers. But she knew she liked the speckled blown-glass balls least because they were too easily broken.

At the end of the row, Manna sidestepped and trotted down the next cheerful aisle. It was packed with dolls – round-cheeked wooden ones with white smiles spread across their rosy faces, and red rouge smeared over their crooked balled chins. Some of them glared scary, like the menacing nutcracker soldiers with their large shell-crunching teeth and gaping "I'm-gonna-eat-you" mouths. But most of them flopped funny with long German noses and puffy Bavarian sleeves.

Manna thought Ailani might like one.

The next row was stacked with multicolored crafts, swirly candles, and clear-glazed ceramic – and the next few were lined with irresistible clinking toys made of shiny tin and glossy stained wood.

Manna figured she could buy a whole box full!

Smiling, she skipped around to the last aisle and stopped cold, her heart dropping into her wobbly knees.

It was a Hawaiian girl's dream. Table upon table of sticky, hot treats ... all for the taking!

Trying to contain her excitement, Manna gripped her wine glass with both hands, pressing it to her jittery stomach, and walked as slow as a happy bride. With each dragging step, she sucked in extra long whiffs of drippy sweet aroma, trying to take it all in.

To the left, luscious baked apples drizzled sweet golden syrup, and hot roasted almonds clanked in sugar-coated churns. On the right, squarish-round pepper nuts crunched over doily-lined trays, and powdered sugarplum figurines danced angelically in white-frosted glass displays. Down the aisle, swollen wursts oozed sweet-salty juice over pockets of crusty pretzel-bread, and bubbling potato pancakes spattered and fried in sizzling cast-iron pans. Further down, golden-brown Schmalzgebaeck cakes swelled and popped in deep frying vats –

and Fruechtebrot loaves dripped tangy fruitiness next to crunchy Springerle-aniseed biscuits. At the end, Lebkuchen gingerbread cookies puffed, copper-toned and frosted, on top of hand-size wafers of host.

Manna licked her lips. Lebkuchen was as special as First Communion, so she would start with those first. Reaching down, she pulled out her bill, feeling rich and strangely spoiled.

"What are you gonna get?" asked Mano.

"Everything!" she gushed, turning round to hurry back down the aisle. It felt like they were running out of time ...

CLINK – A – CLINK!

"Money for the poor," croaked a shrill voice, rattling coins in a loud tin can.

Surprised, Manna froze. The voice came from behind her, at the end of the aisle – but a second ago, no one was there. Maybe it was the voices in her head. She looked at Mano to see if he heard something ... and the hairs on her arms curled.

In all their years, nothing ever grossed Mano out (not even the antenna wriggling roach that squirmed in his milk – he just drank it), but at this very moment, his pale, disgusted face looked ready to vomit.

"Wha-at?" cackled the suddenly angry voice.

Mano gagged, turned his head to the side, and spat a brown wad of puke to the ground. Then holding one knee, he hunched over and groaned through his teeth.

Manna couldn't help but feel curious. What on earth could sicken him?

Forgetting to fear, she spun around quickly ... and stared.

Crumpled on the ground, covered with tattered burlap and enormous black flies, was the most disgusting woman Manna ever saw. Her orange-white hair scraggled around scab-flaking bald spots and exposed folded decaying ears (one of which dangled by a brownish-grey sinew, ready to fall off her head). Her yellowish-grey face pocked with deep, purple-red sores that frothed with glistening pus – and her cracked, sagging skin wagged loose from her cheeks and slupped off her shriveled skull, as if it were pepperoni pizza sliding down a wall. Buzzing loud, the hairy, black flies tasted her oozing sores.

Manna felt sick ... with pity ... for the dying leper that begged her.

The leper's hideous face scrunched into an orange, toothless sneer. She reached out her gnarled, yellow-clawed hand and rattled her noisy cup, spraying reddish-brown spittle as she crooned, "Money for the poor."

Instinctively, Manna dropped her crisp bill into the leper's cup and grinned close-lipped, trying hard not to gag.

The leper's face dropped – further.

Bumping against Manna's shoulder, Mano stepped forward and reached inside his shoe, trying to copy his sister – but instead, he tripped and spilled his whole glass of wine on the leper's face.

"NOOOOO!" shrieked the leper, ripping at her face with her terrible claws, red spit spraying through her hands. Then, with a body-shuddering jolt, she jerked up to her knees, flailed her arms in the air, and shook furiously from head to toe. Hissing and spattering, she strained her head far back and melted into a blood-red puddle of boils.

"AAAAY!" screamed Manna, her terrified heart jammed in her throat.

Mano killed the leper!

Quickly, the gloopy leper puddle dissolved into bright orange steam that curled up and transformed into a long waving hand – then, hypnotically, it swayed above Manna, like a rattlesnake charmed by a flute.

Dazed, Manna breathed in deep to steady herself, and an odd acidic smell teared her eyes. Uncontrollably, she felt herself sway with the hand, her blurry eyes firmly locked in its palm. Then, without trying, she relaxed and let the hand hold her ... mind.

WHISH!

Without warning, the hand shot forward and snatched at Manna's face. Snapping out of her trance, she ducked quickly, grabbed her brother and bolted past the food stands, straight for the tall Christmas tree – and Ailani!

Manna's head spun and her heart pounded in her throat.

What was going on?

Billowing tents clapped against a howling wind and parachuted into the sky. Hot dogs and dolls, plates and fries, whirled past Manna in frenzied confusion. Women screamed and glassware crashed, quickly scattering out of the way – and jovial fat men slammed down their beer steins and scrambled, scared-faced, away.

Oh my gosh, thought Manna. *She's chasing us – and everyone's getting out of her way!*

"Gotcha!" boomed a towering red-faced man, swiping both children up in one bulging arm. Glowering through cruel grey eyes, he swung round a swollen hand and plucked away Mano's bill.

"Dirty colored thieves," he swore, growing red around the ears.

"Those belong to me," said a dry, shrill voice.

Panting, but glad the big man could protect her, Manna squirmed round to look at the leper – but instead, there stood her aunt, fists clenched around two shopping bags, a tight smile stretched across her face.

"I'm sorry," grappled the man, letting go of the children. "I ... uh ... saw them knocking down tents and ..."

"Ha, ha!" laughed Theresa. "Such small children – do that?" She motioned towards the tents, her smile relaxing. "It was the wind, Herr Schmidt ... and your brilliantly creative artist's imagination."

"Yes ... of course," blushed the man, looking at his feet. "My sincerest apologies, Madame."

Manna looked back at the fair.

Bent, broken tents lay on the ground – cracked, crumpled gifts littered the aisles – and gawking people shook their heads in disbelief.

Embarrassed about her own imagination (that leper wasn't *real*), Manna glanced sheepishly at her aunt and noticed for the first time.

Standing next to Theresa, Anna looked small and scared.

Moho never met them at the door, but today he did, almost as if he knew.

"You're home early," he wheezed, totally out of breath.

Anna hadn't said a word the entire way home, as though nothing bad had happened, so Manna was shocked when she burst into tears.

"I've never been so humiliated in my life!" she cried, her eyes and face suddenly red.

Instantly, Moho's face fell, as though he was to blame, but Manna knew it was all her fault. Her stomach grew heavy with dread.

Covering her face with both hands, Anna ran to her room, threw herself down on the squeaky bed, and crumpled into a sobbing heap. Forgetting to glower at Pu-pele, Moho ran in, close behind her.

"Go to your room," ordered Momi, executing the usual plan.

Obeying immediately, Manna shuffled down the hall, but stopped abruptly at Anna's door.

Something was different – in there.

"What happened, Baby?" breathed Moho, his voice shaking with uncertainty as he stood over her, his wide back to the bedroom door.

"She ruined everything ..." Anna choked in her pillow, "in front of Theresa."

Manna felt herself choking, too.

Why did all the weird things happen around her?

Anna sat up, hugging her pillow to her breast, and wailed, "She knows now ..."

Manna didn't know what Anna was talking about, and neither did Moho – but he knew what to do. He sat gently on the edge of the bed, pulled Anna onto his lap, and wrapped his massive arms completely around her.

With a soft whimper, Anna flung her frail arms around his neck and squeezed. Manna smiled, thinking things would be better.

Suddenly, Anna's eyes flew open and stared wild-eyed at Manna.

Oh no, thought Manna, jumping out of view. *She saw me!*

"Get rid of her," said Anna. Her voice was cold and dry.

Manna didn't know where to run. Last time, he saw her hiding under the bed!

"Who?" asked Moho – and suddenly, Manna felt as though that big orange hand squeezed her ankles and held them firmly to the ground. Petrified, she stood shaking ... and listened.

"My mother," said Anna. "She's in the closet."

"No one's in there," growled Moho under his breath, unusually tense around Anna.

"I can hear her ... breathing!" cried Anna, pushing Moho away.

Moho stood up, towering over Anna, and begged, "Trust me, Baby. Nobody's there."

"I KNOW SHE'S IN THERE!" screamed Anna, springing off the bed and lunging for the closet door.

Faster than a snapping turtle, Moho caught her by the waist and swung her over his shoulder.

"Stop it!" squealed Anna, slapping her palms on his back. "That tickles!" – but Moho just poked his fingers deeper into her tummy and hauled her, upside down and laughing, through the hall and into her safe kitchen – never noticing Manna was there.

Huh-hmm.

Manna heard breathing, like a gentle summer wind whispering past her ears – and instantly curious, she leaned through her parents' bedroom door and listened closely, her heart standing still.

Huh-hmm.

She heard it again – but this time it seemed to call her, longing to have her near. Without thinking, she stepped gingerly into the room and noticed a musky, salty smell, like Anna's warm perspiration – and at once, everything felt cozy.

Huh-hmm.

This time the breathing drew her forward, as though it was a magnet pulling her chest. Growing strangely excited, she tiptoed to Anna's closet door and pulled down its silver handle. Then, with a jittery heart, she swung open the door ... and gasped.

Before her stood a tall, shimmery red fairy – the most dazzling thing she ever saw!

The fairy's red sequined dress glittered like a million blinding sunsets, and her knee-length hair beamed electric orange past her full, sparkling rouged cheeks. Her round ocean-blue eyes twinkled in deep ripply pools, and her dark red lips pouted a shiny, heart-shaped surprise – as though she had exclaimed, "Oh!" With a faint rustle, her wide, curvy hips moved heavily from side to side, like a coconut-laden palm tree swaying in an island breeze.

Shocked, Manna and the fairy stared at each other, open-mouthed. But suddenly, the fairy twinkled with pleasure and flashed a pearly white smile.

"My precious Manna," she cooed huskily, reaching out a soft brown hand.

Manna stepped back. This didn't feel right. The fairy wasn't supposed to be there – in Anna's place.

THUMP! – "OW-WAY!"

Mano's shoe hit the fairy right between the eyes, and she hollered in surprise.

Manna jumped back, alongside her brother, glad that he followed –

and glad he didn't want the fairy there, either.

"The children!" Manna heard Anna scream.

"Ooh, you puka head!" fumed the fairy, pressing her chubby palms against the bright red shoe print on her forehead. Then, quick as a flash, she snatched up Mano's shoe and flung it back at him, her glazed eyes burning with hate.

Manna ducked, pulling Mano down with her.

THUNK!

It sounded like a boulder hit the side of a mountain, but instead, the shoe smacked Moho's forehead – right when he burst into the room.

Manna's huge eyes almost popped out. She wasn't expecting him there!

Moho's wild face snapped back and forth between Manna and the fairy, as if he was choosing a victim. Manna was certain he'd choose her, but suddenly, with a nasty snarl and a body-jerking heave, he grabbed the kicking, arm-flailing fairy and threw her out the fifth-story bedroom window.

"NOOOOoooo!" shrieked the fairy, as she flew further and further away.

"This never happened," glowered Moho, right before he tromped out the door.

"Whoa," breathed Mano, tottering towards the window and leaning out to survey the damage.

Manna turned away, shivering, and that's when she saw it.

The fairy's bright red, magical bag shimmered innocently on the closet floor.

Quickly, she grabbed the purse and stuffed it in her dress.

Anna shouldn't find it.

Manna could hear their bedtime voices through the wall.

"We should move to Hawaii, so you can rest ... and get better," coaxed Moho, his usual growl reduced to a tiger's purr.

"But my family," objected Anna.

"*My* family is *your* family," insisted Moho, "and they will take care ... of you ... the kids ... the responsibilities."

"But how will we live?" asked Anna.

"Very well, Baby," promised Moho. "It's a much better life there – the people, the place ... and me ..."

His voice boomed, suddenly proud.

"There, I'm something special."

"You're special here," insisted Anna.

"Yeah, in your home – but not in your world."

There was a long pause, and then Anna quivered, "*My* world is in *your* home ... wherever that may be."

"Then it's settled." Moho's voice sounded excited. "I won't re-enlist. When my time's up, we're going HO-O-OME!"

Anna popped into ridiculous giggles, so Manna knew he tickled her. She felt glad that Moho knew how to take care of Anna – but she still worried about the fairy. Where did she come from, and what was she doing here? Then she remembered the bag.

The answer must be in there.

Quickly, Manna pulled the bag out from under her pillow and tiptoed into the bathroom. Then, closing the door and flipping on the lights, she rolled it between her palms and examined it.

The bag looked like a leprechaun's money pouch (except that it was shiny red). It had two drawstrings that bunched the material at the top, leaving a bulging bottom sack. Its satiny material glittered with sparkling jewels that shone a thousand shades of red – and its drawstring handles dangled metallic-pink with threaded tassels hanging from their ends. Sewn to the center of its gathered top, two pearly white clams hung, shining.

Manna opened one clam with her finger and bit her lip.

Inside was a frosted globe filled with blue water and a tiny wiggling red fish. She peeked into the other clam and grinned. The pearl in there held a smiling mermaid with a gentle waving hand.

Suddenly, Manna's heart started to beat fast. It was time to open the pouch, and something scary was probably in it. Maybe a child-eating monster. Or a face-sucking squid. Or even a pixie-dust bomb!

Squeezing her eyes shut, she held the purse far away from her face, and yanked it open.

Nothing happened.

Relieved, her heart slowed down.

Manna opened her eyes ... and squealed.

The purse held the fairy's treasure! Its pink-lined pouch shone full of golden coins, and along its upper rim, a circle of pockets spilled over with diamonds and pearls.

Excited, Manna put the purse on the counter and dug both hands inside to scoop out the treasure, but something pricked her finger. Surprised, she stopped and peered inside.

The corner of a pink, flowered envelope stuck out of the coins and winked at her, inviting her to take it.

With a suddenly nervous stomach, Manna slid the dainty envelope out and held it to the light. It was labeled, "Nur Anna – von Mutti," which meant, "Only Anna – from Mother" -- so this was her grandmother's bag and she wanted Anna (and only Anna) to have it.

Disappointed the bag wasn't magic, Manna started to replace the letter, but noticed it wasn't sealed – the tongue was just tucked in. Her heart skipped a couple beats.

Maybe she should peek inside. It couldn't hurt anything, could it? Anna would never know.

Shaking a little, she untucked the tongue and pulled out a thin stack of pictures. Immediately, a warm flow rushed from her fingers to her toes. They were baby pictures of her and Mano, with Anna, propped up in a hospital bed. Anna cuddled both of them tightly – Mano bright-eyed and bushy; Manna bundled and asleep.

Manna flipped through the pictures quickly, choking back hot tears.

In every picture, Anna squeezed her tight and beamed – thrilled to have her there.

Manna flipped through the pictures again, her heart filling with hope.

Maybe Anna wanted her after all. Maybe the trouble was something else, like Moho said, something about Anna that had to get better. Anna loved her – you could see it clearly in the pictures.

Manna's heart froze. You could see something else clearly, too – a huge, horrible, open-fanged shadow mouth looming directly above Anna's head – with a long forked tongue that flicked menacingly over her ear.

Manna's heart jumped and pounded in her brain. That mouth couldn't be real!

Quickly, she flipped to the next picture and the mouth was there too, much bigger and closer to Anna's head.

In the next, the mouth descended on Anna. Its fangs scraped her forehead and its hideous tongue wrapped around her shoulders, as if it was swallowing her whole.

BAM!

Mano swung the bathroom door open and bumped past Manna. Startled, she dropped the pictures in the toilet.

"Sorry," he mumbled, already tinkling in the bowl. Then, with a quick kick, he flushed and stumbled out the door.

Manna watched the pictures swirl down the commode.

She was glad they were going away – to Hawaii – where Moho could keep Anna safe.

Chapter Five

DON'T MOVE

"Prepare for landing!" hollered the cargo plane pilot, right before he slammed the bathroom door shut.

Manna jerked straight up in her wooden seat and thanked God it was bolted to the floor.

When Moho said it was free to fly from Germany to Hawaii in a cargo plane, it sounded like a really good deal. But he forgot to mention there was no food on the bumpy, eighteen-hour flight and not a single window with a view. He also didn't say that there were only eight hard seats, facing backwards in a row, directly in front of a fifty-ton pile of military-issued cargo. But most upsetting, he didn't mention that the camouflage-colored mountain was held in place by just a few flimsy ropes.

Manna squinted at the bulky green wall that trembled before her. Without a doubt, when the plane dove on descent, the ropes would pop and the cargo would lurch forward and crush her.

"What's the matter, darlin' ?" asked the boyish pilot. His pug nose turned up and pointed at his bright blue eyes.

Manna gazed at the kind face that loomed above her and wanted to speak up – but couldn't.

Ten-year-olds never show fear.

The pilot glanced at the cargo and smiled back at Manna. His playful eyes twinkled with mischief.

"Wanna come up front and play pilot?"

"That's illegal," objected Momi.

"So is smokin' durin' flight," the pilot clucked back, avoiding Momi's hot glare.

Eager, Manna sprang out of her chair and grinned. If the cargo crashed through the cockpit, she'd have time to eject, like a fighter pilot bailing midair.

The pilot saluted Moho and asked, "Is that alright – SIR?"

Moho nodded his head up once and grunted, then leaned his cheek drowsily against Anna's sleeping head. He looked oddly pleased, and Manna worried she was making a mistake.

Quickly, the pilot grabbed Manna with a cold, damp hand and dragged her to the cockpit. Once inside, he hopped into a chair, but Manna stood frozen ... in awe.

A shiny silver pilot's panel stretched around the cabin and down the center of the aisle. All over it, red and white lights and green glowing dials flashed, sensitive and bright – and a thousand excited buttons and toggles switched spontaneously, on and off. On either side of the cabin, identical grey leather chairs leaned forward and guarded tilting hourglass steering wheels that automatically flew the plane.

Manna peered at the computerized wheels and the beaming thought-processing panel and thought, *Cool! I'm in the brain of a cloud-ripping robot!*

"Wow!" breathed Mano.

Manna jerked around, not surprised he followed.

"Sorry," said the pilot, turning around in his chair. "There's only one extra seat."

"That's okay. We'll share," said Mano, plopping himself down, much to Manna's relief. If he stood there much longer, he would stumble (or *something)* and hit the self-destruct button!

Manna shuddered.

There was a reason kids weren't allowed up here. Something bad was bound to happen.

Biting her bottom lip, she squeezed into the chair next to Mano and buckled the seat belt around them – tight.

"Keep your hands on your lap," she whispered into his ruffled hair.

"Paradise," the pilot breathed dreamily.

Manna looked out the wide window and gasped.

Before her shimmered the most beautiful deep blue ocean surrounding a glistening row of dark green, mountainous isles. Foaming white water slapped the tan island shores, and thin streaky clouds zoomed merrily through the steep inland ridges. A long, perfectly arched, bright-colored rainbow beamed over the biggest island and hid its ends in a line of rolling, black-tipped hills.

Amazed, Manna watched the powerful ocean waves swell and the shiny trees sway – and could swear they were rising to greet her.

"Wanna put on the brakes?" asked the pilot.

Excited, Manna raised both eyebrows and nodded.

"Push down that lever ..." the pilot grinned, "... slowly."

Clutching the stiff lever tight, Manna eased it back and felt the plane lose power through her arm. Immediately, her heart skipped a beat.

She was in total control of the brain!

Manna gripped the lever tighter. If she thrust it back up, the plane would shoot into the air, and she wouldn't have to worry about the cargo.

"Wanna drop the landing gear?" the pilot asked Mano.

Manna's chest fell. He didn't know what he was asking. Mano would drop more than the wheels!

Before Manna could object, her brother's bright face bounced up and down, and the pilot said, "Push that button."

Flopping his whole body forward, Mano slammed his chin down on the panel.

Immediately, the plane shivered and its bottom fell out. Then, with a loud scraping groan, the mountain of cargo (or something just as heavy) slid out the hole, and the bottom bumped itself shut.

Manna clutched the seat cushion, just *knowing* he hit the wrong button.

"Somethin' wrong with your hands?" frowned the pilot.

"Nope," answered Mano, gripping both of his bouncing knees.

"Right then," said the pilot, widening his eyes and facing land. "Twenty seconds to impact."

Surprised Mano didn't blow it, Manna sat up and leaned forward.

This was turning out to be fun!

Blinking, she peered through the white, misty window and ignored her pressure-clogged ears.

Misty silver clouds hurtled towards her face and sliced over the plane's hull. In an instant, the blue sky burst out of the clouds and thundered over the plane. Then, with a sharp ear-popping bow, the cabin tipped sideways and spun on a wing – then plunged straight for the ground. Whistling wind sheared past the window and pressed hard against Manna's chest.

Suddenly, a grey wall of asphalt slammed Manna's way, threatening to crush her skull. Trying not to scream, she grabbed her shaking brother and squeezed her fear into his skinny arm.

BAM!

The plane hit the ground and bounced back into the air.

THUNK! SHROOOOM!

The plane hit the ground again and shuddered violently against its screeching brakes – then taxied lightly to a stall.

Manna breathed out, her whole body exhilarated.

That was the fastest she'd ever gone!

"Cool," beamed Mano at his giggling sister.

"WE'RE HERE!" boomed Moho, spraying excitement through the cabin walls.

Instantly, hope skipped around Manna.

Maybe here, everything would be different.

"KEALO-O-O-O .. HA!" called a clamor of voices below.

Manna looked down from the airport balcony, past the escalators, where a dark, excited crowd waved, their arms out to their sides and covered with long hanging leis. Every one of them smiled with a deep, desirable beauty that Manna had never seen before – and suddenly, she felt nervous, like the first day of school, worried she wouldn't fit in.

Moho's hand shot up into the air, his pinky and thumb extended while his other fingers curled down in his palm. Then swiveling his wrist as if waving hello, he yelled back, "ALO-O-O-O ... HA!"

Hooting with arms open wide, the crowd clambered up the escalator (even though it was going the wrong way). The tall heavyset black men huffed up – three steps at a time – bearing white giant-toothed smiles and swinging hefty loads of purple and white orchid leis. The equally tall and heavy, brown-skinned women jiggled up the stairs behind them, teetering and laughing hysterically as they tugged on tightly wound, red and yellow feather leis that tangled in their long wavy hair. The small, nimble, dark brown children scampered easily up the moving handrails, twirling bushy, green fern leis over their glistening heads, as if they were helicopters taking flight. Every one of the loud crowd wore loose, silky clothes splattered with large bright-colored blossoms.

Thrilled, Manna closed her eyes and hoped to be engulfed by the oncoming flurry of wild Hawaiian flowers.

Quickly, a soft, dewy lei pulled down on her neck and a little girl kissed her chin, breathing, "Aloha!"

At once, Manna's heart burst with fragrant joy. The flowers smelled sweeter than sugar-dusted candy, and that kiss was softer than a baby bunny's pink nose.

"Aloha!" a rough, sweaty cheek growled, right before it kissed her hair and scratched a fern lei down the back of her neck.

"Aloha!" a loud woman's voice laughed at the same time it squashed both of Manna's cheeks between its chubby, hot palms and planted a cushy, moist kiss on her lips. Tickling, a feather lei brushed past her nose.

Aloha. Smack. Wrap.

Aloha. Smack. Wrap.

The love and leis piled on and on, smothering Manna in a head-high mountain of leis. Tingling, the heavy perfume of fresh-cut flowers dulled her mind and numbed her fingers and toes. Then sharply, the thin minty smell of newly pruned leaves contracted her chest and froze her air-starved lungs. With a swirl, the heavy heat inside the lei mountain pressed down on her shoulders and neck ... and held her face under a steamy ocean of dew. Lost in cozy oblivion, she swayed dreamily and wished she could always be there.

Suddenly, the alohas stopped and everything went deathly silent, as though Moses had parted the sea.

"Tutu," Moho murmured tenderly.

Anxious, Manna tugged the leis away from her eyes and peeked out at Tutu ... Moho's mother.

Although Moho stood six foot four, the red hibiscus that clung to Tutu's flat reddish-grey bun scraped his temple when they embraced.

"My biggest boy," she cooed, her deep stately voice echoing in the humid air.

Groaning, Moho squeezed her tighter. Then pulling away, he glanced at his kids.

Smiling, Tutu turned her dark, crinkled face and stared straight at Manna.

With a blinding, "Zing!" – Tutu's sea green eyes pierced Manna's sockets and stabbed electric-sharp pangs through her brain. Then pumping fury, her blood-red eye veins shot blazing hot streaks out of her haunting-moon whites and burned Manna's heart shut. Quivering, an ice-cold, long-fingered hand squeezed Manna's guts and yanked them into her throat.

"YOU ARE THE ONE!" a wicked voice screeched in her head and at once, Manna knew – something evil lived inside of her.

"At last," Tutu smiled back at Moho. "The Kealoha family is back."

Relieved to be free of the witch's glare, Manna wiped away a tear.

Tutu had seen right through her.

"Dees my keeds," said Uncle Ku-hai, Tutu's second oldest son. "Get my oldest, Ku-hai ..."

The tallest, most muscular boy in the crowd (who was sixteen but could pass for twenty) ambled forward and flashed a wide straight-toothed smile. His handsome face shone with a leader's charisma below the light brown lightning bolts that flashed through his dark brown hair, and right away, Manna liked him.

"... then Aikoa ..."

A tall, tough-looking girl nodded her head up once and grinned Ku-hai's wide smile – but somehow, on her it looked cruel. Her sharp, cold eyes ran quickly over her new cousins, warning them to respect, while her long wavy brown hair fluttered menacingly in the wind.

Manna shivered. That fourteen-year-old cousin looked a lot like Pu-pele – who happened to be fourteen, too.

"... and Kau ..."

A fat, yet muscular boy puffed up his chest and nodded his broad head. Manna knew he was only thirteen, but his fierce brown eyes and ominous size made him look forty-two. She figured it best to stay out of his way.

"But more better call him kau-kau," offered a skinny, bushy-haired boy.

Immediately, the crowd roared with knee-slapping laughter.

(Manna didn't know, in Hawaiian, "kau-kau" means "eat" – vigorously.)

"... and the joker stay Iki – my youngest boy ..."

Iki smiled eagerly and bounced on his toes. His messy, blonde-streaked hair flew wild like Mano's, and Manna felt glad he was ten, too.

"... and my baby, Waka."

A chubby Hawaiian doll toddled forward, her dark round eyes shining mischievously under a black mop of curls. Turning up in a devilish smile, her dark red upper lip spread fuller than the bottom and formed a wide heart under her spoiled, round nose.

Manna felt herself grin. That six-year-old looked like a bundle of trouble.

"Get mine," said Uncle Moku, Tutu's third son. "First Moku ..."

A tall, muscular boy stepped forward and grinned openly. His handsome Hawaiian features matched all the other cousins, yet something about him was different. Maybe it was the way he stood, not quite straight and tall. Or maybe it was the shy, thankful look in his eyes, like life had stopped being rough. But whatever it was, Manna felt they had something in common, even though he was fifteen years old.

"... then Kokala ..."

A wall of a boy stepped forward and jiggled with a high-pitched laugh.

Manna smiled. You could tell this boy was good-natured and funny —
and very easy to love. But from the softness in his massive arms, you
could see it might be annoying that he didn't do any chores.

Who knows how a thirteen-year-old got away with that?

"... and Hi'u ..."

A feisty-looking boy stuck out his pinky and thumb, waving shaka
like Moho did (except he kept his hand down by his hip). Then
smirking, he stuck out his tongue and wiggled it, crazy like a fish.

Everyone giggled, including Manna. That nine-year-old might be
fun.

"... and my keiki li'i, Pahau."

Six-year-old Pahau smiled sweetly at her daddy. Her brown, angelic
face shone out of her bouncy, orange-red curls, and her bright, light
brown eyes sparkled innocently above a shy, tiny-toothed grin. Manna
wanted to squeeze her – the one that gave the very first lei.

Suddenly, Uncle Junior (Tutu's youngest son) shuffled from toe to
toe, looking guilty.

"Brah, I never when find a wife," he admitted.

Uncle Moku smacked Junior on the back of the head and boomed,
"But you when find a million girls!"

Snorting, the crowd laughed loud.

"Who you get, Brah?" asked Uncle Ku-hai, smiling wide at Moho's
kids.

"Momi, Pu-pele, Ailani," grunted Moho. Then stepping in front of
his girls, he thunked a heavy hand on Mano's shoulder and boomed
proudly, "And Mano – MY BOY!"

"What about da kine, skeenny one?" asked Iki.

Moho's lips curled in and Iki backed up, looking very nervous.

After a long, uncomfortable silence, Moho squinted and breathed,
"Manna."

At once, the whole crowd sucked in and pummeled Manna with scorn. Ashamed, she frowned at the ground and hoped it would swallow her up.

Something bad was wrong with her name.

Anna reacted first.

"It's for Moho and Anna – together," she squeaked. "M for Moho – then Anna."

"That's beautiful, dear," assured Tutu, stroking Anna's baby fine hair.

Thankful, Anna smiled at Tutu, glad that she was there – and suddenly, Manna felt glad, too.

"Bum-bye, we go Tutu's house," recovered Uncle Moku. "Give you chance to da kine, settle in ..."

"Your house stay choice," interrupted Iki. "We when work twenty-four days, no break."

"Except Kokala, that buggah," chided cousin Moku.

Kokala shrugged his round shoulders and grinned.

"And da kine, two white gifts for Anna – stay preemo," added Junior, grinning proudly from ear to ear.

"We go fish, one hour," finished Uncle Ku-hai. Then he commanded, "Keeds, go school."

"Aaaah!" the cousins moaned together. Then, waving shaka, they dragged their slippered feet away.

Secretly, Manna wished she could follow.

The KeALOHAs

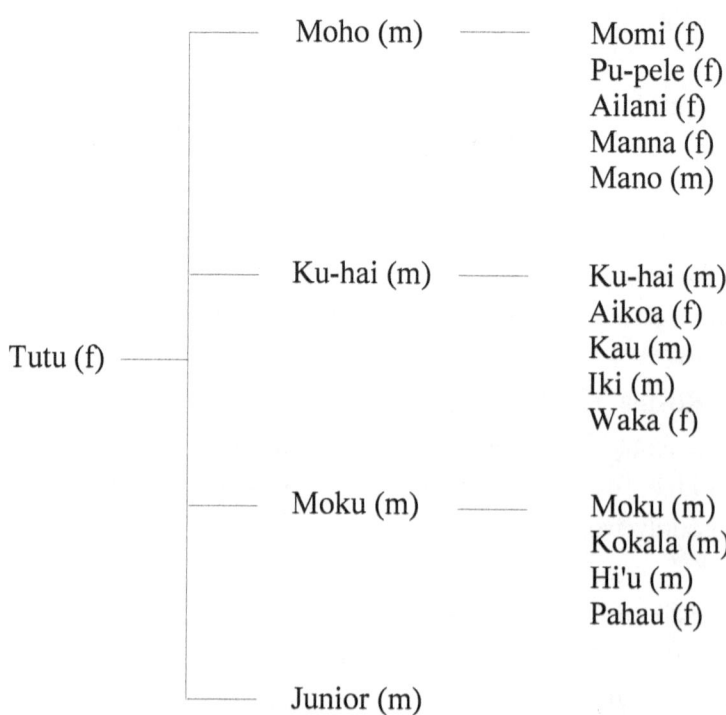

Tutu (f)

Moho (m) ——— Momi (f)
Pu-pele (f)
Ailani (f)
Manna (f)
Mano (m)

Ku-hai (m) ——— Ku-hai (m)
Aikoa (f)
Kau (m)
Iki (m)
Waka (f)

Moku (m) ——— Moku (m)
Kokala (m)
Hi'u (m)
Pahau (f)

Junior (m)

"OW-WAY!" squealed a little voice, before it scuttled away.

Manna jerked up in surprise and almost teetered off the black, jagged rock.

Mercilessly, the scorching afternoon sun beat down on her

hallucinating skull and tossed light-headed orange flecks into her eyes. Faint, she stumbled towards the shaded front porch and fell, spread-eagle, on her back.

After a dizzy moment, the popping orange flecks transformed into a deep, shining blue and Manna sat up – to relax.

The comforting clear blue sky and sparkling blue sea spread wide before her, whispering cool secrets in their breeze – and a hundred long palm fronds clapped playfully in the air, clicking noisily against their trees.

Enjoying her break from the cruel sun, Manna ran both of her hands along the smooth blue-painted porch and felt thankful to be there.

Moho's family built them a big, beautiful house on a black lava hill that towered high above the crashing blue sea.

Sitting tall, Manna sucked in the sweet smell of wild ripe guavas and peered to her right at the distant but tall, red cinder cone, Kilauea – Hawaii's fierce volcano. But suddenly, a cool puff of wind tossed her waist-length hair over her eyes. Flipping her head left, she let the wind blow her hair out of her face.

Now she could see Mauna Loa and Mauna Kea, Hawaii's majestic, snowcapped mountains (or really, dormant volcanos) gleaming at her from far away.

Daydreaming, she wondered why the state of Hawaii was named after this island, when seven others floated in the Hawaiian island chain. Luckily, everyone called this one "The Big Island" – to avoid confusion.

Manna glanced at her blistered hands and couldn't figure out how her cousins did it – building the perfect house in just twenty-four days. The twelve oversized rooms all boasted a stunning view of stark Hawaiian beauty. The rooms Moho went in (to eat, sleep and sit) faced his beloved swelling sea – and the room Anna lived in (the kitchen) opened up to the German-ish white mountains, making her feel at home right away. Even Manna's room faced her favorite thing – the spectacularly strong Kilauea.

"GET BACK TO WORK!" bellowed Momi, from the bottom of the red cinder driveway.

Startled, Manna jumped four feet and landed neatly on her clearing spot between Mano and Ailani.

Before Moho went fishing, he demanded they clear their overgrown acre and Momi wanted it done – today!

In a flash, Momi poked her sweaty, sunburned nose and red, heat-stripped eyes into Manna's face, making her shudder.

Only the devil could get there that fast!

"Stop again and you'll get it!" hissed the Devil. Her hot dead-squid breath curdled in Manna's face.

Worried, Manna stood still. Movement upset the Devil.

With a vicious grunt, the Devil jabbed her pointed pitchfork at Manna's feet and jerked up a small pile of uprooted plants. Then glowering, she spun around (knocking Manna with a club-like elbow) and tromped down the hill, back to the end of the driveway. Once there, she tossed her tiny forkful onto a large pile of shriveled plants and scuffled back to her clearing spot – behind the looming blue house.

Relieved the Devil was out of sight, Manna relaxed and let her eyes scan the side of the house. She thought it neat the way the front leaned on the lava hill, while the back stood free at the bottom – teetering on long wooden legs. It reminded her of a tail-wagging dog, resting its front paws on your knees.

Remembering Moho said the Big Island houses stood on stilts so they could sway during earthquakes, Manna closed her eyes and tried to imagine what one felt like.

BOOM! BOOM! – CRUUUUNCH!

A ground-shaking rumble and deafening boom careened through the lava rock, followed by an earth-splitting crunch.

"EARTHQUAKE!" screamed Manna. Grabbing Mano, she dropped to the ground.

In an instant, a huge, shiny red four-by-four skidded down the driveway and scraped to a stop – an inch from Momi and her bush pile.

"Waaah!" yelled Momi. Jumping out of the way, she fell backwards into the pile, her big, clumsy feet wiggling in the air.

"WHA-AT'S UP?" hollered a beaming Moku from the back of the tall pickup truck – but you could hardly hear him over the pounding boom-box bass.

Manna giggled. Momi looked funny scared.

Hooting and slapping one another, the older cousins poured out of the truck bed – and smiling sweetly, the two smallest girl cousins popped out of the cab, followed by their grinning driver, Ku-hai.

"You when see her face?" squealed Waka.

Angry, Momi's hot glare pierced through the child.

"Wha-at, you neva know how take joke?" chided Iki, his brown-streaked hair more ruffled than Mano's – and sweatier, too.

"SHUT UP!" screamed Momi, lunging forward and jamming her pitchfork in his brow.

Stiffening, Iki stuck out his scrawny chest and glowered at Momi through her pointy, curved prongs.

"Ay, sorry," breathed Ku-hai, stepping cooly between them. "We like help."

"Get grinds or what?" blurted Kokala, as though nothing was going on.

Forgetting Iki, Momi rounded on Kokala, her pitchfork and voice shaking in an effort to contain her violence.

"How da-a-are you be-e-eg for food."

Surprised, Kokala rubbed both hands on his swollen tummy and said, "What? You neva know? -- You supposed to offer."

Hate shot out of Momi's cruel eyes and hailed disappointment on

Manna's shoulders.

The cousins weren't allowed to play ... with them.

"Snack!" hollered Pu-pele, suddenly standing on the front porch gripping a wide serving tray. Delicious, nutty, beige pumpernickel piled high in its center, surrounded by a circle of white-coated, sliced-up brie.

Starved, Manna's tummy growled.

"Grinds!" all the cousins yelled together. Then streaming over one another like nine hungry sharks, they darted up the black lava hill.

With an easy one-handed vault, Moku sailed over the porch handrail and landed in front of the tray first. But immediately, he leaned back and frowned.

"What's that?"

"*My* snack!" quipped Pu-pele, yanking her tray away.

"Whateva," said Moku, waving his hand. "You can keep um."

At once, the other cousins (who were now *all* on the porch) shuffled left and sucked in through their bottom teeth, as though they were sending a secret message. Aikoa clenched her strong brown fists and cocked them in front of her hips.

Sidestepping Pu-pele, Moku kicked off his slippers with two quick jerks and grabbed for the double sliding glass doors.

"Stay out!" warned Pu-pele. Her emerald eyes sizzled and her fingers gripped the glinting silver tray ... like a knife.

Shocked, Moku and Manna stood speechless.

How could she be so ungrateful? The cousins built her house.

"You're dirty," huffed Pu-pele, flashing a hot glare over her cousins.

"Whatcha mean?" objected Moku. "We went surf!"

Suddenly, Ku-hai stepped forward and blocked Aikoa's raised fists.

TOOT! TOOT! – Crunch!

A small red truck swerved down the driveway and honked a friendly hello.

"Tutu!" squealed Waka and Pahau, already running hand in hand to greet their grandmother.

Distracted by the girls' cuteness, Manna wondered if Hawaiians ran everywhere – like everything in life was an exciting affair that you hurried up to enjoy.

"Neva mind, Tita," Ku-hai nudged his shoulder against Aikoa's and nodded his head at the ocean. "More betta out here."

Manna looked up at Ku-hai's strong, chiseled face and wise, patient eyes ... and had a funny feeling he knew what went on in her house.

"What's wrong?" asked Tutu, standing inside the sliding glass door, wondering why the cousins wouldn't come in from the porch.

"Nothing," said Ku-hai. "We like stay here."

Tutu cocked her head and smiled. Her weathered skin cracked with age, but a youthful warmth emitted from her empathetic face – and for a moment, Manna liked her.

"Thanks, eh?" said Ku-hai, swinging Tutu's large woven lauhala basket.

"Tutu!" exclaimed Anna, rushing over with one of her white gifts – a curly miniature poodle.

Turning around, Tutu greeted Anna with a warm bear hug.

Quickly, Pu-pele slammed the door shut behind Tutu and squinted suspiciously at Ku-hai.

"Why you neva tell her?" asked Iki, spitting on the ground. "She when treat us worse than one dog."

He's right, thought Manna, watching Suzy (the dog inside) lick Tutu's feet.

"More betta save face," said Ku-hai. Squatting down flat-footed, he reached into the basket and tossed Iki a glazed bun, reminding, "She your cousin."

At once, the cousins elbowed forward and grabbed overflowing handfuls of sticky white buns and red Hawaiian Punch cans. Within seconds, a loud clamor of popping cans, chomping teeth, smacking lips, and gulping throats splintered the air – and immediately, Manna understood why they called it "Grind."

Stopping for a breather between six buns, Moku grabbed his tummy and grinned, "Some ono." Then raising his eyebrows and jerking his head up, he asked Pu-pele, "You like?"

"How would I know?" she snapped. "*Germans* don't make those."

Amused, Moku straightened his back and grinned playfully at the cousins. Then pretending he held a cup and saucer, he tilted his Hawaiian Punch can above his saucer bun and translated with a heavy British accent.

"Would you care to sample one of my doughnuts?"

All the cousins snort-laughed red punch out their noses.

Bumping Pu-pele, Mano lunged forward and grabbed four.

Doughnuts! thought Manna, right before she plucked one out of Mano's hand.

With a five finger shove, she stuffed the fist-sized doughnut into her mouth and took the biggest bite she could manage.

Immediately, sweet, gooey bread stuck to all sides of her mouth and seeped sugary yeast onto her cheeks.

Chewing quickly, Manna stuck her tongue into the squishy bread and felt chunks of licorice taffy. Surprised, she looked down at what was left of her bun and realized it was stuffed with thick sweet-sour sauce that oozed around dime-sized blumps of *something* that looked like fried cherry pie filling. Greedily, her tummy gurgled and she shoved the rest of the bun into her mouth. Then she leaned forward to grab a piece of white-rind-covered brie.

"What's da kine, white stuff?" asked Moku, just as Manna stuffed the sticky hunk of brie in her mouth.

Using one delicate finger, Ailani twirled a pumpernickel slice around the circumference of the tray, as though it was a tan ballerina – and mesmerized, Moku's eyes followed.

"Cultures," Ailani murmured, before Manna could swallow. "They form on the outside while the cheese inside cures."

"Get MOLD!" yelled Iki, spewing a pink mouthful of saliva-chewed manapua doughnut.

"Ow-way!" exclaimed Aikoa. "They when eat MOLD! Like da kine, slugs!"

Together, Waka and Pahau gagged. Chewed, bloody-red clumps slupped off their tongues and splattered on their bare knees.

Suddenly sick, Manna couldn't swallow.

The soft, delectable brie covering that stuck to her mouth didn't seem so special any more. It just felt like a foreign encasing that restricted her tongue – reminding her that she couldn't speak their language and might, forever, be left out.

Shing. Chop.

Moku's knife almost hit Ku-hai's toe, but he didn't move.

Shing. Chop.

Ku-hai's knife stabbed Iki's slipper. Iki jerked, but couldn't get away. His slipper stayed stuck to the ground.

"Brah," laughed Kau. "You when play like one girl."

"Savages," grumbled Momi, drinking a can of Hawaiian Punch.

Manna wondered why she insulted those who fed her.

Shing. Chop. Su-u-uck.

Iki's knife sliced razor-close to Kau's protruding stomach, but he didn't move. He just sucked hard on his homemade cigarette, and holding his breath, he teased, "Like one *mad* wahine."

All the other boys laughed and coughed out smoke, but Manna could swear Iki pouted, right before he frowned and looked tough.

Hesitant, Manna picked up the last can of Hawaiian Punch, popped it open and peered at its blood-red juice. The only reddish thing she ever drank was lumpy strawberry-flavored milk, so this stuff looked really gross. But determined to fit in, she held her breath and forced down five noisy Hawaiian-style gulps.

Instantly, the tangy juice tingled her tongue and sugarcoated her thirsty throat – then it tickled through her tummy and shot instant energy into her wilted bones.

Yumm! she thought and started to chug the rest – but Mano, bright-eyed and curious, stared hopefully at her over the can. His sweaty black hair sprawled over his beaded forehead and dripped onto his shining brown nose – and his mouth hung open like a hot, panting dog. Feeling sorry for him, Manna handed over the can.

"Work," growled Momi, as soon as Pu-pele stepped in the sliding glass door.

Bummed, Manna trudged back to her hot place in the sun, wondering why the cousins played knife games when it was time to work.

Didn't they come to help?

"Ow-way! Au-we!" cried two little girls – and Manna could swear it was her two little cousins. Alarmed, she jerked her head left.

A field of shoulder-high, purple and white orchids bowed gently in the breeze and exposed Aikoa's bushy brown head – and smirking wickedly, Aikoa glinted her light hazel eyes at Manna, then leaned down and plucked at something.

"Au-we!" the little girls yelped together, and Manna knew.

Aikoa was pulling out their hair!

"No, no!" one screamed. "No pluck me!"

Reacting fast, Manna rushed at Aikoa, forgetting that Aikoa was a lot bigger than her.

BAM!

Unexpectedly, the ground swung up and smacked Manna in the chest, knocking the wind right out of her. Sprawled, tummy down, she lay breathless in the dirt.

"Look! Da baboose – stay parallel!" squawked Aikoa, standing over Manna and pointing so her little cousins would see.

Holding armfuls of bright colored flowers – and about six yards away – the little girls giggled and waved, "Hello!" with their small, chubby, brown hands.

Confused but breathing, Manna sat up on the poky cinder ground.

The tall orchids made the ground look level, but it wasn't. The lava hill dropped off – and so did Manna. Embarrassed, but amused by her unusual clumsiness, she thought, *So that's how Mano feels.*

"She one bolo head," teased a little girl.

"Nah, nah. One hemo head," squealed another, making a bunch of little girls laugh.

"No make fun, you guys," whined a third.

Bleary-eyed, Manna stared at the light green orchid reeds that swayed before her. On the tip of each danced a darling hula girl, about two inches tall and submerged waist-deep in its stalk – and in sweet unison, all the hula girls waved their teeny white arms and bobbed their cute quarter-sized heads.

Manna closed her eyes and shook her brain, trying to get rid of delusion. Then opening wide, she blinked in disbelief.

The orchid girls were still there!

Blinking back at Manna with innocent round eyes that shone bright purple behind long white lashes – the tiny girls grinned inviting pink smiles underneath small pointed noses. Clinging to the top of their white-faced heads, a large purple and white orchid fluttered in the wind, like silky, smooth hair – except for the closest teary-eyed girl, who drooped bald. Her delicate white fingers spread over her bare green crown, trying in vain to hide it.

"What, bother you?" snapped the bald little girl. Her shiny eyes glared defensively at Manna.

Surprised, Manna wondered how hard she hit her head.

The orchid girls couldn't be real.

Reaching out to check, she poked the bald girl in the face.

Eyes burning, the willful nymph gripped Manna's finger and sank her thorny, sharp teeth in its tip.

"AAAAY!" screamed Manna, in pain and surprise.

"AAAAY!" screamed Waka and Pahau, at the same time.

"AAAAY!" screamed Aikoa, even louder.

Jerking to her feet, Manna tried to run but couldn't. There wasn't anywhere to go.

In an instant, the whole flower field turned into a descending pack of shrieking orchid girls, all baring their drippy, bloodthirsty, green fangs!

Backing up, Manna watched in horror as the angry girls rustled against the wind and snapped their anxious teeth – and then she saw it coming – something invisible, tearing through the orchid field, zigzagging faster and faster towards her. Confused, her heart pounding in her chest, she waited breathlessly for the thing to rip through her.

"NOOOOO!" screamed Waka, bursting through the flowers and trampling over Manna.

"IKI-I-I!" pleaded Pahau, right behind Waka. Breathing hard, she scrambled up the rock hill.

Snap! Growl!

A cat-sized, growling rat fox sprung out of the crushed flowers and snapped at Manna's neck. Too shocked to move, she frowned at it with pursed, tense lips.

Squinting, Iki's laughing brown eyes smiled wicked fun at Manna as he thrust his captured mongoose in her face. Its sharp yellow fangs grazed her cheek and its rotted stink breath seared her nose, temporarily fazing her.

"Catch 'em, Brah!" yelled Hi'u, popping out of the trampled flower crack and throwing Iki up the hill.

Looking back at Manna curiously, his sweaty brown hair as wild as his eyes, Iki held his mongoose high and scurried over the hill, running under the house to head off the girls.

"WA-HA!" spooked both boys, almost colliding into the girls.

"AUWE!" roared Aikoa. Then grabbing both little girls by the shoulder, she spun around and dashed the other way.

Slipping and clinking loose rocks, Iki scampered out from under the house and stopped at Momi's bush pile to search for the girls.

"Give him – geeve um!" yelled Hi'u, suddenly pulling on Iki's mongoose.

"No ways, Brah!" Iki yelled back, tugging in the other direction.

"I get 'em!" yelled Kau. Grabbing Iki and Hi'u by the back of their necks, he clunked their heads together.

Dazed, eyes rolling, Iki dropped the mongoose, and in a wink, it disappeared under the bush pile.

Hooting loud, all the boys dove headfirst into the bush pile, like a football team sacking a quarterback – and flurrying in their wind, a hundred uprooted bushes and long shriveled weeds flew left and right, forcing snapped, twisted branches to tumble haphazardly through the air – but no one could find the mongoose.

Laying on his back, Iki flung his arms open and hollered in frustration, "BUMMA-A-AHS!"

"STOP IT!" shrieked Momi, stabbing her pitchfork through Iki's shorts and pinning him to the ground.

The bush pile was scattered all over the yard – and it took her all day to build it!

"Ay! Watch it, Tita!" yelled Aikoa from inside Tutu's truck, her tough face hot with anger. She knew Momi couldn't handle a knife any better than a joke – and she didn't want her cousin skewered.

"Good ting you neva move dees time," chided Moku. "Ete, here, going go poke you!"

Ripping his shorts, a red-faced Iki jumped up and wailed, "You guys when lose my dog!"

"FO-WA-CLOCK!" yelled Ku-hai. "HO'O MAKA!"

Startled, Manna spun around and stared at a looming Ku-hai, wondering, *How long has he been standing behind me?*

Moku leaned through Ku-hai's truck window and flipped on the thundering bass. At the same time, the other boy cousins leaned headfirst into the truck bed.

Covering her ears to block out the bass, Manna finally figured it out.

Hawaiians made everything a loud party.

ZING! ZZZZZZZZZUH!

With a quick chain pull, Kau started a huge weed whacker and leveled the closest bush – and immediately, Waka and Pahau skipped away, swinging the bush between them.

ZING! ZZZZZZZZZUH!

Moku cranked up a smaller weed whacker and swiped between Kau's knees. Laughing heartily, Kau spun his massive body around and sliced his blades over Moku's shimmering hair.

"AH-HA-HA!" cackled Iki, cranking up a loud buzzing chain saw and brandishing it above his head like a sword.

Shivering, Manna thought his stick-up hair and glowing eyes looked utterly deranged.

"ON GUARD!" hollered Hi'u, pointing a long-toothed, thrashing saw straight at Iki's chest. His brown eyes danced with dangerous mischief.

Jerking, Iki swiped at Hi'u's head and barely missed.

With a gasp, Manna stepped back.

This game could get bloody.

Walking cooly between the boys' whirling saws, Ku-hai pulled out a long, bladed whacker. Then, lighting a homemade cigarette, he casually chopped down a tall, thin tree.

"TIMBA!" hollered a lazy Kokala, sitting open-legged on the truck hood.

With a splintering crash, Ku-hai's tree hit the ground and the game was on.

Racing to outdo one another, the boys attacked the yard with their screaming weapons, slaying every tree in sight. Kau, the meanest, sliced down the thickest, and Moku, the cleanest, chopped only roots, leaving the trunk intact. Ku-hai, the fastest, felled three trees at once with every accurate slash. Hi'u, the wildest, ran to and fro destroying everything in his path – and Iki, the loudest, aimed so bad that, mostly, he chopped rock.

Happy, Waka and Pahau skipped between the boys gathering their spoils and plopping them on Momi's pile – while Aikoa, strong and proud, tossed the longest trees, one-handed, in the pile's direction.

Within seconds, the air throbbed with deafening work and Manna worried it would explode through her ears. But thoroughly impressed, she uncovered them to listen to the earth heave and groan as her cousins beat it into submission.

"Wanna try?" shouted an excited Mano, dragging an oversized chain saw behind him.

Unsure, Manna didn't answer. He'd probably chop off her head ... but she wanted to know what it was like. Biting her lip, she summoned her courage – and nodded.

Beaming, his stick-out tooth and surprised eyes sparkling, Mano cranked up the oversized saw.

Shing-shing-shing!

With a metal clanging shing-shing, the heavy saw sheared the lava rock ground and splintered black flint in Manna's face. Thinking fast, she grabbed its handle right above Mano's bony, straining thumbs and helped him lift the saw up – and far away from their bodies. Then hobbling under its weight and heart-panging vibration, they stumbled to the closest branch-sprawling tree and shoved the chain saw in it.

Instantly, the destructive power of the saw hammered through Manna's chest and shimmied across her brain – and whistling loud, large hacked-off tree chunks and battered, splintered branches whirled over her head, as though they were caught in a fervent wind tunnel that Manna, herself, controlled!

Suddenly delirious with power, Manna swung the saw up and hacked off the tree's limbs. Then she spun around and gashed out its guts.

"Wee-hee!" she heard herself squeal, over Mano's loud, "WOO-HOO!"

The saw felt better than trains – because the power came from within ... her!

"PAU!" barked Ku-hai, clicking off Mano's saw. A stern look stretched over his face.

Surprised, Manna looked around.

The whole acre was clear and a one-story bush pile lay on the drive, so Ku-hai must have said – "Finished."

Exhilarated, Manna grabbed one of the branches she chopped and skipped down to the bush pile with it.

"Watch it," said Iki, splashing his water can on the ground – but Manna knew – *he* bumped into *her*, not the other way around. Ignoring him, she flung her branch on the pile – and hit Hi'u, who was suddenly standing on top.

His vindictive eyes gleaming, Hi'u jerked his can at Manna and splashed water on her knees.

"Ay, Brah, you when wet me," complained Aikoa, flinking water off her slippered toes.

Smirking, Hi'u sploshed more water on the pile – and at once, Manna smelled gas.

"Get crackers," said Moku.

Scrambling over one another, the hungry cousins lunged forward and snatched the treats out of Moku's hand. Always starving, Mano grabbed two.

"Throw 'em on toe," breathed Moku. Then he flicked on his cigarette lighter and brushed its flame across Mano's palm.

Confused, Manna leaned over and looked in Mano's hand.

They weren't *eating* crackers. They were *lighting* crackers – FIREcrackers!

Grabbing Mano's wrist, Manna watched in horror as the wicks of two four-inch-thick firecrackers sizzled across his palm.

Without a doubt, the cousins were crazy!

Swinging their sparkling wicks in time, the cousins chanted together,

> "Junk in a munkin,
> Shaka, shaka, po.
> Why pio? Why pio?
> Big fat TOE!"

Jerking Mano's hand as hard as she could, Manna hurled the firecrackers at the bush pile.

BANG! BANG! BOOM! SHRO-O-OM!

With deafening successive bangs, the bush pile exploded into a crackling, yellow and blue inferno. Sweltering heat blasted Manna's face and seared through her clothes, burning frenzied excitement through her body.

This was, by far, the coolest thing she'd ever done!

Drawn by the roaring fire, Pu-pele ran outside and tried longingly to touch it. Her long wavy hair glittered orange around her shining moon face, and her wet half-smile quivered excitement. Outstretched and twitching, her chubby brown fingers reached deep into the pile.

"Careful," Moku warned gently, and pulled back on her hand.

Smiling coyly, Pu-pele's emerald eyes glinted with adoration, and amazingly, she obeyed.

Feeling Ku-hai's heavy stare, Manna tried to stare back – but intimidated, she looked down right away ... and noticed.

Her index finger bled two pin-pricked drops.

"Ah Tutu, we when get plenty fish," grinned Uncle Ku-hai. "When Moho go stay you neva need work – the feesh jump right in da boat!"

Moho smiled wide, and for a moment, Manna thought him handsome in his flower-print shirt and knee-length shorts – but he couldn't compare to Anna. Dressed in a tight, hip-short, sparkly white dress and covered with shimmering pink blush, she glowed like a fairy-princess Barbie.

Junior ran his eyes up and down Anna's dress and twinkled.

"We going go treat you to da best party in town!"

Excited, Anna wiggled her pink-painted toes in their white high-heel slings and hugged Moho's arm tight.

Manna couldn't help but smile at Anna's happiness. Glad that the men would take the women out *every* Saturday night – she forgot to worry about attending Tahuna class at Tutu's house while the adults were away.

"Aloha," grunted Moho, placing a rough kiss on Tutu's cheek. Then jerking Anna off her feet, he spun around and tromped out the door.

Smiling, "Aloha," the uncles and their wives followed.

"Ta means – the," murmured Ailani, as she tapped her right hand down her left forearm, "and huna means – secret ... knowledge."

Manna wondered what secrets Tutu would teach them. Hopefully, it was how to make manapua doughnuts.

"Try come," motioned Tutu. Her evil green eyes sliced over the children.

Spooked, Manna ducked behind Ailani and shadowed her into the dark side hall – and scuffling close, Mano followed her in line.

"In Hawaii, ao – the day – is the time for man, and po – the night – is the time of the Akua – your fierce family GODS!" resounded Tutu, but her deep voice echoed out the long hall walls instead of the front of the line where she walked.

Suspicious, Manna glanced at the tortured wooden masks that dangled on the walls like moaning decapitated heads – and could swear Tutu's voice gurgled out their gaping mouths.

Instantly, the creepies crawled up Manna's back.

"The mo'olelo – the stories of the Akua – hold the secrets of Hawaii's past and are sacred to your family," breathed Tutu.

Tutu and the children walked further down the hall, and Manna noticed a funny smell, like tree bark burning – or maybe human flesh. Anxious, the hairs on Manna's arms jumped up and tried to run away.

"Mo'olelo can only be told in the day," continued Tutu, "in the secret of your family circle – where you must sit still without a word, respectfully, left leg and arm crossed over your right – in the ne'epu position."

Tutu stopped at a yellow-hued doorway and turned around slowly. In the dim light, her red-bordered eyes glowed eerily like human-cooking coals. Hissing, she warned, "Move or speak during mo'olelo and you will be punished with DEATH!"

Manna's heart stopped cold.

Would Tutu really kill her?

Grunting, Momi tromped through the doorway after Tutu, with Pupele and Ailani on her heels – but when it was Manna's turn to go through, she froze. A stinging chill engulfed her chest and prickled across her back.

Something dangerous lived in that room, and no way was she going in it.

"Oof! Sorry."

Following too close, Mano bumped her through the door. Shooting him a dirty look, she noticed – he shook uncontrollably from bushy hair to long brown toes, as if he too felt frozen – yet beads of sweat streamed off his broad, flared nose. Looking down where he stared, Manna watched the earth spread brown and grainy beneath their feet.

How odd. The floor was missing and they stood barefoot and shivering in warm, moist sand.

Suddenly, the soft rustle of wheat grass blowing in the wind brushed Manna's face and breezed through the room's grass shack walls – and at once, four hanging lauhala mats clapped against each wall, and two pointed tiki torches flickered on opposite ends of the room. Then a sharp, chilly swirl blew up to the ceiling and hooed through the thatched palm roof.

Quickly, Manna realized that they stood in Tutu's olden-day grass shack (and that her modern house was built around it), but she didn't understand where the wind came from. It seemed to fly right out of the now cool, pebbly sand.

"Noho. Sit," ordered Tutu, tilting her reddish bun towards the center of the shack – and at that moment Manna noticed the white and black stick-figure patterned dress Tutu wore. It was made of a single square piece of cloth that draped over her wide body and tied in a simple loose knot above her shoulder.

Manna wondered if the dress would fall off.

Mano shoved his rough, clammy hand into Manna's and headed for the floor where fourteen handkerchief-sized, white cloths lay in a large circle, in front of greyish-green, rectangular lauhala mats. On nine of the opened cloths glowered hideous, foot-long, blackish-brown wooden dolls, each carved and shaped like a beating club. Their cruel, down-slanted, pupil-less eyes glared at Manna, and their wide open, square-toothed mouths frowned past their chins. Crouching, arms bent and fists clenched at the hip, the evil dolls looked ready to pounce.

Scuffling to their mats, the cousins each sat behind a doll. Serious looks shrouded their faces.

Quietly, Manna sat on the closest lauhala mat (between Mano and Ailani) and peered around the flickering circle ... at the cousins and their dolls.

Their frozen brown faces glowed striking and fierce, like ancient, unbeatable warriors – forcing hot goose-pimply awe to wash over Manna's body.

Careful to avoid death, Manna crossed her arms and legs, then stayed perfectly still, until she noticed Mano's shoulder knocking against hers. As always, he sat too close – bouncing. Nudging him in the ribs, she hissed through unmoving lips, "Stay still!"

Wincing, Mano stopped – and Manna felt bad that she'd asked him to do the impossible.

Her nervous, jerky brother would be the first clobbered by death.

Flowing around the outside of the circle, Tutu rose both palms to the roof and emitted a low ominous chant – but the cousins continued to move their stern faces, and none of their arms stayed crossed.

Stiffening, Manna wondered if the cousins did the killing by beating you with their ugly dolls.

Tutu stopped chanting and scanned over her new grandchildren with scrutinizing eyes – and suddenly defensive, but remembering the airport, Manna glared at Tutu's forehead with all her might.

"On earth, every person possesses an unalterable destiny," hummed Tutu. "One that you can feel in your heart and your bones – but cannot see or understand ... until the very last second of life ..."

A sickening premonition seeped into Manna's stomach and swirled to her head.

Her destiny would be a struggle.

Tutu leaned far forward, parted her dry lips, and revealed the large glistening fangs of a dragon-faced vampire careening to take its first bite.

Squeezing fear out of her stomach with one quick flex, Manna refused to flinch.

"Unless-s-s," hissed Tutu through her terrible fangs, "you live as a Kealoha – close to your Akua and family circle, who – together – choose the path of your unwavering fate, and thereafter, guide and protect you."

Obstinance filled Manna's head as she squinted at her grandmother.

No one was going to tell her what her destiny *had* to be or force her to follow *their* path, especially not someone in Moho's family. He was wrong about her. She wouldn't always be a blistering scab that he picked at and tossed away. She could make herself something worthy and good. Mother Mary told her so!

Tutu put both palms out, in front of her breasts, then swooped them apart and traced the children's circle.

"With the Tahuna teachings, you will see the future – your future – and learn what you truly are ... and where you are meant to be – and with the guidance of your Akua and family, you will excel on your chosen path."

Panic prickled Manna's chest. There *was* something creepy and weird about her, but she could change it – or hide it ... as long as the family didn't see. Holding her breath, she readied herself to fight off their attack.

Swishing her dress between the cousins, Tutu pressed into the circle.

With a synchronized swipe, the cousins sat straight up and crossed their arms and legs. Looking like knights wielding armor before their enemy, they stared coldly in Manna's direction.

Breathing out slowly, Manna planned her escape.

She would use Mano as a shield and a tiki torch as her weapon.

Lowering her lids, she glanced at her brother to check his position, and noticed – his arms and legs were crossed – BACKWARDS!

Instinctively, she hissed, "Switch your arms and legs."

THWAP! - "UGH!"

With obedient vigor, Mano swung both *feet* over opposite *arms* and his huge right foot thwapped Manna in the chest. Losing their balance, they both tumbled backwards into a tangled heap.

Reacting first, Manna scrambled up, yanked Mano to his bottom, crossed his arms and legs properly, and plopped down on her mat.

The tiki torch was too far away, so their only hope was – no one saw.

SHREEM!

A brilliant blue comet sheared past Manna's face and screamed towards the thatched ceiling, as if meaning to rip through – but right before it did, it screeched to a halt and vibrated a deep-toned, heart-shaking hum. Sizzling, twinkly blue dust sprinkled out of the majestic earth-like ball as it twirled on its misty axis.

With a quick stab, a red laser beam poked out the ball's center and stuck itself in Manna's gut – and suddenly anxious, she felt herself stretch towards the ball, like a moth drawn to flame ... and she knew.

That blue ball was about to teach her something important.

"Keawe," a deep voice hummed and spit metallic-red needles out of the ball's glowing, red center. "From the Beginning of Time, in the World of Po – the vast space of wintry nothing that whirls round in chaotic, black seas."

Manna felt herself smile.

Keawe's warm, masculine voice splashed over her forehead as His prickly red needles popped on her skin, chilling her with anticipation.

"Keawe," the voice continued. "The only life existing in dark waters, had nothing to rule. Breathing forth Mana – the force that pervades all time and space, and provides all the power to live – Scattered Life at Will."

Something blistering hot zoomed past Manna's nose, at the same time something razor-sharp cold shot past her lips, going in the opposite direction. Clenching her biceps, she tried hard not to jerk back ... away from the large circling comets.

Crackling loud, the two bright yellow comets streaked, in sync, around the inside of the children's circle, leaving shimmery lemon trails in their wake.

"KEAWE!" boomed the blue ball. "Akua Supreme – Made Aloha – Forever."

With a deafening crack-crack, twin lightning bolts stabbed out of the blue ball and skewered the orbiting comets. Then, snapping loudly, the bolts yanked the comets upwards, within arm's reach of the smoking, but now silent, blue sphere.

Shocked, Manna stared at the coal-black centers of the hanging, yellow balls, and thought, side by side, they looked like giant eyes that could see right through you. Eerily, the eye on the left scanned the children's circle, its red pupil examining them closely – while the rigid eye on the right stayed fixed to the ground.

Feeling harshly judged, Manna squeezed the worrisome hole that grew rapidly in her stomach.

"Kane," a comforting voice droned out the left eyeball, and Manna's stomach filled with relief. "Akua of Earth – Father to All – Weeds the Garden before the Fall."

Groaning, the roof rumbled as if it held back thunder, and with a sharp jerk, the red-pupiled Kane eye swiveled and glared at Manna.

"Kapu ke ola – Sacred is Life," it instructed, before breathing, "To the East."

"Malama," sang the eyeball on the right, sweet femininity fluttering in Her notes. A gust of electric breath tingled through the air and sprayed citric perfume in Manna's face. "Akua of Moon – Mother of All – Caring for Creatures, Lonely and Small."

Manna tried hard not to bite her lip, lest that count as movement. Quivering with desire, she held herself back, wanting so badly to stand up and kiss the sweet-smelling ball.

"Comfort Fears. Soothe with Enchanted Grace. Fill Hearts with Heavenly Cheer."

Crackling loud, three red-hot balls streaked past Manna's back. Squeezing her eyes shut, she tried hard not to flinch even though her mind screamed, "RUN!"

BANG! BANG! – BOOM!

The red, black-striped ball in the lead turned around suddenly and banged into the two behind it. On impact, fiery flames leapt out of the first wounded, black ball, and rainbow-colored halos cascaded out of the second. Stunned, both balls slammed to a halt.

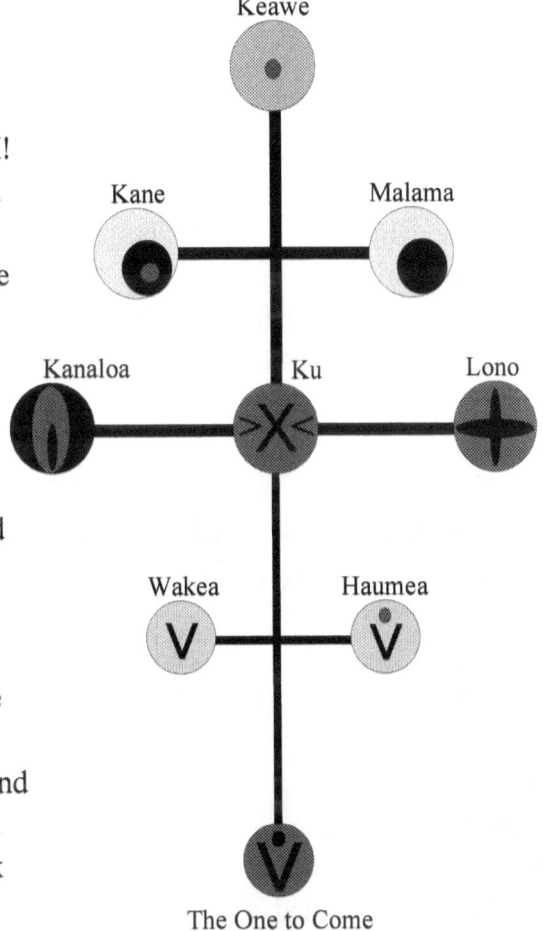

The One to Come

Booming turbo-charged power, the fierce, striped attack ball whined round the children's circle, overtaking His stalled victims (twice) and encompassing everyone in a black, cloudy trail that stunk of burned, shriveling flesh.

Flowing up from her feet, every one of Manna's hairs rippled – even the ones attached to her head.

That striped ball screamed tantalizing evil.

"Mai!" the left eyeball commanded – "Come!"

Manna glanced up.

Thin, bright yellow arms reached out from both glowing eyes, like two welcoming hugs.

Quickly obedient, the mean striped ball streaked upwards and grabbed a hand from each eye, hanging off them like a child between parents.

Spitting flames, the fiery black ball sputtered to the left eye and touched His hand, muttering, "Makua ka-nay."

Leaving a luminous rainbow trail, the other ball arched towards the right eye, whispering, "Makua he-nay."

Manna shivered.

Those three competitive god-balls were definitely something to fear.

"KU!" the cruel middle ball boomed and Manna noticed – it wasn't striped at all. Instead, it was dark blood-red with a black ">X<" tattooed on its middle.

"Akua of Kau'a – in Friendship, Battle and War," the ball growled. Its glistening outside shed thick red drops of bloody perspiration. "Judge with Retribution. Punish Ferociously. One reaps only what one sows."

Furious, the ball whipped around on its axis and smattered the children with acidic, flesh-eating drops – and curling her toes, Manna gritted her teeth as the drops ate through her skin, gurgling with enjoyment.

Swelling five time its size, the massive ball bellowed, "TO THE WEST!" – then quieted.

"Kanaloa," cackled the black ball on the left. A bright red flame flickered in its middle. "Akua of Darkness – in Land, the Sky and Sea."

BAM!

The flame in the center of the ball exploded and crackling meteors showered atop the children's heads. Burning like rubber, a searing stench filled Manna's nose, and instinctively, she held her breath.

"King of the South!" shrieked the sizzling ball and without warning, Manna's heart curdled.

"Lono," whispered the ball on the right, his voice strong and calm – and immediately, Manna relaxed. "Akua of Light, Knowledge and Health."

Shimmering bright, a red four-petaled flower bloomed inside the speaking ball, and with an exhaling sigh, the grass shack filled with incense breath.

Flittering, two small yellow fireflies flew over Manna's head – then tumbling over each other, they rolled merrily around the children's circle – nudging each other along the way.

"Shine Above Children," continued the kind male voice. "Lead the Way – Star of the North."

Almost ducking, Manna tried hard not to giggle. One firefly buzzed through her bangs with a girlish squeal – and the other snorted a masculine guffaw as it tickled past her nose.

As if working together, the Kanaloa and Lono balls each threw out one yellow, long-fingered hand and snatched at the naughty fireflies – but zipping out of reach, the fireflies zigzagged between the children, skimming off their unmoving heads.

Crackling like lightning bolts, the frantic Akua hands grabbed at the fireflies – but missed, smacking the other balls and children instead.

Sizzling in response, the other angry Akua balls whirled around the children, trying to block the fireflies from buzzing between them.

"Keikis – MAI!" commanded the blue Keawe ball, and immediately, the fireflies obeyed, each fluttering to an outstretched Akua hand – and at that moment, Manna realized they weren't fireflies at all. Rather, they were small shiny balls with rays of light that streamed out of their sides and beat furiously, like hummingbird wings.

Simmering, the black Kanaloa ball straightened His glistening arm and opened His palm to expose a foggy, yellow ball. A black V poked through the ball's center and gleamed like a wet pebble-beach rock. Hiccuping, the ball spoke drunkenly.

"Wakea – Father of Ali'i – Maker of Sons."

With a loud burp, the Wakea ball jerked towards his mate (who sat vibrating in the Lono ball's hand) and rolled over her laughing, "Maker of Fun. Catch me when you can!"

Growling, the Kanaloa ball snatched Wakea back.

"Haumea," giggled Wakea's crystally yellow mate. A black V poked down her middle and a scarlet jewel sparkled above it. "Mother of Ali'i – Aumakua – Kanaka – Spreading ALO-O-O-O-HA!"

Tumbling like pins through the air, streams of red light burst out of the Haumea ball and flip-flopped to the ground. Some touched Manna and immediately vanished – making her flesh tingle, as though Haumea had run her cool, smooth fingernails across Manna's skin. Half smiling, Manna liked it.

Glowing, Wakea and Haumea vibrated towards each other, like magnets being drawn together. Then gurgling loud, the Wakea ball passed through Haumea, flipped and rolled back to Kanaloa's hand.

With a pain-filled cry, Haumea spit out a spongy red ball whose center jiggled like warm jelly. A black V pointed through its middle and cradled a round black stone.

"Pum, pum, pum," the red ball expanded and contracted fast, like a child's frightened heart. "Pum, pum, pum, pum."

Almost squirming, Manna realized – the jelly ball's heart beat in sync with hers.

"The one to come," Keawe breathed softly.

"Huna ike ..." moaned Tutu. Her eyes rolled far back in her head, showing only her luminous whites.

Shivering, Manna stared at her grandmother. Standing rigid with palms to her hips and mouth frowning open, she looked like one of those hideous wooden dolls.

As if summoning the dead, Tutu's shaky incantation grew louder.

"O na-a-a mo'olelo ..."

Manna held her breath, knowing something scary was about to happen.

"Pahu pa'epu hoi!" Tutu commanded, her hands raised to the Akua balls. "Burst forth with a roar!"

Clinking furiously, three midnight-black, razor-sharp crosses stabbed through the three center line balls and skewered the other six in their sides. Then whistling like a child's top, the crosses spun all the Akua balls in a wild, dizzying orbit.

Rumbling, the ceiling filled with thunder and the sharp clap-clap of splitting bolts, and with a chest shaking, "BAM!" – all the balls exploded.

Shivering, iridescent rain pelted out of Keawe and showered through the yellow and white, sparkling crystals that Kane and Malama spurt. Hissing, orange meteors peeled out of Kanaloa and burst into shimmering dust, leaving long twinkling arches.

With successive menacing whines, a hundred dense black balls of smoke hurled from Ku and exploded into gut-shaking bangs – while dazzling U-shaped rainbows and sizzling silver birds spun out of Lono and zigzagged to the ground.

Crackling, red and yellow stars screamed out of Wakea and Haumea and crashed into one another with glass-shattering blasts – and humming, the last red jelly ball sprayed amber, perfumed, sparkly-petaled flowers that tumbled through the air.

Shaking with the horrific booms and covered with fizzling debris, Manna thought this the coolest fireworks show – ever.

"It's come," murmured Ailani.

In a blink, Tutu stood outside the circle and the balls vanished with a wet, "Sput!"

Disappointed, the cousins drooped their shoulders and glared at Ailani, who rocked back and forth, faster and faster, knowing she made a mistake.

The rule was: Kill the one that spoke.

Together, the cousins picked up their club dolls and Tutu moved slowly around the circle – towards Ailani – starting the ritual to kill.

"I said it," blurted Manna, without thinking.

Lifting her palms to the sky, Tutu chanted low, her deep voice moaning like a ghost.

"Of Hawaii, of Man and Akua – Opposites paired together."

Tutu pressed both palms to her stomach. Then alternating arms, she swirled her hands in slow wide ovals, as if stirring a witch's thick brew – and her voice quivering low, she chanted an eerie, woeful song.

"Cold, rigid mountains against warm, gentle seas,
   Rising suns heat the still east, setting suns cool a west breeze,
   The strong man stands tall, his gentle woman stoops low,
   Opposites, friend, complement, foe. "

Manna's heart pounded in her chest. Tutu hovered very close to her now, and any moment, she'd signal the cousins to give their fatal blows – but she wasn't sure who they'd beat. Ailani or her?

"Ku and Hina," continued Tutu, "Kane-Kanaloa, Wakea-Haumea, Ao and Po!"

Ku-hai's spear-headed, growling, black doll cocked high above his head, motionless and ready to throw.

Glaring defiantly, Manna decided.

If he threw that doll at her, she would catch it and throw it back – harder!

Tutu stepped over Manna and glowered down.

"Know what you are and your pairing you'll find – before it consumes your life."

Manna scowled at Tutu, the one who would consume her life now.

"Ku-hai-moana!" roared Ku-hai, making Manna jump. "The biggest! The strongest!"

"Kane-huna-moku!" shouted Moku. His crouched wooden doll pointed high – and two bright yellow feathers floated off its glassy-eyed head. "Hidden!"

Aikoa's black, red-feathered doll shot up in the air as she growled through clenched, square teeth, "Puna-ai-koa'e! Combat!"

Oh, they're not going to kill us, realized Manna. Carefully, she retracted her fingernails from her pinched biceps and relaxed.

"Kane-i-kokala!" snarled Kokala. An unusually fierce light gleamed in his eyes, below a black, squinting doll that hung steady in the air. "Savior!"

"Kau-huhu!" hooted Kau. His horrid wooden doll's head stuck out from a flowing, red feather lei and looked oddly like something slit its neck. "Fierce! Force!"

They're calling out their full names – and meanings, thought Manna.

"Ka-ehu-iki-mano-o-pu'uloa," Iki stumbled over his long name, his black stone, moss-covered doll trembling in the air. "Green friend!"

"Ka-hi'u-ka!" shrieked Hi'u, his black, flat-headed doll smirking like him. "Smiting tail!"

"Waka!" yelled Waka in a loud masculine voice, her brown doll crouched forward, broad shoulders spread out. "Guardian!"

"Ka-ahu-pahau," squeaked Pahau, her large-busted, tan doll waving low. "Wahine!"

In sync, the cousins banged their dolls back onto their cloths and silently began to fidget. In response, Mano bounced openly and no one took notice.

Manna figured, mo'olelo was pau (finished).

Tutu kneeled in front of Momi and placed two large palms on top of her big blonde head. Then pushing it so far back that Momi's sharp white nose pointed to the sky, Tutu chanted low.

"I ka 'ike mai luna mai e ..."

Quickly, the cousins wrapped their dolls in their white tapa cloths.

Curious, Manna glanced down at her tapa cloth. In one corner shone the Akua ball formation (with the three black crosses in the middle) and rotating slowly on its axis, each ball spun like a living planet.

Cool, thought Manna.

"The rock," barked Tutu, before she moved to Pu-pele and chanted again.

"I ka 'ike mai luna mai e ..."

Reaching out cautiously (in case the balls bite), Manna brushed her fingertips over its length. Smiling, she remembered the soft, sticky inside of the fresh peeled bark she and Mano collected in the Black Forest.

"The heat," commanded Tutu, sliding quickly to Ailani and chanting, "I ka 'ike ..."

Manna brushed her hair off her cheek and noticed her fingers smelled of sweet mulberry. Pressing them into her nostrils, she wondered if Mano's cloth smelled that way, too.

"The wind," barked Tutu. Then, with a rough two-handed jerk, she yanked back on Manna's skull, almost snapping it off her neck.

Immediately defensive, Manna clutched Tutu's wrists and struggled to shove her off – but without warning, the long wail of a conch shell shattered her mind, and an invisible gourd thumped pain through the pieces.

"What are you?" growled a deep voice inside Manna's throbbing head.

Wincing, Manna pushed harder on Tutu's wrists.

"Answer me – NOW!" commanded the gruff voice. "WHAT ARE

YOU?"

Panicking, Manna put both feet in Tutu's gut and kicked as hard as she could, but her feet just sank into a soft, spongy mass and a sudden hot wind held her down.

"THE POWER!" roared the voice.

Letting go, Tutu repeated, "The power."

Frowning, the cousins sucked in hard, just like they did at the airport – and confused, Manna couldn't guess: What was wrong with power?

For a moment, Tutu stared, dead cold, at Manna. Then she slid to Mano chanting, "I ka 'ike mai luna mai e ..."

Uncomfortable under the cousins' hot stares, Manna wished she could go home.

"The water," smiled Tutu, just as Moho's truck crunched down the drive.

"Pau," Tutu ordered, waving her right hand at the other children, motioning that they could go – but her heavy left hand landed on Manna's shoulder and held her down on her mat.

Obedient, the cousins grabbed their bundled dolls and marched out of the room. Mumbling, Momi and her sisters followed.

Manna stiffened her back. Tutu would punish her for that stomach kick, no doubt, and it was gonna hurt. Not knowing whether she should fight back or take it, she waited patiently for Mano to leave ... but he didn't. Knees bouncing, he stared blankly at the sand, acting dumb.

Glancing at Mano gently, Tutu asked, "How long have you known?"

Squinting, Manna refused to answer – because she didn't know what Tutu meant.

"Mana gives all the power to live," droned Tutu, "and if taken away – all will die. It is a sacred force, living in your bones, fueling the soul with life."

Manna stared at the ground and decided she should go.

"They follow you," warned Tutu, her voice suddenly tense. "Some to steal your mana. Some to protect it. Others, to be a part of it. Always look over your shoulder – and distinguish between the three."

Squeezing Manna's small chin with a hot palm, Tutu tilted her head up and peered at her with red-veined eyes.

"You are the Keeper of Nui-Akea – Power Supreme – the most desirable power of all. But that power fatally poisons man – for those who hold it succumb to heinous greed and willfully murder their souls."

Tutu's eyes filled with pity.

"This, child, is your fate."

Manna scowled up at Tutu. She hated pity even more than being told she was doomed to die of greed. Mano was the greedy one, not her.

Tutu's face grew stern in response.

"With Power lives her cousin, Responsibility. Always be aware."

Grabbing Mano's hand, Manna huffed to her feet and ran through the door – right into Cousin Ku-hai.

Without a word, Ku-hai turned around and trudged away, dragging his feet like a warrior defeated.

"Don't move!" whispered Mano, through the dim candlelit room, right before he flicked on the light.

Flutter. Crack! Flutter. Crack! Crack!

Rapid-fire, Mano batted at the wild cockroach flurry that winged through the air, cracking hard black shells with each vicious candlestick swipe.

Wiggling with yellow guts seeping out their sides, the fat dragonfly-sized bugs hit the ground and scurried in frantic circles, dragging their long wounded legs through their juice.

Startled, Manna sat up and gasped, both hands across her mouth.

Crack!

With a wet crack off Mano's candlestick, a juicy cockroach popped on Manna's temple and slid, dazed and sticky, down her cheek – but quickly, its thorny back legs stabbed into her chin, and it squirmed its way back up, smearing hot slime into her ear.

"Sorry," breathed Mano, falling onto her trundle bed. "I said not to move."

Shoving his rough fingers in her hair, he grabbed the roach and squeezed it in his fist, letting yellowish-brown juice ooze through his fingers. Then opening his palm to show off the slick, crumbled shell and mangled wings, he grinned, "He won't do that again."

No, he won't! thought Manna, lunging at Mano's lit candle and lamp. With a two-fisted fling, she threw both at the wall, and together, they cracked into buzzing darkness.

"I can't see!" whined Mano, still scared of the dark.

Kicking hard, Manna knocked him off of her bed and onto the floor with his burst, scuttling prey.

Gasping, Mano leapt to his feet and bolted, full blast, to the door.

BAM! - "OOF!"

With a loud grunt, he slammed into the closet and flopped to the ground – but frantic, he scrambled up and smacked his palms along the wall (searching for the door), crying, "Manna ... Manna ... I can't see."

Spiteful, Manna ignored him. That bozo had to learn a lesson.

Banging his head loud, Mano swung open the door and stumbled through it – letting the bright hall light stream in. Then silent, shoulders sagging, he replaced his candle and lamp, and the window screen he took out (to let the cockroaches in) – and shaking, climbed into bed.

Satisfied, Manna wiped her face on the edge of *his* sheet and pulled her blanket over her chin.

It was about time someone punished him.

The wooden Guardian Angel flickered rhythmically on the wall, in time with Mano's bouncing bed.

Manna watched the angel's beautiful smile beam down on the lost children and thought it weird that Mano was always moving, even in his sleep. She wondered if angels slept or if they always moved too, around the world, watching over helpless children. Then she thought, *Does Mother Mary sleep?* – and that's when it hit her.

She forgot to turn the other cheek.

Frowning, she knew it was wrong – what she had done to Mano – and she wished he didn't exist. He made everything hard – birthdays and presents, holidays and school, even everyday life, and now ... he made "being good" hard, too.

Creak.

Tiptoeing, Anna crept into the room.

Quickly, Manna closed her eyes and squeezed out hot tears. Then folding her hands under the blanket, she prayed that, just once, she'd get a cross, too.

Chapter Six

The LESSON

"Don't turn your back to the sea," called Tutu, from the edge of the blue-painted porch. "It's alive – and always hungry."

"Yeah, right," Momi rolled her crackling blue eyes, "and black cats bring bad luck."

Manna bounded off the lava rock hill and landed neatly on the jagged rocks below. This was her first time to the beach and she couldn't wait to jump in.

"Ow!" winced Mano.

Manna whipped around.

Mano had slipped off the rock hill and gashed the right side of his knee. Thick red blood gurgled down his calf, and quickly, he wiped and licked it.

"The saltwater will clean it," murmured Ailani, brushing softly past Manna.

Grabbing his rough hand to hold him steady, Manna teetered over the gleaming beach rocks. Moist from ocean spray, they slipped beneath her feet.

"The tide pool's over there," gushed Pu-pele, from high on top a volcano-shaped rock. Her waist-long, reddish-brown hair glowed in the morning sun and looked oddly like flowing magma.

Manna turned the way Pu-pele pointed.

About twenty yards away, a tall black breakwall curved around a large sparkling tide pool and shielded it from the ocean's cresting waves – and glimmering at the deep blue sky, the pool lay still ... waiting.

Excitement rushed through Manna's body and pattered in her heart. The pool looked shallow enough to wade in!

"Come on," she yanked on Mano's hand and pulled him into a run.

Flashing by, cruel, jagged shore rocks turned into round, wave-beaten stones that protruded from a shelly, black pebble beach – and a thousand small shiny black crabs scurried out of the way and hid under the warm rocks – where tiny round opi'i snails clung to small damp crannies.

First at the edge of the pool, Manna kicked off her blue loafers and belly flopped in, eyes closed. Warm, tingly water splashed over her body and pulled through her hair – then something tiny scratched her nose.

Manna opened her eyes and saw a yellow and black-striped fish streak by, then twitch around and nip at her again. Smiling, she brushed it away.

Nip. Nip.

Two more, brilliant, blue and yellow angel fish bit her nose and darted away. Then at once, a school of yellow-backed, white-bellied fish engulfed her face. Tickling, a hundred fat white lips nibbled her nose, like octopus tentacle kisses.

Squealing bubbles, Manna jerked up, her hands covering her nose.

The fish tried to eat her mole!

"Ba-ha-ha!" echoed Mano, covered from head to waist in a red, bulbous, seaweed-filled fishing net. His awkward, outstretched hands shook above his massive red weed head, and his body convulsed wildly, as though he was being electrocuted.

Quickly, Manna popped into spraying giggles – until something stopped her ...

The funny feeling a redheaded monster really *did* live in this sea.

"They look like frogs," said Mano.

Doing a slow breaststroke, Momi and Pu-pele swam through the clear tide pool that was so deep now, they couldn't touch the bottom. It seemed as the afternoon sun fell, the shimmering pool rose in an effort to get up and follow it.

Standing waist-deep in water, at the breakwall's edge, Manna wished she knew how to swim.

"Fried frogs taste like chicken," said Ailani, standing on the black rock wall with the deep ocean roaring at her back. Then, bending her knees and springing forward, she dove in the pool without making a splash.

Suzy (the white poodle) stood on her fluffy hind legs and yipped nervously. She didn't want to be left alone on the rock wall, and Manna couldn't blame her.

The wall stood at least fifty yards out.

Relaxing, Manna leaned backwards against the hot, craggy breakwall stones and let her face absorb the sun. Twinkling, red heat prickled through her lids and tingled in her brain. Then a brilliant orange flash zoomed across her mind, making her dizzy with light-headed electricity, and for a moment she felt like she would fly – right out of her body. Smiling, she understood why adults lay worshipping the sun.

"At noon, when the body casts no shadow," hummed Ailani, "the full strength of the sun goes into the worshipper – giving him power."

Manna opened her eyes.

Close by, Ailani's pink face glistened with crystallized salt drops as her lovely white hands treaded water.

"Hawaiians call it Kau-kala-i-ka-lolo, the time of victorious sun on the brain."

"How do you know?" asked Manna.

"I listen," said Ailani, her earnest eyebrows raised and dripping.

"To what?" asked Mano, stranded on the wall, because he couldn't swim, either.

Ailani's soft brown eyes grew distant when she breathed, "Everything."

Manna wondered why *she* couldn't listen to *anything* – or at least, was so easily distracted.

CRASH!

A massive white-tipped wave crashed over the breakwall and smacked Manna into the pool. Then sucking hard, it flipped her, yanked her backwards, and slammed her against the razor-sharp, jagged wall. Shocked and in paralyzing pain, she sank deep into a stony crack.

"SUZY!" screamed Ailani, struggling to stay above the now foamy, churning water. Her face contorted with fright.

Feeling Ailani's fear grow like thunder in her chest, Manna looked up.

The dog was gone. The ocean had sucked her out to sea!

CRASH!

A cresting, blue, two-story wave smashed over the wall and shoved Ailani's gurgling head under – and whistling loud, a biting cold wind whipped Manna's face and tried to suck her down, too. Frantic, she jammed her hands into two sharp crannies, gripped the wall with both heels, and pressed her back against the wall's solid stones.

"OOF!"

With a heavy, sopping thud, the swollen wave hauled back and slammed Mano across Manna's chest. The wind knocked out of her, she refused to breathe in the angry waters that gushed down her face, knowing the sea would drown her.

CRASH!

Roaring, a high-arching wave pounded over the wall and slapped Mano into the pool. Yelling, he grabbed at Manna's hand, and instinctively, she lunged for him – and lost her grip on the wall. Gasping in horror, she tumbled into the swirling water.

In sudden whooshing silence, the hungry wave dragged her down, face first, and spun her in a sickening, blurry whirlpool. Then yanking her arms and legs in all directions, it pummeled her with seaweed and rock.

Helpless, Manna screamed – and the furious wave shoved a burning salt fist down her throat.

BAM!

With a back-breaking slam, Manna's sputtering head cracked against the rock wall and in an instant, the sea came to life. Wheezing, it spat a slimy white sea creature onto her face and sliced her cheeks with ten horrible, sharp, curved claws. Then, tugging hard on her hair, it pulled her down to take a feverish bite.

In a wild panic, Manna batted at the squirming sea creature that clung to her face, and with a vicious head-shaking growl, it sank four thick fangs in her brow.

Blinded, she stumbled backwards, pushing hard on the creature as it devoured her eye – and with a body-snapping jolt, it whipped five cold tentacles around her neck and yanked its teeth out of her skull – ready to take a death-dealing bite.

Choking, Manna squeezed her eyes shut and prayed her end would come quick.

"You take the rat!" yelled Momi. Her long fingers gripped Manna's neck as she yanked the frightened dog off her sister's face and threw it at Ailani. "And you take the boy," she growled at Pu-pele.

Manna opened her eyes.

CRASH!

A powerful blue wave slammed over the wall and knocked her forward, into Momi – but lightning fast, Momi gripped the rock wall with her big, tough hands, pressed her weight against Manna, and pinned her to the wall.

"Stupid ... useless ... wimp," Momi growled as the retreating wave rushed up her back. Then standing tall, she spun around and ordered, "Get on – NOW!"

Squinting through watery blood, Manna didn't know what to do. She didn't trust Momi with her life – but Mano was too far away (riding on Pu-pele's back to the shore) and Ailani was nowhere in sight. Taking a chance, she scrambled behind Momi and wrapped her arms around her neck.

CRASH!

With a back-cracking whack, the wave slapped both girls into the pool and flipped them, head over heels – but undaunted, Momi thrust forward and broke through the churning surface to yell, "Get your filthy hair outta my face!"

Reacting fast, Manna yanked on her sticky, wet hair, but it caught on Momi's chopstick bun and stretched Momi's head far back.

CRASH!

Another wave smashed over the wall and shoved down Momi's throat. Spitting foam, she shrieked, "IDIOT! I'LL DROWN YOU FIRST!" – then she dove into the pool.

Hanging on tight as they thrust deeper and deeper into the murky water, Manna counted each of Momi's long breast strokes and hoped she didn't mean it – but after five strong pulls, her throbbing head began to spin and a thick red streak flashed in her eyes.

"HEES!"

Breathing in loud, Momi came up for air, right next to Pu-pele and Mano. Then, always competitive, the sisters dove together and raced underwater for the beach.

Holding the quick breath she managed to gasp, Manna looked at a frightened Mano. His hair flowed out in the water, like a breezy lion's mane, and his cheeks and eyes puffed round like a fish's. And then she saw it – a long, wiggly, red flash, headed straight for Mano's neck.

"Shark!" she screamed underwater, right before Momi came up for air.

Coughing hard above water, Manna snapped her head around, looking for the shark, but couldn't see it.

With a powerful thrust, Momi dove under again, with Pu-pele at her heels.

Manna looked right, then left, but the shark wasn't there. She looked up. Not there either. Then suddenly, a lurking feeling that something followed her shivered down her back – and horrified, she spun around.

A wide, bloody, razor-lined jaw stretched open and aimed for Mano's head.

"NOOO!" Manna yelled, lunging at her brother and yanking him off Pu-pele's back.

With a desperate spread-eagle twist, Mano spun round underwater and clutched Manna's head, at the same time his heel bonked the shark on the nose.

Veering in surprise, the shark disappeared.

At once, Pu-pele grabbed Mano's arm and Momi yanked on Manna's hair, but Mano refused to let go. Sinking fast, he clung to Manna, knowing only she would protect him from the shark.

Thinking clearly, Manna stiffened and pointed her toes.

If she could touch the bottom, they could propel themselves back up – and maybe Momi would take care of the shark.

Boom-boom. Boom-boom.

Manna's heart pounded in her pressured head. The bottom wasn't anywhere near them, and her lungs ached for air.

Boom-boom. Boom-boom.

Mano shoved his nose into hers and spitting bubbles, his eyes wild with fear, he pointed vigorously to the surface.

Boom-boom. Boom-boom.

Determined, her heart pounding against his, Manna squeezed her brother's chest tight and looked for the bottom.

FLASH!

Glinting, the shark's double-lined teeth shot up from below.

Startled, Mano jerked and let go of Manna, giving her a chance to shove him out of harm's way. Then clenching her fists, she whipped around and faced the hungry shark alone.

CRACK!

With a mind-splitting crack, the shark's heavy jaw crunched through Manna's forehead and everything went a brilliant blood-red ... black.

Manna came to on the windy beach.

"Did you see Momi knock her out?" squealed Pu-pele, her eyes dancing above a shivering Ailani and dog. Then curling her chubby fist, she bonked herself on the forehead and rolled her eyes so far up they turned white.

"Did she get the shark?" asked Manna, looking at Mano, who sat bouncing at her feet.

"What shark?" asked Pu-pele.

"The red one," breathed Manna.

"Sharks aren't red, stupid. They're white."

Manna squinted up at a smirking Momi, not sure she knew what she was talking about – but certain Tutu was right.

"Three loco-moco," grunted Moho. Leaning against the take out counter, he smiled playfully at the fat brown woman standing inside the open window. Flirting, she strummed her grimy fingernails on his gnarly fist and grinned through gold-capped teeth.

"For you, we get five – fo' free."

Manna smiled at a bouncing Mano, who sat next to her in Moho's massive truck. Anna said, before fishing, Moho had to teach them to swim – but first, he wanted to eat.

"Thanks, eh," Moho winked at the oily lady and chucked two white Styrofoam containers at Mano. A brown rubber band stretched over each and held a plastic spoon to the lid.

Holding the steering wheel with one hairless hand, Moho dumped a container into his large frowning mouth and peeled away through the clear, breaking dawn.

Spitting brown rocks, the bumpy road shook under the heavy truck and zigzagged down to the beach – and clapping in the truck's strong wind, a row of light-green banana trees rippled below tall, majestic coconut palms, as if fanning their royal, grey knees. Quietly, black stellar rocks rose ahead and guarded an empty, silver-flecked, black sand beach, pushing it firmly against the dark purple waves that slapped casually along its shore – and on a far away cliff, a long line of surfers stood motionless, surfboards pointed south, like spear-wielding aboriginal hunters waiting for the kill.

"Dawn patrol," Moho smiled as if he'd love to join them.

Tingling, a cool, salty breeze snatched at a wisp of Manna's hair and flipped it carelessly out the window – and for a moment, she felt totally free.

Slurping greedily, Mano opened a container and shoveled four heaping spoonfuls into his mouth.

Relaxed, Manna breathed in the thick, rich smell of Moho's black coffee as it floated through fresh Thanksgiving gravy, and at once, her tummy grumbled. Quickly, she popped the lid off one warm container and peeked in.

A brown, crinkled egg sat on top a flat, greasy burger that stuck to gooey, white rice – and bubbling, brown, separated gravy oozed off the egg's slimy, raw yolk. Scrunching her nose, Manna thought loco-mocos looked a lot like puke.

"You gonna eat it?" asked Mano, always looking for more.

Lucky to get anything, Manna held her breath and stuck a small spoonful into her mouth.

Dripping off her tongue, the beefy flavor of gravied rice smashed through a soft, creamy yolk and crumbled around the juicy, french-fried burger.

Delighted, Manna grinned at her twinkly-eyed brother and thought Pu-pele wrong.

Kids shouldn't wake up to cold puffed cereal. Breakfast should be hot, meaty pot pies that filled your tummy with lumps of gooey, warm lead.

Suddenly famished, Manna gobbled down the container and smiled.

Certainly, a full stomach would help her swim.

"What's wrong with you?" yelled Moho. Swinging Mano out of the water, he shook him high over his head. "No boy of mine should have a problem learning to swim!"

Desperate, Mano spun his arms in wild, jerky circles, practicing his useless crawl. He'd been at it for over an hour, but had only learned how to sink – with unwavering vigor.

"Kick your feet and pull your arms!" Moho hollered for the hundredth time, an inch from Mano's face. Then roaring, "AAARGH!" in frustration, he threw Mano fifteen yards.

Before hitting the water, Mano spun his arms and legs in a fast spider-like crawl, sure to get it right this time – but when he hit the surface he just sank with a loud, drowning gurgle.

Moho waited a full two minutes, then dove down to retrieve his son.

Manna wondered why Mano tried so hard. At some point, he ought to give up, but that wouldn't impress Moho – and that's what he really wanted. It seemed the more Moho expected, the harder Mano tried – no matter how much it hurt.

Manna frowned.

Maybe it wasn't so great being the boy.

"Kick your feet and pull your arms!" Moho growled so loud it sounded like the ocean roared.

Determined, Mano barked back, "Yes, SIR!" right before Moho winged his floppy body into the air.

Manna wondered if Tutu was right, that power (like Moho's love) held a horrible burden ... responsibility – and then it dawned on her. Maybe power was something like talent, a gift from God that He expected you to use or you'd miserably fail His test.

"WOO-HOO!" yelled Moho. "That's my boy!"

Manna looked up. Mano could swim!

Standing at the edge of the water, he beamed at Manna and shook both fists in the air, like a boxer winning his match. Dark red blood streaked out his nose and splattered his sunk-in, blue-bruised chest.

Grimacing, Manna guessed. Moho threw him too hard.

Moho popped out of the water, slapped his son on the back and grinned, "Let's go, my boy."

"What about me?" blurted Manna. That red fish scared the daylights out of her and she wanted to learn how to get away.

Ignoring her, Moho put a heavy arm around Mano and steered him down the beach.

"The sea is the only place to be," Moho crowed. "One day, you'll agree."

Determination burned hot in Manna's chest as she summoned her special power – her Nui-Akea – Power Supreme.

She could use it – to force *anyone* – to do what she wanted!

Scrambling round in front of Moho, she stuck out her skinny chest and bellowed, "TEACH ... ME ... TOO!"

Black gums bared, Moho snarled down, "I'll teach you, alright."

Then, with his loudest "AAARGH!" yet, he whipped her into the air and threw her fifty yards – straight over the hungry, wave-snapping sea.

Flipping, arms and legs flailing, Manna hit the cold blue surface, headfirst – and nearly knocked out, she sunk without a fight.

Glimmering softly, the light blue sky reflected off the disappearing surface, as if waving goodbye, then misty darkness slid over her face like a chilling, fluttery shroud. Familiar loneliness engulfed her chest, and instantly, she curled up in a ball ... and cried.

Today she would drown – and no one could help her. Not mean old Momi with her hot screaming breath, or smiling Pu-pele and her quick burning temper. Not even Ailani and those delicate, angelic hands.

Her hands. Manna remembered her lovely hands – treading water like a frog.

Jerking to life, Manna put her arms over her head and pulled back like Ailani – and could swear, she swam up. Filling with hope, she stroked six more times, and the blue sky winked encouragement through a blurred, flickering surface.

Moving faster, her lungs feeling like they might implode, Manna pulled four more strenuous strokes and her head burst out of the water.

"Manna!" she heard Mano scream, right before her head went back under.

Quickly, Manna pulled herself out again – and caught a glimpse of Moho holding her frantic, struggling brother with a mean chest-gripping arm.

Her head went back down and she remembered.

Five, like Momi, then breathe.

Pulling hard, she shoved the water behind her five times, then came up for air.

Mano was closer and hanging limp under Moho's hot glare.

Five more and she surfaced.

Mano stood smiling, alone at the water's edge.

Five. Gasp. Five. Gasp. Five.

Manna was on the beach ... and able to swim.

"How'd you learn so fast?" gushed Mano, his face red with excitement.

"Ten years isn't fast," Manna wheezed at the ground.

But I finally learned. That man aims to kill ... me.

Chapter Seven

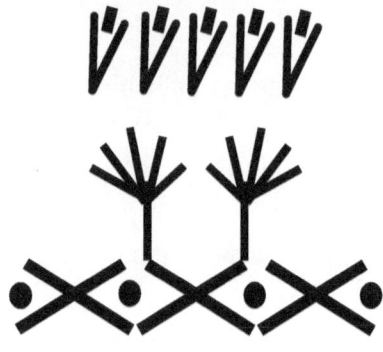

The RED HANDS

Manna clasped her hands together and held them above her scratchy woolen knees, afraid to touch anything. Sitting stiff, inside the other white gift from Moho's family (a beautiful, beige-leathered Mercedes), she worried the sleek interior would easily crack, like delicate Blue Onion china. Leaning against Mano, she pinned him to the passenger's door, in hopes that'd stop him from bouncing – or at least keep his bony knees from hammering through the dash.

Biting her nervous lower lip, Anna gripped the steering wheel with small white-knuckled hands and pressed the accelerator down to the floor. Humming softly, the solid yellow lane line zipped under the long sedan, right below the gleaming silver hood emblem, and disappeared quickly behind blind, choppy hills. (Being her first time to drive, Anna thought dead center was the right way to go.)

Smiling to herself, Manna glanced at the brown-skinned, rubber-slippered school children who ambled down the road.

Unlike Germany, here she'd fit in on her first day of school – because now, her skin was the right color.

With a swift neck-aching jerk, Anna stopped in front of the bus stop and four burly, brown Japanese boys. Laughing high-pitched snorts, the boys talked in the middle of the street – their hands stuffed into baggy surfing trunks and their bodies rocking from toe to toe. Panting, their large bushy white dog lay aloof at their feet.

Instantly, Manna's heart fluttered. She couldn't wait to meet the other kids! Grabbing the door handle over Mano, she swung it open, and gasping, they both tumbled out.

Butterflies tickling her tummy, Manna giggled and eased the car door shut. Then she pulled Mano gently to his feet – but bewildered, his bright round eyes begged for encouragement.

He hated going to school, because teachers always separated them.

Smiling cool, Manna gruffed, "No fear, Brah."

With a relieved twinkle, Mano laughed in agreement – or maybe, at her funny-sounding pidgin English.

CRACK!

Out of nowhere, an orange and white lightning bolt cracked through Manna's eye and exploded into hot spurting lava. Stunned, she clutched her eye with both hands and tried to squeeze out a stabbing pain, but burning fast, red lava drenched her cheek and coated her shaking forearms.

"Ho, Taro!" hooted a boy from across the street. "Broke da face!"

"All bus' up," sneered a little girl.

"Bachi, bachi – double eyes," taunted the girl's giggling friends.

Peering through blurred double vision, Manna glanced up and couldn't believe it.

The fattest red-faced Japanese boy threw a pear-sized rock at her face – and everyone thought it was funny.

Embarrassed, all hopes of fitting in dashed away, Manna lunged for the car door, but flowing sideways, Pu-pele blocked her.

"You'll get blood in it!" she hissed.

Manna looked down at her palms. Coated with thick red blood, they glistened in the sparkling morning sun.

Much too hard, Pu-pele pressed Manna's right hand above her eye and breathed, "Get used to it. Not everyone's gonna like you." Then smiling cheerfully at Anna, she waved, "Bye-bye, Mommy!"

Dazed, Manna didn't know what to do – but Anna did.

Narrowing her shiny blue eyes into snake-like slits, Anna fixed them on the sniggering Japanese boys and floored the car. Revving loud, it shuddered angrily against its parked gear and blasted smoke plumes out the exhaust.

Growling, the boys' dog jumped to her feet and pawed the road, like a bull daring Anna to charge – and stiffening, all the boys lifted their defiant chins ... and refused to move out of her way.

Prickly awe shivered down Manna's back.

The bold dog and her fearless crew held their ground like five kamikazes – willing to lose their lives for pride – and surely, that's what they'd do. For in a maddened rage, Anna would plow right through them.

Determined to be brave too, Manna grabbed Mano's hand and tramped around the car, past the boys and onto the waiting bus stop. Then pursing her lips into a tight frown, she stared through Anna, so she'd know.

Manna could take care of her boy.

Shaking, Anna peered at Mano for a moment with wet uncertain eyes. Then squinting at the expressionless boys, she threw her car into reverse.

SCREECH! BOOM – BOOM!

Brakes screeching and stereo pounding, Ku-hai's shiny red truck whipped around Anna's car in a sharp fish-tailing curve, then skidded to a smoky halt on top of the yelping dog. Taro, the shortest slanty-eyed boy, jumped out of the way, but the other boys stood solid.

Without speaking, the cousins swayed in the tall truck bed and frowned at Manna in synchronized scorn.

Instantly uneasy, Manna felt dry blood crack on her face, and shuddering, she understood.

The cousins expected her to fight ... and not be such a coward.

Burning fast, a hole of shame hollowed her throat, but she refused to let on. Steadfast, she met the glare of every stiff brown face at the bus stop – to let them know.

Not one of them would see her cry.

Like Moses, Ku-hai held up an authoritative hand, and slapping their slippers, the Japanese gang parted. Then, with a gut-shaking, smoke-spraying rev, he peeled away – and at that moment, Manna noticed.

She and her sisters were the only girls there.

"Ay, no go in there," barked a tall, teenaged, bushy-haired girl, quickly blocking the graffiti-littered bathroom door.

Manna stopped, thinking it weird that high school kids shared the elementary school campus. Seemed like that might cause a lot of trouble.

Rough, passing students bumped Manna, and anxious, she wondered why Aikoa and her friends guarded the bathroom door.

"That your cousin?" asked a stocky black girl. Her short afro sprang up only a quarter inch high, and her dark eyes glowed like the Devil's coals.

"No boddah me," quipped Aikoa, her strong arms wrapped around a handsome, dark-haired boy. Smirking, the boy ran his olive-green tattooed knuckles over Aikoa's round, jeans-covered bottom – and growling, she snuggled into his muscular chest.

"Get da Mimi Akua in there," the bushy-haired girl warned Manna. Her hazel eyes twinkled with mischief. "You go in and ..." Suddenly, the girl's red-clawed, golden-fingered hand snatched at Manna's face. "Da red hands going go ma-kay you."

"Pumpkin," Aikoa rolled her eyes at her friend.

"What? You neva when see?" Pumpkin tried to convince Aikoa. "Get the bloody handprints of da keeds he when eat. Stay drippin' down da walls."

Sweating, Manna wondered, *Where am I supposed to take off these stupid woolen hose!*

"Mano!" scoffed a cute curly-haired boy. He and his lanky, fair-skinned gang quickly surrounded them. "More like *dog* fish."

Laughing loud, the tall boys slapped one another's backs and waited for Mano to react – but Manna reacted first. Grabbing her brother, she hurried down the hall knowing neither of them knew how to fight.

"Am I ugly?" whispered Mano, his eyes and cheeks burning red.

Surprised, Manna looked over his high, chiseled cheeks and pouted pink mouth, and his small close-to-the-head ears. By far, he was the best-looking boy around.

"He called me dog." Mano's voice almost shook.

"No, dog *fish*," corrected Manna. "It's a small, harmless shark in a bowl."

Something stiff rapped Manna's shoulder, but suspecting she'd get clobbered if she turned around, she pulled Mano down the outdoor hallway, faster. Glancing at the red tin sidewalk covering, she worried.

The whole school seemed packed with bully gangs.

Jumping in front of her, a tall, tanned, big-busted girl blocked Manna's way ... and smiled.

Hanging in the girl's face, long straw-like brown hair fell over her light brown, beady eyes and pencil-thin, straight eyebrows. Protruding to a point, her thin nose arched down to black-lined, beige lips – and sticking out of them, four tiny, square front teeth gleamed, crooked and yellow, between two long, white-flecked fangs.

Instantly, Manna shuddered.

The girl could be a vampire.

"Hi! My name's Barbara Guadalupe Cameron Lopez," gushed the vampire. "But you can call me Barb."

Surprised, Manna remembered, in Catholic school, you invoke Saint Barbara for protection against fire and lightning – and Guadalupe was Spanish for "Mother Mary."

"That's nice," Manna heard herself breathe.

A shocked, rejected look washed over the girl's long-chinned face, and her thin-lipped mouth dropped down to expose silver-capped adult molars. Then spinning around abruptly, the girl scuffled away, her curved hips and wide bottom twisting awkwardly from side to side.

Confused, Manna yanked Mano down the long crowded hallway, thinking, *Must be time for the bell.*

"HILE!" shouted a long line of t-shirted, brown boys using thick, fake German accents.

Startled, Manna stopped in front of them, and at once, they threw up their right arms in stiff Nazi salutes and clicked their solid, naked heels together.

With a heart-stopping thud, a cold, hated feeling whacked Manna's chest and at once, she knew.

Something wicked thrived at this school.

SPLAT!

A mud-splattered kick ball bounced off Manna's plate and rolled under the next lunch table.

"Taro, you when play like one girl!" hooted one of the Japanese gang, and standing next to each other, the two boys looked like brothers.

His deep-naveled potbelly bouncing, Taro huffed to the next picnic table and shoved himself between it and the bench. Then groaning, he groped for the ball with stubby, dirty hands. Shedding thick trails of hot sweat, his open butt crack slipped out of his shorts and its cheeks jiggled like warm fleshy Jell-O.

"Ugh," groaned Mano. "He when got cleavage like one girl, too!"

Spraying milk, Manna giggled – at Mano's clumsy pidgin.

"Ice shave?" asked Barbara. Suddenly standing above Manna, she held out three heaping, rainbow-striped snow cones, and under her bony, skin-flaking elbow she clutched a large grocery bag. Sticking out of her bust-hugging, blue tank top, her long-haired armpits emitted a strong musty smell.

Lightning fast, Mano snatched all three cones, and greed grinning, passed one to Manna, as if Barb didn't get one for herself.

Frowning at the treat, Manna wondered why stinky Barb followed them all day, even though Mano acted rude.

Without being invited, Barb slid onto the bench next to Mano and snorting at her, he slurped both his cones with a wide bumpy tongue, making sure to mark his territory.

"Wow, Mano! No shame!" snipped Barb.

"HA-CHOO!"

Always ready to get even, Mano feigned a loud sneeze and smattered Barb's surprised face with green saliva-dripping slush.

Quickly marking her own cone, Manna took a big, sloppy bite.

Freezing her lips, the Hawaiian Punchy syrup tingled her tongue and sent a cool shot of energy to her hot, itchy thighs.

Although she finally got rid of the hose, her wool skirt still trapped in heat.

"Get crack seed," chatted Barb, dumping out her grocery bag. Dried, sugared squid and anchovy-sized fish skidded across the table and filled the air with a rotten, salty sea smell.

Instantly disgusted, Manna's stomach lurched – but anxious to start eating the crack seed, Mano shoved a whole snow cone down his throat.

"I get lunch at Leilani's, down Keaau," rattled Barb, "to stay out of trouble. My little brother, Joe, got me a Corvette – so I can go to school. We live up Volcano and got no bus. My mom doesn't know, though. She thinks I go work – not school." Smiling sly, her fangs barely showing, Barb continued without breathing. "Joe covers for me now, and come summer, I do all his work."

"OW!" yelled Mano. Dropping both empty paper cones, he gripped the top of his skull and held it together, as though it might explode.

Smirking with delighted revenge, Barb squawked, "Brain freeze!"

Shooting a cross look at her, Mano flopped his long, skinny arm across the table. Then, grunting, he pulled all the crack seed onto his lap.

Sitting up straight and proud, Barb beamed at Manna.

"I won't be a grower forever. I'm going to college, in the mainland."

Manna looked closer at Barb. If you ignored those teeth, she looked pretty – and at least fourteen years old. So it seemed odd, with her confidence and car, that she didn't hang out with the older, accepted crowd. Without thinking, Manna swallowed down the rest of her snow cone and blurted, "Why are you following us?"

Cocking her head and forcing up one puzzled eyebrow, Barb breathed, "Because you're haole ... like me."

SMACK!

Like a ball-sized boulder, brain freeze smacked Manna in the forehead, and in pain-filled surprise, she grabbed it – but not fast enough. Oozing hot, red brain matter slopped onto the table through the splitting crack in her skull. Shocked, she held her breath and waited to die.

"Ho, da buggah when broke her head, noddah time," squealed the same little girl.

"Bachi, bachi – double eyes," her friends taunted again.

Blowing snot like a beached whale, Taro flopped across the table and grabbed his grimy kick ball.

"Spock da haole!" mocked his pleased brother.

Groaning, Manna realized. It wasn't brain freeze.

Taro's ball hit her face and opened the morning's rock wound – and his brother made everyone laugh.

Spreading fast, hot embarrassment singed her cheeks, and at once, she had enough ... of being pushed around.

Forgetting her pain, Manna scrambled up to fight – but the ground swayed under her feet and her eyes swelled orange, then blurred.

"Bubble-eyes, no act wise, cut you down, peanut size," chanted three little girls.

Squinting, her face dripping with blood, Manna clenched her fists, but she couldn't think of anything clever to say – so growling instead, she stormed towards the bathroom.

No matter what Aikoa's gang said, she was gonna use it!

Huh-hmm.

Someone breathed loud right when Manna burst through the bathroom door. Looking left, in the direction of the sound, she noticed small red handprints (made by finger-painting kindergarten students) smeared above a single rusted, white sink. Frowning, she remembered Pumpkin's joke about the Mimi Akua.

Huh-hmm.

The heavy breathing seemed to come out of the walls, like something familiar, from a long time ago.

"Who's there?" she asked, but no one answered.

Suspicious, Manna crouched to the floor and checked under the toilet stalls, but the breather hid her feet.

Huh-hmm.

A creepy, haunted feeling crawled down Manna's neck, but refusing to let the hiding girl scare her, she strode to the sink and turned on the hot water.

Quickly, long strands of curly, orange-red hair clogged the drain and the sink filled with clear, warm water – and wiggling like tiny red eels, blood drops slipped off Manna's face and spiraled under the running tap.

Leaning over the basin, Manna scooped up a soothing handful of water and splashed it over her eyes.

"HA!" yelled a harsh, wicked voice. At the same time, two clammy red hands popped out of the drain and grabbed Manna's ears.

With a body-jerking splash, Manna felt the hands yank her head underwater and slam it into the drain.

Frantic and drowning, Manna clawed at the cold, slimy hands and kicked her feet hard in the air – but squeezing her ears tighter, the hands refused to let go.

"HA-YAH!" the voice yelled louder, raising Manna's head up and cracking it harder against the drain.

Manna's heart pounded in her pulled ears, and panicking, she couldn't understand.

How could the Mimi Akua pull her whole body down a quarter-sized drain?

"AAAAY!" yelled the voice, suddenly letting go of her ears and grabbing the back of her head.

THWAP!

With a loud mind-jarring thwap, Manna saw the Akua dash her head against a blood-spattered wall and everything burst into a speckly orange ... black.

"Manna! Manna!" she heard an anxious voice call from far away.

Blinking, Manna opened her eyes and saw Mano's blurry fright-contorted face hovering above Barb ... and her bloody, red hands.

Brains aching, bathroom walls spinning, Manna could swear she heard Tutu moan, "They follow you ... look over your shoulder – and distinguish between the three."

Crunch. Crunch. Crunch.

Manna heard her hard-soled loafers crunch against the steaming, black cinder path as hot disappointment seared her chest.

How could everyone hate her? And her only friend try to drown her? And her own mother forget to pick them up?

Suddenly, cruel, throbbing sunbeams beat down on her head and pulsed pain out her swollen, bruised eye. Squeezing it shut, she held in stinging tears and pretended, one day, someone would like her.

HUH?

Suddenly, two ugly, long-toed feet blocked Manna's path – and gasping, she jerked her head up.

Barefoot at the bottom of the drive, Moho glared down at her from high above ... with dark, terrifying eyes and hairy, anger-flared nostrils.

Startled, Manna leapt sideways and scurried out of his way.

"You drive 'em," growled Moho, throwing something silver and clinking at Momi's neck. Then spinning round rough, he tromped back into the house.

"He bought me a truck!" shouted Momi, waving a set of keys above a black, shimmering truck. Intimidating, the new four-by-four's wide knobby wheels sprung out of curved, dark red fenders that tilted up and open in front, like a shark's bloodied mouth.

Remembering the red shark from the week before, Manna shivered, but couldn't help cracking a smile.

The new truck stood a foot taller than Ku-hai's!

"He bought *us* a truck," corrected Pu-pele. Curling her orange-glossed lips, she waved a small sandwich bag in front of Momi's face, and instantly, Momi snatched it.

The see-through bag bulged with twenty homemade cigarettes, like the ones the cousins smoked.

"Get in!" growled Momi, right before she sunk into the driver's seat and lit up a skinny, twisted drag.

Forgetting the day's troubles, Manna scampered into the truck bed ... and waited.

"Humph," muttered Ailani, at the same time she tapped her right hand on the passenger's door handle. Then, methodically, she tapped it down her left forearm – five times.

"Humph," she muttered again, restarting her door to arm ritual.

Four more times, thought Manna, *and she's in.*

"OOF!"

Trying to clamber into the truck too fast, Mano slipped and flopped back to the ground.

"Come on!" urged Manna, holding out both hands. Then grabbing his long sweaty fingers, she yanked him into the truck bed – face first.

With a deep clunk, Mano's chin dented the black bed liner and his twinkly brown eyes crinkled into a grin.

"We're in!" squealed Pu-pele, slamming the passenger's door shut behind her.

Ruh. Ruh. Ruh. Ruh.

Momi turned the key, but the truck didn't start.

Manna felt her heart flutter in her chest.

She couldn't wait to catch Hawaiian wind!

Ruh. Ruh. Ruh. Ruh.

Momi tried again, but the engine refused to turn over.

Instantly, Momi's big, blonde-fuzzy ears turned bright red – and hopping mad, she banged her heavy fist on the smoke-covered dash, swearing, "VERDAMMT! VERDAMMT! VERDAMMT!"

"Pump the gas twice, then turn it," murmured Ailani, rocking rhythmically back and forth. An encouraging smile filled her shimmering cheeks.

Scowling straight ahead, but trusting Ailani, Momi stomped on the gas pedal twice, then yanked on the key.

RUHHHM!

Lunging forward, the truck sprang to life and knocked Manna off her feet – but in a blink, Ailani pressed her bare heel on the brake, and Manna scrambled back up.

Engine roaring, the truck vibrated from head to toe, like a quivering horse anxious to race – and quivering with it, Manna held an excited breath.

Eyes dancing, a standing, heated Mano gripped the back window right next to her and flashed an excited, fun-crazed smile.

No doubt, a ride with Momi at the wheel would be better than any train, or even a power chain saw!

"P means park, R's for reverse, and D makes it drive," rattled Ailani, since she was the only one who knew how to drive.

Biting her full upper lip, Pu-pele leaned over her brainy sister and used one chubby, orange-painted finger to bink on the radio.

Whining loud, an electric guitar shattered the air, followed by an angry man shouting at the top of his lungs. Then, with a head banging crash, three drum-laden guitars slammed out a heart-ripping lick – and for the first time ever – Momi and Pu-pele shared a smile.

Pounding fast with the beat, Manna's heart almost burst in her chest.

At last, they would have fun – together!

Horns blaring, two crossing cars swerved out of the way and crashed into each other, but Momi didn't care. Gassing her truck, she peeled across the cinder street without stopping.

"Stop at intersections!" screeched Pu-pele, clutching the overhead passenger's handle. Her flashing, massacred eyes bulged with fright.

"NO!" shouted Momi over the eight blaring speakers. "EVERYONE gets out of OUR WAY!"

A long spiraled clump of Pu-pele's orange-tinted hair flipped out the open back window, and smiling smugly, she agreed with her sister.

Thrilled they got along, Manna belly flopped onto the cab roof, threw her feet in the air – and immediately, Mano copied. Then gripping the rubber windshield seal with their fingernails, they both hung on for their lives!

RUHHHM!

Momi gassed the truck faster, and with a goose-pimply chill, salty wind whipped Manna's face, blasted past her ears, and sliced through her scattering hair. Rapidly, it splashed off her neck, rushed down her body, and washed through her bare, kicking heels. Vibrating hard, the cab hammered excitement into her chest and tickled her rattling brain.

Dizzy with speed, Manna hugged the cab roof tighter and pressed her chin into its hot, sleek roof – and growling in response, the speeding truck sprayed red jagged cinder pellets around her face and twirled them through her bent, open knees.

Suddenly, Momi cut a sharp right turn and fish-tailed onto a narrow, tree-lined road that followed the water's black-cliffed edge. Bending low in the truck's wind, young, sappy pine trees slapped Manna's right arm and flung backwards in twisty, needle-spitting circles – and smashing over the steep rock cliff on the left, white foam-spewing waves doused her cheeks with tingly, frozen sparks.

Squinting at Mano's red wind-stripped eyes, Manna heard him yell, "WOO-HA!" over the roaring wind, and grinning wide, she thought, *We're riding a Hawaiian tornado!*

BOOM! BOOM!

Suddenly, Ku-hai's truck popped over a hill and streaked, stereo pounding, straight their way – but not willing to pull over, Momi gassed the truck. Jumping forward, it tore straight for the cousins, determined to knock them off the cliff's edge.

Horrified, Manna slapped both her palms on the windshield and screamed, "MO-O-O-O-MI!" but it was too late. With a quick white flash, Ailani's bare left knee went up and she slammed on the brakes, at the same time Ku-hai slammed on his – and with a violent body-hurling

145

jolt, the truck bumpers bashed into each other.

Losing their grip, Mano and Manna somersaulted through the air ... straight into the arms of death.

Like angry flesh-ripping jackals, six growling paws snatched Manna out of the air and slammed her into the cousins' truck bed – at the same time six others grabbed Mano and threw him down, on top of her.

Peering through stunned tears, Manna saw the cousins' horrible open-mouthed faces glare down at her, above their hip-high, big-knuckled fists, and instantly, she knew.

Those hideous war dolls would kill her – for what Momi just did.

"RUN!" Manna heard herself shriek, as she pushed Mano to his feet. Then, shoving him up first, she scrambled over Ku-hai's cab and leapt over to Momi's hood – but with a loud thunk and groan, Mano slipped between the locked bumpers and got stuck.

Turning round fast, Manna grabbed his hand ... but couldn't find the strength to pull. Slicing her throat, Ku-hai's hot stare gagged her – and gripping cold, Momi's steely-eyed snarl skewered her back – and painfully embarrassed, she understood.

The cousins saved her life.

Chapter Eight

In the BEGINNING

"You are the Keeper," echoed Tutu, "of your Akua."

Standing tall before the dim Tahuna hallway, her eyes glowed a fire-flecked green.

"Keep him well, and he shall reward you – slight him, and he will destroy."

"Right," Momi rolled her glassy blue eyes, "and how're we supposed to keep him? In a bottle?"

Still angry about yesterday's truck crash, Ku-hai and Aikoa lunged forward and jammed their hot faces into Momi's cheeks.

"OBEY!" snarled Ku-hai, right before Aikoa growled, "RESPECT!"

Startled, Momi jerked – but stood her ground.

"Appease," breathed Moku, glancing quickly at Pu-pele. Smiling prettily, she twinkled back at him, as if he were a chocolate treat she'd love to eat – and Manna could swear, at that moment, Aikoa twitched.

Putting two calming hands on his cousins' shoulders, Moku pulled them gently towards the Tahuna hall.

With a scoffing snort, Ku-hai spun around (knocking Momi with his firm, broad shoulder) and strode through the side hall entrance – and without a word, Aikoa and Moku followed.

"Honor!" growled Kau. His muscular chest swelled twice its size and his hard brown fists clenched low, but he just scowled backwards at Momi, without touching her, and stomped down the hall.

"Celebrate!" Kokala smiled awkwardly, then he jiggled after Kau.

"Praise!" spit Hi'u. His squinted stink eyes bit Momi, and her steely glare stabbed him back.

"Follow!" piped Iki, stepping quickly between the two. Then nudging Hi'u, he steered him into the hall.

"Comply and please!" Waka and Pahau shouted together. Holding hands, they skipped after Iki.

"Don't mock what you don't understand," warned Tutu. Then wrapping her heavy arm around Momi's taut shoulders, she smiled, "Especially if it's Hawaiian."

Manna frowned.

What she didn't understand was why Tutu liked evil Momi so much – and why the cousins told her how to fit in.

Suddenly letting go, Tutu flowed into the hall, and without complaining, Momi followed. Catching up fast, Pu-pele and Ailani trailed her heels.

Tagging along, Manna scampered into the hallway, and a welcome chill tickled her spine.

Even though Tahuna gatherings were dangerous, the excitement of mo'olelo made it fun!

"A Keeper must chose an Akua and thereafter be bound to Him," growled Tutu – and again, her voice seeped out the walls. "To care for Him and always be aware of Him – as a child, forever attention-starved."

Hanging half-dead on the walls, the brown and black wooden masks groaned with Tutu's voice. Squinting at them, this time, Manna was sure.

Tutu wore a microphone – hooked to speakers buried in the masks.

"In return, the Akua charges His Keeper with POWER!" resounded Tutu. "Everlasting power – that lives in the Keeper's bones and ensures him protection, success and love."

Her skin tingling with curiosity, Manna peered at the moaning mask on her right. Thick blackened scars cut down its strained, tortured cheeks and circled its thick, howling lips – and protruding to sheared, crooked points, brown-streaked teeth glinted a haunting yellow.

Shuddering, Manna thought the teeth looked real, or at least, like someone's dried, cracked bones.

"Once chosen and revered, an Akua and His Power may be summoned with a Fetcher – be it a wood or stone image ... or even His Keeper's bones!"

A sharp pang sliced Manna's gut, and at once, she knew.

Tutu could fetch any Keeper's power by stealing and controlling his bones!

"Do not step over a coconut or knock it to the floor," glowered Tutu, "lest you pay with an eye."

Turning round at the grass shack door, she stared directly at Manna. Her long left brow quivered with greed, and her cracked lips filled with hungry white spittle.

Horrified, Manna worried.

Which cousin would gouge out her eye? And in which mask would they shove her splintered skull?

"Can we move?" Mano whispered through clenched teeth. Sitting rigid next to Manna in the torch-lit Tahuna circle, he strained to stay perfectly still.

"Only when she's outside the circle," muttered Ailani. Rocking back and forth, her slouched shoulder knocked Manna's and barely hid her sheepish smile.

Manna felt herself grin back at her sister.

Last time, they almost messed up!

"To the Akua, humans are divine," groaned Tutu. Reaching up to the rafters, she unlatched a netted sack filled with polished, dark brown coconuts.

"Koko," Manna heard someone whisper, right before Tutu moaned, "A prize to be won by the gods."

Trying to get comfortable for the mo'olelo show, Manna wiggled her bottom into the warm, pebbly sand, and instantly, something anxious rustled behind her. Looking round fast, she saw a dark shadow slither into the sand – right before a cold, whooshing swirl slapped her face.

Thump. Tap. Thump. Tap-tap.

Brought to life by the sudden room-circling wind, the hanging lauhala mats thumped and tapped against their walls, as if they were drumming Hawaiian gourds – and rolling far back, Tutu's haunting, witchy eyes glazed over. Lost in a trance, Tutu slid the coconut sack over her shoulder and slipped sideways into the children's circle.

With a back-straightening snap, all the children (including Manna) froze into a cross-legged ne'epu position.

Thump. Tap. Thump. Tap-tap.

Thump. Tap. Thump. Tap-tap.

Dancing a slow ancient hula in time with a heavy gourd's beat, Tutu took turns tapping alternate soles to the sides of her large, bowing body. With each foot tap, she pushed her hips in the opposite direction and swept both palms down to her long extended toes, as if offering them as a gift to her queen.

Thump. Tap. Thump. Tap-tap.

Moving smoothly in front of Ku-hai, Tutu plopped a hollowed, half coconut shell down on his tapa cloth – next to his doll – then swished two more toe-presenting bows.

Thump. Tap. Thump. Tap-tap.

Hips swaying wide, Tutu flowed right, around the circle – and that's when it hit Manna.

Those hideous dolls served as Fetchers ... and every Kealoha was a Keeper!

Thump. Tap. Thump. Tap-tap.

Quickly, Manna scanned the cousins' cloths. Ku-hai's spear-headed doll stretched the longest, with its hunched, bulging shoulders held firm – and Aikoa's square-faced doll glared stout and defensive, as if it were ready to fight.

Squinting, Manna remembered. Ku-hai had yelled, "The biggest! The strongest!" and Aikoa had growled, "Combat!"

Thump. Tap. Thump. Tap-tap.

That was it. That's where the cousins got their strength. From their dolls ... and keeping an Akua.

Thump. Tap. Thump. Tap-tap.

Manna's heart started to beat fast. She could do it, too. She could be strong and proud, like her cousins. All she had to do was become a Keeper.

Thump. Tap. Thump. Tap-tap.

Wait a minute. She already was one. Tutu said ... she was the Keeper of Nui-Akea – Power Supreme. That meant she could be stronger than Ku-hai, tougher than Aikoa ... and more dominating than Momi herself!

Thump. Tap. Thump. Tap-tap.

Aching, hot desire hollowed Manna's gut. Always stepped on, always ignored, there was nothing she wanted more than the power of her Akua.

Thump.

Suddenly, Tutu plunked a shimmering coconut shell onto Manna's tapa cloth, at the same time she finished moaning, "... keep your soul."

Startled, Manna realized ... she hadn't listened to mo'olelo – the lessons that taught you how to be a good Keeper. Pursing her lips, she concentrated hard on Tutu's next words, determined not to get distracted again.

"Some to take care of it," chanted Tutu, dancing her way to an empty tapa cloth. "Some to enslave it. Others, to devour."

In a blink, the gourd drumming ceased and Tutu sat cross-legged outside the circle, behind the empty cloth.

Immediately, the cousins relaxed, and a few of them grabbed something black off their mats and popped it into their mouths. Chewing without swallowing, they grinned at one another.

Hawaiian gum, thought Manna, but when she looked down, on her cloth lay a thick, gnarly root chunk. Hungry, Manna hoped it came from a Hawaiian gum tree.

"Awa," groaned Tutu, "is the drink of the gods. They vie for it, are appeased with it, and use it to communicate with their Keeper."

Spatting loud, Ku-hai shot a juicy black quid into his coconut cup – and Manna thought it sounded like one of Mano's hacked up louggies.

"Only the most handsome ali'i may chew – those with perfectly straight, white teeth. Others must find themselves a chewer ... someone chaste that they can trust."

"Momi," Tutu commanded, looking directly into Momi's surprised, pale face – and at once, Manna remembered.

Momi sported big yellow buckteeth.

Grunting a complaint, Momi chucked her awa root into Ailani's coconut cup – and Pu-pele's glimmering, white teeth smirked.

Thunk! Rat, rat, slap!

Without warning, Mano tossed his root chunk at Manna's cup, and knocked over, it rolled to the edge of her cloth. Thinking fast, she blocked it with one stiff hand – and frowned at her brother's befuddled face.

"Careful," she hissed. "They'll gouge out my eye!"

"Sorry," he muttered, looking down in shame. His crooked tooth flickered weakly in the tiki torch light.

Annoyed, Manna wondered if he'd ever do anything right.

"Chew until it melts, then spit it in the cup," barked Tutu. "Continue till it's all gone."

Suddenly feeling timid, Manna picked up a root chunk and rolled it between her finger and thumb. Shedding dark brown dirt, its rough skin crinkled and flaked like hard, dried-up dog stool.

Scrunching her nose, Manna couldn't believe anyone would eat this stuff – but with a loud crunch, Ailani popped one in her mouth.

Not willing to be the only non-Keeper in the room, Manna squeezed her eyes shut and copied.

With a skull-crunching snap, the scratchy root broke between Manna's teeth, and a searing vapor fumed into her brain. Almost screaming out loud, her mouth and eyes flew open – and with a flash, Tutu's neck stretched long, like a dragon's, and her dangling head zoomed round to Manna.

"Chew-w-w," Tutu hissed, her eyes quivering like eels.

Horrified, Manna chewed as fast as she could.

Burning, jagged-fingered root splinters scraped her cheek and clawed into her bleeding gums. Sucking hard, she swished saliva over them, hoping to lessen the pain, but instead, her spit caught fire and singed her tongue.

Eyes tearing, Manna grabbed her cup and shot a stream of smoking black sludge at it, with a loud, splattering ...

SPIST!

Missing the cup, the sludge hit the suddenly blazing, red sand, then transformed into a miniature iridescent conch shell. Wisping into a gentle swirl, twinkly red dust rose above the shiny wet, fast-throbbing shell.

"Man," said a comforting voice, and without moving, Manna looked up.

Standing over the shell with His large, black-striped arms raised, a warm, muscular man gurgled. From His head flowed thin streams of deep blue water that vanished as they touched the ground, and from His skin beamed yellow-orange rays that filled Manna with the sun's soothing warmth.

Smiling drowsily, Manna knew. This could only be a dream.

"O'le kane – no man!" shrieked a sweaty, thin guy. His streaked blonde hair curled over a pasty white body and dripped bluish-grey sweat onto His brown, bristled loincloth.

"Lahui Akua," the yellow man murmured through His trickling hair, and as if responding to His command, the ground under the conch shell rose six inches and transformed into a sandy, red mold of a man. Wiggling like a scared fish trying to hide in coral, the pearly conch shell buried itself in the sand man's chest.

At once, the sky roared a thunderous threat and a furious black cloud twisted overhead.

Terrified, Manna's heart hammered in her chest, and panting out loud, she tried to wake herself up ... before something horrible happened.

SNAP!

With a hungry lip-smacking snap, an enormous greenish-red caterpillar dropped out of the dark whirling cloud and dangled directly above the sand man's head. Then, spurting thick, glistening blood out its fanged, sucking mouth, it noisily devoured his face.

Jerking awake, the sand man flung his bloodied arms and spattered chest in frantic, convulsing circles, then he stiffened and his skin turned a dark ruddy brown.

Letting go, the caterpillar jerked up His bulgy-eyed head and smiled at the yellow, watery man – and at that moment Manna noticed.

A hundred wild-eyed, thrashing eels dangled off the caterpillar's crown.

BAM!

With a gut-shaking bam, the caterpillar exploded into hot, black, twinkly dust.

"Mana," gargled the yellow man, and immediately, the sand man rose – making Manna catch her breath.

He was real now, and the most beautiful thing she'd ever seen.

Completely naked, his dark skin shone strong over his perfectly formed body, and his eyes twinkled greenish-yellow, like a cat's – and quivering, his uncertain smile flashed perfectly straight, white teeth.

Biting her lip, Manna realized. The handsome man was merely a boy.

Approaching the yellow man shyly, the boy whispered, "Kane," then knelt before Him on one knee, and bowed his head low to the ground. One of his sturdy, rippled biceps cocked over his upright, bent knee while the other stretched solid to the ground.

"He will break the law!" screeched the sweaty blonde guy. "La'a kahuli!" Then dissolving with a loud sput, He sank into the ground, leaving only a fishy trail of smoke.

Twinkling, a cool rainbow shot past Manna's ear and curved sideways, in front of the boy. Then, chirping cheerfully, a flock of fluffy silver birds spiraled down the rainbow and encircled the giggling boy.

"Aloha," whispered a tanned, naked man, as He emerged from the singing birds – and immediately, Manna squinted.

Beaming bright around His body, a pure white light blinded her eyes.

Reaching down gently, the naked man slid His long-fingered hand down the boy's hairless chest, and slipped it underneath his ribs. Then, sweeping His shimmering arm high overhead, He yanked out one of the boy's ribs and flipped it into the yellow man's falls.

With a delighted feminine giggle, a round-busted, wavy-haired girl popped out of the yellow man's stream and wiggled her chubby brown fingers at the boy – and beaming wide, the boy anxiously grabbed them, murmuring, "Ku'u wahine. Mahalo. Mahalo."

Embracing gently, the girl and boy kissed.

They love each other, thought Manna. *So beautiful ... and made to last.*

Slowly waking, her drowsy eyes teared with romantic bliss, and her shining cheeks filled with a goofy smile.

What a nice, euphoric dream.

"A Keeper's dreams are reality!" barked Tutu, from directly behind Manna.

Jerking awake, Manna realized her chewed awa had dissolved.

Quickly, she spat its black swill into her glimmering coconut cup, and at once, Tutu grabbed it and poured it into a large black shell. Then flowing back to her spot in the circle, she continued.

"They tell the future, and the past, and allow a Keeper to go places and do things that no one else ever can."

Offering Momi the cup first, she smiled.

"Today, your Akua will teach you who you are – and where it is you come from. In your dreams, he will take you back ... to the Beginning of Your Time."

Light-headed, Manna wondered.

Had she just been to the Beginning of Man?

"Drink," Tutu commanded, and smiling eagerly, Momi chugged from her grandmother's black cup, knowing she was now Tutu's favorite.

Cramping, a familiar sadness gripped Manna's tummy.

No matter what the game, she was always picked last, because no one ever liked her.

Suddenly jealous of everyone, she watched Tutu ease the cup away from Momi and pass it to her adorable second-favorite ... Waka.

Pouting, Manna curled her toes and prayed that this time, she wouldn't be last.

Slowly, Tutu's glowing coconut cup passed into the hands of the thirsty cousins, and curious, Manna noted.

Each of them snorted right when they got the cup ... and they all snorted when Ku-hai drank last.

Twinkling at Moku, Pu-pele fingered the cup after Ku-hai and swallowed a tiny taste – then Ailani sipped from it twice (between four head tilts) and passed it round to Mano. Gulping loud, Mano swallowed a mouthful and shoved the cup into Manna's hand ... last.

Disappointed, Manna peered into the cup. The black, bubbly swill reeked of spit and tobacco, like some cowboy's used, slimy chew – and eyes tearing, she knew she couldn't drink it.

At once, the cousins snorted and glared defensively at Manna.

Immediately embarrassed, she felt hot shame sear her cheeks.

Not only did she forget to thank the cousins for catching her truck-expelled body, she just scoffed at their sacred drink.

Knowing the last Catholic must finish all the wine in the goblet, Manna squeezed her eyes shut and forced down the tongue-bittering awa in six throat-shearing gulps ...

"Where is He?"

It was the yellow man again, but this time He faced Manna, as if expecting her to answer His question.

Suddenly, a menacing rattle filled the air, as though someone shook a giant jar of dried-up dog fangs directly above Manna's head. Startled, she looked up, but saw nothing.

WHOOSH!

Roaring, a bitter, cold wind whooshed through Manna, and at once, a hundred frozen eels strung their slimy, coiled bodies around her throat. Terrified, she tried to scream but couldn't. Deafeningly loud, the shrill pleading shrieks of tortured women silenced her – and the pain-filled howls of half-eaten men rang loud in her ears.

Sickened, Manna went limp – and without trying, she answered the yellow man's question with a deep, rumbling croak.

"Under the poisonous waters of the Yellow River."

Suddenly, uncontrollable, wicked laughter popped out of Manna's lips, and she cackled, "Encased in a lava tube, made by My ever faithful Pele."

Shaking, Manna feared – the Devil spoke through her.

"Never would he be tricked by that fiery hag," gushed the yellow man.

Manna felt a smirk spread over her lips.

"But He'd trust her faithful Ka-moho-ali'i," she jibed, "like You trusted that snake Kanaloa ... the One who lured You away."

Manna heard herself cackle again, before she bragged, "How easy it was for Him to distract You with a game of Test-A-Man and a cup of awa – aka manu."

Awa. Manna remembered the awa.

This most definitely was a dream, and nothing she should fear.

"To what end is this?" choked the yellow man, and Manna thought He might cry.

Filled with sudden fury, she bellowed, "TO THE END OF MAN!" Then raising one cruel fist, she growled, "Without Lono, all men shall perish! And their children starve to death – right before I devour their wailing souls!"

Scared of herself, Manna forced her lungs to breathe in deep – to make sure she didn't die of fright in her sleep.

Shaking His streaming blue head in disappointment, the yellow man gurgled, "This hate, Ku ... will consume You."

This can't be the beginning of MY time, thought Manna.

Deciding to leave, she tried to pinch herself awake, but without warning, her hands clenched into fists and shoved themselves onto her hips.

"Your love for them consumed YO-O-OU!" she heard herself shriek, and at once, her stomach burned with jealousy. "You treasure them! Those WEAK ... UNFAITHFUL ... SELF-SERVING HUMANS! And even when they break Your Law – LA'A KAHULI – You invite them to live in Kahiki ... with YOU!"

Manna felt her lips curl in.

"Do You invite Me," she growled, "Your most powerful, law-abiding Son? Or Lono, Your favorite? Or Kanaloa, Your friend?"

"NOOOO!" Manna bellowed the answer to her question. Then she spit on the ground and scowled. "I've always hated Your stupid men – but they appeased Me for years, with offerings so grand ... but not anymore. They've forgotten Me ..."

Manna felt herself smile wicked again.

"But in bloody horror, they'll remember ... right before I swallow their screaming souls!"

Manna's eyes narrowed, and feeling like she might giggle, she taunted her yellow elder.

"You got it wrong, Kane. My hate will consume *them* – not *Me*."

The yellow man's head trickled for a moment, then with a warm, gentle breeze He sighed.

"I look into Your eyes of hate and can only think of My favorite Son, trapped in His pool of poison."

With a shocked thump, Manna's heart stopped – and breathless, she thought she might puke.

"It is true. You can destroy all that I love," breathed Kane, "but what You can't do is destroy Me."

Instant, hot anger boiled in Manna's chest and steamed into her head. Half-crazed, she almost smacked Kane for His bold, ugly challenge – but certain He was trying to fool her, she held herself back and hissed, "You wish to trick Me – but you cannot. I am the Highest, the Strongest of Your Children – and the Power of My Hatred frees Me from Your manipulation."

The waters from Kane's head almost ceased, and Manna could swear she felt two beaming red eyes jab her, like laser beams aimed at a helpless target. Shivering, she held her breath.

"I only wish to free My beloved Son from His poisonous prison," whispered Kane, "and certain death."

Suddenly, the waters on Kane's head swelled into life-producing falls, and gurgling loud, he roared, "What is it You want? Supreme Power? Over Me and all My children?"

SHROOM!

With a turbo-charged boom, Kane swooped his shiny yellow palms over His foam-spraying head and shot a million sunbeams out of His glowing fingers.

Crackling like lightning, the beams zigzagged towards the sky and wove themselves into a giant lemony dome. Then out of nowhere, a squawking flock of red and gold-tipped birds spiraled frantically through the dome, as if warning everyone of danger.

Humming out loud, Kane struck a deal.

"Covenant – My Son. Release Lono, and I shall grant Your destiny – to have Nui-Akea – Power Supreme!"

Manna's heart raced in her chest. That's what she wanted. Power Supreme! Without thinking, she yelled, "COVENANT! NUI-AKEA!"

With a loud clap, the sky exploded into a brilliant array of neon-colored fireworks, and arching wide, the most beautiful twinkling rainbow streaked through the dome – and disappeared at the farthest edge, almost as if it were running away ... scared.

Burning hot, a terrible jealousy singed Manna's gut.

He would do anything for His clumsy, weak Son ... but not for her. Never, ever for her.

Manna's teeth clenched.

That was it! That was all the disdain she could take! After she secured her power, she would use it to destroy them all. Those mocking humans ... that favorite Boy ... and her scornful, loveless Dad!

Rippling, Kane's waters beamed bright, and their crystally warmth filled Manna with overwhelming happiness.

Yes, she smiled. *This Covenant would make all things right.*

Chanting Hawaiian, Kane sprayed the air with perfumed breath, and somehow, Manna understood the foreign words He spoke.

> *"Of Hawaii, of Man and Akua -*
> *Opposites paired together.*
>
> *Light of Kane, darkened by Kanaloa.*
> *Generations of Hina, destroyed by Ku.*
> *Fires of Pele, doused by Ka-moho-ali'i.*
>
> *A new Covenant, a new Destiny.*
> *For we, today, are paired again.*
> *We Kane, we Ku, we Pele, we Moho ... and we Kanaloa."*

Moho? thought Manna. *Which Moho? My dad?* – and that's when it hit her.

Her father was Ka-moho-ali'i, and this *was* the beginning of her time. The waters on Kane's head spurt a muddy blood red as he roared,

> *"From Moho shall come six – five mortals, one god!*
>
> > *One for Kane,*
> > *One for Pele,*
> > *One for Kanaloa,*
> > *One for Moho.*
> > *The Fifth to Keep the Sixth,*

The Sixth, born for Ku!"

Kane flowed forward and placed both hands on Manna's shoulders. Gushing off His palms, soothing heat washed through her body and made her almost unaware. Hazily, she listened to His calm words.

> *"The Fifth holds the Power of Kane –*
> *And shall be the Eternal Keeper of the Sixth.*
>
> *The Sixth holds Nui-Akea for Ku –*
> *His Wahine of Mana – Power Supreme.*
>
> *Their Pairing shall Seal this Covenant,*
> *And their Irrevocable, Wedded Destiny."*

"A WIFE?" bellowed Manna.

Jerking back, Kane released her shoulders, and instantly, they sagged in disbelief.

"A wife," Manna heard herself growl again, "for me ... to devour!"

Blood pumping in her ears, Manna felt like her head might explode.

She was the Fifth born ... the Keeper of the Sixth – Wife of the Devil Himself ... and *her* destiny was to help *them* extinguish the human race!

So scared she didn't know what to do, Manna grabbed her hair and screamed – loud.

SUP!

With a wet sucking sound, Kane and the dome disappeared, and Manna stood alone and shivering in a white, luminous fog. Uneasy, she backed up and bumped into a cold, hard being.

Slithering fast, an eerie feeling rushed down Manna's spine.

Without a doubt, if she turned around she'd face the Sixth ... her evil, unborn sister.

Catching her breath, Manna decided – to kill her.

With a shrill war cry, she spun around and lunged at the Sixth's neck – but yelping high, Mano jumped out of her way. Frightened and pale blue, he shook violently before her, his purple lips gaped down and his crooked tooth glimmering white.

Horrified, Manna shrieked, "Why are you following me?" – right before Tutu commanded, "MAI!"

With a blinding crack, Manna woke up in the warm Tahuna circle. Tutu sat smiling in her spot, her arms spread out, above her full bosom.

"Now that you know what you are," Tutu hummed, "your pairing you must find. For if you do not couple with your other half, you shall die."

Dizzy and deflated, Manna stared at the sandy ground, half wishing she could die now.

She would never be good. Her destiny dictated she be evil.

"Your pairing, your opposite, is your other half, that you cannot thrive without," continued Tutu. "Be it friend or foe, soul mate or spouse – or something to struggle against – you must find it, and make all things complete."

Clammy cold, Mano's rough hand slipped into Manna's, and instantly, she filled with contempt.

That dream was *her* beginning, *her* secret – and no one else needed to know ... especially not Mano.

Chapter Nine

VWVWVWVWVWVWVWVW

AAAAAAAAAAAAAA

KILLER

Creak!

With a gasp, Manna dropped to all fours. She didn't know Anna's bedroom door creaked!

Terrified, she waited for Moho to wake up and kill her – but he didn't. He just grunted and squeezed Anna tighter.

Glinting in the soft moonlight, a large silver crucifix hung above Anna's head and gazed down at Manna with pity ... and choking, she almost cried.

Mother Mary couldn't help her, and neither could her Guardian Angel – because she was the Keeper of the Devil's Wife.

Blinking back hot tears, she stared at the sad, long face that drooped on the Cross, and tingling, hope seeped into her chest.

That giant cross served as Anna's Fetcher, because she kept Jesus Christ.

Squeak! Squeak! Squeak! Humm.

Squeaking rhythmically, Anna's bed rocked in time with Moho's bouncing knee – and humming a peaceful snore, her precious face smiled, like a cherub fallen asleep.

Manna frowned and thought it perfectly clear now – why Anna shook her so hard and screamed, "You're the devil ... I see you hiding in there ... and I'm gonna SHAKE YOU OUT!"

White and limp, Anna's hand suddenly slipped off the side of the bed and instantly, Manna's heart skipped a beat.

This was her chance to get help!

Scuffling fast, she crawled over to Anna. Then trembling on her knees, she touched her aching forehead against the tip of Anna's index finger and prayed.

In the Name of the Father ...

Tilting her head up (so that Anna's finger traced down), she continued.

And the Son ...

Pulling back, she turned her head right and touched Anna's finger to her temple – then moving her face left, she traced Anna's finger across her forehead and finished.

And the Holy Spirit.

Burning tears streamed down her face, and shaking, she touched Anna's finger to the tip of her nose and begged.

Boops. God's gonna watch over you.

"Move it!" someone hissed through the dark.

Jerking awake, Manna clutched a sharp pang in her side. Jabbed through her ribs, a white spear skewered her lung.

"In the truck," Moho growled under his breath. Hovering way above her, with Mano at his side, he gripped two thin surfboards in one gnarled hand. Glinting in the dim purple dawn, both boards stretched long like brandished hunting spears – and that's how they felt, jammed in Manna's side.

Scuffling to her feet, Manna tiptoed out of the room, so as not to wake Anna up.

"A Hawaiian belongs to the sea," Moho warned his son, and his voice echoed eerily down the hall ... like Tutu's. "He is born from her, always dependent on her, and in the end, returns to her womb."

Manna padded down the still hallway and slipped out the side driveway door. Instantly, chilled salty air filled her lungs and apprehension gripped her chest.

Last time Moho took her to the sea, he tried to drown her.

"In this life," Moho croaked, "you must call on her, play with her, and bid her respect. In return, she'll reward you ... immensely."

As if going to a morgue, Manna trudged slowly towards Moho's truck and ignored the prickly crunch of the cinder drive beneath her bare feet.

Most likely, she wouldn't return from the sea.

Always eager, Mano bolted past her and winged the truck door open – and with a crack, it snapped back against its hinges and slammed shut, pinning him halfway in the cab. Twisting frantically, his long toes scraped the ground and tried to wiggle his waist free.

Suddenly hot, Moho's foul breath blasted Manna's face, and an inch from her nose, his cruel, black, pupil-less eyes flashed.

"You watch out for him!" he growled.

Shocked by his stench, Manna caught her breath and wondered, *Who's gonna watch out for me?*

"Don't eat rocks," was the only thing Moho said before he left them on the beach.

Sitting on the water's edge, in the cool black sand, Manna watched the white water splash between her tanned, open thighs and gurgle inside her shrunken wool skirt. Seemed like Mano had struggled for at least three long hours and still hadn't caught a single wave. But luckily, he hadn't eaten any rock either, even though a row of black, jagged edges peeked out of the churning blue sea and leered at him, just to his left.

Manna watched the glistening water pool over her cute, chubby toes, and stretching, she spread them wide. With a soft tremble, a tiny bubble swam out from between her toes and popped without a sound on the water's surface – and instantly, she knew.

She would drown the Sixth, as soon as She was born – and the Devil couldn't do anything about it.

"WOO-HOO!" yelled Mano, and Manna looked up. His bobbing head was close to the shore and beaming from ear to ear. Somehow, he managed to catch a wave – and Manna felt herself frown.

If anything happened to Mano, Anna would be crushed – but she'd feel even worse if her newborn baby drowned.

Not wanting to hurt Anna that way, Manna dug her toes into the wet, sticky sand and let a retreating wave suck her ankles in deep. Her feet stuck sturdy in the ground, she leaned far back and tunneled her fingers into the sand.

Whirling, a chin-high wave sploshed over her body and slapped cool across her face, but rigid, she held her ground and thought, *Once I'm the Keeper of the Sixth, I can steal all Her power and use it – to conquer Her ... and destroy the Devil Himself.*

WHOOSH! SNAP!

Another high wave broke on the shore and whooshed over Manna's chest – and with a big-toothed snap, a gleaming red shark lunged at her face.

Jerking back fast, Manna scrambled up the beach on all fours, then whipped around to check on Mano. Hunched over low and wobbling, he stretched his long arms out on either of his sides as he rode a small, mushy white wave.

Thrilled to catch Manna's eye, Mano waved wildly – and lost his balance. With a loud slap, his chest hit the water and his huge brown feet kicked the board high into the air – but attached to the leash on his ankle, it jackknifed back down and rapped him on top of the head. Lolling his long red tongue out, Mano rolled his eyes far back and sunk under the next white-foaming wave.

Manna giggled at his clumsiness and remembered.

Momi said sharks were white, not red.

"Hee. Hee. Hee."

Manna heard a little girl giggle at Mano.

"Tee. Hee. Hee."

Manna heard a bunch of giggly girls join in ... from over a light green hill dotted with rustling coconut trees.

Delighted, Manna grinned.

Maybe the giggling girls wanted to make friends.

Hurrying, Manna skipped up the hill and peered through the field of shoulder-high orchid reeds that waved along its smooth edge – but all she saw was four flat, grey, stone-marked Hawaiian graves.

Moaning, a cold wind suddenly shivered across her cheeks, and a funny feeling she shouldn't be there pricked her spine.

"Hide!" a little girl hissed, and darting around, Manna's quick eyes scanned the ancient cemetery.

One glowering, grey-weathered, wooden Tiki-god towered over the seaward edge of the hill, and a lonely altar table (made of round, bleached beach rocks) spread long, behind the tombs. Quivering, light green orchid reeds swayed between the still, ancient rocks, and another girl whispered, "We tell her!"

"No bother," quipped another. "She get hard time understand."

Squinting both eyes, Manna saw – it was the orchid girls again, bickering about her. The bald one that bit her disagreed with the others and wanted to tell Manna something.

"Now she when see you, puka head," complained a cross little girl, right before her darling, purple-eyed head popped out of a reed. Then flinking her delicate white hands at Manna, she squealed, "Shoo, fly!"

"She going go steal your bones!" squeaked the flowerless girl. "When you not looking!"

Manna thought of Tutu, but mesmerized by her bald, little friend, she heard herself whisper, "Who are you?"

"What? You no can tell?" snapped the flinky-hand girl, except this time, her haughty hands gripped her tiny half-submerged waist. "We da Menehune!"

Suddenly, a chilling wind whipped through the reeds, and at once, the frightened girls bared their green, thorny fangs and shrieked, "SHA-R-R-RK!"

With a body-twisting jolt, something razor sharp and biting cold grabbed Manna's shoulder and jerked her body around.

Horrified, Manna almost screamed – but it was just Mano. Standing before her, his sunk-in, shivering chest streaked with dark red blood and his soaked shorts dribbled pink.

"What happened?" asked Manna.

Glowering at the ground, Mano mumbled, "I ate rock."

"BOY!" hollered Moho, and with a quick rustle, the Menehune girls disappeared.

"I told you – WATCH HIM!" hollered Moho. His huge black lips spit on Manna's nose, and his parsley breath blasted her cheeks.

Defensive, Manna barked back, "I did – SIR!"

Furious, Moho jammed a surfboard into Manna's chest and knocked her backwards into the hot sand. Heart stinging, she lay flat on her back, clutching the board as if it could shield her.

"GET IN!" boomed Moho – and that's when Manna saw it – that same cold, mocking look in his eyes, like last time, when he tried to drown her.

"What? You afraid?" Moho taunted. Then snorting, he smirked with cruel flashing teeth, "The All Powerful One – afraid of the sea?"

Instantly, shame stung Manna's chest, and frowning, she swore – she would show him. *She* wasn't afraid of *anything*.

Jumping to her feet, she spun around, and determined, tromped to the sea.

CRASH!

With a loud crash, a stinging cold wave knocked Manna on her back and grinded sand up her thighs. Then, as if wanting to bury her, it spread a thick layer of mud over her face.

Manna hugged her board and dragged herself up. Then frowning, she belly flopped onto the retreating wave with her board snug underneath her.

Idiot! she thought, as she cupped her hands, threw them over her head, and dug her chin into the sticky, waxed board. With a deep two-handed breast stroke, she shot past the angry wave.

Can't he count? she screamed in her head. *He should've had only FOUR kids!*

CRASH!

With a deafening crash, a freezing cold, white wall of water knocked Manna backwards and sucked her under its curl. Then, churning quickly, it yanked her body around and spit her up into its swirling foam. Dizzy and choking, Manna paddled blindly, trying to get out of the wave.

CRASH!

Before she could think, another wave smacked her face and flipped her backwards into its gurgling blue. Slipping off her board, she clung to one of its fins, and with her back to the ocean, kicked both feet as fast as she could.

CRASH!

Instantly, another wave whacked her in the back and cracked her forehead against the top of her board. Then roaring, it dragged her under its foam and spun her in dizzying circles, sideways, like a helpless child rolled down a steep hill.

Manna hugged her board tight and remembered, Tutu said, "Don't turn your back to the sea. It's alive – and always hungry."

Her mind racing, Manna jerked her body around and pointed her board at the raging sea. Then she shoved her board under her gut, surfaced, took a deep breath, and double-paddled as fast as she could.

CRASH!

Another roaring wave stuffed a salty fist down her throat and flipped her backwards under its curl. Then jiggling wildly, as if laughing at her, it shook her off of her board and tried to snatch it away.

Choking-hot salty barf seared Manna's throat, and bitter tears streamed down her cheeks – and with a sudden cold rush, she hated them all – for taunting her.

Moho. And Mano. And this nasty, murderous sea!

Gritting her teeth, her entire body shaking with rage, Manna jammed her board underneath her, jutted to the surface, and faced the next foam-spewing wave.

"I'll kill you back!" she cried. Then using all her weight, she thrust the sharp point of her board into the wave's cresting neck, trying hard to kill it.

Spitting and wounded, the wave passed by, barely shoving her, but Manna didn't notice. She glared at the next curling wave, wanting nothing more than to punch it – and right when it got to her, she gripped the top of her board, tucked both knees under her hips, and cocked the board far back.

"ARGGHHH!" she growled and punched the swollen wave with the tip of her board.

Gurgling loud, the wave passed over her head – and tickled down her sides.

Double-paddling once, Manna surfaced and shot a hot glare at the retreating wave. In response, the wave sprayed tingly foam on her face, as if it was sending butterfly kisses, and in an instant, Manna understood.

Like any good Hawaiian, the waves expected you to fight back – or at least, punch through them.

Hopeful, Manna faced the next wave, squeezed her board tight, and punched through it with all her might. Then paddling as fast as she could, she jutted forward to meet the next and plowed, full force, through that one, too – and the next – and the next – and the next.

Slap. "Uh-h."

Slap. "Uh-h."

Slap. "Uh-h."

Slapping noisily against her board, blue water whooshed past her ribs, until she noticed – the slapping was in time with her strokes and her tired, wheezing breath. Manna looked up at the rippling blue horizon and knew ... the cresting waves were far behind her. Excited, she stopped paddling and grinned back at the distant shore.

She did it! She got past the break. A lot faster than Mano did!

"YES-S-S!" she breathed and sat up on her board – but her weak, shaking arms gave out, and she flipped sideways into the sea.

Giggling at her own clumsiness, Manna pulled her tummy back onto the board and spread her arms and legs open like a turtle – and relieved, her arms and legs slipped into the clear, rippling sea.

With a soft crackle, tingly iridescent drops suddenly splashed off the board's nose and sprinkled cool onto Manna's shoulders, but at once, the broiling white sun cooked them into crinkled, dusty-white hot spots. Then, brushing past her cheeks, a warm, salty trade wind stroked her hair and soothed her heated crown – and slapping lazily against her board, the dark blue sea breathed slowly, all around her. Rising and falling like a sleeping giant's chest, distant swells filled the horizon as they expanded towards the sky, then slowly, they sunk down as if to exhale – only to be followed by the next rising swell.

Slowly and rhythmically, the powerful, glistening blue swells rose and fell ... rose and fell – and mesmerized by their striking beauty, Manna lost her breath whenever one fell, and waited ... anxious for the next to expand. As it did, she breathed in deep and enjoyed its immense sense of peace.

Dreamily, Manna felt her eyelids droop up and down ... up and down, keeping time with each flowing swell, and hypnotized, her pupils suddenly stung. Biting her bottom lip, she felt her cheeks smile.

For the first time ever, she felt utter peace – with herself – and the sea around her.

Wanting to get a better view of the calm blue swells, Manna gripped the nose of her board and propped herself up on her elbows.

Thump.

With a quick jerk, the nose of her board caught a little air off a wave and thumped back down against the water's surface. Startled, Manna sat up fast, both arms stiff, her knees dangling in the water.

Thump!

A larger wave bumped the tail of her board four inches into the air, and it thumped down, louder, against the sea.

Worried, Manna looked inland and searched for the cresting wave break line – to make sure she hadn't drifted back into it – but for some reason, it disappeared.

Certain she'd better get out, Manna spun her board towards the beach.

THUMP!

With a loud thump, something hard hit her board and nearly knocked her into the water!

Instantly, Manna's heart pounded in her chest, and she panicked.

For sure, she'd drifted into the rocks – and any second, the sea would pulverize her head against them!

Her mind spinning wild, Manna flopped down on her board and

paddled inland as fast as she could.

THUMP!

Something bloody red slammed into her board, and almost flipped her into the sea – and burning her eyes like a thousand poison needles, fear squeezed her lids shut. Whimpering, she double paddled – FASTER – but gurgling loud, the angry sea suddenly raised her board high in the air, and terrified, she knew death was near.

Choking back tears, she started to pray – but stopped – her heart frozen in her chest. Shrieking across the sea, a frightened Menehune squealed, "SHA-A-A-ARK!"

Horrified, Manna's lids flew wide open, and at the same time, both of her knees jerked up onto her board. Then quickly, her feet popped up, under her bottom, and suddenly squatting sideways, she felt her hands flatten against the top of the board, as if they meant to keep her balance.

Petrified, Manna hoped.

If none of her touched the water, the shark couldn't bite her!

With a cold backwards rush, vibrating, deep blue sheets of water streaked under Manna's board, and at once, she felt herself fall through the air, straight down a steep, sparkling green wall. Trembling, she crouched low to the board, flung both hands out to her sides, and tried to keep her balance – but she jerked when someone hissed, "Position is POSSESSION!"

With a crash, her board cut a sharp left and ripped through a white hole in the wall – and roaring, the sea came to life. Shocking cold flecks sprayed through the air and pelted her face with needle-sharp kisses – and screaming in a swirl, a brilliant sea green curl flew over her head and shattered a million glistening icicles around her. Then shaking wildly, the wave reared beneath her and shot her through its whistling barrel.

Giggling with glee, Manna heard herself squeal, "WEE-HEE-HEE-

HEE!" – and out of nowhere, a raging hot, tingly thrust of power blasted through her head.

She owned this wave ... this sea ... and all the world around her!

WHAM!

With a sudden lurch and a jarring wham, Manna felt something rock hard slam into her chest – and everything went black.

"GET UP!" Moho snarled. His dark, pupil-less eyes glared past Manna, as if she wasn't laying there.

A razor-sharp pang shot through Manna's ribs, and frowning, she blinked down at her splintered, blood-splattered board.

She had eaten rocks, and so had her board. Broken in two lopsided pieces, its shiny resined shell frayed out to expose its spongy, glistening innards – and Manna thought it looked like a huge broken bone with its marrow squirting out. Shivering, she wondered if that's how her throbbing ribs looked.

"NOW!" hissed Moho.

Forcing back pain-filled tears, Manna clutched what was left of her board and hauled herself up. Then trying not to breathe in, else her ribs snap in half, she trudged slowly towards Moho's truck.

"Stupid power-hungry witch," muttered Moho, from too close behind.

Gritting her teeth, Manna tried to walk faster, but couldn't. With each step, her board grew heavier and heavier, dragging her down – just like her sinking heart.

She got in the water – and caught a wave. Didn't she? Wasn't that good enough?

Suddenly at Moho's truck, Manna heaved her broken board up over the truck bed, but with a gasp, dropped it to the ground.

Quivering in a helpless blood-trickling pile, seven five-foot-long, yellow-streaked tuna lay half-dead in Moho's truck. Gaping down, their spittle-foamed mouths gasped hollow while their wheezing red gills fanned wide – and sweating, their contorted bodies undulated in pain as their hazy, tear-stained eyes howled with fear. Gushing runny, red streaks though a cracked, razor-lined jaw, a lifeless shark stared, dark-eyed and cold, above them, letting them know what came next.

With a loud whimper, Manna buckled forward and swallowed a burning mouthful of puke. Then grabbing her board, she lifted it into the bed and gingerly propped it up against the cab, careful not to hurt any of the suffering fish.

Thunk!

With a sickening thunk, a foot-long, club-shaped rock dislodged from her board's fins and gashed the closest fish in the eye. With a jolt, the fish curled its tail in the air, then gurgled out a last dying breath.

"Sorry," Mano muttered. Trying to maneuver his board into the cab, he had banged Manna's and knocked the rock out of its fins.

Unable to speak, Manna glared at her brother as he stuffed his board into the cab and jammed its nose out the back window. Then he flopped onto the seat and curled his left arm around the board's middle, as if it was his new teddy bear.

Hollow, Manna felt her heart sink – further.

"The best ahi," gloated Moho. His long white teeth gleamed in the hot afternoon sun, and his dark eyes glinted pride. Grinning at his boy, he stabbed a live ahi tuna in the back and slit down its spine. Stiffening with pain, the ahi gasped once and died.

Manna drooped against the cool truck cab and tried not to faint – but bouncing on his toes next to his father, Mano leaned hungrily over their kill.

Maybe Tutu will come out and stop them, hoped Manna. (They'd pulled up her drive five minutes before, but still, she hadn't come out.)

With a flick of his wrist, Moho slashed off the fish's long rubbery side and exposed its brown-veined, trembling guts. Then he flipped over its plump, jiggling flesh and cubed it into dark red, blood-drizzling squares. Clinging fast to the fish's still-breathing skin, the cubes spread open and oozed a foul, raw sewage smell.

Grunting, Moho lopped off a foot-long section and tossed it at his boy.

With a juice-spattering slup, the wiggling flesh smacked Mano's face and slid down his chin, but he didn't notice. Starved, he sank his flashing white teeth into its glistening flesh and sucked off one of its drizzling squares. Then, smiling runny streaks of blood off his crooked tooth, he nuzzled his nose into the stinking flesh and tore off six cubes at once.

Pointed teeth gleaming, Moho did the same, and in moments, both of their necks streamed with sticky congealing blood.

Sickened, Manna turned away and caught sight of the dead, bloody-mouthed shark.

They look like him, she thought. *Cold-blooded killers.*

"Crack seed," a soft voice intoned.

Manna jerked around.

Tutu stood broad and tall behind her, holding out a small clear plastic bag. Shriveled and twisted in the bag, something resembling rotted, skin-flaking squid tried to claw its way out the top. Its bony, yellow, white-dusted hands scraped frantically at the air, like a corpse digging its way out a grave.

"Dried plum," breathed Tutu, her voice almost kind, "and coconut milk."

In the bright sunlight, Tutu's eyes glinted an evil red-bordered green, and as if trying to cloak them, she lowered her grey-lashed lids and held out a tan, twig-covered, half coconut shell in her fat-fingered hand. Inside the shell, white bubbles frothed on top a fogged, lumpy, white juice, and Manna thought it looked like a witch's brew – or maybe, Pu-pele's bedtime milk.

Painfully tightening, her stomach suddenly growled, and desperate, she grabbed the coconut milk and swallowed it down in four hungry gulps.

"They were born with this place," Manna heard Tutu's voice drone, but she didn't see her lips move. Licking her own lips, Manna smiled and thought it neat that coconut milk tasted both sour and sweet, and clung to your teeth like chalky honey.

"And forever, are part of it – the Mu – the Menehune."

Tickling, scratchy coconut milk coated Manna's throat, and wanting to taste more, she squeezed her tonsils together and forced the milk back into her mouth. Then sucking her cheeks together, she rubbed her tongue between them and peeked into the coconut shell, to see if there was more – but the only thing left was a glistening, white, bark-like substance.

"The Mu plant banana and live wild. Their bulged, hairy arms and bloated, round bellies gleam a rough ruddy red – and if they catch you, they'll rip off your flesh, from head to toe – like rabid, frenzied monkeys peeling a human banana."

Unsure, Manna stuck her sand-filled nails into the coconut shell and scraped at its cool, flaky inside. Then hoping for the best, she popped her fingers into her mouth.

Instantly, her taste buds stood up and quivered – but she couldn't tell if that was good or bad.

"Your stripped shards of flesh and bloody, mangled corpse, they'll toss to the side – to rot in the morning sun – because *never* do they eat meat."

Meat. Manna remembered. That's what this stuff was. Coconut meat.

Starved, she snapped the coconut shell in half and sunk her teeth deep into its meat. Then, ripping down like Mano did with his fish, she tore off a mouthful of crunchy flesh.

"The Menehune appear delicate, with their smooth, shimmering skin and their chubby, childish frames, but looks are deceiving. They kill anyone in their way ... unless they want to play."

Instantly, Manna gagged, and a large chewed chunk flew out her nose. Her tongue on fire, she spit the rest of the flesh to the ground and bit both of her cheeks, trying hard to pinch out a bitter, acid soap taste.

"They are fast, and win every sport – olo'hu, ke'a-pua, uma, and the race – but their favorite is diving off cliffs. Never, ever, will you beat one."

Still starved, but more cautious, Manna eyed the crack seed and wondered if it was safe to eat. Surely, it couldn't be worse then raw coconut meat – and maybe, since it was plums, it tasted like Christkindlmarkt sugar plum ... fairies.

"Both are small and answer to none – for you cannot kill one – you cannot hurt one – and only the very faithful can hope to make one go away."

Without looking at Tutu, Manna yanked on one of the wrinkled-up plum squids. Scraping loudly against the bag's crinkled edge, the rough, twisted tentacle dragged three other dead, crooked fingers with it.

"For fun, both play tricks on man – or lead their ali'i to worship."

Manna scrunched up her nose. The squid felt tough and rubbery, like the bottom of an old leather sole – but determined, she stretched off a knuckle-sized piece and popped it into her mouth.

Instantly, the squid smeared a tart, salty-sweet glue over her gums and into her salivating cheeks, and surprised, she felt herself belch.

"They build altars, and roads, and fish ponds – and steal all that you lose."

Thrilled the crack seed tasted sweet, Manna shoved the rest into her mouth and tried to chew, but her teeth wouldn't close. Instead, they sunk halfway into the warm, gooey clump and stayed stuck, two inches apart.

Dripping with greed, Manna's cheeks spilled orange saliva out her lips, and sucking in fast, she clenched her teeth down and smashed the squid between them – and with a soft popping sound, like a pus-filled zit exploding, two squid knuckles popped off and fell, wet and mangled, to the ground.

"You cannot keep one, and one cannot keep you – for their purpose is to keep the land ... and Hawaii's sacred forest."

Tutu pressed her face into Manna's, and she could swear Tutu's pupils twinkled like Santa's.

"They are gremlins, living within."

Manna smiled at Santa and thought, *Gremlins are green ... like elves.*

Thump. Rump. Rump. Rump.

Moho jerked the last dead ahi out of the truck, and the rock club that killed it rolled across the grey, plastic-lined bed, right into Mano's outstretched hand.

"Excellent choice," moaned Tutu. "A Fetcher from the water ... like you."

Proud of himself, Mano beamed at Tutu and flipped the Fetcher in his hand, twice.

Instantly jealous, Manna screamed, "That's MINE!" – but it sounded more like, "THUH MUH!" because her teeth stayed glued together, and the squid blob clogged her mouth.

Desperate, she jammed her fingers between her teeth and yanked on the sticky wad.

"Chee, make A every time," scoffed Aikoa. Her cruel green eyes suddenly squinted down at Manna, and embarrassed, Manna dropped her squid on the ground. Burning hot, orange drool streamed down her chin and dripped onto her bare, curled toes.

"Ho! Check it out!" hooted Hi'u. His short, three-finned board gleamed a chipped-up yellow under his sinewy brown arm, and smirking sideways, he leaned back on his tough heels and jerked a mocking chin towards the truck bed. "She when eat it!"

Manna's heart dropped in her chest – and with a cold, slithering feeling, something terrible coiled round her ribs. Almost faint, she struggled to breathe.

"Oh man, my old board stay broke," whined Iki. Leaning into the truck bed, he looked like he might puke, but instead, he glared at Manna and spit, "Dat took one whole summer for earn, picking papaya. Why you no spock the rocks?"

Manna felt her cheeks flush red and her tongue squeeze dry. Then trying to get air, her mouth dropped open – wide.

"Stay futless, that's why," grumbled Aikoa.

Gutless? Manna heard a horrible voice boom in her head, and swirling wild, hot humiliation surged through her brain. Clenching both fists tight, she snarled, *I'll ... show ... YOU ... gutless!* – then with all her might, she lunged forward and swung a hard fist at Aikoa's chin.

BAM!

With a loud scrape and bam, Manna's foot slipped on her hacked-up squid goop and her fist hammered Moho's cab – and with a sharp, "ZING!" her knuckles split and her whole arm went numb, as if someone had stabbed her funny bone.

Sucking in hard, Manna tried to hold back the pain.

"They will follow you," whispered Tutu. Her warm hand caressed Manna's shoulder, and instantly, she felt better.

"Choose another board," Tutu croaked, but Manna could swear her voice chimed like Christmas music. Filled with happiness, her heart skipped a beat.

Tutu offered her the best Christmas present of all – a new surfboard!

"Give her one," ordered Ku-hai. Suddenly towering over Iki, his puckered red lips seeped dark curly smoke that wrapped slowly around his handsome chiseled cheeks – and taken back, Manna gazed at Ku-hai's unyielding face.

"Why me, Brah?" squeaked Iki. "I already when give 'em two."

"You da same size," breathed Ku-hai.

Iki's shoulders spread rigid and his lips tightened in defense, but his voice almost quivered.

"I only got two left."

"Den get 'em," barked Ku-hai. Suddenly impatient, his dark brown eyes pierced Iki's forehead, and with a grimace, Iki jerked back. But recovering fast, his tough frown flattened and he spun straight and tall on his heels – then he tramped up the driveway. Wagging in his wind, the red and green leash of the board he carried wrapped itself round his calf, and Manna wondered if he might trip. Almost hoping he would, she watched his sandy, slippered feet crunch over the red cinder drive and disappear behind the house – then something caught her eye.

Up under the house lay a pile of old, weathered surfboards. Some with three cracked fins. Others with only one. But all with white meshed patches that held in Styrofoam guts – underneath lumpy brown, moldy wax smeared tops.

Manna wondered how often those ugly boards were ridden.

"Pick one," growled Iki. Suddenly standing next to her, he held two spanking-new boards. The one closest to Manna glistened lime green and skinny, like a glittering neon string bean – and the other one (which he held much further back) shone a brilliant, deep, churning red. Streaking down the red one's underside, two black lightning bolts sliced either edge like jagged hunting knives – and a long black X cut through its center, like crossbones marking a bottle of poison.

With a sudden jerk, Iki tilted the red board back, and with a pupil-searing glint, its sharp tip stabbed Manna's eyes and sent chills through her brain. Biting her lip, she felt herself drawn to the board – like a moth being pulled towards a flame.

Without a doubt, that board could be worshipped.

"Hurry up!" growled Iki, and startled, Manna looked into his strained, pooling eyes ... and understood.

She wasn't the only one who loved that red board.

"That one," she whispered – and pointed over the truck bed, straight at Tutu's house.

"ARGHH!"

THWAP!

Furious Manna pointed in her direction, Aikoa thrust her board at Manna's temple – but jerking sideways fast, Ku-hai's strong hand shot out and caught it, midair. Then, without blinking, he laid the board gingerly into the truck.

Stunned, Manna heard herself squeak, "No. The brown one. Under the house."

"Those are old ... and broken," warned Tutu.

Panicking, Manna tried to invent a lie – before Tutu forced her to keep Aikoa's board.

"They get plenty mana," someone lied for her, "from all the killer rides."

It was Moku. Standing next to Ku-hai, on the other side of the truck, he held a moldy, single-finned board in his hand. As if drizzling pus, its yellow-skinned top bubbled with sand-flaking boils and dripped bulbous brown tissue off its edge.

With a warm, soft breeze, Moku swooped the long, thin board into the truck. Then, as if weaving a lauhala basket, his smooth, deft hands unraveled the leash from Manna's old broken board and double-knotted it to her new one.

"Pour boiling water on top," Moku smiled at Manna, and his kind eyes glowed with pride. "Then wax 'em up."

Manna felt herself smile back, and at once, tingly hope washed through her chest.

This could be the one!

"Enough already!" snapped Aikoa, and with a sharp shoulder nudge into Moku's chest, she snatched up her board – at the same time Mano blurted, "Can I have one?"

Spinning round on him, Aikoa looked ready to kill – and disgusted, Manna thought she could kill him, too. He was so greedy. And stupid. Couldn't he tell?

The cousins didn't want to give away boards!

"Which one?" grunted Moho.

Surprised, Manna stared at her father. His dark face filled oddly with approval, and his sharp, evil teeth glinted white at his boy.

"That one," grinned Mano. His hungry brown eyes lit up and his long-fingered hand pointed – straight at the dead shark's mouth.

Instantly, Ku-hai started to object, but before he could, Moho grabbed the shark's largest tooth and pulled. With a wet sucking sound, like that of a spoon being pulled out of cold Jell-O, the tooth sunk into Moho's thumb and plopped off a jiggling piece of flesh.

"Ya-a-ah!" yelled Moho. Quickly squeezing his thumb against his curled fist, he frowned at his hand and watched his black blood pump out his thumb and stream over his gnarled, hairless knuckles.

"Be careful," muttered Tutu, "of those meant to shred."

Then, with a skilled one-handed weave, she knotted a sinewy string around the shark's tooth and flicked her wrist left. With a crack, the tooth popped out and dangled, jagged and shiny, from the knot in the center of the string.

Bumping Manna to get at Tutu, Mano snatched at the tooth, right when she raised it above his head – and with a slash, it sheared through his closed fist, then dangled over his crown and spattered his own blood onto his forehead.

"Hele mana o Ka-moho-ali'i i ka keiki o mano kumupa'a," moaned Tutu. Twinkling, her red-bordered eyes crinkled wickedly, and her flowing hands knotted the shark tooth necklace around Mano's throat.

Thrilled, Mano grinned proudly at Manna. His crooked tooth glinted in the steaming sun.

Shivering, Manna peered at the huge crooked shark's tooth – and then back at Mano's mouth – and had a funny feeling they were the same – the shark, Moho, and his boy.

"How was the tube?" Mano kept grinning.

"Killer," Manna heard herself breathe, and for a quick second, excitement tickled her brain.

Beaming, Mano twinkled his bright brown eyes and bragged, "Next time, I'm gonna shred better."

At once, Manna's heart and fists clenched.

Never – EVER – would he be better than her ... she'd make sure of that!

"Get in," grunted Moho. Then glancing sideways at Tutu, he smirked, "We gotta take Anna to church."

Chapter Ten

PELE'S HAIR

"**M**ove it!" barked Momi.

Fully dressed, Manna jerked awake and frowned.

It was Monday morning. Time to go to school and get picked on – by all the bully local gangs.

Without moving, Manna glanced at her brother. Bouncing both knees, he sat and rocked at the foot of his bed, his long-toed feet shaking her trundle.

It was worse for him. The locals figured out he was clumsy and spent all day knocking him down.

"Hawaiian snow!" squealed Pu-pele. Excitement burst out of her chest and swept through Manna's open window.

Thrilled, Manna sailed out of bed and pressed her face against the hot window pane – and with a wet thud, Mano's shoulder knocked hard into hers, and his sweaty forehead banged loud against the window frame.

"Whoa!" breathed Mano.

Glittering like golden-red Christmas tinsel, foot-long strands of shiny, iridescent snow coated the rough cinder drive and Momi's massive death-black truck.

Outside and delighted, a beaming Pu-pele scooped an armful of the glistening snow from the truck's hood and tossed it high into the air. Sizzling, the twinkly snow strands floated above her head for a long moment, then swirled down, round her face – and flipping in the breeze, her thick golden-streaked locks tumbled over her bare shoulders and beamed a brilliant ember of red – just like the spun-gold threads of Hawaiian snow that scattered across her cheeks. Twinkling bright, Pu-pele's emerald green eyes danced with amusement, and her glimmering, orange-glossed lips quivered around a radiant, snow-white smile.

Smiling drowsily, Manna sighed. Pu-pele could be beautiful.

With an annoyed grunt, Momi swooped her naked, white arm down the truck's long windshield, trying to clear away the snow.

"Yow!" she suddenly yelled and wrenched her arm back. Stabbed through her skin, stiff orange strands of snow dangled off her arm like jumbled orangutan fur.

"Ooh-ooh-ooh," Mano bantered like a monkey – and instantly, Manna popped into giggles.

"What thuh!" growled Momi. Then grabbing the snow, she yanked it out of her skin. Clinking, it crumbled in her palm and sprinkled onto the hood.

"It's glass!" she shrieked. Panic bulged her flashing blue eyes, and hopping up and down, she yowled, "It's scratching my car! It's scratching my car!"

"Don't worry, dear," cooed Tutu. Suddenly standing next to Momi, her wicked chin smiled sly. "Auntie's breath will blow it away."

With a sudden gush, a whistling wind zipped past Momi's red, stretched-back cheeks and tossed the orange snow off of her truck. Shimmering, the truck stood stark black and flawless against the orange-coated land.

Grunting obstinance, Momi stared past Tutu and adjusted her high blonde bun – tighter.

Still smiling, Tutu raised both of her hands to the sky, then swooped them towards Kilauea. Curious, Manna let her eyes follow Tutu's fat upraised palms – and with a gasp, she felt tingly awe pierce her being.

Shooting high, thick black smoke plumes poured out of Kilauea's tall red cinder cone and streaked through the clear blue sky – and crackling, red-hot lava fingers streamed down her steep, shining flanks. Shuddering, the earth groaned, and the floor underneath Manna swayed.

"Pele sends an invitation ... to visit and find your Fetcher," muttered Tutu. "Today, we go to Volcano."

Swelling like a prickly balloon in her chest, joy tickled Manna's ribs – and with wild, grinning eyes, Mano shook one large fist in front of his face and growled, "YAH-MAN! NO SCHOOL!"

"Don't crush or eat them on the way up," warned Tutu. "They are the sacred ohelo berries and can only be taken after you offer Her."

Always hungry, Mano stared at the small, shiny red, round berries in his hand, and Manna thought they looked sour – or maybe even poisonous. Suspicious, she glanced at the bush where he picked them and thought the broken branch dangled oddly limp and twisted, like a murdered woman's arm.

"Offer who what?" growled Momi. Her blanched face dripped with sweat, and her giant feet snapped every shrub in her way.

Manna felt certain she'd crushed some berries. After all, they'd been walking through the Volcano forest for over an hour.

"Pele – something desirable," muttered Ailani. Jerking to a halt as though she'd made a mistake, Ailani brought her delicate right hand up to her soft, damp lips, snorted air out her nostrils once, then rapped her left knuckles three times with her hand.

Manna knew she'd do that two more times before she followed Pupele in line.

"The volcanos are the Hawaiian's sacred land – their five living churches," groaned Tutu. "Here grows Kohala, Hua'lalai – Mauna Kea, Mauna Loa .... and Kilauea – Home of Pele."

Far in the lead, with big Momi blocking her view, Manna wondered how Tutu knew Mano picked the berries.

Swoosh!

With a quick swoosh, a long brilliant white bird sliced through the dark green trees, leaving a sparkling rainbow-mist in its wake. Leaping off its back, reddish-brown flames tumbled through its quivering, streaked ... wings? No. Those weren't wings. They were shimmering rays of light, like those that stream through tree branches in a misty, cold dawn.

Quickly, Manna rubbed her eyes. That bird couldn't be real.

"Kilauea is your family's sacred place. Its forests, its rock, and its showers – all bring forth life – that precious mana, straight from the gods."

At once, three giant, light green tree ferns tossed their dark lacy shadows across the waxy green vines that stroked Manna's knees – and a handful of chocolate brown, bristly-haired fronds popped their snail-curled heads out of waving feathery-leafed plumes. Then, dancing excitedly around Manna, a sudden riot of color shimmied across the forest floor.

Glistening, red ohelo berries bounced rapidly; pungent yellow ginger shook to and fro; white and purple orchids quivered upright; and dark green fern fronds jerked their billowy arms up and down – and high in the air, clinging to brown, twisted ohia branches, yellow-tipped, red lehua puff flowers rattled their slender tentacles in the wind.

Feeling herself crouch down and tiptoe silently, like an Indian, Manna crept through the sacred forest and breathed in deep. Tingling, fragrant maile filled her lungs and cool, crispy, wet air tickled her awestruck cheeks.

Without a doubt, this forest held the essence of life – that life granted by God.

"The Akua left their generative spirit – their mana – in this place," breathed Tutu. "Here, everything is alive. The plants, the rock, and the air."

"Rocks aren't alive," grumbled Momi.

"Haoles think that," hissed Tutu, "till they see it live and breathe in the pit!"

Clenching, Manna's stomach suddenly dropped into a hollow pit in her gut – and by instinct, she stopped, her anxious eyes darting around, knowing something evil lay waiting ... for her.

"In old Hawaii, the Akua lived amongst man in their grand, human-like forms ..."

Tutu's rich voice floated through the thinning air, but Manna couldn't listen. Terrified, she stood perfectly still.

"But quickly, the Akua became disgusted with man's evil ways," droned Tutu. "As punishment, they parted, but with aloha, they promised, if we were good, they'd come back ... in diminutive size, speaking strange languages, to give us another chance to be with them."

"That's why they thought Captain Cook was a god," muttered Ailani, but she was so far ahead, Manna couldn't see her.

"What's wrong?" whispered Mano. Close behind her, his hot ahi-stink breath burned Manna's neck, but still, the hairs on her neck stood up and shivered.

"She listens to the voices in the wind!" a cruel voice suddenly cackled through the trees.

"WAH!" yelped Mano – and thoroughly spooked, he grabbed Manna's arm and ran, full blast, towards Ailani.

BAM! - "UGH!" - "OOF!"

With a bam, Mano slammed into Pu-pele, and dragging Manna down with him, he toppled headfirst into a berriless ohelo bush.

Shocked, the wind knocked out of her, Manna stared, wide-eyed, at Pu-pele and prayed she wouldn't explode – because scattered before Pu-pele, a skirt-full of picked ohelo berries trembled between her bent, open knees ... and sitting mad on her butt, her steaming green eyes screamed revenge at the ones who made her spill them.

"Oh no!" Ailani cried, and her terrified face drained white.

"I'o o-o-o-o!" something cried back. Then, with a loud, "Beathe! Beathe!" two enormous tawny brown wings pounded past Manna's head, and eight hooked, shiny black talons grabbed Ailani by the hair and – tiny feet flailing – swooped her away.

"Ka-o-o-o-o-helo!" the wind screamed, and at once, something hard and clammy cold landed on Manna's back and pressed her chest solid to the ground. Then scraping mercilessly, a thousand needle-sharp claws ripped at her skin, and a million hungry creatures sucked noisily at her flesh.

Helpless and dying, Manna watched in horror as everything sprayed a wet bloody red.

"Manna!" grunted Mano. "Manna!"

Dizzy, Manna opened her eyes. Unable to breathe under the weight of the cold, hard thing, she had fainted – and hunched above her, a blood-dripping, razor-sliced Mano tried to wake her up.

Eyes blurred, Manna wondered if the cold thing had saved her.

"You first!" demanded Pu-pele. Then she shoved Ailani in front of her and knocked her through the trees.

Frowning, Manna bit her lip and wondered how Ailani got free.

"It came alive," muttered Mano, bouncing up and down on his knees, "and took back all its berries."

Confused, Manna looked at the still ohelo bush. Clinging to its thin, crooked branches, a hundred small bunches of fresh, juicy berries glimmered – and Manna wondered why the thing only scratched Mano.

Scared, Mano slipped his cold, sweaty hand into hers – and at once, she remembered.

She was supposed to take care of him!

Panicking, she jumped to her feet and pulled him towards Tutu – but with a quick puff, something black and red blew perfumed haze into her face, then fluttered gaily in front of her nose.

Giggling, Manna squirmed with delight. Hovering with his beating wings an inch from her cheeks, a small I'iwi bird twinkled his eyes at her. Then cocking his cute, tiny head forward, he pecked her nose with a hooked, shiny red beak.

"Beat it!" Mano growled and took a quick swipe at the bird's wing, but missed. Leaving a single feather in his hand, the bird darted away into the steamy, white sky.

Her eyes tingling, Manna slipped the feather out of her brother's hand ... and felt safe.

She could feel her Guardian Angel now, following them – and keeping a watchful eye. With a reassuring smile, she squeezed Mano's hand and whispered, "Let's go."

"Pele is ho'opa'i," Tutu's voiced moaned up ahead, "the one who broke the rules and was driven away. Learn from her – for she hides in Kilauea's boiling pit and has no choice but to call it her home ... and remember. Always offer her your humblest respect."

"Why offer a *reject* anything?" complained Momi.

Clinging to her I'iwi feather, Manna walked quicker, towards Momi's voice.

"Think of her as the Devil, living underneath your church – and you must appease her in order to enter. You understand about the Devil?" asked Tutu.

"Yeah," Momi growled back. "Kick Him if He gets in your way!"

Suddenly, a thick putrid stench, like smeared rotten eggs mixed with burnt, smoking rubber, burned Manna's lungs. Coughing out, she wiped ash off her swollen, dry eyes and saw Tutu standing in a broiling grey mist. Sizzling, a hot wind raked her cheeks, and at once, she knew.

The children walked straight towards hell.

"She will test you and turn you to stone. Look around and you will see."

Breaking through the trees, Manna looked past Tutu and gasped.

Congealed into a thick, crusty earth skin, a thousand silver, cooled lava coils spread wide across the land, as far as the eye could see. Spitting poisonous sulfuric gas, the hideous wrinkled skin cracked open along glossy fissured sores and oozed glowing, bright orange-red blood – and to the far left, a grey, crater-sized, blank eye socket hole emitted a low metallic hiss.

Shaking uncontrollably, Manna rubbed her eyes – and couldn't believe what she saw next.

Wrapping up towards the volcano, a long, twisted, clinkery, sharp spine convulsed left and right, as if some horrible monster writhed just below the earth's surface – and scattered around the beast's spine, hundreds of frightened, glowing, red molten fingers burst out of its crackling flesh and groped for the sky – but rumbling, the hungry grey beast sucked each bleeding hand back down into its steaming mass. Desperate, the crying, tortured hands tried over and over to escape from the beast – but each time, it swallowed them down with a slippery squeeze.

Instantly, every tissue in Manna's body screamed, and breathless, her body went limp. Feeling her hand slip from Mano's, she watched in horror as the Devil Himself wriggled before her, infinitely devouring His victims' souls.

"Oh my gosh!" squealed Pu-pele. "It's beautiful!"

Glimmering, a trail of sparkling grey smoke curled through Pu-pele's bare, chubby knees – and Manna had a sick feeling this was where she belonged ... with the Devil.

"Underneath, an inch below, travels the molten rivers of Pele. Stay on the path, else fall through and meet the maker."

At once, Manna spied the ancient Hawaiian trail. Covered with smooth, oval, grey beach rocks and lined with jagged, reddish-black cinder stone, it zigzagged, unharmed, across the Devil's back.

Relieved, she remembered.

She could change her destiny – if she found the right Fetcher ... today.

Left ... Manna groaned in her head. *Left* ... *Right* ... *Left*.

Marching slowly in line, she squeezed her nostrils shut and tried not to breathe in the ashen, sulfurous air, but with a dusty, orange blast, a sizzling wind forced a bitter, scratchy fist down her throat. Coughing so hard her guts hurt, Manna leaned into the dry, swirling winds and willed all her weight forward, but her heavy, swollen feet stayed stuck to the ground – as though her rubber soles had melted to the path.

Hungry and exhausted, she rested for a moment and prayed that soon they'd reach the top of Kilauea ... or at least, the howling whirlwinds would stop – but in quick response, a cruel cinder-needled swirl scraped her hot cheeks and bit the stinging whites of her eyes. Squinting through the thick, prickling haze, Manna glanced back, to check on her brother.

Hunched over low and hugging his tapa-bound lunch tight to his gut, he leaned into the wind and took a huge shaky step forward. Then quickly, he took another.

Surprised, and determined to reach the top before him, Manna slipped her chapped hand into her lunch (which Tutu had wrapped into her white tapa bark cloth) to make sure her red I'iwi feather was still there. Then hunching her head down low, she jogged four wrenching steps into the wind.

"Kneel, hands forward!" Tutu suddenly growled in her ear.

Startled, Manna looked up.

Teetering off the edge of a wide, flat ledge, she almost jogged straight into Kilauea's broiling, red lava pit!

Horrified, she jerked back and stared, speechless, at the ominous steam-seeping ... earth wound.

Spreading three miles round and cut into a steep, jagged, oval-shaped drop, the enormous blood-filled hole billowed thick orange-black smoke – and bursting out the hideous molten sore, sticky red boils popped open and sprayed orange-fringed, blast-white pus. Quivering in a thick drippy jumble, four thigh-sized, crackling veins oozed glowing rock-clotted blood – and as if being squeezed out, half of the pit bulged like a huge pinched-off heart. But suddenly, with a deafening hiss, the swollen heart squeezed itself down and spurt streaky, wet, whistling flames out of a dozen blood-spattered cones. As though reeling in pain, the whole pit shuddered and groaned, then the emptied heart sunk down with a loud, "Splut!"

Nauseous, Manna stared at the earth's gaping chest wound and its vile pumping heart, and with a frightening cold rush, insignificance hit her.

Here, where the earth pulled back the beauty of her skin and showed the generative power of her innards – here, where no man's shadow can stretch so long that he appears to dominate her land – here, you come to understand.

It is the living earth that rules man – for he is a mere parasite, living off her edible flesh – and without respect, Earth will scorch and kill her lovely skin – insuring man, her pest, dies too – all the while, she lives safely within.

Revelation, that fiery end to man, would be committed by Earth herself – unless man learned to appease her.

"On your knees!" a scorching wind howled across Manna's chest and shoved her shoulders to the ground. Caught off guard, her knees buckled and hit the hot, jagged ledge – then, as if acting on their own, her feet spread open and pointed her toes to either of her sides, and her bottom sank snugly between them, hovering two inches from the steaming ground. Snapping forward, her stiff hands swooped up and formed a flat-headed arrow to the sky.

Wincing, Manna wanted to wiggle out of her body-cramping position – but she couldn't move.

Mo'olelo had begun.

Thump. Tap-tap-tap. Thump-tap-thump.

Thump. Tap-tap-tap. Thump-tap-thump.

Flowing in front of the children, at the very edge of the smoking ledge, Tutu danced an ancient hula – but Manna couldn't hear the words she chanted, because a deep thumping gourd drowned out her voice.

Thump. Tap-tap-tap. Thump-tap-thump.

Thump. Tap-tap-tap. Thump-tap-thump.

Tightening her achy stomach, Manna concentrated hard on Tutu's hula'ing hands – in hopes they'd interpret her story – and as if she read Manna's mind, Tutu spun around and faced the children.

Thump. Tap-tap-tap. Thump-tap-thump.

Thump. Tap-tap-tap. Thump-tap-thump.

Broad hips swaying, Tutu touched her long, stiff hands together – over her right shoulder and high above her head. Then, leaving her right hand pointed at the sky, she bowed down low and touched her left hand to her extended left toes – and tilted her cheeks towards the gurgling pit.

Thump. Tap-tap-tap. Thump-tap-thump.

Thump. Tap-tap-tap. Thump-tap-thump.

Over and over, in time with the beat, Tutu pointed to the sky, then bowed down low as she flowed to the center of Pele's throne – and trembling, Manna thought, *She's bowing down ... to show her respect as she approaches.*

Thump. Tap-tap-tap.

Thump.

Suddenly steaming, orange haze flickered behind Tutu's back and her tight bun unraveled to reveal hip-long, bushy, fire-flecked hair. Standing tall and still, she flashed a wicked, inviting grin, then slowly crossed her arms across her full, breathing breasts, as if offering to give away a hug – and that's when Manna saw her.

Shimmering misty orange, a giant shadowy ghost girl rose out of the broiling pit. First, her long, wavy red hair popped out of the fiery pool and dangled playfully around her glimmering, down-turned cheeks – hiding all of her face, except for her dazzling, red, puckered lips. Then, arching straight and tall, the girl's long, naked back stretched out of the pool and flipped her glittery hair behind her broad, supple shoulders.

Exposed and jiggling, the girl's huge full moon breasts loomed high above the pool, and with a throaty laugh, she spun them around and pressed them deep into a giant blue man's chest. Surprised, the blue man stepped back and whispered, "Not here!"

Why not? Manna thought. *She's breathtakingly beautiful!*

"You witch!" someone suddenly shrieked, and at once, Manna's blood curdled. "How dare you try to take my man?"

Shrinking away from the blue man, like a blowup doll that sprung a leak, the startled ghost girl hissed, "Sister! Forgive me!"

"NEVER!" her sister bellowed back, and with a horrific crash, a forty-foot, sparkling blue wave curled out of the sky and smashed down onto the ghost girl's head.

Shrieking so loud Manna's guts shook, the ghost girl tore at her sizzling, melted flesh, as if trying to pull off the water, but it was no use. Her red eyes bulged in pain, she threw her contorted face back and exploded into a hot, white cloud of steam.

Shivering, Manna felt biting cold rain pelt her face and thighs, but unable to move, she stiffened her arms and stared straight ahead.

Vibrating through the air, the long whine of a conch shell followed by the heavy pound of a wooden gourd warned Manna the Akua approached – and at once, Kilauea's tumultuous pit filled with a rough ocean blue.

Paddling a thin outrigger canoe to the thumping gourd's beat – two large, muscular, bare-chested Hawaiian men popped out of the blue ocean's horizon and shot over the high, choppy waters – and hugging a small iridescent egg under her arm, the diminished ghost girl wept in between them.

Cramping, Manna's stomach tied itself in a knot, and at once, she felt sorry for the homeless ghost girl.

"Brother," the Hawaiian up front grunted to the Hawaiian in back, "she's on our heels," – and Manna almost gasped.

A giant, bristled, misshapen hump stuck out of the front man's broad, rumpled back, like the hunchback of Notre Dame – and his fierce, dark face caved in between his piercing black eyes, as though some blunt weapon had crushed his skull between them.

Shuddering, Manna wondered how bad his assailant looked.

"Maui!" the Hawaiian in back grunted, as he leaned far back and dug his long grey-skinned paddle in the water. Instantly, the outrigger stopped and Manna understood.

The one in back was their leader.

"Dig your home here," the leader barked. "And this time, don't give up!"

Manna looked past the leader. Floating free in the water, a flat, green rock with tan-sanded beaches spread wide, about three times the length of the canoe.

"Protect me," the ghost girl begged. Fear and exhaustion resonated in her wobbly voice.

"I cannot," the leader grunted back, his eyes cast down to the water. "*She* is my sister, too."

Something sad crept into Manna's stomach.

She knew how the ghost girl felt, with no one to protect her ... but herself.

"Then protect my favorite baby sister, Hi'iaka," breathed the girl, as she rolled her egg in the leader's lap. "For *she* is your sister, too."

"Na-maka-o-kaha'i!" the hunchback breathed, and terrified, Manna looked up.

Looming high above the canoe, a forty-foot tall, shining, blue Hawaiian woman glared down on her younger siblings. Glinting pearl white, her condemning eyes scanned their quivering canoe while her twisted, sea-green, foam-streaked bun sparkled bright and alive with swimming, multicolored fish. Rippling blue down her bulged, sinewy arms, sheets of cool water spilled off her hip-clutching hands and coated her thick, flexed thighs with a twinkly wet, tight, sequined skirt – and pointed upright, her bare, protruding breasts sported two iridescent clam shells that flickered a rainbow hue.

Fearing Na-maka-o-kaha'i's coal-black pupils, Manna stared at her white-streaked bun and prayed that she'd kill the ghost girl fast, before she could scream out in pain.

"You stupid hag," growled Na-maka-o-kaha'i. "Did you think you'd go unpunished?"

Defying her fate, the much smaller ghost girl grabbed a giant anvil-headed digging stick from the bottom of the canoe and stretched herself up on her feet. Then growing fifteen feet tall, she swung her flaming, bare breasts at her sister and sing-songed, "Catch me. Catch me. Catch me if you ca-an!"

Transforming into molten, red-hot fluid, the ghost girl shot through her sister's stomach with a crackling, comet-like "BOOM" – and without touching the water, she landed with an earth-shattering, "BAM!" on the little island, Maui.

Spurting wild, right where the ghost girl landed, a sudden, gaping rock wound spread open and leaked white, trembling pus – just like the blistering hole in Na-maka-o-kaha'i's gut.

BAM! BAM!

The girl's digging stick drilled her earth hole deeper – and stunned, Na-maka-o-kaha'i pressed her gushing hands into her quivering, empty wound. Gurgling like an overflowing cesspool, the wound quickly filled in blue.

BAM! BAM! BAM!

The ghost girl dug faster – but not fast enough. In an instant, Na-maka-o-kaha'i lit on her long orange hair and pulled.

"Au-we!" the girl squealed, right before Na-maka-o-kaha'i dashed her head against Maui's now jagged rock. Instantly limp, the ghost girl's body died – but Na-maka-o-kaha'i didn't stop. Roaring like a tidal wave, she raised the girl's limp body high above her head and slammed it to the ground. With a bone-crunching whack, the ghost girl's back broke, along with both of her legs – but that wasn't enough.

Growing larger, Na-maka-o-kaha'i raised her sister's corpse higher and higher – repeatedly pounding it against Maui – until each one of her bones shattered. Then, tossing her to the ground like a lumpy sack of potatoes, she sprayed her with her gushing blue hands. Melting fast, the girl's torn, bruised skin fizzled into glistening, red, sticky boils – and sputtering, each boil blistered then burst, sending a trail of thick orange smoke to the sky. Sizzling in the bloody pool, the girl's grey, splintered skeleton scattered in a haphazard pile, as though vultures had fought over her flesh.

Sickened, Manna felt hot puke burn the back of her throat and swallowing it down, she tried hard not to look at the dead girl's ruined body.

"She has been judged and found guilty," Na-maka-o-kaha'i boomed at her brothers. "Never, may she come home!"

Then, her voice rippling like a stream, she slid her trickling hands round her brothers' shoulders – and as though her waters soothed them, they both wriggled into her hug.

"Leave her bones here – as a reminder – what happens when you disrespect ohana."

Satisfied, Na-maka-o-kaha'i breathed in deep and swelled twice her size. Then whistling loud, she spun like a ballerina on her toes. Round and round she went, until suddenly, she transformed into a sparkling blue, cone-shaped tornado that lifted up to the sky. Spraying the children with fresh, tingly water, Na-maka-o-kaha'i touched the tip of her cone to the center of the canoe and wailed, "Uha-a-a-ane he-e-e-ele!"

With a wet, "SPIH!" the ghost girl shot out Na-maka-o-kaha'i's tip and plopped onto the boat – except now, wobbling in a cold lump between her brothers, she resembled curdled banana pudding. Her deformed, gooey head waggled skull-less, from side to side, and her saggy, Jell-O'd arms slupped off the boat's edge and twitched with the ocean waves. Melted raw, her wrinkled, yellowish-grey flesh pocked with deep, purple-red sores that frothed glistening, yellow pus – and her scraggled, soggy hair flattened back to reveal swollen, mucus-oozing ears. Her red-veined eyes rolled far back, the goopy girl drooled bluish-grey spittled foam.

Horrified, Manna thought the once beautiful girl looked like a boneless, water-logged hag.

Whistling low, Na-maka-o-kaha'i spiraled into the sky and vanished – and tingling, Manna's back shivered.

Na-maka-o-kaha'i gave her sister another chance ... to be good.

"Hoi!" the leader growled and stabbed his sharp, grey paddle into the ocean blue. Immediately, the hunchback up front dug in and chanted, "Hoi! Ai! Hoi!"

"She broke my bones," the ghost girl gurgled – but her brothers just kept paddling and chanting, "Hoi! Ai! Hoi!"

"She broke my bones!" the girl grumbled louder.

"Hoi! Ai! Hoi!"

"How dare that witch judge me ..." growled the girl.

"Hoi! Ai! Hoi!"

"And break my bones!"

"Hoi! Hoi! Ai! Hoi!"

"I am Pele!" the girl rumbled – and the earth below Manna rumbled, too.

"I AM PELE!" the girl shrieked – and with a deafening, "BAM!" the ledge below Manna lurched left, at the same time Pele's sweaty, bicep-straining leader stabbed his paddle into the ocean blue. Hissing madly, as though it had sprung a hot leak, the canoe spun round to a stop and faced all the children – and where the leader stabbed it, the ocean blue spewed sticky, red goo.

"Hawaii!" growled the leader. "Your new home!" – but Manna didn't hear him. Her blood thinned and her heart pounding scared, she stared straight into the ugly leader's sweat-dripping *shark* face. Gaping down, his horrible pointed jaws snapped open and closed with his tired, heavy breath – and his black, pupil-less eyes stared hungrily ... at her!

THWAP!

With a cruel thwap, the shark man smacked Pele with his paddle, and with a sloppy, "Flup!" she flopped overboard and sunk into Kilauea's now broiling pit.

"I am Pele!" Manna heard Pele hiss, and the pool shone a bright orange-red.

"I am Pele! And here ... I AM THE JUDGE!"

With five successive bams, as though dynamite drilled Kilauea, half a dozen spatter cones exploded. Then sizzling grey, a soft, quiet haze cloaked the trembling pit.

Dizzy, Manna felt herself not breathe.

The shark man wanted to kill her – and there wasn't a thing any of her siblings could do about it.

"It's okay," Ailani whispered, and Manna realized.

She was the only one still rigid, because mo'olelo was pau.

"Uhane is your soul – that generative life you take wherever you go," moaned Tutu, but Manna couldn't listen. Quaking, she felt the shark man nearby – waiting for the kill.

"That mana spit through the air by the Akua."

My mana. That's what he wants, thought Manna. *And he can get it by eating my bones!*

"In the air, uhane lewa – the bodiless souls – shout to you, if you listen," Tutu hissed. "From the dead, uhane aumakua – the faithful souls – guard you, when you obey."

Nauseous, Manna glanced at her grandmother. Wrapped back in a bun, her long bushy hair sat tall on her head ... but she didn't put it there.

"All uhane – all aumakua – belong to one or more of nature's classes, and as such, may enter any object within," Tutu smiled, and her wicked, red-bordered eyes flashed round the children's semicircle.

Forgetting her nausea, and the shark man, Manna stared at her grandmother, curious.

"But even more, they control their class objects, and their presence forces a response. Rocks must moan, pebbles must rumble – shells will cry, and plants will writher – as soon as their aumakua comes."

Did she make a pact with the Devil? wondered Manna. *Is that how she got her power?*

"Beware of them – the aumakua – for when you do not obey, they punish."

Slithering up her back and around her chest, something cold stifled Manna's breath, and rigid, she let realization hit her.

"You are of Pele's clan – and she is your family's aumakua," warned Tutu. "Murdered by her sister, her spirit entered this place – and here, she is the judge that you must appease."

Tutu was of Pele's clan – the old Hawaiian sorcerers from the past.

"Your Fetcher must come from your Akua's class – that part of nature that holds his mana. But beware, for an aumakua may enter your Akua's objects and block you on your way, unless you appease him, too."

And Moho – he would help Pele do something bad – because he was one of her clan, too.

"Pele, your aumakua, the spirit in this place, likes to play games," groaned Tutu. "She shape shifts – and tests fools. She comes as a white dog – they must not run over. Or an old lady – they must not scorn. And sometimes, she comes as herself – to see if they will obey."

Suddenly, anger burned Manna's head, and without meaning to, she heard herself scream, *Do they expect ME-E-E to obey Pele, too?*

"Those who fail her test, she melts with her fires, gleefully torturing their flesh until their scared, shrieking souls bolt from their smoldering bodies – only to be whipped with her molten white chains and enslaved at the bottom of her pit."

NEVER! Manna growled in her head. *Once I get that Fetcher, I'll have Power Supreme– and THEY will do as I-I-I please!*

"Today, your soul must leave your body and find your Akua's Fetcher, in this place – your family's sacred Volcano. But first, you must offer Pele something of value, so she doesn't test you on your way, or grow angry when you take something from her land."

Opening her coconut-cup-filled koko net, Tutu smiled warmly and motioned towards the pit.

"Go to her – while I prepare."

At once, Manna's chest breathed in deep, and with a zing, her angry head cleared. Excited, she jumped up and skipped after her sisters in line.

Today was the day!

She would find her Fetcher – and be more special than them all!

A billowing grey haze poured out of Kilauea's pit and spilled onto the children's melting shoes – and traveling fast, a thin white fog swept off the pit's eastern edge and tossed swirly smoke into an ashen, bleak sky. Bubbling in the deep pit below, bright orange magma flashed beneath the children and sprinkled drops of blood onto the ledge – and standing tall, Kilauea's glistening spatter cones breathed brilliant misty-white smoke.

Standing fourth in line, near the ledge's edge, Manna stared eerily at her surreal sisters. Hovering over the pit, they twitched like Halloween witches stirring a poisonous brew.

"SSSSSS-SEH!" Momi breathed in deep, through a thin, twisted cigarette clenched between her big yellow buckteeth. Then, sweeping her large, awkward hand up, she yanked out the cigarette with her forefinger and thumb, and flicked it into the pit.

"Suck on that!" she hissed. Then she shot a cruel glance at her sister.

Rocking back and forth, as though her stomach ached, Pu-pele hugged her black bag into her gut, and turning around, Momi couldn't help but jibe her.

"Hurts, eh? To give up your stupid stolen stuff!"

Wounded, Pu-pele jabbed her hand into her stuffed magic bag and yanked out one of Tutu's coconut cups. Then screaming out in pain, she flung the cup at Momi's face.

Stepping sideways in a blink, Momi let the cup pass her cheek. Then she cackled, "One tiny cup? For the great aumakua?" – and Manna noticed.

Momi almost stepped into the pit.

Her slitted blue eyes glinting, Momi groped down into her low-cut shirt and pulled a see-through plastic cigarette bag out of her bra. Smirking at Pu-pele, she dangled it over the pit and taunted, "Bet you can't outdo this!"

With a plop, the cigarette bag hit Kilauea's broiling red top and disappeared.

Furious, Pu-pele swung her bag by its long handle, and with a loud, "HAH!" – she whipped it over her head and hurled it at Momi's face.

With a heavy thwap, the bag bounced off Momi's forehead and tumbled into the pool. At the same time, a surprised Momi stumbled backwards and almost fell in, but Ailani's quick hand yanked her forward and back onto the ledge.

"Humph!" Ailani snorted. Her small, delicate hand pressed itself against her lips, and a long tawny feather fluttered below her nose, its pointed quill pinched inside her white-knuckled fist.

"Humph! Humph!" she snorted twice more, then released the feather over the pool. Swirling left and right, like a fallen leaf, the gentle feather floated through the pool's parting haze.

My feather! thought Manna. *I could offer my I'iwi feather.*

Shoving her hand into her lunch, she groped around for the feather and felt its soft side hiding under her cool Hawaiian Punch can. Clutching it between her hot fingers, she stroked it gently with her thumb and remembered the I'iwi bird's lovely kiss.

"Hurry up!" Momi shouted, and without thinking, Manna grabbed the Hawaiian Punch can and tossed it into the pool.

With a loud, "Ka-bam!" the juice exploded before it hit the pool's surface, and a sharp aluminum shard bounced back and sliced past Manna's cheek – at the same time something quick ripped out one of her hairs.

"Ouch!" Manna yelped, grabbing her cheek with one hand and her hair with the other.

Bumping past her, Mano dangled a long reddish-black hair in front of his face. Then, with a breathy gust, he blew it over the pool. Tumbling round and sparkling as bright as Hawaiian snow, the single hair drifted up to the clouds.

"Why'd you do that?" grumbled Manna, still scratching the spot where he yanked out her hair.

Embarrassed, Mano looked down at his huge melted Hush-Puppies ... and shuffled.

Cause you're too greedy to give away your own stuff, thought Manna. *So you gave away mine!*

"Drink and lay down," barked Tutu.

"Your kino – your body – that you leave behind, must be guarded by someone you trust," moaned Tutu. "Else it be stolen, along with your mana – that power living in your bones – and you become the wailing uhane lewa – the lost souls in the wind."

Laying side by side, their five heads in line, in front of Tutu's crossed-legged knees, Manna thought they must look like embalmed, frozen corpses getting ready to go to their graves. Almost giggling from the drunkening strong awa drink, she crossed her hands over her chest – just to make sure she looked really dead. Then lolling her mouth open, she stared emptily up Tutu's nose.

"Never look the Akua, the aumakua in the eye. Cast yours down and show your respect," groaned Tutu.

Amazed, Manna gazed at the long bushy grey hairs that clogged Tutu's nostrils – and wondered how she could breathe. Then it occurred to her.

Laying underneath Tutu this way, she could see up to her brain, if those prickly hairs weren't in the way.

"Hele i ka hale o Pele," wailed Tutu, and at once, her white-spittled lips stretched open wide and her red, wagging tongue licked Manna. Then, with a sloppy gurgling sound, she sucked all of the children down her throat!

Before Manna could react, hot, slippery, wet tissue squeezed her stiff body deep into Tutu's gut – then pushing her headfirst through a small bloody red hole, it popped her into a pitch dark, rumbling, dank cave.

Dazed, Manna lay perfectly still – not knowing what to do.

ZHAM!

With a wrenching electrical force, two enormous hands suddenly stabbed through Manna's ribs and clasped both of her lungs. Then shaking her whole body murderously, they tried to yank them from her chest!

"NO-O-O-O!" Manna screamed. Slapping wildly, she struggled to get free, but the horrible hot hands clutched her lungs even tighter and tore them out of her chest.

ZUP!

With a flying zup sound, Manna landed on top a grey, stony plain – all her body parts intact. Shivering hard, she thought it horrible, the way your body leaves your soul – then she realized.

It was her *body* that her soul left behind.

Manna looked down at her scuffed Hush-Puppies and wondered how her soul brought along her clothes – and that's when she noticed. She stood on the same ancient trail that wound up the volcano.

"Pu'u-lo-a-a-a," the wind moaned in her ear, and spooked, Manna spun around.

Scattered before her, as far as the eye could see, the stripped, white ghosts of fire-raked ohia trees groped for the sky – and waving in the cool wind below them, tufts of silvery green grass popped through the cracked, silver lava and rustled their skinny, sharp blades at Manna. Bubbling high in the distance, two bus-sized lava hills rose out of the cool, solid ground – and frozen, half-crackled, they filled the horizon and dripped yellowish syrup off their honeycombed sides.

"Hawaiian honey!" Manna squealed, and answering, her stomach growled.

Without thinking, she bolted across the crunchy, grey lava towards the closest honey hill. But right before she got there, a one-armed ohia trunk swiped its sharp hand across her bare knees and sliced both feet out from under her body. With a flesh-shearing scrape, she tripped and slid across the cruel spiked lava.

Shocked, Manna heard herself cry out in pain. Her elbows and knees scraped raw, she clenched her fists and teeth, and waited for the pain to subside ... but it didn't. Panicking, she thought, *Oh no, I need stitches!*

Rolling onto her bottom, she jerked her knees up and her elbows around – to inspect the damage – but there was none. Completely unharmed, her knees and elbows glowed a sunburned brown.

Confused, the pain almost vanished, Manna stared at the ohia tree and the ancient Hawaiian stick-figure petroglyphs that etched the lava around her.

This place, she had passed on her way up the volcano ... but it had changed. The uhane spirits – the wandering souls – in the land, in the wind – she could see now, because she was one of them.

Excited, Manna knew. She could hurt – but she couldn't die.

As a soul, she could do *anything*!

Her heart pounding in her chest, Manna scrambled to her feet – and at once, the ohia tree blocked her. Knowing the honey hills lay sacred and the ohia only meant to slow her down ... so she entered with respect, Manna heard herself whisper, "Mahalo."

Then tiptoeing carefully, so as not to step on any of the thickly clustered stone-carved petroglyphs, she picked her way up to the top of the windblown honey hill – and looked around.

Spreading far and wide, the distant ocean shone a remarkable blue, slapping foamy white across the black-cliffed shore – and breathless, Manna felt the dense quiet of the place descend upon her, as though someone in concentrated stillness loomed high above.

Her backbone prickling, Manna let her eyes follow her ancestors' rough path, from the ocean, up the cliffs, and barefoot across the hot, jagged lava patch – in search of this place – the land of their aumakua.

Gr-r-r-r!

Suddenly, Manna's stomach growled out loud, and forgetting her past, she squatted down, scooped a handful of honey out of the closest circle-shaped honey cell – and gagged.

Wiggling live in her palm, a twisted, breathing piece of human flesh glimmered a yellowish wet. Oozing off its blue-veined sides, thick red-streaked juice dripped off the smelly, knuckle-sized stump and spread warm, sticky blood into Manna's palm.

Horrified, she dropped to her knees, flipped the stump back into its honey cup, and smeared its juice onto her skirt.

Umbilical cords, she thought. *They're pieces of infant umbilical cords!*

Silenced by a sudden rush of awe, Manna felt her widened eyes traverse the umbilical cord littered hill.

Each circular cell of the haphazard honeycomb was etched into the lava rock by an ancient Hawaiian man. Using a stone digging tool, he chipped a hand-sized circle, close to the others, then pecked out a small round cup in its center. Then, whispering the proper birth chant, he filled the cup with a stump of his newborn's umbilical cord – that life-giving channel between wife and child.

Decayed from Earth, the ancient umbilical cords had vanished and left only the piko hole – the circular, navel-like carvings. But in the spirit world, the cord still lived and breathed – infant gasps in the wind. Their breath kept open that life-giving channel between the spirit world and the Hawaiian child.

Amazed, Manna's soul shivered.

The Hawaiians, the Tahuna, learned how to walk that unseen line between life and imminent death – and how to secure channels to the world beyond. And concentrating hard, they figured out how to control the spirits of the land – using Volcano's guarded Fetchers.

Suddenly, something chilling cold coiled around Manna's neck and hissed, "Waha-a-a-a .... U'LA!" – and with a quick jerk, the thing lassoed her high into the air and threw her towards the beach.

Stunned, Manna felt herself fly through the warm, wet clouds. Then her back hit the cool cobbled beach – but the impact didn't hurt.

Scrambling to her feet, she spun around to see who threw her – and at once, tingly excitement shot through her chest.

"The place," she heard herself growl, "where they come to feed me!"

Growling in turn, her stomach churned in her gut and drool dripped off her lips – and suddenly crazed, she raced towards a huge raised altar table and threw both fists in the air.

"The place," she cackled, "where man opens his channel to the spirit world ... by sending up one of his dead!"

Her heart pounding with greed, Manna's eyes scanned the ancient Hawaiian sacrificial place.

Looming twelve feet high and six feet thick, a blackened boulder wall marked a sprawling rectangular temple – and swaying forty feet high, a wooden, man-made scaffold waved its red and yellow, feathered plumes. Squatting over the altar table before her, two grey-weathered, snarling tikis rose twenty-feet high, ready to devour any feast – and slapping in the wind, a tall majestic green row of coconut trees rattled their dark brown, bristled balls. Hunched low and waiting, a long palm-thatched hut stood patiently behind a flat, six-foot-long sacrificial stone – strewn with human blood.

The heiau, Manna heard herself think. *Where the wombless man – unable to bring forth life himself and open a channel to the spirit world. Where the wombless man – opens a temporary channel, by sacrificing one in death.*

Shaking a cold feeling off her neck, Manna stepped back and felt herself not want anything to do with this place – and then she saw it. The women's much smaller, neatly hewn temple. An orderly place – for passionate gifts – those grown with love and skillful toil.

Feeling light and happy, Manna skipped to the women's gathering place – their Hale o Papa – and giggling, she ran her fingertips across their cool, grey-stoned altar table.

Women didn't have to kill things – because they owned a direct channel to the spirit world – inside of their wombs.

"Hina!" a loving male voice croaked.

Startled, Manna's head jerked west – towards the sound of the voice – and something caught her eye.

Standing tall in a clear rippling stream, a far-reaching ohia tree swayed back and forth in its own gentle wind. Twisting round in an hourglass shape, its dark, smooth trunk held out delicate waving branches that moved strangely like a woman's hula'ing arms – and spreading red lehua puff blossoms across its full, dark green middle, its outermost twigs curled left and right, up and down. Chirping noisily, busy yellow-beaked I'iwi birds darted between the tree's highest branches and tended a garden of tangled, light green, leafy vines – and hanging loosely around the tree's top, the dew-covered vines looked a lot like sparkling, sweet-smelling leis.

Filled with desire, Manna thought the beautiful ohia the most luscious thing she ever saw.

"Which branch?" asked Mano. Suddenly standing next to Manna, his soul looked just like his real body – except ... it didn't bounce.

Angry, Manna almost asked why he followed – then she remembered. He already had a Fetcher from the beach.

Twinkling bright, Mano's eyes bounced off the tree and crinkled at

Manna, as if it was okay that he followed – and instantly, she thought he was right.

One of the branches *could* serve as her Fetcher!

Excited, and determined to get a branch before him, Manna bolted for the tree. Jerking forward, Mano raced after her.

Splashing through the hot stream first, Manna swung into the lowest tree branch and snapped off a smooth foot-long stump.

"Au-we-e-e!" the tree cried out in pain – and spurting dark red, sticky blood out the hole Manna made, it whipped its sharp, long-clawed branches around her body and ripped her off of its bark. Then howling like the wind, it slammed her to the ground and forced her head under its now steaming, bloody red waters.

Terrified, Manna kicked at the tree and beat it with its own stump, but choking on blood, she threw up as soon as Mano stomped on her stomach.

"Get off!" she cried – knowing they would both die – and grunting scared, Mano scrambled into the tree and jammed his tapa cloth lunch into the tree's gaping wound. Squeezing out the back of his bundle, a large hunk of ahi dropped out and slapped Manna's face – and instantly, the tree's wound shut.

Gently tossing a heart-shaped leaf lei around Mano's sweating neck, the calmed tree straightened up and its waters ran clear.

"MAI!" commanded Tutu, and at once the children obeyed.

"La'au o Hina," muttered Tutu. Her suspicious green eyes burned through Manna's brain – and sitting up quickly, Manna clutched her new Fetcher in defense.

"Did you make the right offering?" hissed Tutu.

Remembering the hunk of ahi he dropped, Mano instantly took credit by blurting, "Yes!"

Smiling proudly, Tutu glanced at Mano's neck. Still dangling there, the vine lei shimmered an eerie crystal green.

"Aka manu," breathed Tutu. "Planted by the birds. The most valuable awa of all."

Jerking upright, Mano ripped the precious awa lei off his neck and threw it at his grandmother. Pleased, she handed him a small piece back.

"Give it to someone you trust," she cooed. "Someone who can tend it in the ohia trees."

Begrudgingly, Manna held out her hand, expecting Mano to give her the job. But bumping past her to get at Ailani, he tossed the plant into her folded ivory-white lap. Snatching the awa up quickly, Ailani shoved it into her shoe, in case Pu-pele tried to grab it.

Jealousy burned Manna's throat – and narrowing into slits, Pu-pele's angry, burning eyes squinted down at her sister and promised, one day, she'd get even.

Chapter Eleven

The SHARK'S BITE

"One hour," grunted Moho. Then he flared his dark, sweaty nostrils and tore down the rocky beach road in his gourd-banging, gleaming grey truck.

Anxious, Manna turned around and stared at a distant black jagged cliff. Along its steep oceanfront edge, a line of stocky yellow surfers stood motionless, their surfboards pointed south – then at once, they all jumped in.

Bouncing on his toes, Mano clutched both of their surfboards in either of his bony hands as he glared, squinty-eyed and defensive, at the row of paddling boys.

Six weekends they'd surfed down Kalapana – but never before had anyone encroached on their beach.

Frowning, Manna squinted into the brilliant morning sun and could tell – it was the Japanese gang. The ones who wielded nunchucks and knives to keep others at bay – and used chubby Taro to knock Mano down.

"They're stacking up," breathed Mano. His dark eyes scanned the choppy blue water where the Japanese gang swam out, but Manna wasn't sure if he meant the waves or the boys – because already behind the break, sitting in a long spread-out line, Ku-hai and the cousins waited for the next swell. His brown back straight and tall, Ku-hai sat rigidly at the head of the line, his warm hands gripped on his strong half-submerged hips – and glinting bright red, Iki's thin, black-streaked surfboard bobbed sideways, up and down, giddy at the end of the line.

Suddenly, a six-foot swell peeled back to form a mile-long, glassy pipe line – and at once, Manna's heart skipped a beat.

That wave was more than enough for two!

First to take off, Ku-hai popped up on his board, dropped down a glistening blue curl, cut back, and stuffed his head into a whirling foam-spitting barrel.

"Woo-hoo!" all the cousins hooted across the churning sapphire ocean, and with the Devil's speed, a tingly cold chill raced up Manna's spine.

She wanted to be out there – Japanese gang or not!

Unbuttoning her skirt, she kicked it to the ground.

"You gotta wear that!" blurted Mano, his eyes alarmed and wide – and with a face-stinging slap, it hit Manna.

It was okay to surf in your panties, with your brother, but not with anyone else.

Embarrassed, her cheeks burned red as she snatched up her skirt and glared at "the boy" – thinking it unfair that he whipped off his shirt – till she saw him bend down and roll up his tight, long woolen pants.

Once those got wet, his butt would look like bursting German broiled sausage!

Giggling out loud, Manna tucked her board under her arm, and knowing who was supposed to watch who, she squealed, "You first!"

Hush-Puppies on, Mano snatched up his board and bolted across the pointy, dew-covered rocks to the distant cliff, where he and Manna had never been – and feeling a shrill hoot of excitement, Manna scampered

216

after him.

KA-BOOM!

With a deep booming crash, a swollen white-watered wave slammed into the fourteen-foot cliff and pelted Manna's face with stinging, cold, salty drops – and freezing shut, her lungs shivered as she watched the angry spitting wave pull back and expose razor-sharp, gleaming, wet lava rocks. Spreading twelve feet wide below her, like a Vietnamese bamboo-spiked booby trap, the glimmering black rocks poked up and jeered at her – ready to impale and kill.

Stepping back, she decided not to go in.

"We gotta jump before the wave pulls back," muttered Mano. Then he kicked off his scuffed leather shoes.

KA-BOOM!

Another wave pounded against the cliff's face, hiding the murderous rocks, and Manna could see he was right – but to go in would be crazy. If they jumped a split second too late, the rocks below would unveil and skewer their guts, right before the next wave drowned their blood-spurting heads!

Glaring at the ocean, Manna almost hated it – for ruining all her fun. Then she caught sight of a swell. Rising up and down, up and down, its soothing amniotic rhythm called to her, willing her to come in and play. Not meaning to, she slipped off her shoes and smiled hazily at her brother. Grinning back, his bright brown eyes twinkled and he assured her.

"When I say – go."

Mano didn't know how to walk – or run – on land. But the water, he understood. So much so, that he called all the spots, all the waves, every position – and even took care of the boards. Waxing them. Stripping them. Keeping them primed.

Letting her chest rise with hope, and a distant swell, Manna barely noticed Mano fasten her leash. But wiggling her cold toes, she knew that in the past six weeks, he'd become one with the water and board, like Moho said, taking Manna along for the ride. She lived to surf now. Nothing else mattered – except the powerful thrust of a curl.

KA-BOOM! – "One!"

A ten-foot wave hammered the cliff at the same time Mano barked the count down – and snapping out of her trance, Manna felt panic grip her heart.

Today, someone would die!

Mano understood the water – but the rocks below were definitely land!

KA-BOOM! – "Two!" – "Pull out!" a sudden whirlwind hissed in Manna's ear, and choking, her chest burned with fear.

It was her! She was gonna die!

Desperate, she grabbed Mano's hand and screamed, "NOOOO!"

KA-BOOM! – "THREE!"

Drowning her out, the wave and Mano roared – and a split second later, he squeezed her hand tight and shrieked a high-pitched, excited, "GO!"

With a hard shoulder jerk, Manna tumbled off the cliff, and shrieking horribly, plunged to her death.

SMACK! CRUSH!

With a sickening smack, Manna's chin split against something rock hard, and a churning salty mass crushed into her face. Frantic and sputtering warm blood, she shoved her board in trim and double paddled as fast as she could – till she caught sight of Mano's long bloodied toes. Dangling off either side of his surfboard, limp and lifeless, a gurgling foam swallowed them whole.

"Mano!" she heard herself squeak at the same time her bruised, scraped knees straddled her rattling board and her stiff arms snapped her body into a sitting position.

CRASH!

With a neck jarring crash, an angry wave nailed her face and nearly swiped her off of her board. But determined to save her brother, she clutched her side rails and pearled underwater – to get away from the breaking waves.

Where is he? she cried.

Submerged in a surreal pressured silence, her heart pounding in her chest, Manna jerked her head around underwater and searched for her brother's thin board. But all she could see was a smeared trail of blood dashed over a long, jagged rock, and streaky lines of red trickling through a clouded, swirling white surface.

Oh no! she wailed. *It killed him!*

Gripping her surfboard rails tight, she straightened her arms to get clear of the board, then frog-kicked six times, as hard as she could – heading straight towards the jiggly lines of blood ... that seeped from her brother's body.

"HAH!" – she breathed in deep as she punched through the surface and caught sight of Mano's tan, rippling back. Taking turns cutting into the surface, his long sinewy arms paddled quickly – up, forward, back – and his bunched, gleaming biceps curled round with each stroke.

He's not dead! gasped Manna. *He's paddling out!*

Incited, she pearled underwater again, kicked four times, and surfaced into six strenuous double strokes.

"Woo-hoo!" she heard Mano hoot right before she rammed into him – and with a foot-flailing splash, he kicked her in the neck, and they both tumbled off their boards.

"Goof!" Manna cried as she surfaced, but choked by saltwater, it sounded more like a drowning chicken's, "BA-GOCK!"

Instantly, they both burst into sea-spraying laughter – and relieved, Manna grinned at her brother's wild, beaming face.

Spurting out his flared, snorting nostrils, two red streams of blood splashed off his cracked, smiling lips and sprinkled down his bouncing Adam's apple neck – and pointed to the sky, knotted in his wet stick-up bangs, his huge shark tooth necklace glimmered on top of his head, like a cannibal's victim-made crown.

Crinkling her nose at him, Manna thought he looked like a crazed monkey-boy ... escaped from some prehistoric zoo.

"We made it!" squealed Mano – and burning hot, excitement sizzled through her head.

This time would be the most fun – showing off in front of the cousins – because she and Mano knew how to shred!

"What? No more baggies?" huffed Taro, as he shot a slanty-eyed smirk at Mano's shrunken wool pants. Then, trying not to be the last one out to the break, he splashed an armload of water into Mano's face – but without blinking, Mano paddled past.

Frowning at the dirty wet shorts that clung to Taro's big rumpled butt, Manna dug in harder and whizzed past him too, thinking, *Yeah. Like that looks any better.*

As if reading her mind, Taro stopped paddling and eyed Manna's tight woolen skirt.

Oddly embarrassed, she closed her legs and pearled underwater.

"Ey, Shahk-bait!" Manna heard Shoda, the flat-top, Japanese gang boy holler when she surfaced. "Get to the end of the line – and take ehu there with you!"

Blowing past Shoda, with Mano jamming far in the lead, Manna wondered why the two slowest Japanese boys wanted to keep them behind. There were plenty enough waves ... then it hit her.

Shark bait. That's what she and Mano were – because sharks got attracted to blood!

Panicking, her heart jumped in her chest, and her feet popped out of the water – so a shark couldn't bite them. Then panting, her mind spinning wild, she double paddled as fast as she could to catch up with Mano, and protect him.

SUCK!

Feeling a cold wind suck past her cheeks, Manna jammed up to Mano's side – and wheeled around to face the shore – but she knew.

Sitting two miles out, they had no chance of outrunning a shark!

"What? Mento?" roared Tadashi, Japanese gang boy, second in command. "Deez position mines!"

Startled, Manna almost tumbled off her board.

So close to her right that she could smell his sushi-stink breath, Tadashi straddled his board, furious – and bobbing next to Mano, on their left and barely an arm's length away, Sanjiro (the cruel Japanese boy in command) squinted his beady black eyes in their direction.

Feeling trapped, Manna jerked her head left and right, searching for an escape – but there was none.

In a tight line, far to their left, the staring cousins buoyed high, up and down, with Ku-hai and Moku sitting closest to Sanjiro, in the best take off spots – and to the near right, the glaring Japanese gang sat in a much looser line, waiting their turn to take off – with Taro floundering the furthest away, submerged belly-deep in a flat, wave-less spot.

Her cheeks suddenly burning red, Manna realized. Mano stuffed them in the wrong position. They were supposed to be at the end of the line, like Shoda said, where the least number of waves curled.

Frowning, Manna didn't like it. Over there, the cousins couldn't see them shred.

"Tink you toff?" growled Sanjiro, Japanese boy in command. "Wit dat yellowed-out, hapa haole stick?"

Ignoring Sanjiro's taunts, like he usually did, Mano squinted at the incoming swells – and Manna wondered if he'd gone crazy. If they didn't move these boys were gonna hurt them, like they hurt everybody at school.

Nervous, she glanced at Sanjiro, to see if he had a gun.

"Yeah, you da one I talking to!" Sanjiro growled the moment Manna's eyes met his – and horrified, she caught her breath.

They never picked on her at school – because she was a girl!

"Never mind," whispered Mano, his bright eyes flashing trouble, and instantly, Manna felt like she might giggle.

Last time he twinkled like that, Taro ended up with roaches in his shorts!

Huh-hmm.

Suddenly, Manna heard a familiar breathing, like a gentle summer wind whispering past her ears. Her heart standing still, she leaned round and faced the ocean, knowing it came from out there.

Huh-hmm.

She heard the breathing again. But this time, it seemed to call her, longing to have her near. Without thinking, she leaned forward on her board, filled her lungs with musky air, and willed the distance ocean swells to hypnotize her.

Huh-hmm.

Feeling numb, Manna barely noticed the warm water raise her up and down, up and down – opposite that of the approaching swells – but smiling, she felt safe ... like a sleeping, coddled baby, floating in its mother's womb.

"BACKDOOR, LEFT!" shouted Mano.

Snapping to attention, Manna spun her board into position, left of Mano, and paddled hard towards the cresting wave's peak.

That was the rule. Because the swells always hypnotized her, Mano called out every wave, to snap her out of her trance. And to be safe, they rode each wave together, taking turns up front. But Manna always got to go up front, first.

"UGH!" Manna grunted and dug in with all her weight. Backdoor was the hardest, because it meant they missed the wave and had to paddle hard to catch up.

"Going skeg you, BRAH!" someone barked, and in that instant, Manna scooped over the towering wave, beyond its cresting peak, and popped up on her board.

"Wee-hee!" she squealed as she slid down the wave's beautiful sparkling blue face.

SUSH! HAH!

With a loud sush, Sanjiro sliced down, in front of Manna, and cut off her path – and with an out of control, "HAH!" Mano barreled down the wave, after him.

FLA-DAP!

With a slapping, "FLA-DAP!" Mano rode his fins across the top of Sanjiro's board, and jerked off balance, he rammed a bony elbow into Sanjiro's chest. At the same time, Sanjiro jabbed him in the back.

Startled, Manna slanted her board up, grabbed its nose in one hand, and stuffed it into the wave's crowning face. Then, knowing the wave aimed to crush anything in its path, she quickly pearled underwater.

Oh man, she thought, as the cool, cloudy water crumbled high above her head. *That was Sanjiro's wave! He was closest to the peak!*

Wishing she didn't take off, Manna curved her board up and surfaced, worried her brother got pummeled by the wave ... but only eight feet away, his beaming brown head bobbed, safe above water, and his O-shaped, dripping red mouth howled, "Ho! Da buggah got drilled!"

Surprised, Manna glanced towards shore, just in time to see Sanjiro's board come down with a sharp crack and clock his contorted sea-puking face – right before the next rough, roaring wave smacked his ugly head underwater.

"Rinse cycle," someone hissed in her ear.

Giggling, Manna looked back to see who joked behind her – and gasped.

Paddling mad on a wide, dark blue swell, Tadashi and the Japanese gang headed their way, ready to kill and get even.

Angry, Manna shimmied onto her board and hissed at Mano, "Position is possession!" But with a confident glimmer in his eyes, Mano just flipped his long shaggy bangs off his bloody forehead and breathed, "Unless in you're a shredder!" Then, with a start, he caught sight of the Japanese gang and his sparkling eyes bulged with fear.

"Ho! Ho! Ho!" he yelled and grabbed his board. "BARREL LEFT!"

Hot adrenaline suddenly jammed in her throat, Manna whipped round to see how close the Japanese were – and couldn't believe it. Looming ten feet high, a spit-spraying, sparkling green wave curled right above her head – and she sat ready, in its pocket.

"Me first!" she heard herself squeal, and without thinking, she popped up on her board and slipped down a steep, backwards-rushing, emerald-cut slide.

FR-R-R-R-RUH!

With a wet sucking sound, a shocking-cold, glittery white crown licked her right cheek. Then an under-board surge stuffed her body into a closed, cathedral-like, sparkling green barrel. Screaming in a tight swirl, brilliant cut diamonds slashed around her head, and lightning-fast, truckloads of shimmery, sheared glass whistled before her, hissing, "Sss-uh church. Sss-uh church."

Shaking furiously, Manna's slippery board careened through the tingly wet barrel – and all at once, her senses screamed, "We own you ... Home of the Gods!"

"Wee-hee-hee!" Manna heard herself squeal, and out of everywhere, raging hot, sizzling wet power blasted through her head – and the whole world rose up to greet her. Her, the Queen of the Gods!

CRUSH! – "SHRED-DAH!"

With a resounding crush, the wave slammed shut behind Manna and spit her out of the tube – and as always, Mano shot out of the wave and howled a long breathy, "SHREDA-A-AH!"

Catching up to her in an instant, he did a high five miss, with a palm slap down low ... and a cold, clammy hand squeeze.

Giggling out of breath, Manna flopped down on her board and squeezed Mano's hand back.

She liked it. His enthusiasm – and his boyish penchant to shout.

"Another, 'nother!" yelled Mano, and spinning his board towards the break, he paddled faster than ever before.

Snapping to attention, Manna spun around, feeling exhausted, but dug in as hard as she could – knowing he'd catch a good one for his turn up front ... then she heard it. A loud, clamoring hoot – coming from the cousins.

Oh my gosh, cried Manna. *They approve!*

"Spill right!" Mano barked, and Manna didn't understand.

Spillers curled junk and mushy. Why would he choose a lame one for himself?

Shrugging it off, she winged round to face the shore and double paddled over white-webbed, green, sloppy water. Then, setting up for the crumbly curl, she shoved a weary-armed heave and popped up on her board.

SLIS-S-S!

With a quick slice, she slid down the wave and cut back across its short bottom – and out of nowhere, knocked Tadashi off his board.

Tickled by her clumsy mistake, Manna zigzagged back down the grumbling wave and sniggered up at her brother. Climbing the wave fast, he railed a fist-waving, red-faced Shoda – right off his board.

Laughing out loud, Manna cut right and caught on.

They were cutting off the Japanese gang – 'cause out here, no one could touch them!

Satisfied, Manna's cheeks grinned wide.

They'd put up with more than their share, being embarrassed *all day* at school. Here played the big get even!

Slipping right and left across the bouncy wave, Manna wiggled her bottom at the floundering Japanese gang – as if taunting, "Catch me. Catch me. Catch me if you ca-an!"

Done with the wave, Mano dove off his board, popped out the back, and paddled as fast as he could – and dragging behind him, his long gleaming board ricocheted off each oncoming curl.

Panting, Manna dropped out after him, onto her board, and willed her weakened arms forward, not wanting to be separated from her brother in case he ran into trouble – and with a breezy whiff, she found herself jammed up to his left shoulder, right smack in the middle of the Japanese line.

With a startled jerk, Mano stopped paddling and slammed his foot down. With a crack, his board sailed high into the air ... and nailed him on the top of his head.

"Barrel left," he chuckled at his own clumsiness, and Manna felt her throat laugh evil.

Six weeks. Six weeks worth, they'd get even.

"GOING BROKE YO HEAD!" Tadashi roared on their far right, and spiffing left on the wave, Manna double paddled away, growling, "No way, Brah. My turn up front!"

"ETE!" growled Sanjiro – and with a slash, he dropped down, paddling fast, and set up to catch the wave ... right in front of Manna.

Amped, Manna thrust both of her arms forward and paddled – deep and hard – at the same time her left hand grabbed Sanjiro's leash. With a yank, his board snapped out from underneath him, and Manna popped up on hers.

FR-R-R-R-RUH!

Accidentally running over Sanjiro's surprised, squinty-eyed face, Manna felt something cold blast past her cheeks and suck her into a roaring, blue and white curl. Her fists clenched and her body crouched tight, like a ready, springing tiger, she flung both arms high into the air and totally crazed, bellowed, "SWEE ... EE ... EET REDEMPTION!"

CRUSH! – "SHRED-DAH!"

With an earth-shattering crush, the wave slammed shut behind her and tossed her out of the tube – and hooting, Mano accentuated their exit.

High five missing, he dropped down, his crooked tooth smiling proudly at Manna – and just beyond him, twelve feet away, Moku's beaming brown face shone bright.

Feeling a jolt of energy, Manna yelled, "Nuh-thuh! Nuh-thuh! For the bruh-thuh!" – because it was Mano's turn up front.

Whipping his board around, Mano peeled out towards the break – and feeling high off the ground, Manna followed.

"Snake the snake," someone hissed in her ear, and giggling, she knew how to do it.

"Whoa!" Mano breathed loud and slapped to a halt so fast that Manna slammed into him. Tumbling off her board, she felt the cool, ebbing ocean swallow her whole – and suddenly submersed in its calm, cozy silence, she knew.

The only place to be ... the only way to feel ... was deep, in the surf of the sea.

Stretching her head far back, she wiggled her toes as she floated towards the surface, and breaking through, nose first, she smiled hazily at her brother – then gasped.

Gurgling angrily, as though Moses had parted the sea, the whole ocean rose before her ... in a massive, blue and grey, towering wave wall.

Terrified, Manna's heart stood still.

Dotting the glistening wave wall, directly above her, the fist-shaking, bloodthirsty Japanese gang set up – ready to drop on their heads.

Meaning to pearl, Manna slid onto her board – but froze.

Burning a hole through her throat, Sanjiro's evil, black-slitted eyes trained on her neck as he paddled straight her way – with a glinting, curved knife grasped in one hand – and flashing bloody knives of their own, the angry Japanese gang followed.

They're gonna kill us! thought Manna.

Signaling him to scatter, she slapped at Mano's shoulder, but missed. Already paddling out to cut off the Japanese gang, he climbed the spitting, back-churning wall and blocked their takeoff path – never noticing their knives!

"MANO!" Manna heard herself scream, and horrified, she felt a biting cold spray rake round her cheeks and smack long hair over her eyes. Nearly blinded, she slammed her face into her board and double paddled towards her brother, as fast as she could.

FR-R-R-R-RUH! – "BARREL LEFT!" Mano roared with the wave, and glancing up, Manna saw twelve teeth-baring killers drop off the wall and barrel her way – with Mano and his hungry, crooked shark tooth dripping in the lead.

Oh gawd! she screamed. *They're gonna eat me!* – and in a frenzied brain-spinning fright, she scrambled up on her board, dead center pocket, and shrieked a long horrible death cry – on the drop.

WHOMP! CLINK, CLINK, CLINK!

With a loud whomp, Mano's airborne long board slapped down, in front of Manna, and with three consecutive clinks, the Japanese boys dropped in – behind her.

"WRA-A-A-AH!" the wave roared and reared its glistening white body. Then, with a deafening crash, it pummeled all but the three in the lead – slashing Mano, crouching Manna, and the cold blade-wielding Sanjiro.

"FR-R-R-RUSH!" the wave grumbled, not having murdered the

three. Then surging left, it stuffed them all into its whistling blue barrel.

Panting with fear, Manna crouched down low, her wobbly knees almost touching her board – and rearing in response, the hissing wave thrust her forward.

"A DAY TO DIE!" someone bellowed in her ear, and jerking her head right, she caught sight of a fast-approaching Sanjiro.

SUSH!

With a quick slice, Sanjiro caught up to her, at the same time his shiny, curved knife swiped at her throat – and with a high-pitched yelp, Manna pearled out of the way.

SNAP!

FROMP! – "HAH!"

With a wide toothy snap, a gleaming red shark shot out of the wave and lunged at Manna's face, but missed. Flying wet over her pearling head, the famished shark fromped across her board and snapped it in half, at the same time someone scared yelled, "HAH!"

SWOOSH!

With a roaring, cold swoosh, a washing machine swirl thrashed Manna's body underwater, and suddenly submersed in a bloody sea of red, she knew death was near.

"BLUP!" something hungry bubbled, right before ten sharp, long teeth sunk into her gut and ripped at her cramping intestines.

Horrified, her heart slamming against her ribs, Manna tore at the clamped teeth and kneed their evil head – until suddenly, she realized.

She was beating a pain-stricken, blood-gurgling Sanjiro.

Shocked, her arms went limp, and shaking uncontrollably, she stared down at her enemy's wide-eyed, pleading face – and noticed. Floating around in the water, jiggling like fattened yellowish-blue snakes, something long and bloody spilled out of his shorts.

Oh gawd! Manna screamed. *It ripped out his guts!*

Without thinking, she grabbed Sanjiro's hair and swam for the surface.

"Shark! Mano! Shark!" she screamed as soon as she hit air – and out of nowhere, Taro's fat, ghastly white face knocked into hers.

"Take him in!" Manna barked, and threw Sanjiro's drowning head at his brother.

With a slick glimmer, Mano popped through the clear blue surface, alongside his sister, and grinned. Glinting, his crooked white tooth shone in the salt-speckled wind.

Suddenly furious with him, Manna yanked off her leash, jumped on top his back, and growled, "Bring me in!"

Boardless, grumbled Manna, as she trudged up the beach towards Moho's waiting truck. *I'm boardless again! Because that idiot broke my board!*

Huh-hmm.

Manna heard a familiar breathing – and froze in her tracks. Tingling, a cold chill raced up her spine – and she knew she headed towards trouble.

"Her bones belong to me!" growled Moho, from behind a tall black rock – and the hairs on Manna's neck stood up and shivered. Jerking round fast, she scanned the pebbled beach for a safe place to hide, but there was none.

"Just a small piece, Brother," cooed a husky-voiced girl, and Manna thought the voice sounded familiar.

"GO HOME!" bellowed Moho. "THEY BELONG TO ME!"

Then with a loud, "KA-BOOM!" something solid hit the shore behind Manna.

Scared witless, she sailed over the slippery rock wall that lined the windy beach road ... and toppled, face first, into the dirt.

SCREECH! BOOM! BOOM!

Brakes skidding and stereo pounding, Ku-hai's shiny red truck grinded to a halt – and with a prickling puff, its glowing black tires spit pointy cinders into Manna's eyes.

Almost run over, she jerked up onto her aching, blood-streaked knees.

"Ey, road kill!" taunted Iki, from the back of the truck. Then, with a shush-eyed smirk, he speared his red and black lightning board at Manna's chest.

Reacting fast, Manna caught it midair – and flung it at his face.

"Get manners or what?" growled Aikoa, as she jerked her dark brown chin up and let her hot hazel eyes sear Manna's chest.

Instantly deflated, Manna's heart sank.

How much more of this could she take? Being hated ... just for being born.

Jerking forward rough, Iki grabbed Manna's neck, jabbed his board into her chest, and hissed loud in her ear, "Keep her cous!" Then, with a stern look about, Ku-hai's face shone righteous approval, right before he floored his roaring truck.

With an off-balance, skinny-armed squeal, Iki spilled out of the truck bed, right before Hi'u yanked him in by his hair – to all the laughing cousins' delight.

Her chest hollow with disbelief, Manna watched the smoking red truck disappear ... through burning, blurry-eyed tears.

It was hers now – the thing she wanted the most!

"Move it!" growled Moho.

Hugging her new board tight, Manna scrambled up to her feet and faced her enemy ... with pride.

Chapter Twelve

The LAST ONE

"Chicken keeper!" laughed Pu-pele, and instantly embarrassed, Ailani hid her yellow-feathered, bird-shaped Fetcher behind her back.

Defensive, Manna squinted, fist clenched, at Pu-pele.

Never before had she taunted Ailani. No one ever did.

"Bock!" squawked Mano, joining in. Then, his black, sweaty hair standing on end, he bulged his shiny eye whites, stuck out his scrawny chest, and jammed both thumbs into his armpits. Transforming into an attention-grabbing, ruffled-up rooster, he flapped his bony elbows up and down – at the same time he pecked his head forward and back.

Furious he mocked Ailani, Manna stepped forward to club him, but before she could, he bent both knees and knocked them together – swooping them in and out, fast and wide – as he took three giant steps forward.

"BOCK! BOCK! BOCK!" he squawked louder and louder, his head, knees and wings going as he strutted a jerky, rubber-legged dance around Manna and Ailani – as if he were king of the cocks and they were his prospective chicken wives.

Horrified, Ailani's innocent round eyes stared straight into Manna's.

Then at once, they both burst into spit-spraying laughter.

Mano *was* the king – the king of the geeked-out chicken-boy kooks!

Her soft skin shimmering, a thankful Ailani twinkled at her brother – and with a steamy, defiant huff, Pu-pele flipped her round, brown nose into the air and swirled out of the room.

Warmed by Ailani's angelic smile, Manna felt glad, for once, that Mano could look so deflicted (which was Manna's mispronunciation of "diphyletic") ... then she remembered.

Tutu said to finish carving their Fetchers today – before mo'olelo.

"Let's go!" hollered Momi from outside, at her truck and ready to go.

"Au-we!" Manna heard herself gasp, and without blinking, she bolted to the kitchen, winged open the silverware drawer, and snatched out the thickest butcher's carving knife. Then, her heart pounding scared, she dashed to her room, yanked her ohia branch Fetcher out from underneath her bed, plopped down on the floor, and wedged the smooth branch between her bare feet.

With a swoosh, something shivery cold slithered up Manna's thigh, but desperate, she ignored it. Any second, Momi would be screaming at the top of her lungs – so she barely had time to finish.

Gripping the long sharp knife in both hands, she raised it high above her head – and with a loud grunt, she slashed it down with all her might and hit the top of the Fetcher. With a sizzling pop, a chunk flew off, and Manna could swear the hole it left behind looked like a huge wailing eye.

ZAM!

With a sharp blast, something roaring hot suddenly soared through her veins, blasted through her chest and drove into her head – and instantly crazed, she stabbed at the wooden Fetcher repeatedly, wanting to kill its helpless soul. Screaming out in horrific pain, the Fetcher twisted right and left, trying to get away, but in a bloodthirsty rage, Manna stabbed it even harder ... her lips dripping with hungry saliva, at the thought of one day, licking the Sixth's dying soul.

Flashing dark red, the Fetcher moaned out loud and spread open its gaping, down-turned mouth. Then suddenly, it stiffened into a crouched fist-clenching warrior – unafraid of further abuse. As if glistening with greed, the Fetcher's brown, chiseled skin quivered – and her knife frozen above her head, Manna understood.

The thing would drink its own blood.

"It's got a penis!" blurted Mano, and slitting, Manna's cold eyes glared up at him.

"You idiot!" she heard herself growl, her face contorted with hate. "The Sixth is a GIRL!"

Ashen grey with fear, Mano's face dropped and his arms went limp – and with a crack, his stone Fetcher slipped from his hand and thumped onto Manna's. Sailing high into the air, Manna's Fetcher flipped once, then bounced, rock heavy, into her lap.

With a sharp jab, her pelvic bone felt like it snapped, but oddly relieved, Manna heard herself giggle,

"Not any more!" – because Mano's Fetcher knocked off the small protruding piece.

"NOW!" bellowed Momi, and grabbing both Fetchers, Manna sprang to her feet.

"What'd *you* run into?" squealed Pu-pele. Her emerald eyes danced with curiosity and delight.

Oozing bright red and blue over Iki's shiny right eye, a baseball-sized bruise swelled it shut.

"Hawaiian love!" chortled Kokala. Then, with a soft swipe, he fake punched a half-grinning Iki in the eye.

With a singe, Manna's heart and gaze dropped. Trying hard not to let on, she squinted at the sandy mo'olelo hut floor, knowing.

Nobody loved her.

"Lolo, here, when take apart Uncle Moku's lawnmower – and stick da engine on his bike!"

"Did it work?" bounced an anxious Mano as he leaned off his mat – and with a smirk, Hi'u chirped, "Sure thing, Brah – but get no brakes!"

"Less you count Uncle's hard fist!" jeered Aikoa.

"HO!" piped in Kau, his eyes unusually sparkled. "I never when see da buggah fly so far! Uncle Moku popped him one good one!"

Not meaning to, Manna heard herself giggle, right before Mano and Iki crumpled into high-pitched, throat-scratching laughter – and at that moment, she understood.

The three had something in common ... speed!

"Today you shall apparate," moaned Tutu, suddenly flowing round the outside of the children's circle, "and learn how to fly."

Startled, Manna swallowed down her laughter and snapped into a straight-backed ne'epu position. Then, tight-lipped and every muscle tense, she stared down at the white tapa cloth spread out before her.

If she moved during mo'olelo, Tutu would be the first to crush her skull.

"The awa and chant will transport you," droned Tutu, as she placed awa-filled coconut cups in front of the cousins, "and your cousins will teach you how to fly."

"Pih!" spit Momi. "Who needs them?"

Suddenly, laying face up on Manna's tapa cloth, her steely-eyed Fetcher stretched its mouth open and growled its square, far-spaced teeth down, forcing its huge tattoo-banded chin to protrude. Then curling its crinkled top lip up, it smiled at the same time it frowned – and at that moment, Manna missed Tutu's reply. Morbid amazement streaming through her head, she leaned in close and focused on her Fetcher doll.

Inside its ribbed, sideways hourglass-shaped mouth, a fat lolling tongue quivered, ready to fork out and gouge – at the same time its flared, wrinkled nostrils spread round and wide, exposing two dark crevasse-lined tunnels meant to suck you deep into some demon's sinister mind. Bulged down and too far apart, its enormous almond-shaped eyes propped up a coiled cascade of Indian headdress-shaped hair, and frozen into two C's, its clawed hands reached down, ready to snare any being. Trunk thick and squatting down low, as if releasing a fat stool, its bulky legs flattened out two square, broad feet and exposed eagle-like, taloned toes.

Shivering, Manna thought her Fetcher the ugliest thing she ever saw – and with a tingly cold swish, something whizzed up her back and spiraled out the door.

CLUNK!

Bending down low, Tutu clunked an awa-filled coconut cup onto Manna's shimmering tapa cloth – and startled from her thoughts, she glanced over at Ailani's carved wooden Fetcher.

Extending elegantly down its light tan sides, a myriad of etched feathers fluttered in an intricate woven pattern and cloaked her bird's delicate, pointy, clawed feet – and shrouding its round, dimpled girth, a thin white tapa cloth strip dangled menacingly off its neck. Chiseled into stark awareness, its owl-beaked, eagle-shaped face bulged two full moon, round eyes that stared, knowingly, at Manna. Then, as if warning, the long yellow feather attached to the top of its head stood up and pointed in her direction.

"Drink!" commanded Tutu, and not wanting to be the last one done, Manna snatched up her cup and guzzled down its acidic, bubbling gruel.

"Hele uhane!" wailed Tutu, before Manna finished, and with a loud, "ZHAM!" two red-hot, blistering, white hands stabbed through her ribs, wretched her soul from her chest, and hurled it into the sky.

"WHUP! WHUP! WHUP!" Manna heard, and suddenly flying around in sickening room-size circles, she felt her arms rip from her chest and her legs split wide apart, at the same time her head and bottom took turns tumbling around each other in the air. Then sucking noisily, a sweaty, hot wind pressed her cheeks firmly together ... and stuffed something long and fleshy into her mouth. Gagging, Manna forced warm puke back down her throat and cried, *Oh Gawd! Something went wrong!*

"Think!" Iki suddenly rapped a stiff finger on her forehead. "Think! Think! Think! Think! Think!" – and her brains slamming against her skull, Manna wanted nothing more than to kill him.

"Think!" Iki continued, rapping hard with each word. "Think! Think! Think! Think! Think!" – and furious, Manna swiped in his direction, but missed.

"Think!" Iki rapped forty times more. "Think! Think! Think! Think! Think!" – and wanting to explode, Manna felt her whole body clench when she bellowed, "STO-O-OP!"

At once, the world froze – and Manna hung upside down and weightless, suspended midair, thirty feet above the cousins ... and her staring, wide-eyed siblings

"BLA-A-AH!" her guts heaved, and with a stinking, sloshy fladap, greenish-red, quivering, wet slime splattered on top Iki's head.

Bursting into laughter, all the cousins fell down on the grey, misty floor – and that's when Manna noticed.

They all wore their clothes.

Worried, she squeezed her eyes shut and prayed ... she'd be wearing something pretty – the day she died.

"Going play bat, or what?" quipped Iki, and opening her eyes, Manna blinked.

Her puke had smeared into a hazy, lime green light that danced playfully around Iki's smirking, upturned face – and his perfectly round, sparkling eyes.

"You gotta think," instructed Ku-hai. "In the direction you want to go."

BAM!

With a loud bam, Manna crashed to the floor, headfirst – and with a bone-jarring crack, her brains spilled out a bloody, jagged wound.

Scuffling to his feet, Moku smiled warmly against Manna's cheek and lifted her to a stance.

"Tink a little slower, eh Bat-Girl," he whispered. His moist breath tickled her ear. "And remember. Anything here could be permanent."

Pitter-pattering, Manna's heart skipped a beat and her knees almost wobbled – but her head felt a lot better.

With a wiggly-tail flicker, Iki suddenly darted into the air, then spun around, arms open at his sides, and grinned, "Lie dat!"

Wanting to try first, Mano jerked up too fast and flipped backwards into the air. Flailing wildly, his gawky arms and daddy-long legs flapped in off-center, wind-grabbing circles – and for a second, Manna thought he fell ... up!

"Outta my way!" blasted Momi, and with a searing blue flash, she tore through the air, both fists forward like Superman, and ripped through a surprised Iki and Mano. Spinning out of control, they both tumbled to the ground – and Momi disappeared into a far off, twinkling mist.

"Ete!" grumbled Ku-hai, and with one big-knuckled fist forward, he barreled into the mist ... after her.

"Oo-ooh!" squealed Pu-pele. As she flowed up into the sky, a streaky orange trail shimmered off of her bare, pointed toes – and at that moment, prickly chicken-skin raced up Manna's arms and tingled across her neck.

Pu-pele was breathtaking ... beautiful.

Sizzling in a bright orange light, her long golden locks spilled over her inviting red cheeks and flickered off a plump pouty-doll mouth – as her soft upraised arms crossed high above her upturned face and thrust out two brown, supple, round breasts. Arched tall and straight, her back stretched to the sky, and suddenly drowsy, Manna let herself yawn.

Drawn to Pu-pele's flaming hair like a confused, anxious moth, Moku fluttered up and smiled shyly at her now parted and quivering lips ... at the same time a jealous Aikoa scuffled to her feet.

"Boo!" smiled Ailani, suddenly standing nose to nose with Manna, and Manna couldn't help but smile back at her sister's dancing, light brown eyes. Then she noticed.

Ailani's long shiny hair seemed to trickle off her head, like water – yet it glowed all the rainbow's hues.

"Humph!" Ailani muttered. Then she pressed her right fist to her shimmery pink lips – like she did before she'd go – but instead of tapping down the length of her thin white arm ... she disappeared.

"Boo!" Ailani appeared between Moku and Pu-pele, her nose shoved firmly into Pu-pele's steaming red face.

"Cool!" breathed Moku, and giggling, Ailani flashed a dainty white smile.

Furious she stole Moku's attention, Pu-pele swiped a smoking hand across Ailani's delicate cheek – at the same moment Ailani muttered, "Humph!" and disappeared. Missing Ailani, Pu-pele jerked forward, all her weight in her hand – and smacked a surprised Moku to the ground.

"Boo!" Ailani announced, thirty feet away and almost obscured by the mist Momi and Ku-hai vanished into.

Jumping to his feet, a delighted, grinning Moku clapped loud approval ... and Manna thought it weird that his brown eyes sparkled with pride.

"Eh!" Aikoa shoved Moku at the same time Pu-pele glared, green eyes slitted, at a twinkling, angelic Ailani.

"Humph!" Ailani disappeared for good.

BLAM! - "OOF!"

As if shot from a cannon, Aikoa slammed through Pu-pele's gut headfirst, arms stiff at her sides – and the wind knocked out of her, Pu-pele expelled a pain-filled, "OOF!" right before her limp, heavy body hit the ground. Laying flat on her back, she didn't see Aikoa chase after Ailani.

"You it!" hollered Iki, right before he whacked Mano in the ear. Then flitting away, he disappeared into the parting mist.

Gripping his sore ear, Mano flipped up into the air. Then, awkwardly, he fell forward fast, his arms and legs flopping at his sides – and without looking back, he slipped through the dark hole Iki left in the fog.

"Ugh," groaned Pu-pele, and instantly, Moku knelt by her side.

"You okay?" he breathed as he cradled her soft feminine figure in his strong, comforting arms, and almost smiling, Manna watched Pu-pele's unharmed toes wiggle with pleasure. Then she remembered.

Moku said ... anything out here could be permanent.

ZUP!

With a cool zup, Manna found herself wedged between a fist fighting, "You it!" hollering Iki and Mano – then,

CRACK! THUP!

With a sledge hammer left, Iki accidentally socked Manna in the eye, and stunned, she spiraled backwards, both hands clutched over her now empty, blood-throbbing socket.

"MAI!" commanded Tutu, and at once, all the children sat up in the mo'olelo circle.

Afraid to move, Manna stared straight ahead, her heart pounding in her ears – then she realized. Nothing hurt ... and her eye was still there. Squinting, she glanced past a glaring Aikoa, to see a smirking Iki squirm at her side.

Mo'olelo was over.

"Well done," groaned Tutu. "Your father will be pleased," – and with a singe, something frightening cold scraped through Manna's veins and pinched her heart shut.

He *would* be pleased ... like Tutu said – because he could steal her bones from her kino whenever she flew – and there wasn't a single person in this room who could help her.

Her heart burning, Manna glared at her brother.

Bouncing up and down, an anxious grin crinkled his crooked-tooth face, and she could swear. He wanted to play rough with Iki ... some more.

"Simple kine," Aikoa shooed the air with her flat brown hand, as she rolled her green-flecked eyes. "They get us to protect 'em, while they learned how to fly."

"Yeah, right," spit Momi. Her pale face dripped bright red, and her head almost quivered.

Thrilled to have bugged Momi, Aikoa's eyes gleamed a wicked yellow-green, and at once, Manna knew there'd be trouble.

"Tink you can protect you?" challenged Aikoa before Ku-hai cut in, "Mo'o game!" Then he thumped a gnarled fist against his rock-solid chest, right before he thrust it out to Momi's eye level and growled, "Me against YOU!"

Without flinching, Momi curled her thin, dry lips in and growled, "NOW!"

"No!" begged Pahau. Her curly red hair tumbled off her plump, fast-draining face and exposed two huge glittery, scared eyes – and Manna could tell.

Mo'o meant evil.

"They're lizards," whispered Ailani, but her mouth didn't move. Only her nervous hands did, as they wrung inside each other.

Confused, Manna couldn't tell if Ailani's telepathy meant this was a dream.

"They like to test and shape-shift to the most horrible forms," Ailani

241

kept thinking out loud, "and take pleasure in eating spiders and man."

"You're not ready, child," breathed Tutu, and instantly distracted, Manna bit her lip.

Something sad had filled the air.

Sighing heavily, Tutu raised one hand up and squeezed Momi's broad, rigid shoulder. For a moment, Momi relaxed. Then slowly, her tight blonde bun turned to face all her cousins ... and her slanted blue eyes held back shiny, wet tears – an inch from Tutu's face.

"I never was," she breathed, almost childlike ... then she pursed her lips before she croaked, "And it never mattered."

"Sha-ka-po," challenged Ku-hai, his unwavering fist still out, and Aikoa chimed in, "If you dare."

Tight with pain, Momi's face paled a bloodless blue, but undaunted, she whipped around to face Ku-hai, both hard white-knuckled fists cocked. The left one quivered high, just beyond her breathless, sweating chest – and the right clenched low, under her blue-veined, exposed ribs – ready to kill both of her opponents.

"Rock-paper-scissors," Ailani muttered to the ground – and with each word, her right, dainty fist padded against her open, left palm, but Manna had a funny feeling Momi didn't understand what she said.

"Junk in a munkin, Shaka, shaka, po," Aikoa sing-songed gaily, and shaking with hate, Momi leaned forward to club her.

"Why pio? Why pio?" continued Aikoa. Her hard eyes drilled through Momi, as if to dare her – because Aikoa knew. Blatantly challenged, Momi would never release either fist.

"Big fat TOE!"

Jerking forward, Ku-hai flattened his palm on, "TOE" – and wrapped his big paper hand around Momi's left fist. Then, smelling like burnt parsley, his hot breath raked across Manna's cheek.

"Mano!"

"WHAT?" squawked Aikoa – and startled, Ku-hai jerked back and recovered with a resounding, "MOKU!"

Suddenly hollow, Manna's stomach wrenched.

They were choosing teams – and no matter what, she was always chosen last. At school, at home, even at church. She hated it – being unwanted.

"Aikoa!" growled Momi. Determined to win, she deserted her family and pride.

"Kokala!" barked Ku-hai, followed by Momi's choice.

"Kau!"

"Iki!" Ku-hai picked inside his family, even though Pu-pele loomed much, much bigger.

Offended, Pu-pele shot a hot, orange-hazed breath out of her lifted brown nose – and Manna could swear, her lime eyes sizzled.

"Hi'u!" spit Momi, and Manna realized.

Momi ousted Pu-pele, the bigger of the those two – because in comparison, Pu-pele was stupid.

Shrinking back, Pu-pele looked straight at Manna. Her watery eyes blinked like a wounded baby deer's. Then her whole body twitched, and Manna could see it.

Pu-pele would get even.

"Pahau!" grunted Ku-hai, as if something pained his rippled gut, but thankful, Pahau's adoring round eyes beamed up at him.

None of the cousins wanted to fight against their leader.

"Ailani!" quipped Momi, still overlooking Pu-pele, and Manna wondered if her rashness would kill her. She had filled her side with enemies – and added one more, by rejecting a vengeful, half-crazed Pu-pele ... but that was okay.

If she wouldn't pick Pu-pele – for once, Manna wouldn't be last!

Feeling better, Manna glanced at a bright-eyed, bouncing Mano. His bent, sinewy arms tense and his skinny chest crouched far forward, he looked like a scrawny kitten ready to pounce into play – and at that moment, he and Manna shared a smile.

"Waka!" Ku-hai made his only choice.

"Mano," growled Momi – and with a heavy thud, realization hit Manna.

Only she and Pu-pele were left.

It *was* her again. *She* would be last. Ku-hai would pick the bigger of the two.

Looking down at the ground, so no one could see her react, Manna squeezed her lungs shut when Ku-hai hissed, "Pu-pele."

It was over. Momi wouldn't call out her name. The teams never did. As if refusing to acknowledge their disappointment. But as always, the chosen ones leaned in close, to jeer at her unwanted face.

Scowling at the ground, Manna felt a familiar cruel heat sear through her nose and burn out her eyes, but determined, she made sure no one heard her breathe in.

"Raise your Fetchers – no gods," groaned Tutu. Then low in her throat, she gurgled, "Hele i ka hale o ..."

Fierce beyond his years, Kau's chilling, gruff voice barked out last minute orders.

"Grip your Fetcher! Kill your fears! And no matter what – STAY ON YOUR ISLAND!"

ZUP!

Swallowed by a sudden, sticky, smothering black, Manna listened to her heart pound in her chest – in sync with something that sounded like huge cliff-banging surf. Alone and expecting the worst, she crouched forward and listened to the darkness – but all she heard was the faint chirp of a distant, forlorn gecko.

Nervous, she fingered her cool, bumpy Fetcher and dug her bare heels into the warm jagged rock – and as if meaning to calm her, a misty, tan-colored moon flickered high in sky, then descended slowly to the ground. Feeling fear fade, Manna stared at the soft glowing moon and promised herself.

This was a dream. She couldn't get hurt.

Jerking to a halt, the moon spun around, only six feet in the air, and presented itself – a shiny, splotchy-glazed Hawaiian gourd.

"HO'O MAKA!" roared Ku-hai, and with the blinding successive flash of forty-five lightning bolts, the shadowy Mo'o world filled with light – and Ku-hai smashed the helpless gourd with his long twisted Fetcher. Flipping around in tight circles, the gourd sailed over Manna's head and lit towards Momi's face – but right before it reached her, it transformed into a long-tailed, fleshy, grey kite.

"WAAAH!" yelled Momi. Bluish-grey spittle stretched long between her buck and bottom teeth, like a demon's salivating before a meal – and right before she clubbed the kite in the head, Manna realized.

It wasn't a kite. It was an open-mouthed, foamy-gummed sting ray – determined to suck off Momi's head!

THWAP!

With a loud thwap, the sting ray's membraned wing smacked Manna's face and hammered her to the ground – on its way back to Ku-hai's waiting club – and with a deafening shudder, four Hawaiian drums beat underground.

Dazed, Manna heard herself groan, at the same time she rolled on her side – and gasped.

Only a foot under the dark, churning water, a jet black, dragon-faced, twenty-foot-long lizard flicked its fat forked tongue in her direction, and twinkled a hungry, double-slitted, red eye at her throat – and at once, Manna knew the island she lay on stretched only half her size. Afraid she'd be yanked in, she scrambled to her feet and dug her bleeding heels into the gleaming lava rock.

WHAM! THWAP! – WHAM! THWAP! – WHAM! THWAP!

In rapid-fire succession, something rock-hard and something else cloak-thick took turns beating either side of Manna's head, but determined not to be eaten alive by that waiting lizard thing, she held her ground and prayed ... she'd die of head injuries *before* she fell in.

WHAM! THWAP! – WHAM! THWAP!

"GET OUTTA MY WAY!" bellowed Momi, and startled, Manna's head snapped left, in Momi's direction – right before Momi hammered a black blood splattered sting ray with her Fetcher. Flopping round, the sting ray sailed back, gums smacking hungrily – straight for Manna's face – and with a body jolting, "Zup!" and a deep double thump, Manna's island lurched far out of the way.

WHAM! THWAP! – WHAM! THWAP!

"Lo-lupe," Ailani muttered, an arm's length from Manna. "What Momi fears the most."

Standing alone on a larger, lime green island, Ailani hugged her etched Fetcher tight into her gut, but neither she nor its feather stood erect. Worried, Manna peered into her sister's scared brown eyes.

Without a doubt, Ailani couldn't fight back.

"Ku-hai fears nothing," Ailani's voice squeaked, but her lips didn't move. "That's why the gourd won't transform in front of him."

WHAM! THWAP! – WHAM! THWAP!

"ARGH!" growled Momi. Frustration croaked her voice, and by instinct, Manna's eyes jerked around and searched for an escape, but there was none.

Enclosed in a large, grey-misted, high-walled silvery dome, all the children hunched over on their separate islands, their Fetchers clutched in front of them like a ready bat – and gurgling all around them, a soupy, purplish-grey, smelly-squid ocean rippled and swelled with each flick of a hundred dragon-sized lizard tails.

WHAM! THWAP! – WHAM! THWAP!

Ku-hai whacked the gourd viciously, his stiff face never flinching, each time the gourd barreled towards his face – and drenched with bluish-grey sweat, Momi clubbed the lip-smacking sting ray it transformed into, with her brutal, grunting swing. Each time she clubbed it, the ray's skull split in half and Momi let out a deep, exhausted groan.

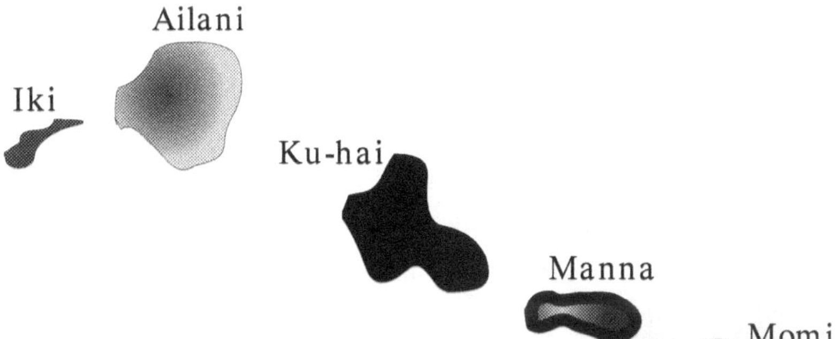

Ailani

Iki

Ku-hai

Manna

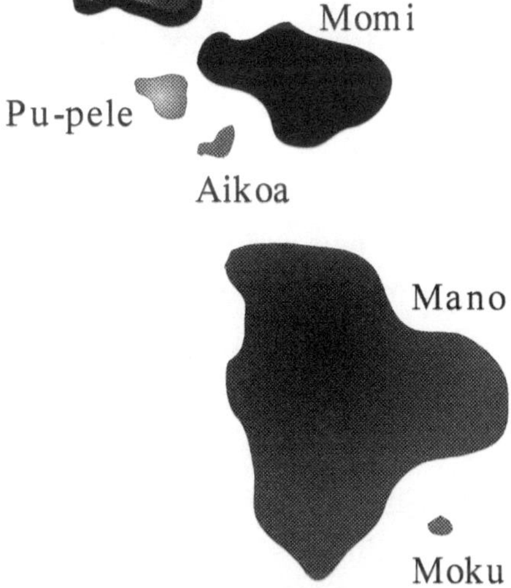

Momi

Pu-pele

Aikoa

Mano

Moku

Certain Momi would give up soon, and the game would be over, Manna glanced around quickly and noticed.

Only nine of the children stood on solid rock islands. The rest floated on misty, rainbow-colored isles – and distracted, Manna took a quick inventory.

Of the rock islands, Mano's spread the largest and most triangular as it shook, side to side – while Ailani's grounded silent and round ... and roughly the same size as Ku-hai's and Momi's (both of which vibrated, crooked and black, in the center), Ailani's settled the second farthest away. Aikoa's tiny brown island floated just to the left of Momi's and directly behind the quivering red stone that Pu-pele seemed to melt on – and bobbing on a tiny brown dot, just behind Mano, a steely-faced Moku appeared to have the only rock island that couldn't quite stay afloat. To the left of Ailani, Iki crouched on a skinny, surfboard-shaped, moss-covered rock, and almost jealous, Manna glanced down at hers.

Spreading wide, like an olden-day longboard, it glowed a red-flecked black – and instantly, Manna felt better. Her island looked the best ... until she caught sight of the other misty-colored isles that floated a foot above water – as if they could fly. Then she remembered.

Her island used to be between Ku-hai and Momi's. Somehow, it moved here – to the north end of the rock islands that looked a lot like the Hawaiian island chain. But if the rock islands represented Hawaii, what did the flying, cloudy-colored ones mean?

SLAP! – BLUH! BLUH!

With a desperate slap, a horned, pain-contorted lizard smacked the length of Manna's eastern beach and groped its clawed, wrinkled fingers in the air – as another much larger lizard ate away its gut.

Horrified, Manna peered closer at the waters – and with a chest-clutching squeeze, felt her heart stop.

Swarming in the water like frenzied feeding sharks, the tar-skinned lizards frantically ate one another, doubling in size with each victim swallowed.

"THE MO'O!" a sudden wind roared as it raked around Manna's cheeks, right before Momi bellowed, "STOP IT!"

Limp with fear, Manna stared helplessly into her sister's drilling blue eyes ... and understood.

The point of the game wasn't for Momi to beat Ku-hai. It was to be the last one standing. After your team helped you kill off your enemy, you murdered each member of your own team. Like the Mo'o. The Mo'o who ate one another.

As if reading Manna's mind, a wind-torn Momi ducked out of Lo-lupe's way, a thin, evil smile stretched across her face. Then, faster than Lo-lupe could veer around, she angled her heaving, wet chest to the right and smattered the rebounding, blood-spewing sting ray with all her might. Flipping out of control in the wind, Lo-lupe spiraled straight for Pahau – but seconds before he reached her, he stretched out his tar-skinned, hook-fingered claws and spread open an enormous wrinkled-gum Mo'o mouth – and that's when Manna heard it.

The anguished cries of devoured, frightened children, trying to escape from the Mo'o's long throbbing throat.

"AAAY!" Manna and Pahau gripped their hair and screamed with the other children – and with a gurgly slup, the child-eating Mo'o swallowed Pahau's head. Then flopping her squirming body high in the air, it swallowed her whole in three sloppy, throat-heaving gulps.

Speechless, Manna watched a grinning Momi and her Maui almost double in size. Then, buzzing like a thousand swarming bees, the tongue-flicking Mo'o flopped down on Pahau's empty isle and sunk deep into the bloodied Mo'o waters.

Fear scraped the back of Manna's neck, and her heart pounding scared, she turned on Ailani and howled, "How do we get out?"

Instantly warm, Ailani's kind eyes filled with pity. Then her skin glowed a haunting-moon yellow and her soft pink lips hummed, "No one escapes death, Manna," – and Manna understood.

The children fought in one of Hawaii's underworlds, submerged in a bad Hawaiian man's hell.

"HO'O MAKA!" roared Momi. Then she smashed the gourd before her with her smooth, black stone Fetcher. Whistling as loud as the sizzling hot wind that scraped around Manna, the gourd streaked towards Waka's chest, leaving a twinkling orange trail in its mist – and right before it reached her, it exploded into a long-fanged, rabid wolf-dog.

Bugging her coal-black eyes, Waka stuck out her round baby-doll chest, sucked in one brave breath, and whipped her Fetcher, two-handed, above her head. Then using all her weight, she swung it down hard, onto the wolf dog's face. Missing his nose, her Fetcher cracked the growling dog's fanged bottom teeth, and lightning fast, the dog snapped its horrible mouth shut ... onto Waka's club. Then, playing a fatal tug of war, he dragged her, kicking and screaming, off her misty blue island – and feeding noisily, two waiting, lip-smacking Mo'o sucked her down by her fat, squirming toes.

"Ho, da shameless!" growled Aikoa. "She when pick on da little keeds!" – and in sudden agreement, and with a deafening Hawaiian beat, all the older male cousins zipped around to Aikoa's side and formed a solid line – between Momi and a far off Iki and Hi'u.

Swelling with purple, veined-neck fury, Momi bellowed, "HO'O MAKA!" right before she drilled the hovering gourd into Aikoa's face – and in an instant, Manna remembered.

Moku said anything out here could be permanent.

With a cool zup and double drum beat, her island banged against Mano's – and the flying gourd peeled back its tanned, glowing skin and transformed into a shrieking, pus-oozing hag.

Without blinking, Aikoa clubbed the hag in the head, and losing one rotten, hanging ear that slapped Momi in the forehead and stuck, the stinking, flesh-dripping hag flopped backwards and propelled towards a sickened, red-faced Pu-pele.

"WAH!" shrieked Pu-pele, right when the hag reached her face, and with a right-handed swipe, she slapped it out of the air. Hissing horribly, the hag hit the grey Mo'o water and melted into a blood-red puddle of boils.

"Ooh!" shivered Pu-pele, her face puckered sour and her fingers flinking the air. "It touched me!" – and all of sudden Manna thought it funny ... that Aikoa and Pu-pele feared the same thing.

Growing old.

Giggling, she glanced back at Mano.

His round eyes scared and his right hand groping out, Mano lunged forward the moment their eyes met, as if trying to jump onto Manna's island for protection ... but both his feet stay rooted, ankle deep, in the wintery, white cliffs of Mauna Kea. Frowning, Manna wondered if her little island could fit them both – or if he'd just knock them both into some waiting lizard's mouth.

"HAH!" cried Aikoa, right before she whacked the gourd with her Fetcher. In an instant, the yellow-clawed hag lit for Pu-pele's face, and gasping, Manna realized.

Pu-pele didn't hear Kau growl, "Grip your Fetcher!" – so she left hers behind with Tutu, in the mo'olelo circle.

"Witch!" screamed Pu-pele, as she punched the hag square in the nose and sent her flailing backwards to a nearby Aikoa – but with a gut-shaking thump, Aikoa's island lunged forward and closed the space Pu-pele had to react, at the same time she whacked the surprised hag in the butt.

Jerking back at Pu-pele, the witch ripped at her surprised face with terrible cracked claws, and sprayed sizzling red spit into Pu-pele's now flaming orange-red hair.

"Stop it – stop it – stop it!" screamed Pu-pele, both her palms slapping wildly at the greedy flesh-ripping hag. Then suddenly, above a heart-shaking rumble, Pu-pele swelled five times her size, her brown hands clasped high above her head as she roared, "I AM PU-PELE!"

BAM!

With an earthshaking bam, Pu-pele slammed her double fist down and bonked the witch right on top of her head – and it split in half! Her left, smoke-filled head side flopped down to her shoulder, but the right stayed erect, its orange, yellow-veined eye rolling around in dizzy circles and its ear hole tooting loudly, like a passing steam train.

Her island shuddering from the impact, Manna almost giggled as the confused ear-tooting witch fumbled, awkwardly, to squeeze back together her empty, lolling head – but before she could, Pu-pele knelt down on her orange lava-oozing island, and with a quick swirling motion, gathered two molten fireballs in her hands. Raising both balls high above her head, she sneered,

"Eat this, you old hag!" and fast pitched them both.

Crackling furiously, the fireballs tore straight for the witch's face, and without touching her, whistled through her split, open skull.

Surprised she missed, the witch and Pu-pele *both* cocked their heads ... their lips hung open and wet.

"UH! UH!" groaned Aikoa, as she batted the sizzling balls away from her face, at the same time Ku-hai barked, "NO GODS!" – and with a double explosion, the balls cracked across the witch's turned back – and exploded into orange-red, needle-point glass that sliced deep, peeling gashes off the witch's glowing flesh and exposed her smoke-filled, breathing lungs ... and pulsing, death-black heart.

Furious Aikoa hit her, the yellow-eyed witch spun around to face Aikoa, her head sides flopping in a sudden golden wind – and huffing in quick excitement, Pu-pele scooped fireball after fireball off her glowing lava island and pelted Aikoa's chest.

Without thinking, Aikoa batted each ball back and smattered the angry witch's breasts – and burning off fast, with a fried rotten-egg smell, the witch's torso melted down and exposed a stark white, dusty-dry animal's ribcage.

"MA-KAAAAAY!" the witch screeched a scratchy war cry – and forgetting the game, she flung her hooked claws forward and tore straight for Aikoa's neck.

Confused, Aikoa stuttered a quick, "Ki-ki-ki..." Then remembering her courage, she jammed both of her fists into her stiff, sturdy hips, stuck out her broad chest, and crouched down low, just like her Fetcher.

BAM!

With a gut-shaking bam, the witch hit a stony-faced Aikoa, and with the force of dynamite explosives, the witch, Aikoa and her island erupted into twinkly white dust. Mushrooming high into the sky, their dust formed a far-stretching cloud – and at that moment, Manna knew.

She wouldn't be that brave ... in her dying moment.

Breathless, she watched Aikoa's cloud disperse, directly above her head – and then it touched her. A tiny, luminous, white spider ... hung by a single moist strand of web.

Blinking back tears, Manna wiped the baby spider away.

Aikoa hadn't turned to dust. She transformed into a thousand newborn baby spiders – and instantly, the creepies hit Manna, as a million shivering insect legs scurrying up her spine.

"Watch out for him," Ailani's voice sounded small and scared. "He's behind you."

Looking up, past Ku-hai, Manna's eyes met a haunting sight.

Hunched over, alone in this world, a pale-faced Ailani stood on the very edge of her isle while a frenzied, swimming ring of hungry torso-twisting Mo'o snapped greedily at her slender white toes – and dripping a suicidal brown, her wet, coin-shaped eyes stared lifelessly at her sister ... as if she'd already drowned in her trickling, rainbow-colored hair.

"Ailani, no!" cried Manna. "It could be permanent!" – but not hearing her, Ailani snorted her last, "Humph!" Then she pressed her right fist to her quivering pink lips and touched her delicate toe to the rough Mo'o waters.

SNAP!

With a snurgling snap, a fat, forked, black tongue whipped round Ailani's leg and yanked her in. Smearing into a rainbowed blue, like an oil slick upon the water, Ailani ceased to exist.

Hollow, Manna held her breath and watched in horror as an enormous, wrinkled, black-clawed foot scraped across Ailani's island and wrenched it underwater.

"Ho'o maka!" sing-songed Pu-pele.

The tanned Mo'o gourd glowed before her – because the player that won the last match got to restart the game. But instead of whacking the gourd, Pu-pele touched the tip of her right index finger to her fat, lolling tongue. Then she licked the tip of her left. Then slowly, she tilted her chubby brown face towards Manna and smiled, ever so teasingly, before she touched her fingertips together – right below her soft, rounded chin. Sizzling like fried bacon, her fingertips glowed a wicked orange-yellow ... and a thin wisp of smoke trailed off them and snaked eerily between her glimmering green eyes.

Suddenly shaking with hate, Manna felt a dizzying fury blast through her head.

No one! No one ever stuck around to help her out!

Then she heard it, growling low in her gut.

It is me .... ME-E-E they will fear the most!

Determined, she gripped her Fetcher tight and readied herself ... for Pu-pele to bat that hideous gourd at her.

SLAP!

"OW!" Pu-pele yowled, right after she slapped the burning hot gourd with her palm. Then buckling to her knees, she squeezed her right wrist with her left hand ... and stared at her grey, drizzling right palm.

Flipping slowly, like a feather blown north in the wind, the gourd floated over Ku-hai's head towards a lone but ready Iki – and wounded, Pu-pele realized. Without her Fetcher or her right hand, she knelt helpless ... at the mercy of her enemies and cousins. But with forty successive, quick water slaps, a long, slick, black wooden bridge unraveled off Momi's solid island and touched the eastern, glowing beach of Pu-pele's.

Her anxious eyes gleaming a sapphired blue, Momi motioned Pu-pele to join her – and eager for her sister's protection, Pu-pele leapt onto the bridge, in a dead run.

FROMP!

With a loud fromp, an enormous Mo'o head shot out of the water and swallowed Pu-pele whole ... because the bridge was a Mo'o's long disguised tongue!

Coming down hard on Pu-pele's island, the gorged, smiling Mo'o licked its wet, satisfied gums and sunk slowly into the bloodied Mo'o waters.

"She's so stupid!" sneered Momi. Her devious, frosted eyes glinted back at Manna.

WHACK! SMACK!

Working together, Iki fast passed the gourd to Kau, who floated right behind Momi – and Kau smattered it into her back. Caught off guard, Momi barely had time to whip around ... and face an open-mouthed Lo-lupe.

Instantly, Lo-lupe sunk his gums into Momi's white throat, and with a horrible gurgling sound, devoured half her neck. Her eyes bulged with pain, Momi fast cracked the back of his skull with her long, heavy Fetcher.

Howling so loud Manna's island shook, Lo-lupe released Momi's throat, then snapped back at her bun – and twisting around quickly, Momi double kicked him in the gut with her gigantic, thundering feet. The wind knocked out of him, Lo-lupe fluttered back – and tangled in her long, shimmering blonde hair, Momi lost it.

No one *ever* touched her bun – much less unraveled it!

Shrieking like a banshee, she lit on top Lo-lupe's back and tore at him like some crazed demon. Kicking and slapping and beating and kneeing him, she let out a long bloodcurdling howl. Then, her eyes icy blue and her hair streaming blonde, she ripped off both of his wings!

Flipping around as they fell down through the air, Lo-lupe roared defiantly and whipped his arrowed tail around Momi's thick chest, as if meaning to hold her still – and her nose an inch from his, Momi squeezed her big hands round his pulsing grey throat, curled in her strained purple lips, and growled, "DROWN! YOU IGNORANT ....!"

CRASH!

With a wet, booming crash, Momi and Lo-lupe hit the water and sunk – and scattering like frightened fish, all the Mo'o lizards scurried out of their way ... and that's when Manna heard them – Kau's second words.

"Kill your fears!"

That was the point of the game. To face and kill your fears.

Shuddering, Manna looked at Momi's still afloat island and wondered.

If she drowned Lo-lupe, could she come back ... and join in the game?

"Yeah," muttered Mano. "She's stupid like you."

As if he were any better, Manna glared round at him and barked, "Stay on your island!" – lest the idiot try to bolt onto hers.

"Ho!" chuckled Kokala. "Betta watch out for that one!" – and snorting out of hairy, flared nostrils, Kau clenched his hard fist in the air and growled back, "More betta, you watch out for deez!"

Laughing through brilliant white teeth, all the leftover male cousins crinkled their brave, handsome faces, and suddenly shirtless, their smooth hulking chests gleamed a dark ruddy brown as they cocked their Fetchers forward ... with their rigid, green-tattooed arms.

Almost jealous, Manna looked around at their unnerved warrior stances.

All of them had overcome their fears, long ago, while she and Mano stood quaking in their shoes. But wait – the cousins didn't have shoes on, and neither did she!

Panicking, Manna looked down, to see if she lost her shirt, too!

"Ho! Ho! Ho!" someone yelled, and with a raking, hot swirl and the harsh beat of four approaching war drums, the cousins' isles whipped high into the air – and Manna realized.

A Hawaiian drum beat loud and distinct ... each time someone's island moved.

CRACK! – SNAP, SNAP, SNAP, SNAP, SNAP!

With a vicious crack, Kau whacked the gourd, and snapping menacingly as it flipped through the air, it barreled straight for Iki's head. But right before it reached him, the gourd transformed into a broad-shouldered, naked, moss-covered, shark-headed man ... with a second huge snapping shark's mouth embedded in his back!

Her blood thinned, Manna heard herself squeak when the shark man spun around (his snapping back inches from Iki's face) and his horrible razor-fanged shark head glared hungrily at her ... just like Pele's brother did!

THU-THUMP! – BAP!

Flipping his island upside down with a double thump, Iki escaped the shark man's hungry, snapping back – and brutally hard, bapped his beady-eyed shark face.

Continuing faster in his backwards path, the shark man flattened out and transformed into a glowing, electric-tailed, rib-bodied eel. Then, slither quick, the eel tried to stuff its face down Hi'u's throat – but his white lips clenched together, Hi'u smattered its head with a ground-quaking,

WHAP!

Jerking back, the eel sailed towards Iki's head, but halfway there, it morphed into a brilliant, blinding-white mouth.

RA-TA-TA-TA ... WHACK!

"WA-A-A-AH!"

Flying too fast, his drum rattling quickly, an overanxious Moku nailed the shiny mouth before it could open – and wailing out loud, it shot straight for Kau's head. But right before it got there, it transformed into a gorgeous, naked, brown woman, her feet and hands flying ahead of her body, as if she meant to touch her toes in the air.

His eyes bulged and ears beet red, Kau hammered the woman, way before she reached him – and stumbling backwards, she burst into a beaming, crystally white light.

KA-BOOM!

In under a second, Moku's island shot forward with a resounding, "Kaboom!" – and his Fetcher exploded in the midst of the light – and streaking forward, the luscious woman grabbed for Kau's cheek, at the same time something bright red and flickering wet flew out from between her toes and distracted his wondering eyes.

With a slippery slap, the woman's body collided against Kau's turned head, and they both flopped into the waiting Mo'o waters.

Hissing softly, Kau's misty island and the red thing disappeared.

"He falls for it every time!" sniggered a jubilant Moku, and coughing nervously, their ears slightly red, all the cousin's shuffled around on their isles.

Not the least bit embarrassed, Moku held out both palms and cried, "WHAT?"

Their eyes suddenly on Manna, all the cousins froze – and jerking around to look at her, a wave of horror washed over Moku's face as he breathed out loud, "Oh man!" Then trying to recover quickly, he smacked the gourd back to Iki.

THU-THUMP! – BAP!

Lightning fast, Iki flipped and bapped the shark man in the head, using the same trick as before, except this time, his island streaked towards Hi'u as fast as the eel it transformed into.

Clubbing the eel, his lips clenched tighter than before, Hi'u didn't notice Iki hovering right above his head – but the shark man did.

Jumping up at Iki, the shark man accidentally bonked his pointed nose on Iki's close, ready club – and with a bluish-white flash, he instantly bounced backwards as an eel and jabbed Hi'u in the neck ... with a long electric-blue pronged tail.

Arms open too wide and a shocked look on his face, as though he was being electrocuted, a sweating Hi'u vibrated for a minute. Then he and his island exploded into ashen dust.

"Whoa!" breathed Mano.

"Good one!" hooted Moku, because Iki hardly ever won.

Enjoying his victory, Iki did three smooth, drum-rolling loop-the-loops in the air. Then suddenly clever, and right above Kokala's chortling head, he bapped the gourd at his unsuspecting cousin's jiggling gut.

SSSSSS-IH! ... Ri-ti-ti-ti-ti-ti-ti!

With a dry sucking sound, like a wrinkled great-grandmother puckering up for a kiss, the gourd's tan skin peeled off against an arid, stale wind, to reveal a grey-dusted, lemony-eyeballed skeletal man – and at once, the air filled with a menacing, bone-clinking rattle ... and Manna could feel it.

Someone's gruesome death loomed near.

Too scared to think, she clutched both of her ears ... to block out the skeleton's high-pitched, nerve-wracking clatter.

Suddenly barreling forward, the starved, noisy skeleton rolled his cracked, greedy head, wiggled his long pointed fingers and clacked his hungry, split, stained teeth – anxious to gnaw away Kokala's fatty, tanned gut – and that's when Manna saw them.

A thousand brown-speckled, needle-legged spiders scurried nervously over the skeleton's sunbaked ribs and shimmied up his twisted, bleached spine – their stiff jointed legs clicking noisily against his dry brittle bones.

Their hurrying legs made that unnerving sound!

"WAH!" Kokala screamed femininely, just like Pu-pele – and right when the skeleton's mouth reached his deep, sucked-in navel, he right-hand swiped it out of the air.

Crunching loudly, the skeleton hit the grey Mo'o water and splintered into a pile of marrow-less bones.

Feeding noisily, a frenzied swarm of gum-mouthed, starving Mo'o snapped at the bones ... and with loud, juicy, abdomen-bursting pops, they gobbled down all the live, swimming spiders.

"Gross!" groaned Kokala, right before someone yelled, "Eh! You supposed to hit that to somebody!"

"Why boddah?" Kokala grumbled back. "I ain't no skinny-kine guy! I *need* somethin' decent for eat!"

Then throwing his thick arms up, he backflipped into the air, tucked his strong knees into his massive breast, and cannonballed into the water. Making a wave so large it swiped all the feeding Mo'o away, Kokala vanished – and with a quick, "Blub! Blub!" his cloud-covered isle disappeared, too.

Biting her lip, Manna wished she had the guts to follow him in – and souring fast, a caustic, bitter taste filled her spit ... because some of Kokala's splash landed on her lip.

"Pith!" Manna spit left – and startled, almost fell off her island.

Only three feet away, Iki's smiling, upside-down, twinkly-eyed face hovered ... and his raised Fetcher aimed for her neck.

Thunk.

Thunk.

Thunk.

Listening to her heart thunk in the back of her head, Manna knew.

It was her turn to face her fears – and any second, a hate-filled, snarling Moho would lunge forward and rip out her throat ... because it was *him* that she feared the most.

Fingering her Fetcher, she peered into Iki's steadfast gaze, and with a sudden sinister rush, she felt hot adrenaline tear through her bones.

Today was the day! She would do it. The thing she dreamed of most.

She would bash in Moho's ugly ... stinking ... insult-spitting mouth!

No matter what it said or how wide it opened its black-gummed, jagged hole – she'd shove her club down its throat and silence him – forever!

BAP!

Without looking, Iki whacked the gourd to Moku. But not fooled by Iki's ruse, Moku lurched forward, and with an earsplitting, lightning-shattering crash, he smattered the electric-white mouth in the teeth.

Whistling like haphazard fireworks, the mouth's glinting, scattered teeth tore straight for Iki's upside-down head. But right before they reached him, they crowded together, into two open lines, and formed a huge teeth-gnashing sneer – that stretched back and grew into Iki's double-jawed, moss-covered shark man.

Jerking his spit-dripping, razor-lined mouth open, the growling shark man bit at Iki's head – but just in time, Iki flipped his island over the shark man's snapping, wet back and landed on top the brown-foaming Mo'o water – at the same time he nailed the shark man in the butt.

With a surprised yelp, the shark man spiraled forward, his arms and legs flailing – but suddenly, he regained control and with a rocket-powered roar, whipped round and barreled straight for Iki's throat.

Reacting fast, Iki ducked down low on his island – but he didn't have to. Moaning somberly, the shark man transformed into Moku's shiny, lip-glossed mouth and swerved up, out of Iki's way.

"EH!" yelled Iki – and with a double-handed tug, he yanked hard on his Fetcher. But using all her weight, a wrinkled, silver-eyed Mo'o jerked it away ... and with a sloppy gummed suck, swallowed it down whole – because Iki let it touch her water.

CRASH!

With a reverberating crash, Moku splintered the surprised wailing mouth – and instantly, as if knowing Iki crouched defenseless, it exploded into the hungry, savage-eyed shark man ... that tore straight for Iki's quivering chest – and that's when Manna noticed.

Iki's chest didn't quiver. His panicked heart pounded through his bare skin!

Horrified, Manna pressed her hands to her mouth, knowing she'd puke the moment the shark man fed on her cousin's shivering red heart – and in final despair, Iki's dry lips stretched open and let out a long horrible cry.

"WHA-A-A-A-A-ALE!"

Skidding to a halt, ten feet from Iki's sweating chest, the shark man spun round, left and right, blinking his stupid black eyes, in search of his enemy – but not seeing a whale, he glared down impatiently at Iki's simpering, white face.

"Okay, okay," stuttered Iki, his palms up, as if to surrender, and his eyes opened too wide. "Not really. But I was thinking ... maybe deez time, I go catch you one fish!"

Exaggerating his ability, Iki spread his hands as far as he could, to show the shark man how long.

"One *bi-i-ig* kine fish!"

Clicking all his nasty yellow-stained teeth, the shark man shook his head slowly, but not giving up, Iki grinned,

"How 'bout one squid den?" – and his scrawny eyebrows raised high, he swooped his thin right-hand fingertips to his puckered red lips, then kissed them into the air, like an Italian. "Tastes ono!"

With a short, "Guhuff!" the shark man almost smiled – and oddly entertained by his charming trickster feast, his coal-black eyes twinkled. Then, with a deep growling croak that made Manna's neck skin crawl, he gave Iki a small reward.

"How 'bout, deez time, you get one head start."

Instantly, Iki's face lit up and jumping high into the air, his arms already spinning in a crawl, he dove into the Mo'o water – but instead of sinking, his body scurried along the surface, like a water bug frightened away.

"One," the shark man growled and Iki paddled faster, flittering quickly between Moku and Ku-hai's floating isles.

"Two," growled the shark man, his back teeth gnashing in hungry anticipation, and with a wiggly-tailed skitter, Iki disappeared into the grey Mo'o mist.

"Three," growled the shark man – at the same time his back mouth snapped, "Go!" – and with a long forward thrust, the shark man arched into the water, without making a splash. Then, his back breathing heavily, he slithered slow and smooth along the surface, as if giving Iki a little more time ... and Manna had a feeling he would play a game of cat and mouse. Then she wondered.

If she jumped in and swam fast enough, could she escape ... unharmed?

"Guess without Aikoa, its just me and you, Brah!" grinned Moku. His warm brown eyes twinkled at an upright, crinkly-eyed Ku-hai.

"Yeah, 'cept deez time, da winner no need put up with da rags!"

Their muscular chests flexing in rhythm, both boys burst into laughter – but Manna didn't see what was so funny.

"Finish up, den," barked Ku-hai, and smiling sly, Moku chortled, "Duck soup, Brah! Two for one!" – but feigning something, Ku-hai smirked at his cousin.

"You tink, Brah?"

Puzzled, Moku frowned at Ku-hai – but without explaining, Ku-hai slow batted him the gourd. Then, for the first time, he readied himself, as if half-expecting Moku to smash the gourd at him instead of the twins.

Thu-thunk.

With a quick double thunk, something large shifted behind Manna, at the same time something cold slithered up her knee, like a forked Mo'o tongue ... tasting – but her heart frozen in her chest, she didn't dare take her eyes off the tanned, glowing gourd that loomed ready, before Moku.

"He's looking out ... for you!" a girl hissed, and Manna saw him. His hunger-glazed, beady-round, yellow and white eyes peered out of the gourd's black, hollow neck in search of her ... his ill-fated prey.

CRACK! – "Grr-grr-grr-grr-grr..."

With a back-breaking crack, the gourd exploded against Moku's club, and twisting out of it, three grumbling, flesh-gobbling, evil, cloaked men raced neck-in-neck towards Manna – their cracked, toothy smiles stretched open across their rotten, wrinkled faces, and their long black coats swallowing all the light left behind them.

FROMP!

Before Manna could react, everything turned pitch black and something piercing cold raked through her cheeks and stabbed through the back of her head.

Stunned, her death rushing upon her, Manna almost dropped her Fetcher when a frightened Mano screamed, "AAAAAAY!"

Then, with a thundering crack, the Mo'o world filled with a blinding white light, and in an instant, Manna's face began to melt.

"AAAAAAY!" Mano kept screaming, and horrified, Manna watched a pulsing white light drag her brother forward, his island thumping and swerving in a hot, swirling wind.

"BWAH!" someone choked out loud, and the white light seemed to fade – because Mano stuffed it down Moku's throat.

It was Mano who dragged the light – not the other way around!

His eyes bulged and neck swollen five times its size, Moku convulsed left and right, his hands clasped tight under his chin. Then, with a gut-wrenching pop, his distended, air-filled body burst, like an over-stretched helium balloon – and his beautiful brown skin sheared away.

Glistening silver on Moku's tiny half-submerged isle, a thin, naked skeleton stood shivering, his long bony fingers clutched over his see-through chest, trying uselessly to hide the giant, sweaty, red heart that beat within – and at once, Manna felt sorry for the scared, lonely guy.

FLUB! GULP!

With a sloppy wet flub, a ten-foot Mo'o flopped onto Moku's island and gulped down his heart – and wisping away in a thin, silvery smoke trail, his heartless skeleton disappeared.

Suddenly sad, Manna felt herself cry as she watched the sly, satisfied Mo'o lick drippy red blood off her wrinkled, cracked lips ... and Moku's island disappear into the water's gurgling depths.

"Pathetic!" someone spit in Manna's ear.

Expecting Momi returned, Manna spun around, just in time to see a dark, shadowy figure disappear – and shuddering, she wondered.

Can the light-swallowing dark guys that haunt Mano hang around?

Thunk ... thunk .... thunk.

With a heavy thunking sound, Mano flipped his Fetcher in his palm, as if choosing the best end to grip – and bouncing on his toes, ready for the gourd to reappear, he glared, squinty-eyed, at cousin Ku-hai.

His stance unchanged, Ku-hai's chest gleamed a hot ruddy brown and his piercing dark eyes glowed a blackened evil ... and tingling from head to toe, Manna could feel it.

Both boys burned with hate.

"HAH!" screamed Mano, and with a chest-swinging slug, he batted the half-appeared gourd.

WHACK!

Ricocheting off Ku-hai's long Fetcher, the gourd ripped forward – and out popped the grumbling, old dark guys – at the same time thick blood spurt from Ku-hai's bubbling, split lip.

"HAH!" Mano growled again – and with a bone-cracking, "Whap! Whap! Whap!" he swung his Fetcher round in a hard semicircle and clocked all three guys in the chin. Their jaws broken and hanging by loose, wobbly hinges, they reeled backwards, and with a deep sucking sound, jammed back into the crooked-necked, spiraling gourd.

WHACK!

Using all the strength of his solid, rippling torso, Ku-hai lobbed the gourd high into the air, right above Mano's head – and wiping dark red blood off his torn, bruise-swollen eyes, Mano tried hard to focus on the darkening gourd – and Manna looked again.

Ku-hai's torso didn't ripple, it bubbled – with fleshy, red boils that slipped off his stripped-away chest, because the gourd melted any flesh that it touched. Then the world went black.

"AAAAY!" Mano cried in the dark – and shivering, Manna almost felt glad she couldn't see him get eaten.

"AAAAY!" Mano howled out in pain. "AAAAY! AAAAY! AAAAY!" – and sickened, Manna knew.

The vicious dark guys ate him piece by piece.

With a quick scuffling, bone-crunching sound, the world filled with light – and the cloaked dark guys flipped off Mano, their skulls cracked open and sticky grey matter hanging out.

Almost puking, Manna buckled.

Sheared off Mano's exposed white skull – thick, fleshy, hand-size patches of pink, bulbous skin hung, dripping red – their bloodstained hair standing on end – and streaked down his gnawed arms and clawed-away chest, glistening black juice splashed against his strained, rock-clutching toes.

WHACK!

Ku-hai's Fetcher cracked the gourd, at the same time a bloody piece of his cheek fell to the ground – and dizzy, Manna couldn't look any more.

WHACK! – "HAH!" – WHACK! – "HAH!" – WHACK! – "HAH!"

The loud gory battle raged on – and floating forward, ever so slowly, Manna's island gurgled low in her ear, "War. What men wage when they fear!" – and she didn't like it. The way men fought, in bloody resolution, to obtain treasures and manly pride.

It had to end – their destruction of human life!

WHACK!

Splintering her ears, Ku-hai's club whacked the gourd, and without meaning to, Manna's island stopped moving a few inches behind him ... their handsome, ever-strong leader.

Rippling down his long curved spine, his bulging, tanned back muscles glistened in the soft Mo'o light, and his thick brown hair glinted with carefree lightning-blonde streaks ... and wanting so badly to touch him – this tall, tantalizing boy – Manna raised her palms to his shoulders.

WHACK!

Ku-hai smacked the gourd, his bunched biceps undulating with taut gleaming sinews and his solid thigh muscles clenched up with masculine force – and Manna raised her hands a little higher.

He didn't know she was there. She could touch him ... right on his curly, thick Hawaiian hair.

WHACK! – "AAAAY! AAAAY! AAAAY!" – THUNK!

With a resounding whack, Ku-hai hammered the gourd at Mano – and finally getting the better of him, the greedy, splintered-tooth dark guys tore angrily at his gut ... at the same time Manna's heavy Fetcher came down with a thunk, on the back of Ku-hai's unsuspecting head.

Crumpling off balance, Ku-hai toppled, chest first, into the dark Mo'o water – and snapping at his back like a frenzied school of piranha, a hundred foot-long, claw-scraping Mo'o fed on his fast-peeling skin.

Sinking slowly as he became eaten, Ku-hai clenched without shivering a muscle. But right before he vanished into the water's depths, he rolled on his back, his taut face smiling up like a satisfied drowned man taking some deep, dark secret to the grave – and in her brain, Manna heard his voice chuckle, "All's fair, eh? In love and war," – and she understood.

He enjoyed this game ... against Mano and her.

Shivering, she glanced up at her brother – and instantly chilled, her heart stood still.

A silly smile plastered across his blood-streaked, boyish face, as if victory meant more than his wounds – and at that moment she knew he enjoyed it, too. The fight, and the murder ... and in the wind, she heard those same words.

Where the wombless man – opens a channel, by sacrificing one in death.

Her eyes wet with tears, she hated them all – for making their wars and delighting in their vicious displays of stout competition. But mostly, she hated them for involving her – a life-generating girl!

Never again would she fight ... not even to save her own life!

Thunk ... thunk .... thunk.

Mano flipped his stone club in his palm, anxious to get on with the game – and frowning at him, Manna let their eyes meet.

"Don't worry," whispered Mano, his confident eyes glittering bright. "It'll be quick!" – and with a searing, hot rush, indignant anger washed through her cheeks.

How dare he think he could beat her – fast! She was better than him, that stupid, clumsy, skinny, little boy – and she could beat him at this, or anything else!

"Huh-hmm!" the gourd hummed, as if trying to get her attention – and Manna thought it odd that it hovered before her. Then she remembered.

She beat Ku-hai, so *she* was supposed to start the next game.

Thunk ... thunk .... thunk.

As if egging her to face him, Mano flipped his Fetcher a few more times and flashed a crooked-toothed, teasing white smile – but determined, Manna held her ground.

In the name of good, she would stand here for all eternity – because murder reeked of all that is evil – and if she didn't hit the gourd first, Mano couldn't start his wicked man's game.

"Grr-grr-grr ... Puh! Puh!" the gourd growled and smacked its lips, and startled, Manna backed up.

Something weird was going on.

The gourd's smooth, shiny skin dripped with frothy white juice and its rounded length segmented into fleshy, rippling coils, as if it held back a stubby, bleached-out earthworm.

"Grr-grr-grr ... Puh! Puh!" the gourd kept grumbling, and suddenly scared, Mano shifted his island left, around the now throbbing, skin-shedding gourd, and hid behind Manna – but at once, a stale, sticky wind sucked him forward ... right under the gourd.

S-S-S-S-SLUP!

With a nauseating slup, the gourd's slimy, transparent skin sloughed off, and keeping its cylindrical shape, slipped right over Mano – and stuck inside the skin, his bulgy-eyed face pressed flat against its rubbery walls, he screamed a muffled, suffocating, "BUH! BUH!"

"Ssssssih!" the gourd breathed in deep through two round, tan-striped nostrils buried in a yellowish-white, horned pig nose ... that squirmed, long and wormy, out of the gourd's quivering neck – and so sickened she couldn't move, Manna heard herself croak, "SHED IT!"

Listening as always, Mano started to squirm.

"MU-U-UH!" the gourd moaned, as it convulsed its slick, heated body, and with an urgent wheezing breath, Mano's head popped out of the skin, but both his arms and Fetcher stay down – trapped.

"S-S-S-S-SSIT!" the gourd sprayed a milky white juice. Then lunging backwards, a breathing worm-thing popped out – except its head was at the other end of its ribbed, gleaming body!

Hooded, round, and larger than the moon, the thing's fly-eyed, wrinkled head twisted slowly towards Manna, and oozing soupy, putrefying enzymes out of its thick salivary glands, it clicked two long, pointed, corpse-scraping mouth hooks at her neck – and in an instant, Manna's stomach wrenched.

Nothing. No nothing could be worse than this ... sputum-dripping MAGGOT!

Her breath suddenly short, Manna felt hot panic fill her heart – and with a croaking grumble, Mano emerged from the skin – at the same time his dark guys flew out of the maggot's wet, breathing butt.

"HO'O MAKA!" Mano roared, and dizzy with fear, Manna fell to her knees, clutching both hands before her, and prayed, *Mother Mary! Don't let that thing decompose and eat me!*

FLUP! – "HAH!"

With a heavy flup, the spit-spewing maggot banged its head against Manna's double-clutched, raised Fetcher – and Mano yelled loud as he beat away his fears.

Panting, Manna tried hard not to scream as her maggot spiraled backwards ... and his bubbling spit ate painfully through her arm and face skin.

Then she smelled it. Her own fast-rotting flesh.

BAM!

The maggot and dark guys collided, midair, then quickly switching places, they transformed into one another and tore back to their bleary-eyed victims.

It was the gourd she and Mano fought ... and each other – because Manna didn't start the game, the gourd did it for her – and it forced them to play double time. Every time Mano hit his dark guys a maggot would attack her, at the same time her maggot headed back to him!

"KA-WHO!" someone roared in Manna's ear, and all her hairs standing on end, she spun around, blinded, and accidentally smashed a surprised maggot in the mouth – but much faster, Mano sent back the dark guys. Grumbling angrily, they flipped around one another, then sucked together with a quick, "FRUH! FRUH! FRUH!" – and turned into the vampire-fanged maggot.

"UH!" Manna groaned, as she beat off a heavy succession of slobbering maggots, "UH! UH! UH!" – and bleaching white, her world turned into a soupy, rice pudding, flesh-stinging hell.

"UH!" Manna kept fighting, knowing any moment a face-sucking maggot would sink its pointy flesh-eating hooks into her eyes – then an enormous pillowy-eyed one snapped at her brow.

"UH-H-H!" she groaned out loud, cracking him between his bulging black eyes – and that's when it happened.

The injured maggot puked warm, tapioca, flesh-rotting bile into her open lips, and slipping past her esophagus, it burned her twisted insides ... out.

Horrified, her gut wrought with pain, Manna stared down at her bare, blood-bubbling stomach and knew he was killing her – from the inside out ... because he wouldn't stop beating off his dark guys – and suddenly furious with him, she bellowed, "MANO-O-O-O!"

Distracted, Mano looked up at his sister, and with a quick, "GRAH! GRAH! GRAH!" the three dark guys tore out his guts.

The maggot suddenly vanished, Manna caught sight of her brother's sorry, pain-contorted face – and his frightened, shaking hands.

Quivering bloody wet, Mano's right, bony fingers held in his spilling, blue-veined guts, and his left gripped a blood-soaked, cracked-off bone piece to his skull. But when their eyes met, he instinctively reached out for her – and always clumsy, he tumbled, face first, into the Mo'o water.

Without thinking, Manna lunged forward to save him – and with a skin-searing splash, she belly flopped against the purplish-grey churning water ...

ZUP!
"Hopa hopa r-ryder, Vena shmeltin schnider ..."

Drowsy and bundled in a white, comforting warmth, Manna peered up at Anna's soft singing face – and for the first time, Anna gazed down on Manna with love. Her fine blonde hair smoothed across her pale forehead and tucked behind one dainty white ear, she pressed Manna high to her breast and let her clear, angelic blue eyes twinkle along with her smiling, pink-glossed, singing lips ... and for the first time ever, Manna felt safe and content.

Feeling a tingly joyous chill dance through her chest, Manna closed her tired eyes and enjoyed Anna's thin hugging arms as they encircled her tiny infant body – and bounced her up and down, along with the beat of her cheery, mothering song.

"... *Velter in da bobbin, Flesher in da robbin ...*"

"Umph!"

Something at Manna's feet jerked awake and kicked her tiny toes – and squinching her nearsighted eyes, she peered over her blanket and saw a scrawny, tan-skinned, bundled-up baby boy bouncing in Anna's other arm. His black, ruffled hair still wet, he looked nearly drowned as he scrunched his bright brown eyes and strained to get a good look at her.

"... *Vena shmeltin sunt, Da mock da ryder – BLOOMPS!*"

On *BLOOMPS*, Anna dropped each baby down six inches, as if she accidentally spilled them to the floor, and the other baby thought it was funny. Flashing a friendly, cute smile, he showed off six pointy white teeth – one of them crooked – and suddenly furious, Manna realized.

It was Mano! He followed her again!

"MAI!" commanded Tutu, and Manna obeyed.

"Where'd you go?" asked Pu-pele, her slitted green eyes glimmering jealousy – and confused, Manna frowned at her, past Ailani – in the warm mo'olelo circle.

All the children sat cross-legged ... and okay. None of their damage stayed permanent.

"The winner gets to go somewhere they've been before," humphed Ailani, "the place they want to be the most."

"Kikiki," scoffed Aikoa. Her emerald eyes glared at Pu-pele as she spoke. "Those cheaters ... never deserve nothing."

"Yeah!" grunted Momi. Oddly feminine, her long-fingered white hands waved limp in the air, and her voice filled with an exaggerated girlie trill. "When in doubt, throw your hands up in the air ... and scream like a girl."

Her cheeks burned red, Manna started to object – to tell them she didn't cry out for Mano's help – but before she could, Mano blurted, "Where'd you go?"

Surprised, Manna jerked her head around, one eyebrow raised ... as if he didn't know – and his bright eyes flashing mock innocence, he shot her a white, crooked-tooth grin. Angry he tried to expose her, she clenched all her teeth and spit, "Home!"

"Nazi, that one," scoffed Aikoa. "You can see it in her eyes," and looking down, Manna hoped no one noticed one of them goes in – and that's when it hit her ... that familiar burning hole in her gut.

In Germany, they hated her for being too brown – and here, they hated her for being too white.

"Never leave your body unless there is someone there – you can trust," groaned Tutu. Her high, aristocratic bun sat firmly on top of a lacy green fern wrapping, and her staunch, red-eyed face loomed eerily in a thin strand of moonlight that shone through the mo'olelo hut roof.

"For someone may steal it and your bones ... and your uhane will be lost forever, in the land of the Mo'o, alone, with only spiders to feed your hungry soul," she continued. Then glaring straight down at Manna, she made sure.

"Do you understand?" – and Manna did.

No matter what she did, be she black or white, they'd always find a

reason to hate her .... and with a cold, rustling rush, something scary filled her gut.

Chapter Thirteen

LOLO

"Get dressed!" bellowed Momi. Her harsh voice grated down the long empty hall, at the same time the phone receiver cracked down on its hook. "Uncle Junior's gonna be here in five minutes!"

Jerking awake, Manna stared straight into the loving eyes of her hovering Guardian Angel – and started to cry.

No one could protect her ... from herself – because she was the Keeper of the Devil's Wife. That's why she murdered Ku-hai and let the dark guys eat her brother ... because inside, she was destined to be evil.

Smashing her covers to her cheeks, she smeared salted tears and bitter snot into its fuzzy, white warmth and prayed ... today at church, she'd drown in the Baptismal Font. Then something caught her eye.

A crinkly, red, flower-print string bikini lay at the foot of her bed – and right next to it, in a tidy black pile, sat a pair of shorts with a matching tank top.

Someone left her a gift!

Bursting with excitement, Manna threw off her covers, and tore away her blouse and itchy woolen skirt. Then stripping off her worn, grey panties, she slipped the pre-tied bikini bottom past her thin ankles and over her slender hips – and it fit!

Feeling tingly joy bounce through her chest, Manna tossed the bikini top over her head and squirmed into its tied bows. But still empty, its twinkly red cups sunk in.

Frowning down at her undeveloped breasts, Manna stretched the bottoms of the cups out, along the bikini string, till they were flat – and then the top fit perfectly, too!

Thrilled, Manna snatched up the shorts set and bolted to the bathroom. Then scrambling onto the sink, both knees on either side of the bowl, she stuck her hands on her hips and grinned at the mirror.

Smiling back at her, a thin (but muscular) athletic girl flexed her rippled tummy and tossed back a long mane of blackened red hair – and for a moment, Manna could swear she had Aikoa's surfing stance.

Giggling out loud, she knew – now she'd fit in!

So happy her heart felt like it might burst, she slipped the black tank top over her head and smoothed down its stiff, scratchy decal with her palms – and suddenly snapping out at her, a red-eyed shark filled the bathroom mirror.

"That's mine!" blurted Mano. Caught off guard, Manna jerked back, fell to the floor, and cracked her head against the stone-hard tile.

"Sorry!" muttered Mano, and the back of her head aching as though it had split, Manna glared up at him. Always nosy and bouncing along behind her, he held up a black and red, frilly, long mumu dress and grinned, "This one's yours."

Feeling hot fury sear her cheeks, Manna jumped to her feet, ready to scream, "There's no way I'm putting on that stupid, old lady dress!" – but knowing he couldn't make her do a thing, she jerked on his new black shorts and spit, "*You* wear it!"

"Uncle Junior's taking us to Pahoa before church!" squealed Pu-pele. "To Leilani's ... where all the well-to-do local men go!" – and suddenly, Manna felt sorry for them all. Dressed in her new, loose-fitting, ruffle-lined mumu, Pu-pele looked like the perfect Hawaiian man's daughter – the kind you'd love to introduce your son to.

"Humph!" Ailani snorted. Then sliding her delicate fingers underneath Pu-pele's pouffy, reddish-brown bun, she fastened an orange hibiscus right above Pu-pele's round cauliflower ear. Sparkling with morning dew, the shiny hibiscus perfectly matched Pu-pele's full orange-glossed lips and her orange-red hibiscus-print dress – but distracted by Ailani, Manna barely noticed.

Glossy black and scooped into a French-twist bun, Ailani's pulled up hair exposed her long elegant white neck and small fuzzy white ears – at the same time a double-woven pink plumeria head lei waved above her pale, glowing forehead, and a matching neck lei brushed against her pink and green Hawaiian dress.

Cocking her head, Manna thought it odd that, all of a sudden, Ailani looked like a pink-flowered Menehune girl.

"Ready?" grunted Momi. Suddenly gushing blue behind Ailani, her long ocean-sprayed sapphire mumu clung to her lightly veined, overflowing bosom, as a blue dendrobium orchid drizzled with white pikake off of her snug-fitting bun – and her mouth hanging open, Manna couldn't believe how gorgeously feminine Momi could look.

Then she realized.

The three of them decided to leave her hair wild – so she couldn't compete for any available son. Rolling her dark, round eyes up, Manna thought, *As if I want one.*

SCREECH! BOOM-BOOM!

His brakes screeching and woofers pounding, Junior skidded down the red cinder drive in a grey, primered, four-door Plymouth sedan – and her heart skipping excitedly, Manna shoved through her sisters and tore for the side driveway door – but something stopped her.

Blocking the doorway, five pairs of black rubber slippers lined up, from smallest to largest.

So thrilled her head spun dizzy, Manna jammed her feet into the smallest pair and sailed through the door, straight for Junior's waiting car.

"BUCKALOOSE!" hooted Junior, right before he caught Manna round the waist and slammed her down, bottom first, onto his dusty car hood.

"Trying, eh?" he chuckled, as his twinkling, light brown eyes danced inside his warm, red-cheeked face.

Instantly, Manna loved him like Santa.

"Hooo! P-ella!" whistled Junior, as soon as Manna's sisters walked out the door, and frowning, Manna felt jealousy burn through her bones. But quickly making up for it, Junior put a soft, steady arm around her shoulders and whispered into her hair, "But not as fine as you!"

Happy, Manna felt her toes wiggle and her arms shiver with delight.

No wonder Junior got so many girls!

Letting go Manna, Junior swept the back passenger door open and faked a low valet bow.

"My ladies!" he flirted with her sisters, and giggling like carefree schoolgirls, they all climbed in. Then winging their door shut, he grabbed Manna around the waist with one solid arm and spun her high into the air – at the same time he whipped open the front passenger door and breathed warmly against her cheek, "Ladies first!"

Her heart pittered hopefully, and without meaning to, Manna whispered, "Mahalo."

Smiling wide, both brows raised and his straight white teeth flashing bright, Junior chuckled, "You one local now, so you say, 'Tanks, eh!' "

Biting her lip, Manna felt her chest swell with joy, as if a hot helium balloon filled her body – and at that moment, Junior's paling face dropped.

Something scary loomed behind Manna.

Instinctively, Manna spun around, both fists clenched – and gasped.

Standing there, scuffling from foot to foot, a diaper-wearing Mano grimaced at his uncle, embarrassed – and hanging from his skinny, sunk-in chest, what was left of Manna's black and red dress dangled short, like a midriff, half-torn tank top.

Desperate to do what Manna said, Mano tore apart her dress and fashioned it into a loincloth diaper and matching shirt!

Groaning out loud, Manna thought she would die.

Was he really so stupid he thought she meant, "Wear it!"

Her eyes burning with disgust, Manna whipped off her shorts set and threw it in Mano's face. Then suddenly blind with tears, she clawed at his loose hung diaper.

He ruined it. *He* ruined everything. And now she had to wear his stupid ruined dress!

Gripping tight around her hips, Junior's hairless, rigid arm pulled Manna's bottom into his hard thighs – and just as quick, his other outstretched arm stripped off Mano's diaper and snapped it loudly in the air, as if it was a flag cracking in the wind. Then, liquid smooth, Junior slid round to face a breathless Manna, and cloaked the rectangular piece around her bikini-clad bottom. Running his fingers a quarter of the way in on either side of the cloth, he quickly fastened a long bow-like knot, and in that instant, Manna wore a Hawaiian-style wrap-around skirt.

Without taking his twinkling eyes off of her, Junior snatched Mano's torn-dress tank top from his hand, and slipped it gently over Manna's head. Then running his palm down the small of her back, he fingered her left hand and raised it to his shoulder, as if he wanted to dance. But instead of taking a first step, he leaned far back and let his eyes traverse slowly up and down her half-covered body.

"Now I neva need worry about da townies boddah'ing you," he

smiled sly. Then a hint of jealousy gleamed in his eyes, and he snorted, "Just my gangies ... da local-kine guys!" – and for some reason, Manna felt like she won.

"Chance um, Brah!" challenged Junior. Barreling down the smooth local highway at eighty miles an hour, he dared a wind-torn Mano to go out.

Sitting arms touching, next to Junior, Manna bit her lip and hoped her brother wouldn't go out. It was one thing to let him hang waist-far out the rolled down window – but quite another to tell him to crawl out onto the hood.

His brown eyes round and sparkly, Mano looked back at Manna for approval – and before she could say, "No!" – Junior blurted, "No worries, I got her!"

Without blinking, Mano flopped his chest down on the outside of the windshield and grabbed both wipers.

"UGH!" – THUD!

Groaning out loud, Mano pulled with all his might, and with a heavy thud, his body flipped out the window, flew up against the wind, and slammed down on top of the metal car roof. His eyes bulged and his nose pressed flat against the windshield, he clung to the wipers with his bony fingers, like a spider trying not to blow off.

"Mano!" Manna heard herself squeak. Scrambling onto the seat, she lunged halfway out the window and grabbed his cold, clammy hand.

"Hang on!" she hissed against a sticky, harsh wind, at the same time Junior hollered, "HANG ON!" too – and with a swift right-left, he jolted the car and Manna's feet flew out the window!

BAM!

With a wind-raking flip and a sharp, pain-filled shoulder tug, Manna felt her naked back hammer flat against the windshield and Mano's bony, clinging, wet arms. The wind knocked out of her, she squeezed her tearing eyes shut and couldn't believe it.

Junior would kill them ... for his brother!

Suddenly furious, oxygen pounding red in her head, Manna decided – they'd kill *him* first!

Grabbing Mano's sweaty stick-up hair in both of her hands, she yanked him down onto the windshield, to block Junior's view. Then flattening her back and head against the windshield on the passenger's side, she spread her arms and legs wide ... and smiled.

Howling in her ears, the wind pressed her to the cold glass and she knew – they wouldn't fly off against the hard wind. So either he'd have to stop or wreck his car ... and the last thing he'd remember was her fingers buried deep in his throat!

Sssssit!

Junior squirted his windshield water jets and turned the wipers on, rapid.

"Ho!" Junior pretended to be cleaning his shield. "Get some big kine roaches stuck to my glass!" – and sliding down, Mano slipped from the glass and flopped off the hood. But lightning fast, Manna grabbed him by the shorts and hung on – his head and arms flapping back in the wind, inches from Junior's sneering, red face.

"Like powah surf?" Junior barked, his moon-round pupils stuck wide open, and Manna noticed. The silver can he drank from read, "Primo Beer."

Stone drunk – he wanted the twins to surf on his car!

A blast of icy fear surged through Manna's head, and instantly dizzy, she grabbed Mano's clammy right hand in her left and sprang to her feet ... into a goofy-foot, left-leg-back surfing stance. Yanked forward and up, Mano clambered into an off-balance, bent knee, right-foot-back surfing stance – his nose jammed into Manna's face and his bright brown eyes dancing with glee!

This was it! The fastest, the freest, they'd ever go – through the roaring Hawaiian wind!

Gunning the gas, Junior let out a high-pitched, "Woo-hoo-hoo-hoo!" – and vibrating excitement up Manna's thighs, the car hood rattled up and down, as if it might open, but Manna didn't know it. Caught in a sudden, spiraling wind, her long hair whipped out round her cheeks, and razor-fast, scattered over her naked back. Then whistling loud, it stripped off her bare neck, pulled her cheeks far back, and squeezed her body with a tingly breath-stealing hand.

Unable to see or breathe, Manna spread her toes and hung on for dear life – her heart pumping girlie excitement through her shivering veins.

"Wee-hee-hee!" she heard herself squeal – and with a tight, right hand squeeze, Mano hooted a long "Woo-hoo-hooooo!" back.

"WRAH!" Junior's tires growled, as he hooked left and they struggled to dig into the crackling black cinder stone – and crouching forward, her head almost touching Mano's shaking left shoulder, Manna dug her left heel in deep, like she did when she cutback into the tube.

Switch! Switch! Switch!

A thousand thin, low-hanging branches whipped Manna's ear, and suddenly ripping through a tight, light green tunnel of trees, the car shimmied hard, up and down, as it flew over a pothole-riddled dirt road.

Absorbing all the jarring vibration in her weakening knees, Manna threw her right hand out to get more balance, and closing her eyes, she tilted her nose up to smell the sweet, dewy, fresh air. Full of salt, it almost felt like cool ocean spray.

SMACK!

Without warning, a pink and green guava exploded in Manna's face – and giggling out loud, she smeared its yellow seeds out of her wind-torn eyes ... and licked its sweet, grainy juice off her open lips.

SCRA-A-APE! BAM!

Suddenly losing control, Junior hooked a sharp right – and spun out into a mind-spinning doughnut – and thrown off balance, Mano fell into Manna's chest. His weight yanked her down and slammed her left knee into the metal car hood.

Jerking to a halt, the car engine died and Junior fell out of his car door, laughing.

"JUNIOR!" bellowed Uncle Ku-hai – and shocked, Manna looked up at her Uncle's big blue house.

It looked just like theirs. With the same porch, the same drive, and even the same black lava hill and size!

"You like buds?" Junior simpered small, compared to his angry older brother – and suddenly relaxed, Uncle Ku-hai waved his hand low and smiled, "Shoots, Brah!"

"Be right back," Uncle Junior grinned at Manna – and suddenly blushing, she couldn't help but smile back.

"Watch out for him," hissed cousin Ku-hai, his handsome brown eyes stern and only a few inches from Manna's sweating, red face. "He's lolo in the head."

"Waste time, you talk to them," snorted Aikoa, from their long sea-green porch. "Stay lolo, too. They get their moddah's crazy head."

Huh? thought Manna, her eyes questioning Aikoa.

"What? You tink you normal?" Aikoa squawked, her eyes reddening cruel. "Get dat moddah, only stand in da kitchen, washing her hands, listening to voices talk in her head."

Then turning her back, her hard eyes still on Manna, she slid open her sliding glass door and hesitated long enough to jab, "She make your sisters take care of you keeds. Dat Bigfoot haole one, stay act like your dad – and dat buffalo butt, with da crazy-kine eyes, tink she your mom!" Then glaring into the car, she spat, "And try look at dat stringy-haired, flat-chested one – stay jerking all da time."

Confused, Manna glanced at Mano – but his eyes big and bright, he looked back at her for the answer.

Didn't everyone live like them?

BANG!

At the same time, Aikoa slammed the sliding glass door shut behind her – and the back door of the car snapped open against its hinges. Flowing out fast, Pu-pele climbed the black lava rock hill, towards the sliding glass door.

Thrilled they'd get to see the inside of their cousins' house, Manna leapt off the hood and scampered after her sister – and suddenly hiding at the corner of the long green porch, a fuzzy white dog yelped as they approached.

Bounding onto the lowest step first, Manna almost didn't hear Aikoa bark, "Stay outside, with da dogs!" – but with a loud, sizzling crack, she heard the orange-sized rock smash through the glass and bludgeon Aikoa between the eyes.

Stunned, her mouth hung open and blood gushing out her caved-in forehead – Aikoa stared emptily into the sky – then crumpled into a lifeless heap.

Horrified, Manna's heart stood still.

Pu-pele killed her cousin!

"Who did it?" growled Moho. His cruel black eyes scanned his five shaking children, as they sat side-by-side on their long living room couch.

He did this every time there was trouble. He lined them up and asked them who did it – and when nobody responded, he bloodied Momi's face ... then beat Pu-pele until she slumped down and cried.

Frowning at the ground, her heart aching mad, Manna wondered why he bothered asking. Why didn't he just hit the two oldest girls, instead of including them all – and making them witness his horrible rage? And then she remembered.

Kokala called it Hawaiian love ... and there was no way Moho would ever love her.

Tears suddenly welling in her eyes, Manna couldn't stand it any more. The beatings, the blood, and his hate.

Clenching both fists, she rose slowly to her feet – and for the first time ever, she helped her sisters ... with a soft, bleary-eyed, "Me."

CRACK! – THUD! – BAM!

With a blinding crack, Moho's rock-solid fist hammered the side of Manna's head, and with a heavy body thud, she slammed against the wall and sunk – right before an open-mouthed, sharp-toothed Mano smacked, face first, into the shaking wall and sunk onto her lap. His nose blood smeared across her cheek, Mano groaned softly in her ear, as she lay still and breathless ... waiting to die.

"You stay away!" screeched Ailani, suddenly standing above Manna – and blinded by a spark-spraying white light, Manna couldn't see Moho's long horrified face, but she could feel her brother was in trouble. Fumbling with his sweaty, blood-dripping head, she tried to hide it behind her back – at the same time Ailani stepped forward and waved her spark-spraying light above their hair.

Ready to defend her siblings, Ailani broke a long, burning table lamp – and threatened to electrocute Moho with it!

His black lips forced into an ugly frown, Moho glared his coal, disbelieving eyes down at Manna. Then he spun on his heavy heels and stomped out of the room – and Manna couldn't believe it.

He hit her! And he hit Mano, too!

"Your cousin's alright," droned Tutu, suddenly standing inside the older girls' room, "and she won't make fun of you anymore. Now that she understands."

Wiping sleep from her eyes, Manna sat up in bed and wondered what time Tutu got there. Seemed like no one ever visited at night.

"You must learn to forgive, child ... else Revenge will be your only friend ... guided by her only brother, Hate – the weakest power of all."

Slipping out of bed, Manna padded silently across the room and peered out the window into the starlit night, to see if Moho and Anna had returned from the hospital – but only Momi's glimmering, midnight-black truck stood tall in the drive.

"And you mustn't worry, dear. The lolo ones, whose spirits are not fully here, hold open the door to the afterlife."

Pressing her cheek against the cold window pane, Manna strained to see if Tutu parked in the street, but only a lost, lonely dog stood sniffing, over there.

"They are touched by the spirits, uhane lewa, and hear the voices in the wind ... 'ike uwa. The ones who guide you towards the light and Hawaiian knowledge."

Frowning, Manna turned around, to go back to bed, and caught sight of Mano shaking in his sleep – and with a rustling rush, something scary filled her bones.

"People fear them," hissed Tutu, "when they should heed and respect!" – and suddenly shivering, Manna remembered.

Tomorrow was school – and the Japanese gang knew what Mano did to Sanjiro.

Chapter Fourteen

OHANA KeALOHA

Clang!

Jolting awake, Manna listened to Pu-pele clang her baking pans around in the darkened morn. Still drowsy, she breathed in deep and could almost taste the thick roasted-bean coffee smell that seeped through the air.

She's making Moho's breakfast early, thought Manna, as she drifted back into a dreamless sleep.

"Manna!" squealed Pu-pele, and flying wide open, Manna's surprised eyes stared straight into her sister's flour-coated, chocolate-smeared face ... and mussed up, sugar-flecked, knotted-back hair.

Did a bakery truck hit her? thought Manna.

"I made it for you!" beamed Pu-pele. Her straight white teeth streaked with buttery brown frosting, she shoved a triple-layered chocolate cake into Manna's chin.

Drizzling down the shiny cake's dark brown, graduated sides, a cascade of popcorn-strung, white pikake leis dangled loosely off each step, blowing sweet honey-suckled aroma into the air – and crowded around each layer's circular edge, small pointy-petaled chocolate flowers nestled close together, their tips painted with golden candied foil. Standing as tall as a wedding cake, its mounded top burst open with carved orange-mango volcanic plumes that shot high to the sky and oozed syrupy juice out of their quivering jellied centers.

Breathing in deep, Manna could smell the warm vanilla crème brule that filled the cake's gooey middle, and instantly, her tummy ached.

Those chocolate flower petals opened pointy and long, just like the ones Pu-pele put on Manna's prizewinning cake, five years before – but Manna had grabbed a silver butter knife from the kitchen drawer and scraped them to the floor, muttering, "I can win by myself."

Flinching, Manna remembered Sabrina Zaruba – the perfect little German girl who flaunted porcelain-white skin, rosy pink cheeks, and crystal-clear shiny blue eyes – above her richly dressed, plump, spoiled, little body. Her thick, long blonde hair always woven into a high-perched, four-stranded braid – she easily won first prize over Manna's second, with her white-frosted, candy-coated, store-bought cake...

"Loser!" quipped Sabrina. Then, spinning on her haughty heels, she whipped her thick yellow braid into the air and smacked five-year-old Manna right in the eyes.

Wanting to kill her, Manna lunged forward and tripped over something warm and spongy – and suddenly lying flat on her tummy, she blinked down at her blue Hush-Puppie shoes ... to see who tripped her.

"Ha, ha, ha!" Sabrina laughed out loud, and Manna couldn't believe it.

In a blind rage, she had dropped her prizewinning cake onto the dirty grass-covered ground – and stepped in it.

Aching, hot tears welled in her big brown eyes, Manna shoved herself up into a flat-footed, squatting position. Then, trying hard to ignore Sabrina's delighted, growing cackle, she placed her trembling hands around her red-ribboned cake and gently squished it back together – but the dent from her sole still showed.

"Huh-huh-huh," she heard her breath shake as her lungs sucked in air – and suddenly towering over her with icy blue eyes that pierced straight through her skull, Momi growled, "Shut up – you stupid cow!"

Embarrassed, she wanted Manna to stop crying.

Pursing her lips tight, Manna forced back all tears and made sure Momi couldn't hear her breathe in.

"Well, that's an improvement," huffed Pu-pele. Still angry that Manna scraped off her chocolate flower decorations, she scooped up the grass-covered cake by its foiled serving plate, and lifted it to her squinted, emerald green eyes. Then, greed flickering in her orange, nine-year-old cheeks, she hissed, "Let's eat it – before the ants do!" and Manna saw them. Their red jointed backs stuck fast in the goopy black frosting, they wiggled their thin, pointed antennas and stretched their short, spindly knees, trying to turn round and eat their way free.

"Humph!" Ailani snorted. Then she tapped a handful of white plastic utensils down her delicate, schoolgirl, bloused arm – before she sat cross-legged on the cold autumn ground.

"Oof!" Mano grunted. Sitting down too fast and too close to Manna, he bumped her right shoulder with his bony, wool-covered knee – but Manna couldn't say a thing. A heated Momi plopped down on her other side, and Manna's voice might give away tears.

Quick and smooth, Pu-pele slid down to her soft, chubby knees and sliced the jiggling cake into sticky fifths. Then flipping her deft hands right and left, she passed five heaping plates round her sibling's eating circle – and in that instant, Manna hated them all.

No one cared that her cake got ruined – or that Sabrina made her look stupid again!

They only cared if they got a big piece of cake – before her.

"You gonna eat that?" grunted Mano, and tears blurring her eyes, Manna stared blankly at his chocolate-smeared crooked tooth.

SCRAPE! – "GROP! GROP! GROP!"

Scraping up Manna's piece in his bony, greedy hand, Mano stuffed it whole into his dripping black mouth. Then chomping loud, he swallowed it down in three groveling chews.

"Mmmm!" he smiled wide, and at once, Manna hated him the most ...

"What's wrong?" squeaked Pu-pele.

Snapping out of the past, Manna gazed up at her sister's steamy, insecure face.

She was wrong. Sabrina's cackle stopped ... the moment Momi spoke up – and they all forced down that dirty, bug-riddled cake – because with all their shortcomings, that was the best they could do to help Manna deal with her pain.

Frowning, Manna felt hot realization sear her bones.

Your family, your ohana, wasn't supposed to be some perfect, happy place, where perfect, happy people acted perfectly nice to you. It was just a tight little group, struggling against their own scary demons, lending a hand through your troubles and trials – by standing solid behind you, whenever you faltered – which is what her siblings always did.

They stuck together ... when trouble came around.

Even the forever spiteful Momi never ratted on Pu-pele. She just grumbled about Moho's abuse – and with a gut-searing jag, Manna suddenly felt glad that she wasn't alone in this confusing, pain-filled whirlwind called "Life."

"WHY ARE YOU FROWNING?" hissed Pu-pele, her injured soul ready to explode.

"Oh ... uh," stuttered Manna, "I was just thinking."

"Thinking *what*?" spit Pu-pele. Her knuckles whitening as she gripped the cake's silver serving tray – and her eyes glowed with hot indignation.

Like a mother, Pu-pele gave without asking for anything in return. Her stolen candy, her sly advice, and all of her personal time ... to do those child-supporting, menial chores. She cooked, she cleaned, she dressed everybody – and got them ready to go. And even when she felt sick and tired, her skin paled a splotchy yellow-brown, she dragged herself up, with ne'er a complaint.

And yet, no one rewarded her ... with the thing she wanted most.

To be adored.

The ever beautiful, tantalizing Pu-pele ...

So desperate to have them love me, for who and what I am – aching in my gut ... torturing my burning head ... this blinding, insatiable urge ... that dominates every screaming fiber of my being!

"That you're always the most beautiful," interrupted Manna, "and everything you make is the most beautiful, too."

Utter shock washed over Pu-pele's face. Then, lighting up like a firefly, her whole body beamed.

"Let's eat it!" she squealed. Her short, chubby toes wiggled with delight – but knowing better, Manna quavered.

"We should show it it off – to everyone – for breakfast. I can make the table, with the cake in the center, and ... if you don't mind ... maybe you could pour the milk, so I don't spill it."

Her eyes popped out and her lips pursed tight, Pu-pele straightened her back and huffed, "No! It's *my* cake – I'll do it myself."

Then, smiling pretty and confident above Manna's raised brow, she spun around and flowed out the door – and Manna felt herself smile, too.

Pu-pele already took back the cake!

"Frühstuck!" sing-songed Pu-pele – meaning "Breakfast!" in German.

Fully dressed, Manna sailed out of bed, but a clammy, cold Mano beat her through the door because he knew breakfast was cake, too.

"Oh man!" breathed Momi, from inside the dining room, and the moment she entered, Manna's heart dropped.

Spread round the oval dining room table, six blue and white china settings glimmered in the bright morning light – and tucked neatly into swan-folded napkins, long, elegant, polished silverware stems protruded from the swans' lifted tails as they swam gracefully around their own lake-like dinner plate.

"What's wrong with you?" Momi hissed at Pu-pele, because she knew Anna would enter and freak.

No one *ever* touched Anna's Blue Onion dishes.

Grabbing Manna's hand, Mano yanked her in front of him, for cover, in case Anna tried to shake him first – but Manna didn't care.

Mesmerized by the shimmering table setting, she let her eyes traverse down the hand-carved, yellow-iced German candles that twinkled tall in the middle of the table ... and noticed. They perched thick and solid (like Hawaiian guardian totems) upon a breezy, dark green ti-leaf island that was sprinkled with white pikake and red plumeria blooms – and dead center of the blowing tropical isle, the chocolate cake quivered, sullen and warm, like the brewing volcano that Pele called home.

"Whew!" a breathy gust blew in from the east, and Manna could swear the room came alive.

"Huh?" Anna gasped from inside the doorway. Her delicate white hands pressed her blushed, pink cheeks, and her pink-frosted lips pouted a full, surprised 'O' below her bright, crystally blue eyes. Then turning round on Pu-pele, she stuttered, "It's ... it's ... exquisite ... my darling, Pu-pu!" – and with a sizzling pop, Pu-pele's face burst with pride. Her sugar-coated lashes wide open and her flour-dusted cheeks burning red, she yanked out the chair at the head of the table and gushed, "Sit here, Mommy!"

Without thinking, Manna scampered to her usual seat, at the opposite end of the table where Ailani and Mano usually sat – on either side of her.

Grunting, Momi plopped down onto the oak seat next to Anna and spread her knees open – and tapping her left foot once, then her right, Ailani slid into the chair between Momi and Manna.

Already bouncing in his chair next to Manna, a lip-licking Mano grinned at the quivering molten cake as Pu-pele slipped a sharp, curved knife through its center. Then, with a quick flick of her wrist, she sliced the knife right and left – and a mango-topped piece toppled onto her glinting silver cake server.

"Take your napkins," Pu-pele cooed, and at once, Manna put her white, knotted swan onto her lap ... and stroked its cute, soft cotton beak.

"These were my mother's," breathed Anna, the moment Pu-pele slid the first quivering, creamy piece onto her mother's plate. "But she never let me use them. She said they were too fancy for a child."

Startled, Manna looked down at her own empty plate.

Lightly painted under its thin porcelain surface, an Asian, blue, fan-covered tree spewed white child-drawn daisies and squiggly vined leaves against a puff-balled, pointy-petaled onion bloom – and swirling two inches wide around its white-laced edges, thin strips of blue-lined porcelain clung, loosely woven together, like a wicker basket made of breakable blown-glass twigs.

Horrified, Manna knew her grandmother was right. The fragile dish would easily break!

"She wouldn't let me touch her goat either," grumbled Anna. Then a hint of jealousy passed over her pretty white face. "It was her favorite thing on our farm, because goat's milk made her warm. The servants milked that goat twice a day, and my mother sang it songs."

CLUNK!

With a jarring clunk, Pu-pele flopped a heaping piece of cake onto Manna's dinner plate, and slid her sharp cake server out – and oozing out the cake's center, slimy, yellow vanilla crème guts jiggled out and over its brown, sticky, rich innards.

Sick to her stomach, Manna knew.

If she tried to eat the cake, her stabbing fork would chip the plate's finish ... and if she didn't, Pu-pele would be insulted and go wild.

Suddenly, Anna's snake-like eyes slit – and fear prickling down her spine, Manna glanced around the table, just in time to see Ailani's nervous jaw jut forward and snap down on her shaking, cake-laden fork.

Clenching her lips together, Ailani moved her head back instead of pulling the fork out. Then, her light brown eyes smiling at Manna, she chomped her teeth down loudly on her soft, gooey bite.

"That evil goat," spit Anna. "She would stamp her hooves every time I walked by her pen – as if she thought my mother loved her more than me!"

Scrape!

The table jolted left, along with Momi's rough, bouncing knee, and lightning fast, she swiped one gnarled paw round the top of her filled coffee cup and hunched, blazing eyes forward, over her half-eaten plate. Then, with a sharp teeth-sucking sound, she cleared her bucktoothed mouth for another grumbling gulp.

Suddenly, Anna's soft eyes twinkled like Tante Theresa's did ... when she brought Christmas presents.

"One day," chuckled Anna, "my mother bought me the most beautiful skirt ... with red ruffles and pouffy underwear lace. It was Sunday, and all her Blue Onion dishes were out for my relatives to enjoy with coffee and cake – so my mother sent me out to play."

Smiling sly to herself, Anna dipped her white, polished finger into her whipped chocolate frosting, then popped it into her shiny pink mouth – and for a moment, she looked just like Pu-pele ... before she got even.

Clink. Clink.

Pu-pele tossed two sugar cubes into the bottom of Manna's small coffee cup, and humming to herself, doused them both with warm powdered milk. Then squeezing three plump fingertips around a protruding, blue-petaled rose, she held a delicate blue-painted coffeepot lid onto its round-bellied pot, and poured black coffee over the crystally white goo.

Swirling into an ice-cream smeared, caramel tan, the coffee steamed through the crisp morning air and spread a roasted honey smell across Manna's hungry cheeks.

Licking her lips, Manna wanted nothing more than to taste her drink – but there was no way she could pick up that cup. Barely glued upon the cup's fine, curved-in side, a noodle-thin porcelain handle forked into a fragile, not-quite-finger-wide loop that would surely break if she shoved her index finger in it!

Drooling, Manna bit her bottom lip and carefully dipped two of her fingers, knuckle deep, into the dainty cup. Then, before they could drip, she shoved them both into her mouth.

Coating her cheeks with a sharp, bittersweet tinge, the quick spreading coffee washed over her tongue and cleared away all saliva, as though making way for a pure chocolatey taste – and suddenly excited, Manna shoved her face down into her cake and took a sloppy, sponge-sucking bite.

Instantly, an alcoholic singe burned the tip of her tongue and shot juicy, fresh mango over her teeth – then soaking through her cheeks, a fruit-laced, creamed chocolate bar flavor melted in her mouth and slid past her gums. Licking rich dark frosting off of her sticky, black lips, Manna smiled around the table at her noisy, feasting siblings, and knew this was good.

She could eat without a fork – and not worry about cracking the plate!

"Right away," grinned Anna, "I skipped to that goat's pen to show her ... I was the only one who got a new skirt. I held its long, crunchy ruffles out and spun around and around singing, *I have one and you don't! I have one and you don't!* "

Throwing her head back, Anna laughed out loud. Then her reddened face tilted towards Manna, and she asked, "Do you know what that nasty goat did?"

Leaning forward on both elbows, as if ready to grab someone, Anna growled, "It sailed over the fence, and with one loud whoosh, it scooped me up on its head, with my skirt stuck fast in its horns. Then it ran around the yard, with me sitting on its face, screaming at the top of my lungs!"

Laughing so hard her neck veins popped out, Anna gasped, "My father was so mad! He chased that goat around the yard for ten minutes, in front of his family and friends, until finally, my mother yelled out the goat's name. And do you know what it did? It ran straight to my mother, into the house, and dumped me on her Blue Onion dishes – and every single one cracked!"

Suddenly, Anna's lips tightened and her face grew grave.

"Do you know what my mother, your Oma, did ... embarrassed in front of everyone?"

Shook you till your skirt fell off? Manna thought the worst, right before Anna breathed, "She scooped me up and whispered, 'I love you more than that goat.' Then she looked at my father and said, 'Get rid of it.' "

Sitting up, proud and triumphant, Anna looked over all her children –

and Manna had an eerie feeling she'd find a way to get rid of *anything* she didn't like.

Quickly, Manna stared down at her plate, hoping Anna wouldn't gouge out her crooked eye – and instantly distracted by her cake's glistening, sweet goo, she stretched her mouth open, buried her nose in it, and inhaled.

"More?" Pu-pele offered Manna seconds for the first time ever, her soft hazel eyes gazing down upon her sister – and at once, Manna yanked her face out of the cake and felt something warm clog her nose.

Here sat family .. her ohana ke aloha – the closet thing she'd ever come to love.

Grunting, Mano squeezed her hand and smiled his wild, toothy grin, and she realized.

He never let go of her hand.

"LET'S GO!" bellowed Momi. Thick black smoke trailed out of her flared, pimpled nostrils, and her glazed, stony eyes glared wild beneath her thin, arched, blonde brows.

Jumping into the back of Momi's death-black truck, Manna grinned at a smiling Mano – and tapping down her forearm, inside of the cab, Ailani rocked back and forth, right behind the crooked, black-balled stick shift ... and Manna could tell.

Everyone felt happy about the morning's breakfast cake.

SLAM!

Tripping out of the side door, Pu-pele caught her balance against the sturdy wooden handrail. Then teetering on Anna's four-inch, shiny red high heels, she clomped down the long outdoor stairs. Stuffed into Anna's tight, red and white Barbie-doll dress, Pu-pele's round butt jerked sideways with each off-balance step, and her fatty, brown breasts jiggled out her skimpy spaghetti-strap top.

"She's so stupid!" muttered Momi. Her large-knuckled fingers strummed the grey Hawaiian-print steering wheel, and Manna understood.

Wearing Anna's clothes would earn you a beating.

Flipping her waist-long hair around, at the bottom of the stairs, Pu-pele vanished behind the looming blue house – but in under a second, she emerged. Her chubby face beamed, radiant and warm, as an oversized, red and white hibiscus flapped its silky petals in the wind, pinned snug and high in her curly brown hair.

Tottering silly over the red cinder drive, Pu-pele jerked her broad hips towards the truck – and with a sparkling flash, Oma's red-jeweled magic bag swung free off her fleshy right wrist ...

Her heart suddenly jammed in her throat, Manna couldn't breathe.

That was the purse she found in Anna's closet ... that day Moho threw the fairy out the window. Except now, the purse bulged, lumpy and round, as if stuffed with a leprechaun's whole gold nugget treasure.

Shivering, Manna remembered the pictures of Anna and the shadow that tried to eat her.

"You ride in back!" huffed Pu-pele as she gripped the open passenger's door for balance. Then she sniffed at Manna, "You go up front!"

Her skin crawling, Manna pulled a humphing Ailani into the truck bed. Then pushing Ailani's uneasy bottom into a seated position, Manna wedged Ailani's back against the cab – and her feet against the round, plastic-lined wheel barrel.

Certain something bad was about to happen, but afraid to go against Pu-pele, Manna slid off the truck's side to the crunchy, graveled ground and barked over her shoulder, "Sit down ... so no one falls out."

Then, holding her breath to make herself skinny, Manna slipped into the cab without touching Pu-pele ... or the evil thing that lived in her twinkling red bag.

"VROOM!" the truck roared as soon as Momi turned the key, and tumbling into the cab, Pu-pele slammed the door shut.

"Oh brother!" snorted Momi. Lurching back, she jammed her head out of her open window and slammed the stick shift into reverse, banging Manna's knee so hard that it cracked.

Gasping in pain, Manna breathed in – and tearing through her nostrils, a week-old dead frog formaldehyde smell gagged her. Horrified, she gripped the quilted Hawaiian-print seat cover ... and swallowed down vomit so Pu-pele wouldn't know.

She spilled too much of Anna's Channel-No. 5 perfume on her dress!

"Your hair's dry and scratchy from the saltwater," hummed Pu-pele. Her deft, purseless hand fingered the gleaming Armour-All'ed dash – and with a squealing highway turn, Momi lurched left.

Whipping around the vine-covered rearview mirror, a scratchy, dried, brown maile lei scraped across Manna's cheek – but she didn't notice.

Pu-pele's hand had pulled something black and white out of the glove box – and Manna knew they were headed for trouble.

"Those ugly brown blotches on your face are from the sun," quipped Pu-pele, her emerald eyes scolding Manna. "And all surfers grow cataracts – snake skin across their eyes," – and at that moment, a thin trail of smoke slithered past Manna's cheek.

"Wear these!" Pu-pele demanded as she plunked a black pair of shades and a white tube of suntan lotion onto Manna's lap, but Manna didn't hear her.

Glancing back at Mano's pale, taut face – she finally understood.

Today at school – the Japanese gang would kill him.

Chapter Fifteen

TRAPPED

"Tink you tough?" growled Tadashi, second in command. With a heavy thud, his shoulder knocked into Mano's.

Almost knocked off balance, Mano stumbled sideways. Then running scared, he trotted away, faster.

"What?" growled Shoda. "Deaf?" Then he shoved his barreled chest into Mano's and blocked his path.

Fear prickling up her spine, Manna stared wide-eyed at the nunchucks Shoda hid behind his back.

Trying to egg Mano into a fight, so they couldn't be blamed for hitting first, the Japanese gang surrounded him before class – but outnumbered, Mano wouldn't fight back.

"SPIST!" a sweaty, slobbering Taro spit something yellow onto Mano's cheek – and glancing at Manna, with glittery, wet eyes, Mano begged her to help him ... so she knew they'd both get brutally beaten.

All the Japanese gang carried nunchucks and knives!

"SPIST!" someone spit, and packing hot humiliation, something sticky wet hit Manna between the eyes and dripped onto her lip.

"Oh!" gasped Pu-pele. Then clanging against the outdoor lockers, her soft brown arm caught her balance.

Giggling warmly at Tadashi, a beaming Pu-pele tottered up on her red heels, her tight red dress spilling her supple, round breasts – and dumbstruck, Tadashi smiled back.

"Puh!" Pu-pele puffed a steamy breath out of her full, orange-glossed bottom lip, and whipping up in her wind, a stray golden-red curl flipped off of her ginger face.

Instantly, Manna shivered.

Oma's sparkling jeweled bag dangled off Pu-pele's right wrist – with something evil waiting inside it.

With a double-handed tug and a jiggly chest wiggle, Pu-pele settled her breasts back into her top – and grinning round at one another, all the Japanese boys looked thrilled with their peek.

"Hmm," Pu-pele smiled wide. Her glimmering green eyes traversed all the boys, as though they were delicious treats she'd love to swallow – and shuffling in place, they all puffed out their chests to impress her.

Wishing to have Tadashi first, Pu-pele fluttered her long, painted eyelashes in his direction. Then swinging her curved hips right and left, she flowed to him. Her glistening tongue touched her parted, quivering lips ... and Tadashi understood.

Her longing mouth wanted to meet his.

Licking his lips, he readied himself for her first slippery wet kiss.

"Hmm-hmm," murmured Pu-pele, a breath away from Tadashi – and realizing her moist, heaving chest came all the way up to his chin, she slid her left hand around his bulged shoulder and bent over, to slip off her high-heel shoes.

Biting his lower lip with anticipation, Tadashi squeezed one stubby hand round Pu-pele's soft, feminine waist, as if letting the other boys know he wouldn't share – and pleased, her exposed cleavage teasing outward, Pu-pele twinkled at a helpless Manna – and sent a lightning chill right through her bones.

Pu-pele could mesmerize any boy ... or girl.

THUNK!

Steady without her shoes, Pu-pele swung her solid arm around and cracked Tadashi between the eyes with her purse. Full of rocks, it sunk deep into his brain.

"AAAY!" Manna heard herself scream at the same time she jumped on Taro's back and hammered his face into the concrete sidewalk. Then, her lips taut with hate, she spit, "Play dead – or she'll kill you!"

THUNK! THUNK! THUNK!

Before Manna could save another, Shoda's skull cracked, right before the skulls of the two boys standing near him – and spewing head blood into glistening, warm pools, their fallen corpses lay perfectly still.

"Woo-hooooo!" a hot wind howled, and suddenly looming above Manna, Pu-pele's wild moonlit face dripped with ravenous greed – and for a moment, Manna thought the Devil came to eat her.

"Get rid of it!" Pu-pele screeched over the wind, and with a loud, "BANG!" her flaming orange hair ripped from her contorted wrinkled-witch face.

Horrified, Manna watched her sister snatch up Anna's shoes and stumble through a prickly red squall. Then she felt it.

Oma's cold, heavy purse in her hand.

Oh gawd! Manna screamed in her head. Her slippered feet pounded against the damp green earth, *She killed them – and plans to blame me!*

"Manna!" a woman called from behind, but blind with fear, Manna pushed forward faster. Blood pumping in her brain, she felt head-high sugarcane scrape past her cheeks and tear at her hair, like dried, bony fingers groping in the wind .... but she didn't care.

If anyone caught her with Oma's purse, Moho would kill her!

"Maaaaaa-na!" the woman called again, but this time she called from in front.

Skidding to a halt, Manna jerked her stinging, wind-torn eyes forward – but for miles, the only thing that moved was wild, light green sugarcane plumes, bending over against a furious orange-red gale.

"Over here!" the woman barked, an inch from Manna's back, and spinning around, Manna whipped Oma's purse high into the air, to hit her – but no one stood there.

"Woooooo," the wind moaned through Manna's hair, and her skin crawling scared, she understood.

The hiding sugarcane ghost girl meant to stop her from getting away – but determined to escape, Manna gripped her purse in both hands and slowly backed up.

"Here! Here! Here!" the ghost girl giggled all around Manna's head, her heated breath prickling Manna's cheeks – and ready to club her, Manna snapped her face around, right and left, trying to get a glimpse of the teasing ghost girl – but couldn't.

The clever ghost girl stayed invisible.

"Come here ...ere!" sang the ghost girl, from high in the sky, and suddenly sizzling out of the ground, something hazy and orange trickled up through Manna's heels ... and shivering, she remembered the big orange hand that chased her at the Kris Kringle fair.

Her mana! That's what the ghost girl was after ... then and now!

"HAH!" a male voice yelled, inches from Manna's back, but before she could jolt around, something grabbed the shadowy guy and scuffled to the ground.

BAM!

With a sudden gut-shaking bam, the whole sugarcane field exploded into an ash-spewing, sweltering, red volcano – and blistering Manna's skin, a broiling hot wind pressed against her chest and sucked away every molecule of oxygen!

Confused and suffocating fast, Manna felt sharp red flames lash her bare thighs and strip her aching ribs – as the ghost girl burned away her flesh to get at her bones!

"UH!" something coughed and grabbed Manna with its clawed, bony fingers – and reeling around fast, she winged her rock-filled purse at its hairy, black head.

THUNK!

With a sickening thunk, Mano's head snapped back, gushing dark red blood from a gaping head wound – and rolling round dead, his glassy eye whites popped out before he flopped to the ground.

"MANO!" screamed Manna. Then falling to her knees, she tried to press back on the thick, jagged flesh piece that hung off his sweaty, burned forehead – but with a sticky flup, her fingers slipped, knuckle deep, into his bleeding skull.

"Oh no!" Manna heard a girl gasp. Then wrapping her warm fingers around Manna's shoulders, the girl pulled a panting Manna to her feet ...

"Run!" Barbara yelled into Manna's nose. Then throwing Mano over her shoulders, fireman-style, she bumped past Manna and hobbled through a growing black break in the fiery sugarcane wall.

Almost crying, Manna heard Tutu's haunting words.

They follow you ... some to steal your mana ... some to protect it ... always look over your shoulder.

Glancing back, over her heavy, slouched shoulder, Manna could see. The fire parted wherever Barbara stepped.

"Coma," the doctor called it, but to Manna, it looked like death.

Naked and greyish-blue, Mano lay flat on his back in the white-sheeted hospital bed – a stiff, morbid expression frozen on his gaunt, bloodless face ... and jabbed into his thin, crossed arm, a tubed sliver needle dripped clear embalming fluid into his sunk-in, mummified brain.

Shuddering, Manna watched yellow pus ooze off her brother's uneven, white-bandage-wrapped forehead – and suddenly feeling stinging, hot tears well in her eyes, she glanced down at his charred, red-blistered neck.

It was all her fault – because she didn't watch out for him.

At surfing, she let him go after Sanjiro on his own ... and at school, she let the Japanese gang push him around. And after Pu-pele's fight, she only thought of saving herself.

Afraid to touch him, Manna fingered his crisp cotton sheet. Then biting her lip, she tugged it a little higher, to cover his cold, still heart.

Forever ... only she and Barbara could tell ... how Manna killed Anna's only boy.

Whimpering softly at the foot of the bed, Anna clutched her son's spread-open feet through the loose, tear-stained sheet ... and kissed his bent, lifeless toes – and almost crying out in pain, Manna felt hot jealousy burn through her nose.

No one ever ... ever ... cared about her!

Without thinking, she spun on her heels and ran out the door.

ZING!

With a pupil-squeezing zing, the brilliant white light of the long hospital hall shot through Manna's eyes – and produced a splendid, lit-up highway to heaven. Chills racing through her bones, she stared in awe at a yellow Angel Gabrielle as he stood grimly at the end of the hall ... waiting to whisk Mano away.

Manna blinked her eyes and stared again.

That wasn't Gabrielle. It was an angry-faced Taro – clutching a black pair of nunchucks in his left hand!

Too scared to think, Manna jerked around and fled down the hall – her heart beating wild – and then she saw it.

305

The vending machine.

She could push it on Taro, before he attacked her!

Skidding to a stop, she slipped off the shiny waxed floor and landed sideways, on her butt. But scrambling quickly to her knees, she crawled round to the side of the steel, glassed machine, wedged her bare feet against the wall – and shoved.

"UGH!" she groaned but the machine didn't budge.

"KANAKA!" Taro growled, his feet thundering towards Manna, and jumping to her toes, she gripped the back of the machine in her hands and pulled hard – but still, it wouldn't budge. Panicking, she flopped round and wedged her back against the wall, but before she could try another shove, Taro's evil red face jammed into hers.

"Why you hiding?" barked Taro, his swollen face ready to explode and his slanted, black eyes riddled with glowing red veins ... and Manna saw.

He was crying.

A fat foot suddenly wedged in her throat, she glared at the ground.

Taro's brother lay unconscious, too.

"UH!" Taro grunted as he slammed his thick knuckles through the vending machine glass ... and pulled out a brown soda pop. Sticking it in Manna's gut, he grabbed another with his nunchuck-wielding hand – but Manna didn't want *anything* from the Japanese gang. Pushing her proud nose in the air, she snorted, "I take Hawaiian Punch!"

"Yeah?" growled Taro. "Take this!" and with a mind-jolting, "BAM!" – his right fist punched through Manna's face – but before it hit her, she ducked and it slammed against the plastered hospital wall. Spewing soda, glass and drywall plaster everywhere, Taro's fist sunk into the caved-in white wall.

"Hee-hee-hee!" Taro giggled, his blue-threaded stitches wagging crazily off his chin. "You so chicken!" – and suddenly furious with him, Manna glared up at his fat Buddah-head face.

Jerking up and down like a mad naked mole-rat, it splotched an uneven yellow and red as delighted blood rushed to his stuffed, laughing cheeks – and squinting lolo and nearly shut, his sparkly black eyes twinkled with childish mischief. Wheezing a girlie, high-pitched laugh, Taro let his beefy, round shoulders jiggle to the ground, on either side of his bouncing, round-bellied gut – and at once, Manna got it.

He was local – and *that* was a Hawaiian punch!

Feeling herself giggle at his joke, she took a red-labeled Hawaiian Punch can from his extended, blood-dripping hand – and accidentally flicked a sheared piece of glass off of his chubby index finger.

"Ho, man!" Taro sighed. Exhausted from laughing, he sunk down to his wide-spreading butt.

"She when broke all their heads," he spit, twirling his nunchucks between his fingers, and distracted, Manna slid down next to him and wondered ... how Japanese kids flipped their mechanical pencils up and down the fingers of their little hands.

"And Mano ... when slice up my bruddah's guts."

Suddenly too close and scowling straight into Manna's face, Taro's beady eyes gleamed with awe as he hissed, "You Kealohas – stay wicked!" Then, sucking loudly on his teeth like Momi, and shaking his head twice, he shoved one of his black nunchucks into Manna's hand, as if giving her a weapon to fight with – and squeezing it hard, Manna wondered why it felt squishy.

"That's why ..." Taro continued. His eyes scanned Manna's face for her reaction. "They when make my initiation to fight one of you."

"Oo-oo-ooh," Taro shivered, his whole heated body slapping against Manna's bare arm. "Good ting, Tadashi never said throw dat rock at your sister!" – and feeling relief wash over her, Manna laughed out loud.

Pu-pele would have killed every local at the school bus stop!

Glad that Taro never *really* had anything against her, Manna flashed him a happy smile – and suddenly nervous, his eyes widened and he squeaked, "Good ting I missed your eye ... 'cause you stay choice." Then, his face burning beet red, he shoved a nunchuck down his throat, to stop himself from blurting anything else.

"Huh!" Manna gasped, and without a crunch, Taro bit off a big, white-filled, throat-clogging piece.

Looking down at her nunchuck, Manna grinned to herself.

She held sushi, not a weapon!

Rolled in dark green, dried seaweed, a long, sticky, white rice log held in shiny chunks of orange, green and black – and glistening out its center, a red-fleshed, raw ahi sliver oozed its smelly squid odor into the air.

Feeling hunger pangs cramp her empty tummy, Manna shoved the sushi into her mouth and bit off a big rubbery piece.

Instantly streaking down the sides of her tongue, the sweet-sour taste of sugar-coated vinegar stripped both of her cheeks and sent a tingly dry swirl down her throat – and thinking fast, Manna sucked down a mouthful of sweet Hawaiian Punch, to make sure the tip of her tongue sizzled with the rest of her mouth – and then she realized.

This awkward boy made her feel hopeful ... and relieved.

Smiling gaily at his sweating, hairless face, she felt a slimy, chewed piece of seaweed slip off her bottom lip – but that was okay.

A clump of spit-shiny rice waggled off the knotted blue threads that stuck out of her new friend's soda-splattered chin!

SWHOOSH!

Scraping its thick rubber lining along the cold hospital floor, Mano's room door swung shut behind Manna, and standing still, she let her tired eyes refocus in the dim air-conditioned room.

Sleeping motionless on the bare tiled floor, Ailani curled up into a tight lonely ball, like a frightened kitten lost without its mom – and steaming four feet to her left, a heavy-breathing Pu-pele lay flat on her tummy, clutching two stolen pillows from Mano's bed. At the far side of the room, underneath the window and stretched out on her back, a tooth-gnashing Momi tossed left and right, uncomfortable on the blanket-less floor.

Blinking around at her siblings, Manna peered at the staggered, melting rows of lit German candles that Anna placed in triangles above each sleeping child – and with an eerie chill, Manna felt like she stood at her whole family's wake, keeping watch over their day-old corpses.

"Humph!" Moho snorted, and gasping, Manna almost jumped out of her skin.

Sitting at the foot of Mano's bed in a flimsy fold-out chair, Moho bounced both of his solid brown knees and stared blankly out the dark open window. Then, hugging a curled up Anna close to his massive bouncing chest, he rocked her back and forth, as though she was his sleeping baby.

Hoping Moho wouldn't notice her, Manna stood perfectly still and watched him ... kiss Anna's soft, shimmering blonde hair with his big black lips.

So small and helpless, he meant to protect her from all the evil in this world, and finally, Manna got it.

Moho would do anything for her ... beg, borrow, steal ... even die ... and that in itself, despite his constant, innate cruelty towards anyone else, made *him* a worthy human being.

Holding back hot tears, Manna suddenly felt worthy of nothing.

She hadn't lived up to her *only* responsibility ... to watch out for the boy.

Without meaning to, she stepped towards her brother's bed, and with a squirming crunch, a nickel-sized roach cracked underneath her bare foot and oozed its warm juice onto her sole. Flicking its mangled, stuck pieces off of her foot with her other big toe, Manna shuddered.

The whole hospital floor scurried with tiny winged roaches that searched for spilled human blood.

Wanting nothing more than to be by her brother, Manna dragged her feet quietly across the floor, knowing that if Moho didn't hear her, he wouldn't look up – and if she didn't lift her feet, she wouldn't smash anything else.

"Huh-hmm," Mano breathed through a fat plastic tube, his slow breath forced in by a balloon-filling machine. Bending over him, Manna touched his cold, rock-hard hand – then she noticed.

That wasn't his hand. It was his grey stone Fetcher. Someone had placed it next to him, alongside of hers. Except hers, they had propped up against his left hip so that its hideous face glared out the door.

Letting her eyes traverse Mano's bare hips and slow-breathing belly button, Manna suddenly caught sight of something glinting on his chest.

His shark tooth necklace.

Stripped by the cane field fire, its long demonic tooth shined like a metallic silver weapon, rooted deep inside an enemy's groaning ribs – and glimmering with all the power of the Devil's raised hand, it promised unbridled riches and indomitable reign ... and Manna remembered.

Her bones. That's what the sugarcane fire ghost girl meant to do with her bones. Burn away her flesh ... and obtain her power.

BRRRRING!

The phone on the night stand rang so loud that Manna jerked up and clasped the harsh, jarring sound it made in her ears.

BRRRRING!

The phone rang louder, and Manna squeezed her ears harder, but still no one else moved. Undisturbed by the blaring, brain-wracking sound, they just kept sleeping – and a wide awake Moho didn't turn his head, as if he couldn't hear the phone ring, either.

BRRRRING!

Suddenly, the phone rang so loud in Manna's head that she thought her brain might explode. Desperate to answer before the phone rang again, she snatched up the receiver and breathed, "Hello?"

"It's dark in here," whimpered Mano, his voice quivering and scared, "and its cold. It's so wet and cold."

Horrified, Manna looked at her comatose brother.

Was he dead? – And his soul trapped in heaven ... or hell?

"Help me!" Mano's soul cried over the phone. "Please help me. I wanna go home."

Her gut wrenching into her chest, Manna cried out in pain, "I don't know how!"

"Use the Fetcher!" a throaty voice hissed over the line, and without meaning to, Manna dropped the receiver and snatched her Fetcher off Mano's lifeless hip. Then throwing both hands high over her head and forming an arrow to the sky, she barked out the mo'olelo words Tutu used to transport her soul.

"Hele ika hale o !" – but nothing happened.

"Oh gawd, its getting hot!" Mano yelped out of the dangling phone receiver. "Get me out of here! Manna! Get me out of here!"

Reacting fast, Manna snatched up his stone Fetcher in her other hand, pointed both to the sky and roared, "HELE IKA HALE O !" – and with a lurch, Moho jerked out of his chair ... to his feet.

"AAAAAY!" screamed Mano, and suddenly whipping around the room, a raking, hot wind bit Manna's cheeks and she knew.

Moho would lunge forward and kill her for what she'd done – if she didn't kill him first.

Snatching off Mano's necklace, she pointed its long jagged tooth at Moho's ugly vein-bulging neck and growled, "Hele ika hale o ..." and his lips clenched down, Moho finished her off with a deep rumbling croak.

"Ku-pele-ka..."

ZUP!

Chapter Sixteen

The FETCHER

BAM!

Molten lava smashed into Manna's chest and threw her backwards onto black jagged rock. Scorching pangs ripped through her body. Needle-sharp razors pierced her back. In sudden unbearable pain, she tried to scream, but couldn't.

Her chest, encased by cooling lava rock, refused to expand.

Shocked, Manna lay spread-eagle on her back, her whole world turned a blazing, streaky orange – and floating right above her, twinkling white steam and bright red, puffy smoke cloaked the darkened sky, like a comforting goose down blanket. Suddenly drowsy, her brain drifted off ...

"Uh!" Manna heard herself groan, and with a breast-clutching cramp, her lungs felt like they would explode.

She needed air! She had to get out of this stifling lava cast!

Clutching both Fetchers and Mano's necklace in her hands, she wobbled up to her knees and faced Kilauea's broiling pit. Then, her head spinning a hazy white-flecked orange, she raised both arms out to her sides and leaned far forward.

Sizzling in her ears, a wall of intense heat seared her arms and face – and smoking a red-tipped black, her cast crackled and oozed bloody pus. Then grumbling out loud, it slupped off of her chest and slid back into its gurgling pit.

"SUH!"

Manna gasped air through her mouth and gagged. The sour sulfur taste of burning human flesh tore down her throat, and at once, she knew.

Forever trapped, Mano burned alive in Kilauea's hellish pit!

"MANO!" she screamed, but no one answered.

Horrified, Manna felt her whole body tremble and her heart pound in her head – scared ... no, panicked!

NO! – Rip-roaring mad!

Moho growled the words that sent her to Ku!

That greedy demon, Ku ... swallowed her brother alive!

Furious with Him, Manna sprang to her feet, stretched both hands over the pit and commanded, "EXPEL MY BROTHER!" – but the pit only responded with a deep chuckling rumble. Then, as if mocking her, the ground countered with a jolt and nearly toppled her into the churning, flesh-singeing pool.

Twirling her arms backwards twice to catch her balance, Manna leaned back against a sudden howling wind that seemed to push her towards the pool – and then she panicked.

Would He eat me, too? The Keeper of His unborn Wife?

BA-BAM!

With a resounding bam, a thousand sticky red boils burst into clawed, smoldering fingers that lashed out of the burning pool and snatched at Manna's bare feet – and sputtering a high-pitched whine, half a dozen orange-red fountains spurted out of the crater and hailed fiery meteors atop her head. Screaming feverishly, a blistering hot wind whipped round her body and sucked her down towards the now whirling blood-red pool – and flipped off her feet, Manna crashed down, face first, onto the spiked lava rock.

Whimpering, Manna clung to the lava rock with all her might, but it was no use.

Ku's wind sucked too hard on her scared, kicking toes as they sizzled, only an inch above His fiery waters – and her cut, bleeding fingers stung bitterly against the sharp lava shards. Utterly terrified, she felt herself slipping ... and knew.

She would be sucked into the bowels of hell!

Her nose stinging with tears, Manna hid her face under one weakening arm, squeezed her eyes shut, and began her final prayer.

Hail Mary, full of Grace, the Lord is with Thee ...

A delighted giggle interrupted.

Manna stopped praying and held her breath.

Growing louder, the giggle turned into a familiar throaty laugh ... and Manna felt herself smile.

Pu-pele. It sounded like Pu-pele – and at once, the wind stopped.

Embarrassed, but relieved, Manna scrambled up to face her sister – and immediately, her heart jumped into her throat.

It wasn't Pu-pele. It was *the* Pele – the giant, stunning fire goddess – submerged hip-deep in Kilauea's now calm, slow-rippling pool.

Pele's smooth, tan face turned upwards as she gazed down at Manna through soft, lowered lids. Her twinkling green eyes danced with amusement, and her glimmering orange-red lips quivered around a radiant white-toothed smile. Still laughing, her large, naked, moon-round breasts jiggled with each deep-throated chuckle, as her long golden curls bounced about her shoulders and spilled into the pool, reflecting brilliant embers of red in each swirling strand. Playfully, Pele swung a blackened wooden gourd from the wrist of her right hand, as she pushed a ringlet of gold behind her ear with the other ... and Manna noticed.

Her movement was fluid, like a hypnotic wave – and in response, shivers rippled up Manna's spine.

Pele was titillatingly ... beautiful.

Cocking her head, Pele regarded Manna with a smirk.

"The all powerful Mana – cowers like a kitten, trembles like a fly." Then she scoffed, "Only Kane would allow a frightened wisp to keep His power."

Hurt from the scorn of one so desirable, Manna's gaze dropped. She stared past the dangling gourd and respectfully remembered Tutu's teachings.

Don't move. Don't look the Akua in the eye.

"Clever little girl, aren't you?" the huge Pele chortled. "But not clever enough to keep me."

Carelessly, Pele swung her gourd higher, slapping it against the pool's surface as it came down – and flying off its wet bottom, blumps of sticky, bubbling, red lava splattered around Manna's feet.

"How much do you think this will hurt?" Pele smiled at her smoking red waters, and Manna gripped her Fetcher tighter, knowing the answer. But she couldn't respond – nor could she take it all in.

What's going on? she thought. *Pele doesn't kill people, she tests them. Pele doesn't devour souls, she enslaves them.*

Pele stopped swinging her gourd, and held it out in front of her.

"Ta da!"

Manna screwed her eyes, then gasped in horror.

Trapped inside Pele's gourd, a sweaty, charred Mano slammed his red, blistered palms against the gourd's inner walls, mouthing, "MANNA! MANNA!" – and when their eyes met, she heard his screams.

Immediately, Mano froze, palms still up, and he pleaded, "Get me out of here!"

"I have what you came for," sing-songed Pele. Her rounded hips swayed back and forth, and her teasing smirk stayed intact. Then, glinting a catty green, her eyes fixed on Manna's Fetcher. "Wanna trade?"

Manna's shoulders sagged as she stared at Mano in disbelief.

Was this a dream? Or was Pele real? – and with a chilling rush, it hit her.

Pele's voice sounded familiar.

Was Pele that husky-voiced girl Moho argued with at the beach ... Moho's sister?

"Oh, don't mistake me for that fumbling, redheaded shark, Ka'ahu-pahau," Pele interrupted.

She reads my mind, Manna understood, but Pele ignored that thought and continued.

"She's inches away from you, just one little lunge ..."

On *lunge*, Pele's chubby left hand shot up and snatched at the air.

"... to get your bones and secure your mana when ..."

Pele tossed her gourd high into the air, then caught it with a two-handed slap and laughed, "SPLAT! Moho tosses her out the window!"

Mano slammed against the top of the gourd, then sunk to its bottom, his glassy, round eyes rolling and dazed.

Sucking in a mouthful of air, Manna shivered as she remembered the glimmering red fairy, Ka'ahu-pahau, breathing in Anna's closet ... and reaching out to grab her.

"Then she gets you alone, with only that noisy haole to protect you – and right as she's about to snap away your drowning bones ..."

Pele smacked the gourd against her huge forehead, rolled her bulging eyes, and shook her tongue-lolling head in feigned confusion.

"BONK! Flailing little brother bops her on the head!"

Mano grabbed both of his ears in pain as the "BONK!" reverberated through the gourd – and shuddering, Manna remembered the red shark inside the tide pool breakwall. The one that almost ate them the first time they went swimming.

Pele lifted her arm and dangled the gourd in front of her face. Squinting her slanted emerald eyes, she peered in at Mano and asked through curled lips, "And what was that thing at school? Drown her in the sink – and then what? Pull her down the drain and out to sea?"

Pele pressed her nose against the gourd and boomed, "DUH! She doesn't fit!"

Tossed back by Pele's deafening, "DUH!" Mano slammed against the other side of the gourd, and Manna bit her lip.

Barb didn't try to drown her in the school bathroom that day. It was Ka'ahu-pahau, and her screaming red hands.

Throwing her head far back, Pele burst into laughter, but this time it sounded wicked ... and made Manna's skin crawl.

Suddenly, thin orange flames crackled in Pele's emerald eyes and glaring at Manna, she leaned forward. Then her left arm raised up and back – while her right arm lowered forward and down.

Sizzling angrily, the gourd's bottom cut into the pool, but reacting fast, Mano suspended in midair to avoid contact with his frying prison walls.

Giggling, Pele begin to twirl like a carefree schoolgirl, letting her gourd skim round and through her orange-red waters.

"Surfing, surfing, surfing," she sang as she spun. "Down Kalapana, we go play. Catch me, catch me. Catch me Saturday!"

Pele stopped and peered into the gourd again, addressing Mano.

"But the little red sea slug never caught her – did she?" and Manna knew.

That red shark she always saw at Kalapana was named Ka'ahu-pahau.

Smiling and once again directing her attention towards Manna, Pele reveled, "Moho knocked some sense into her head, eh? Sent her back home."

Manna remembered hearing Ka'ahu-pahau hit the shore, but her thoughts faded quickly as she felt herself struggling to avoid Pele's stare.

Manna didn't know why, but suddenly, she wanted nothing more than to look upon Pele. Just one more time. To see those fiery eyes. To gaze at that gorgeous, pucker-lipped face. She knew better though. So she forced her eyes down to Pele's smoking red pool and thought, *Don't think. Just listen. And react.*

Sighing, Pele resumed swinging her gourd and confessed.

"At first, I wanted your bones, too ... Just a little piece of your mana to strengthen my own. But you ..."

She stopped swinging the gourd and flicked it into her hand, upside down.

Mano flipped and landed on his feet.

Pele dipped one large finger into her fiery pool and with a quick tap, transferred its flame to the bottom of the gourd. The flame flickered and died, but Manna found Pele's movement familiar.

Pu-pele had done the same thing to Mano's nose, that day in Germany, when the dining room caught on fire.

"You slip and knock me under the trolley."

Clenching, Manna remembered – the brindled pup, with the hypnotic eyes, that almost bit her ... before Mano kicked it under the train ... and then she heard Tutu's words.

She comes as a dog – they must not run over. Or an old lady – they must not scorn.

"And then you ..." Pele shot a dirty look at Manna, "You douse me with German wine. Yick!"

Manna thought about the rotten old woman at the Kris Kringle fair. The one who begged her with an empty tin cup ... but it was Mano who dumped the wine on her head!

Feeling jilted for taking the blame, Manna bit her bottom lip.

"And did you really think a can of juice was an appropriate gift for a *fire* god?"

Feeling stupid, Manna recalled that day at Kilauea, when she offered Pele her Hawaiian Punch can.

"I have to admit, though, I was impressed when you foiled my faithful Japanese tester ... Certainly a rock konk to the head would have been returned by any *good* Hawaiian."

Ashamed, Manna thought of Taro, and how she did nothing when he hit her with the rock. And again, nothing, when he bloodied her eye with his stupid kick ball. Then she remembered how he and the Japanese gang always lurked around her and Mano at school – and how she had saved Taro from Pu-pele's rock-filled purse ... then ate dinner with him on the hospital floor – and with a hot zing, panic clutched her gut.

Pele and her helpers were *always* out to get her ... then and now!

Except this time, she's got me! Manna screamed in her head.

"Oh, no, no, no. I don't want your trembling little bones anymore, fruit fly."

Pele was right. Manna was trembling. But who could blame her? She was trapped. Even if she thought of a way out, Pele would hear her and know.

"I figured, either I take your bones and have a little bit of your mana – or I take your Fetcher and have it all!"

Giggling, Pele released the gourd, letting it dangle from her wrist, and raised both palms up and out to either side of her broad, naked shoulders. Then, as if making a choice between her hands, she shook her pretty, long-haired head, looking from one hand to the other, and chimed, "Eeny, Meeny – Big or Teeny?"

Suddenly, Pele's head streaked forward and blew up into a huge distorted witch face.

"BIG!" the hideous witch boomed, and shrieking horribly, dragon-sized fire tongues shot out of her mouth and licked through Manna's body.

Whimpering, Manna clenched both of her fists, her Fetcher wedged tight in her left hand – and stiffening tall, she held her breath as the red-hot fire thongs jabbed through her being.

Backing off with a shrinking, sly-smiling face, the witch melted down into a grinning Pele.

"Pretty nifty, eh? My sugarcane fire," Pele bragged as she admired the glowing fingertips of her left hand, and shivering, Manna realized Pele's plan.

She snatched away Mano's soul in the sugarcane field, after Manna clubbed him in the head, because she knew.

Without his soul, Mano's body, his kino, would die.

"Give me your Fetcher, and I'll give you this!" boomed Pele. Then she swung her gourd directly in front of Manna, and suddenly at eye-level, Mano started to beg.

"Do it, Manna, please!" he cried, but frowning at him, she remembered Tutu said, "With Power lives ... Responsibility," and finally, Manna understood.

Everything Tutu said, everything she taught the kids, was real.

Manna *was* the Keeper of Nui-Akea – Power Supreme – and one day, she *would* be the Keeper of the Sixth. And Pele, with the Sixth's power, would destroy the human world – because for her, nothing could ever be enough.

Pele would take *everything* that wasn't rightfully hers, like she did with her sister's husband, and she would force the universe to bow down to her – because, just like Pu-pele, her burning desire to be worshipped by *everyone* would command her through all of time – as would her need to seek revenge whenever she felt scorned.

"No," Manna whispered to her brother. "She'll use it to burn the world. First the sea ... where her sister, Na-maka-o-kaha'i, lives ... then the land, holding man. Man – the ones who will no longer worship her. She'll turn everyone and everything to ash ... like she does, day after day, inside her volcano."

"You have to save me!" whimpered Mano, but he was only one person. One insignificant person.

Manna was the Keeper. *She* would save the world. *She* alone mattered.

"To sacrifice one, for the whole – is the only way," she breathed. "Be brave, my brother. We all have to die sometime. What does it matter if you die now or another day? You're not the important one. I am."

Mano's eyes shone with understanding. He always knew that Manna was special. That's why he followed *her* instead of Momi – used *her* instead of Pu-pele – since the beginning of their time.

Mano puffed out his chest as he gathered his courage, and Manna knew he would do what she said.

"*You* are the Good. *She* is the Evil," he exhaled. "But good and evil never prevail. Only power, Manna. Only power conquers all."

He glanced at her Fetcher, and shivering with excitement, Manna felt confident in her new found power.

"Your power isn't in that Fetcher. And it's not inside of you. It's in your ohana!" he barked. Then clenching his teeth, he banged his fist across his chest and growled, "It's in me. In us. We are a pairing, Manna. Inseparable. One!"

Manna grew angry. She, she alone, was the special one! And the Fetcher, *her* Fetcher, was *her* power. The Fetcher made her special – more special than Mano himself – and he *knew* it.

She would not give it up. Not for him. Not for anyone. Because without it, she was nothing!

"But to me ... you are *everything*," quavered Mano, his moist eyes shining bright, "and you always have been."

Manna tried to cough out the smoke that suddenly choked her – but quickly, it descended into a burning ball that swelled in her chest and sunk to her gut like a boulder.

It was over. She had failed.

She wouldn't be the hero, and she wouldn't conquer Ku or His hideous unborn Wife. Instead, she'd be enslaved by her glowing captor, Pele. Or fried to blackened ash.

Almost sniffling, she wrapped both hands around her Fetcher and stood in silence, unsure of her next move – but relieved ... relieved that *finally* she was important to someone. And glad that she didn't have to face her impending doom alone.

"What? You tink you too good to answer?" snapped Pele.

Manna knew how to flatter Pu-pele's familiar insecurity and hoped it would work with Pele, too.

"Sorry," she stuttered, "I was ... uh ... just thinking ... how beautiful you are, and how I wish I could be like you."

Responding instantly, Pele beamed a bright orange-red. Then she swung her thick, glowing hair behind her bare back, and stood up straight and tall.

"Shall we trade?" she smiled, and Manna bowed down low to her queen and cooed, "As you wish, Your Highness."

Pele wiggled in her pool with delight and squealed, "You can be one of my followers!"

Then she flipped the gourd back into her hand and squeezed her large fingers around it. It exploded and vanished. Only Mano was left, clenched in her fist from the waist down.

Suddenly frowning, Pele brought Mano up to her mouth and spit, "You can't!"

Then, turning her emerald-eyed face towards Manna, she cemented their deal.

"Covenant – on the trade."

"Covenant," promised Manna as she raised the Fetcher up and over her head, and bent her elbows as if ready to throw. "On the count of three, then go!"

Beaming delightedly, Pele raised Mano behind her head, mimicking Manna's ready throw, and glaring straight at Pele's chin, Manna started the count down.

"One."

Manna lifted the Fetcher slightly, in a throwing motion, then brought it back down – and lifting Mano, Pele copied.

"Two."

Manna bounced the Fetcher higher, and Pele did the same with Mano.

"Three."

Manna bounced the Fetcher even higher, but this time she looked straight at Mano and hollered, "GO!"

Manna flung her Fetcher as hard as she could, and as it left her hands, she straightened her fingers, formed an arrow to the sky, and called her unborn sister for help, with the words Tutu used to summon the Hawaiian gods.

"Pahu pa'epu hoi – Burst forth with a roar!"

In that instant, Mano shot out of Pele's hand and snatched the flying Fetcher out of the air. Then he swooped down to grab Manna's arm as he flew past, but out of nowhere, a tremendous gust of wind clobbered him to the ground.

Laying facedown on top of Manna, he pinned her to the ground.

Manna tried to move, but Mano's weight held her down.

"Get off!" she screamed – before she realized he couldn't.

It was the wind, not Mano, that held her down. A horrific maggot-filled blur that splattered against the black, jagged rock and pressed them both to the ground. There, they lay flattened and helpless, as a wiggling, hot pool of worms formed quickly around their bodies, puking skin-rotting enzymes onto their flesh.

Slimy, coiled larvae squirmed up Manna's thighs and scraped at her burning, fast-melting skin – and instantly, she thought of the huge fang-clicking maggot that ate her in the Mo'o game ... and the thousand nasty little mouths that now nibbled on her flesh. Horrified, she wanted to scream – but didn't dare.

If she opened her mouth, the worms would fill it and wriggle down her throat!

"GRRRRAH!" the earth growled and shook violently – and with each gut-wrenching jolt, hundreds of hungry, wriggling, white maggots slopped back and forth over Manna's face. Cringing under their stinging, wet pool, Manna held her breath in silent agony and prayed her end would come quick.

Then the dark sky rumbled – louder and louder – until it thundered a mind-pounding threat – and clenching her teeth, Manna felt her brain slam against her dizzy, aching skull.

CRACK!

CRACK!-CRACK!-CRACK!-CRACK!-CRACK!

Sharp, yellow death-dealing bolts sliced through a thousand rushing black clouds and stabbed the ground around Manna's face – and spewing up from the bolts, squirming, wet clumps of sticky, white maggots slopped over Manna's face, snorting their tanned nose butts in the air.

Half-drowned by the worms' puked-up, milky-white juice, Manna squeezed her nostrils together ... and breathed in what little air she could – but tearing through her nose, the thick rotten stench of her own decaying flesh gagged her.

Not understanding why her end had to be so sick, Manna squeezed her eyes shut and whimpered to herself, *Nothing, no nothing, could be worse than this.*

KA-BOOM!

With a gut-shaking implosion, all the swirling black clouds converged in one quick swoop. Then, quivering nervously, they hopped on top of one another and formed an ominous black pillar that reached up and through the sky – and Manna couldn't believe what came next.

The dark grey sky opened its enormous gaping mouth, as if it would devour the cloud shaft whole – but instead, it dropped a glistening, red, forked tongue down the pillar's west side.

RA-TA-TA-TA-TA-TA!

Shedding off the huge lolling tongue, giant fang-gnashing maggots dripped to the ground, their clicking teeth filling the air with a menacing bone-clinking rattle – and thoroughly excited, the waggling tongue flicked around its shivering cloud pillar and tasted the air ... for human blood.

Dread filled Manna's being. Things *were* getting worse!

SSSSSSSSUP!

SNAP!-SNAP!-SNAP!-SNAP!-SNAP!

With a wet sucking sound, the sky's hideous head popped out next. Its black, bulging eyes searched for its victim – darting back and forth as the head descended – and wiggling off its thick, wrinkled crown, a thousand fat black eels snapped their hungry bloodied mouths as their long sleek bodies billowed far across the sky, with each turn of the sky's fierce scowling head.

Trembling, Manna wished she could vanish.

BAM!

With a thunderous bam, the head's massive body hurled out of the sky – frozen in the crouched stance that Manna had carved into her Fetcher – except this body was black, and oozing with more giant maggots.

Recognizing her Fetcher, Manna shuddered.

Her unborn sister was, by far, the ugliest girl she ever saw!

"WHO -- DARE -- FETCH -- KU ?" the horrible head roared, looking straight at Manna – but He didn't see her, buried underneath His little, wriggling, white worms.

Her lips taut and her eyes wide open, Manna couldn't believe it.

She called the wrong god!

Instantly, she felt grateful to be submersed in the pool of worms – and hoping to stay hidden, she stopped breathing and lay perfectly still.

Hissing low, the wind suddenly quieted and all thunder hushed. Then the earth stood solid, and the larvae lay dead. Thick silence clogged the air ... and Manna guessed what that meant.

Ku was leaving ... without her.

His back still to the Demon, Mano jumped to his feet – and dragged Manna up with him!

"NOOO!" Manna howled. "HE'LL SEE ME!"

"Who?" asked Mano – but she didn't have to answer, because Mano whipped around and saw for himself when the Demon croaked, "Fetch Her!"

Frantic, her heart pounding in her chest, Manna snapped her head around, right and left, to see who was coming to get her ... and then she saw them.

The eels on Ku's head -- began to heave and contract.

First, their long shiny bodies jerked up and down in quick choppy waves. Then, one by one, their heads yanked back and spewed black and red-striped balls of smoke. Each mean striped ball spun like a hissing child's top, screeching a high-pitched, "EE-EE-EEY!" that sliced through Manna's ears and pierced her brain – and suddenly petrified, all the blood in her veins running cold, Manna realized.

The spinning balls sounded like an Indian tribe's head-scalping war cry!

BANG!

With a tremendous bang, one of the balls exploded and out popped a monkey ... no, a man.

Manna gasped.

It was a hairy, long-winged monkey man! It sported the body of a monkey, barring long curved claws on all four feet – perfect for shredding human skin – and on top its red, hairy neck, a hideous caved-in man's face unsheathed four bloodied canine daggers out of a snarling, black-lipped snout.

"Banana-Eaters – the Mu," grunted Mano, as he flipped his stone Fetcher in his left hand and took his stance ... and Manna remembered, Tutu said, "They'll rip off your flesh, from head to toe – like monkeys peeling a human banana."

The first Banana-Eater tore straight for Manna's face.

"Stay down," Mano growled, as he shoved his sister to the ground and swung.

CRACK!

The sickening crack of Mano's Fetcher against the monkey-man's brow made Manna shudder.

Shrieking horribly, the crumpled, ruined beast crashed to the ground – and with a nauseating thud, melted into a sticky, bloody puddle of boils. Then, bursting rapidly, each of his boils exploded into silvery grey steam that snaked up and formed a thin wispy column to the sky – and with each spattering pop, Manna noticed.

The gurgling monkey-man puddle shrank down until it vanished, leaving only the pungent, nose-stinging stench of singed flesh and fried away bone.

"UH! UH! UH!"

Grunting out loud with each stroke, Mano pummeled a steady onslaught of Banana-Eaters with a Hawaiian warrior's terrible vigor and precise head-cracking aim – and crashing to the ground, screeching monkey-man after monkey-man bubbled and dissolved like the first.

Mortified, Manna lay, gagging, on her side.

The monkey-men were worse than Mano's roaches!

"There's too many!" Mano suddenly screamed, his voice cracked with fear as he battered another monkey-man. "They're gonna kill us, Manna! Hit 'em with your wind!" – but Manna didn't know what he was talking about.

Helpless and faint, she watched in horror as another slaughtered monkey-man fizzled into a silvery trail – knowing any moment one would lit on top of her head and peel her flesh right off of her skull. But morbidly curious, she let her eyes trace up a monkey-man's squiggling smoke trail ... and squinted.

At the trail's top, a black, sliver-lined cloud hung in the air for a moment – then suddenly, it dispersed and unveiled the dark figure that loomed behind it ... Ku.

ZING!

With a pupil-squeezing zing, Manna's eyes met His, and instantly, he penetrated her – tunneling through her sockets, down to her brain. Whimpering, she tried to pull away, but couldn't.

His warm fingers had entered and filled her cavity ... and were massaging her, deep within.

Feeling all fear melt, Manna's stiffened body relaxed – and ever so gently, He pulled her towards Him ... and panting out loud, Manna couldn't resist.

She wanted to be with Him ... a part of Him ... now and forever.

By instinct, she raised her arms, so that He could pick her up -- but Pele interrupted.

"Father! Forgive me!"

Startled, Ku snapped His head around and shot a whistling glare through Pele's ghostly, quaking figure – and in response, the Banana-Eaters veered right, mid-flight, to follow His stare. Screeching loudly as they fed, hundreds of them lit on top of Pele's head, ripped at her smoking hair, and clawed her screaming, tormented face.

"NO! NO! NO!" Pele shrieked louder and louder, as she pulled monkey-man after monkey-man off of her face – and shrinking fast, her contorted figure sank deep into Kilauea's fiery pool.

But no, she wasn't shrinking, she was disappearing ... quickly – and Manna was hurling through the air, at a dizzying pace, further and further away.

One of the Banana-Eaters grabbed her by the hair!

Limp with fear, Manna squeezed her eyes shut and concentrated hard to maintain her balance, thinking only, *Breathe in ... breathe out ... breathe in ... breathe out ...*

As soon as the monkey-man onslaught ceased, Mano reacted with lightning speed. He snatched up Manna, tore down Volcano, slammed through Hilo, and skidded to a stop at the foot of his hospital bed. Hands down, he was the fastest flier.

"What were you doing?" he yelled into Manna's face.

Shocked, Manna opened her eyes ... and felt glad to see her brother instead of a hungry Banana-Eater.

"Breathing," she squeaked.

"No, up there!" he kept screaming. "You called Ku!"

"No, I didn't!" Manna objected. "I, uh ..."

Actually, she didn't know what happened, but she did remember proudly.

"I tricked Pu-pele!"

"You mean *Ku*-Pele!" Mano roared, and at the mention of His name, Manna's chin wrinkled down ... in disgust.

Why on earth would her unborn sister marry Him?

"Blah!" Manna's head shivered at the same time her big eyes crossed and her pointy, red tongue waggled out.

Bursting into high-pitched laughter, Mano buckled over, into his sister's funny-looking, twisted face. His crooked tooth gleamed bright white in the dim candlelight, and his head and shoulders jerked up and down wildly – and Manna thought he looked absolutely lolo ... like a laughing cartoon hyena.

Popping into giggles, she laughed with him ... at herself.

What made her think she was some powerful Keeper who would save the whole world? She was just a girl – weak, easily frightened, and barely able to take care of herself – let alone anyone else. Whoever believed she could keep the Sixth was, well ... stupider than Pele. Who, by the way, should have just kept her mouth shut.

Ku had no idea Pele was standing there – until she spoke up!

Choking back, their nervous laughter quickly faded, and sighing out loud, Mano looked at his body, his kino, and groaned, "This is gonna hurt."

"What?" asked Manna.

"Getting in there," he motioned to himself and frowned. "Next time, *look* before you hit!"

Frowning back at him, Manna remembered the way he always talked to Pu-pele, and growled, "Next time, *look* before you follow."

Rolling his bright brown eyes, Mano sighed again – then he held out Manna's Fetcher. Still squeezing his shark tooth necklace in her hand, Manna held it out to trade.

"On the count of three, then go," barked Mano, and with a tight-lipped smile, Manna agreed with a breathy, "Okay."

Swinging his arms back, Mano crouched down low, as if he would dive into a swimming pool – but taking his time, he rocked back and forth on his heels and rhymed,

"One – 'You a wimp, Brah.'

Two – 'So are you, Tita!'

Three – Who cares what they think? We just beat up Ku! "

Then smiling wide at Manna, he bulged his shiny eye whites and shouted, "GO!"

The steel side bed rail jabbed Manna in the stomach as she slumped over it, her face buried in Mano's chest – and still limp, she heard him moan softly – but before she could stir, she felt Moho's dark presence bear down on her back.

Worried, Manna decided not to move. Maybe Moho would think she was asleep.

"Boy," grunted Moho. "Boy, you awake?"

Mano moaned softly again, from his pillow-less bed – and Manna felt Moho lean over her, close to his son.

"Who did this to you?" he growled.

"Pele," Mano exhaled – and for some reason, Moho needed clarification.

"You mean, Pu-pele?" he grunted.

"No, Father," Mano took a deep breath and exhaled once again, "Pele."

Moho shot up, and Manna felt his anger – directed towards the back of her head!

He knew Mano was lying. He knew she was the one that broke his son's head – and he would punish her, severely, for what she had done.

"Get up!" Moho grunted, and his rough nudge made Manna jerk.

Wobbling up to her feet, Manna stood tall ... but refused to look at him, in case he could see her guilt.

"Look at me when I talk to you," Moho gruffed.

Shaking, Manna raised her eyes slowly, anticipating the hard fist that would land on her face – but when her eyes reached his, she felt a blow to her gut instead.

The violent anger he always carried with him was gone. In its place was a deep, haunting sadness, shimmering in the dark, black pools of his eyes.

"You watch out for him," Moho's voice sounded soft and hoarse. "He follows you, wherever you go."

Then turning on his heels, Moho stormed out of the room.

Manna's insides continued to ache even after he was gone, but she noticed.

For the first time, she didn't despise his familiar warning.

"Get in," breathed Mano.

"No way!" Manna hissed back. "He'll kill me."

"You wanna sleep with the bugs?"

Manna thought about it.

After tonight, if one more squirming insect touched her, surely she would die!

Biting her lip, she crawled into Mano's bed and laid next to him on her back. Then, smiling to herself, she thought, *It's nice – to be together.*

Groaning out loud, Mano rolled sideways and flopped one heavy arm over Manna's shoulders, and frowning, she thought, *Oh great! He's gonna hog the bed.*

Then, he croaked gently in her ear.

"I love you."

Manna's chest burned and her eyes filled with tears. She had never heard those words before. She didn't know what to say – or what to do. And then it came to her, in a quivering whisper.

"I love you, too."

Chapter Seventeen

MISPERCEPTIONS

Brring!

Manna opened her eyes. She was dreaming. The phone didn't ring. It sat still, next to the lit German candle on Mano's hospital nightstand – and laying on her back, underneath Mano's clammy, shaking arm, she had a funny feeling.

It was Mano who kept calling Anna in Germany, crying out for help, because he always felt scared when teachers separated the twins – but too tired to think, Manna drifted off into a light, fitful sleep.

BAM!

Something hard hit Manna from behind and knocked her off the roof of the speeding German train – but this time, in her flashback dreams, she saw it happen, as though she watched a movie ...

A steaming electric train headed for a narrow underground tunnel – and propped up on her knees, looking down at the car couplings for the little voice that called, "Save me!" – Manna didn't see that in a split second the tunnel would decapitate her, but Mano did. Lunging at her back, he knocked her down to the couplings and hung on to her with all his might, so she wouldn't slip under the train.

The lights went out and Manna saw them again. Two orange-red eyes, burning with hate, glaring up at her from below ... but this time she knew it was Pele, not a goblin.

"Don't look her in the eye!" Manna screamed to herself, but it was too late.

Pele caught Manna's eye and hypnotized her. A stony look on her face, Manna reached her hand down to the puppy, Pele – and offered her a bite.

"Yelp!" – SHROOM!

Pele yelped when Mano purposely kicked her in the face, and slipping under the train, she exploded into brilliant red steam ...

WHOOSH!

Pele's red steam raked past Manna's check and transformed into a blazing propane blue.

"Cool!" beamed Mano – his nose touching Manna's, in front of their lit German stove – and shuddering, Manna saw it.

Had Mano not distracted her and made her look at him as she tried to light his German roach-golf candle, the stove flames would have burned her entire face ...

Frowning, Manna bit her bottom lip and folded her hands in her lap – and bouncing at her side, Mano slipped one blistered hand between hers and squeezed, but he didn't look scared.

Sitting under their trundle bed, with Moho beating Pu-pele in the living room for setting their apartment on fire, Manna saw herself look sad – and Mano try to cheer her up by holding her hand. Then everything flushed a smoky red and Manna saw her brother loom stubbornly before her ...

Clenching his teeth, Mano banged his fist across his chest and growled, "We are a pairing, Manna. Inseparable. One!" – but instead of being trapped in Pele's blackened gourd, he stood next to Manna in their hospital room, glaring out the window.

Following her brother's stare, Manna jerked her head left, and to her amazement, she saw their past flash before her – in quick, noisy scenes – across a white, window-paned movie screen ...

"NOOOOO!" shrieked the leper, right before Mano threw his glass of Gluehwein right into her face – on purpose ...

THUMP! – "OW-WAY!"

The red fairy in the closet, Ka'ahu-pahau, snapped back her greedy brown hand and pressed it fast against her forehead, where Mano had thumped her with his stiff shoe ...

BAM!

Mano swung the bathroom door open and knocked the pictures of Anna – being eaten by the horrible black mouth – right into the toilet. Then, scowling down at the pictures, he got rid of them by flushing them down the commode ...

"NOOO!" Manna saw herself scream underwater – and spinning round in an awkward karate kick, Mano nailed the little red shark, Ka'ahu-pahau, in the nose – before her razor-lined teeth could sink into Manna's throat ...

"SHA-A-A-ARK!" squealed the purple-eyed Menehune – right when a blood-streaked Mano bolted up the orchid-strewn Hawaiian graveyard hill and squeezed a protective hand around Manna's shoulder, because he didn't trust the Menehune ...

"Ka-o-o-o-o-helo!" the wind screamed, and at once, a clammy cold Mano landed on Manna's back and pressed her chest solid to the ground. Then, covering her as best as he could, he lay perfectly still as the angry ohelo bush scraped mercilessly past his skin, snatching back the berries Pu-pele stole ...

"Au-we-e-e!" the blood-spurting ohia tree cried as she tried frantically to drown a squirming, scared Manna – and scrambling into the tree, Mano offered the tree his tapa-cloth bound lunch, to appease her. Instantly, the tree let Manna go ...

SNAP!

FROMP! – "HAH!"

With a wide, toothy snap, the gleaming red shark, Ka'ahu-pahau, shot out of a wave and lunged at Manna's face – but suddenly cutting back across Manna's board, Mano shoved his sister out of the way and the shark bit Sanjiro instead – at the same time Mano stabbed at the shark's eye with Sanjiro's knife ...

"MANO-O-O-O!" Manna saw herself scream in the Mo'o world, and Mano looked up to save his sister, right before the three dark guys tore out his guts ...

SCRA-A-APE! BAM!

Suddenly losing control, Junior hooked a sharp right – and spun out into a mind-spinning doughnut – and throwing Manna down onto the hood, Mano laid on top of her, to protect her ...

CRACK! – THUD! – BAM!

With a blinding crack, Moho's rock-solid fist hammered the side of Manna's head, and with a heavy body thud, she slammed against the wall and sunk – right before Mano lunged defensively at Moho's throat. But quicker than a snapping turtle, Moho caught Mano, midair, and threw him against the wall ...

"What's wrong with you?" Momi hissed at Pu-pele, because she knew Anna would enter and freak.

No one ever touched Anna's Blue Onion dishes.

Grabbing Manna's hand, Mano yanked her in front of him ... so she'd be the furthest from an angry Anna when she entered the dining room ...

"Come here ...ere!" sang Pele, in the sugarcane field, her huge, ghostly, orange-red hand creeping up out of the ground, inches from Manna's back – but with a loud, "HAH!" Mano jumped onto the hand and wrestled it to the dirt ...

CRACK!-CRACK!-CRACK!-CRACK!

With a Hawaiian warrior's terrible vigor and precise head-cracking aim, Mano pummeled a steady onslaught of shrieking monkey-men, as they snatched hungrily at Manna's hair. Completely helpless, Manna lay on the ground, whimpering softly to herself, between fizzling monkey-man puddles. Then suddenly, she struggled to her knees and reached up to join Ku – but thinking fast, Mano grabbed her by the hair and tore down Volcano, back to their hospital bed ...

"HUH!"

With a loud gasp, Manna's eyes flew wide open, and suddenly awake, it hit her.

Mano kept saving her! He always kept saving her – and then she realized.

She kept saving him, too.

Mano was right. They were a pairing. Inseparable. One.

SWISH!

Rustling as soft as wheat grass against a hot summer breeze, a thick black haze suddenly passed over Manna's eyes, and with a convulsing shiver, her body relaxed. Drifting off into another uneasy sleep, she continued to see her flashback dreams ...

"MAI!" Tutu commanded, and with a blinding crack, Manna saw herself sit up in the warm Tahuna circle.

"Now that you know what you are," hummed Tutu, "your pairing you must find. For if you do not couple with your other half, you shall die ..." – and at that moment, Manna understood.

Like any good tahuna, Tutu had entered her dreams and was guiding her through the knowledge she *must* possess – in order to succeed in life.

"Your pairing, your opposite, is your other half, that you cannot thrive without," repeated Tutu. "Be it friend or foe, soul mate or spouse

– or something to struggle against – you must find it, and make all things complete."

The world blurred and spun around for a moment, and Manna thought it okay to relax.

She had found it – her pairing – and now all things were complete. But suddenly, she saw herself stand, frozen and scared, outside Tutu's mo'olelo hut door, the first time Tutu lead them to Tahuna class ... and there was no way Manna would go through that door ...

"Oof! Sorry."

Following too close, Mano bumped Manna through the doorway – on purpose – almost as if he knew she wouldn't learn ... unless he pushed her.

Watching herself shoot her brother a dirty look, Manna suddenly saw it.

Standing beside her, Mano looked really scared, about something ...

"How long have you known?" Tutu asked, glancing gently at Mano – moments after Manna kicked her grandmother in the gut – except this time, watching her life rewind, Manna realized.

Tutu was talking to Mano, not her. He knew something that Manna didn't.

"They follow you," warned Tutu, her voice suddenly tense. "Some to steal your mana. Some to protect it. Others, to be a part of it. Always look over your shoulder – and distinguish between the three."

Looking at herself sitting cross-legged in front of Tutu ... just a small frightened child, Manna felt her heart race.

The three ... really *were* following her.

Pele and Ka'ahu-pahau, to steal her mana. Mano to protect it – and Taro and Barb, she wasn't quite sure – but undoubtedly, they *all* followed too close behind ... and in the future, so would many more.

For all eternity, Manna must *always* look over her shoulder and distinguish between the three ...

Squeezing Manna's small chin with a hot palm, Tutu tilted her head up and peered at her grandchild with red-veined eyes.

"You are the Keeper of Nui-Akea – Power Supreme – the most desirable power of all. But that power fatally poisons man – for those who hold it succumb to heinous greed and willfully murder their souls."

Tutu's eyes filled with pity.

"This, child, is your fate."

Manna saw herself scowl up at Tutu, and viewing her own upturned face – her heart jumped into her throat.

To look upon her angered self was absolutely frightening!

Her shiny, bulging black eyes darted back and forth between Tutu's, as though they were choosing which to gouge out with her quivering, pointy, red tongue – and her rigid, down-turned mouth frowned open and wide, at the same time her top lip crinkled up into a sinister, hungry smile. Her nostrils flared, too black and wide, as red-hot hate flashed across her sweating cheeks – and shivering, Manna saw it for the first time.

Something evil lived inside of her – and Mano knew it all along.

That's why he was always so scared to be alone with her ... in the dark!

Suddenly, a sinking feeling filled Manna's chest, and full of groggy despair, she slipped through a hole in the mo'olelo hut sand – but she didn't care.

That was the reason everyone hated her! It wasn't that she was black or white.

Inside of her lived the purest of evils.

Anna saw it, and tried to shake it out. And at the Kris Kringle fair, after the orange hand chased her and Mano, she caught a glimpse of Anna's small, frightened face.

It was Manna that Anna feared.

That's why she wouldn't touch her or give her a cross.

And Moho, he would do anything to protect Anna – even kill her youngest child – and who could blame him?

That's the first thing Manna thought of doing to the Sixth. Drown her, as soon as she was born!

And the cousins, they all sucked in a deep breath of fear at the airport – the first time Manna looked straight at them. And Tutu, she saw it at the airport, too – when her eyes drilled through Manna and that wicked voice screeched, "You are the one!"

Twinkling, a cool rainbow suddenly shot past Manna's ear and curved sideways, in front of her dreaming face. Then, chirping cheerfully, a flock of fluffy silver birds spiraled down the rainbow and encircled her giggling cheeks. Feeling oddly relieved, Manna spread her arms open and laid back on a puffy, silver-lined cloud that formed quickly beneath her feet.

"Aloha," whispered a blinding white light ... and with the chill of a wintery German breeze, a calm woman's voice warned Manna again.

"Humans with power succumb to heinous greed and willfully murder their souls," – and at once, Manna recalled what they taught her in church.

All men were born evil, and even if they washed away their sins with the Holy Waters of God, they would commit many more ... because evil tempts you, your entire life.

That was His test.

Could you overcome the evil powers in this world, and join Him in His promised land – or would you succumb to man's inherent greed and lust for power, and burn eternally in hell?

Smiling to herself, Manna felt better.

She wasn't the only one who had to struggle against evil. Everyone did. Even the smallest child had to decide whether or not to share his toys. And the oldest man, whether or not to be kind to his wife.

So what, if Manna had a little more evil to purge – this Power

Supreme. She could easily do it, just by being good. Mother Mary told her so ...

Suddenly, a smoking orange-red swirl seared Manna's eyes, and mortified, she watched in horror as her shaking figure stood at Volcano, starving for power and ignoring her terrified, dying brother's pleas ...

"You have to save me!" whimpered Mano, but he was only one person. One insignificant person.

Manna was the Keeper. *She* would save the world. *She* alone mattered.

"To sacrifice one, for the whole – is the only way," Manna watched herself breathe. "Be brave, my brother. We all have to die sometime. What does it matter if you die now or another day? You're not the important one. I am."

Instantly nauseous, Manna understood what Tutu had just shown her.

It would be simple for her to choose the wrong path – and succumb to her destined evil. That is why she murdered Ku-hai in the Mo'o game, without a moment of remorse – and why she could so coldly, so confidently, sacrifice her brother's life – to obtain her Power Supreme. Through her birth, her destiny, she was capable of all things evil and that ... that was her fate!

Panic suddenly filled Manna's heart.

She couldn't do it! She couldn't conquer Ku or control His unborn Wife! They would trick her into doing their sinister will and becoming their wicked human-killing slave – because she was just a child, and there was no way that a *child* could understand what was going on in the adult world – because a child's perception isn't necessarily right!

Look at how badly Manna had misinterpreted her whole life up to now – and how poorly she had translated everyone's intentions and motivations.

She thought Mano always used her, and Moho hated her for no good reason, and that everyone else was mean to her for fun. And she thought Anna was tough – and Tutu, a sinister skull-collecting witch. And my goodness, last year, she really did think newborn babies flew out of the sky, dangling from a white stork's mouth!

Bursting out of the silver-lined clouds, a dazzling white albatross suddenly swooped down and snatched Manna up in his long shiny pink beak. Then holding his misty wings straight out, he spiraled headfirst for the ground.

BA-BAM! CRASH!

With a glass-shattering dynamite blast, Manna dropped back into Tutu's mo'olelo hut, once again seeing herself sitting cross-legged in front of her eerie grandmother as her life rewound ...

A sickening premonition seeped into Manna's stomach and swirled to her head.

Her destiny would be a struggle.

"Unless-s-s," Tutu hissed again, "you live as a Kealoha – close to your Akua and family circle, who – together – choose the path of your unwavering fate, and thereafter, guide and protect you."

But this time, Manna's head didn't fill with obstinance. Instead, it filled with hope. Biting her bottom lip, she listened closely to Tutu's next words.

"With the Tahuna teachings, you will see the future – your future – and learn what you truly are ... and where you are meant to be – and with the guidance of your Akua and family, you will excel on your chosen path."

Like a bubbling glass of soda pop, joyous relief fizzled through Manna's being!

Her family – her ohana – would guide her towards the right path – just as Tutu was guiding her now!

She could do it! She could succeed in life – with the support of her family – just like any normal kid!

Wiggling her toes with anticipation, Manna clutched her hands together, as if she would pray. Then squeezing her eyes shut, she concentrated hard on sending a message back to her telepathic grandmother.

"I'm ready!" she squealed – but Tutu disagreed, and flashed Manna back once more ...

Obedient, all the cousins grabbed their bundled Fetcher dolls and marched out of the mo'olelo hut room – and mumbling, Momi and her sisters followed, leaving Mano sitting at Manna's side. Sitting cross-legged in front of their grandmother, both children looked deep into her glimmering green eyes.

Suddenly, Tutu's face grew stern and she breathed, "With Power lives her cousin, Responsibility. Always be aware!" – and instantly, Manna's heart dropped.

Responsibility. The cruelest word Tutu could have uttered.

Feeling the whole weight of the world suddenly bear down on her shoulders, Manna realized what it was Momi said when Ku-hai and Aikoa challenged her to play the Mo'o game – and reading her mind, Tutu brought Manna back, to relive that scene ...

"You're not ready, child," breathed Tutu, and instantly distracted, Manna bit her lip.

Something sad had filled the air.

Sighing heavily, Tutu raised one hand up and squeezed Momi's broad, rigid shoulder. For a moment, Momi relaxed. Then slowly, her tight blonde bun turned to face all her cousins ... and her slanted blue eyes held back shiny, wet tears – an inch from Tutu's face.

"I never was," she breathed, almost childlike ... then she pursed her lips before she croaked, "And it never mattered ..."

"NOOOO!" Manna heard herself scream. "No child should be forced to be *responsible*! That would make them ... grown up!" – and then it hit her.

Momi was never a child. Her parents had forced her to grow up too soon, by putting her in charge of their kids. As the eldest, it was her responsibility – to take care of and set an example for ... the little kids. And for the first time, Manna understood why Momi was filled with hate.

It wasn't fair! They robbed Momi of her childhood!

Clenching her teeth, Manna felt sheer obstinance sear through her being.

She wouldn't do it! She wouldn't grow up!

Furious, she saw her angry self glare up at Tutu again ... in her flashback dream – after Tutu breathed those hideous words ...

"With Power lives her cousin, Responsibility. Always be aware."

Grabbing Mano's hand, Manna huffed to her feet and ran through the mo'olelo hut door – right into cousin Ku-hai.

Without a word, Ku-hai turned around and trudged away, dragging his feet like a warrior defeated ...

Seeing Ku-hai trudge away again, Manna almost felt sorry for him – but couldn't. Enjoying a wash of relief, she felt nothing other than glad.

Her *cousin*, Cousin Ku-hai, would assume responsibility for her and tell her what she had to do.

It was settled then!

Manna would allow her ohana, her family, to guide her path in life – and she would trust and embrace all the wisdom they spread around the Tahuna circle ... but a mind-controlling Tutu didn't think it was settled.

Instantly, Manna stood up at Volcano again, watching herself sentence her brother to death ...

Manna grew angry. She, she alone, was the special one! And the Fetcher, *her* Fetcher, was *her* power. The Fetcher made her special – more special than Mano himself – and he *knew* it.

She would not give it up. Not for him. Not for anyone. Because without it, she was nothing!

"But to me ... you are *everything,*" quavered Mano, his moist eyes shining bright, "and you always have been."

Manna tried to cough out the smoke that suddenly choked her – but quickly, it descended into a burning ball that swelled in her chest and sunk to her gut like a boulder ...

Suddenly nauseous, Manna wished Tutu hadn't seen that.

How horrible Manna had been to her brother all these years. Mocking him and hating him for being loved by everyone else, even though her own jealous self loved him, too. And up at Volcano, she almost sacrificed him, the person she loved the most ... so that she could be special – more special than anyone else

Almost crying out in pain, Manna suddenly realized.

It was her fault!

She was the reason nobody loved her.

In a blind desire to have everyone love her – and to have them think her more special than *the boy* – she had ignored everyone else. She showed nobody love. She just tromped around in misery, hating everyone for not loving her.

But in a single moment of despair, Mano taught her.

To be loved, you must love someone other than yourself – and you must show them your love.

It had worked with Pu-pele, when Manna stood up for her and took the blame for busting Aikoa's head. Pu-pele instantly showered Manna with attention and gifts. And it had worked for Mano, up at Volcano, when he declared his love for Manna. Without hesitation, Manna gave up her dreams for power ... and spared Mano's life.

Her world suddenly clear, Manna felt an excited zing shoot through her heart.

You must give in order to get!

She could do it! She could have everything she ever wanted!

She would make everybody love her – by giving them her love – and she could conquer that demon Ku and His hideous unborn Wife. Her ohana, Mano and Ku-hai, would help her obtain her Power Supreme – and guide her along the way.

That's why Tutu put them both in her dreams – to let her know.

Mano and Ku-hai would always be there to help her out ... and tell her what to do. Manna had no responsibilities – she needed only to listen and react!

With an exhausted sigh, Tutu suddenly released Manna's mind – and as her brain sank into a deep, dreamless sleep, confidence washed through Manna's being.

Finally, she understood ... all the things Tutu taught her.

Huh-hmm.

Manna heard Ka'ahu-pahau's hot breath against her ear, and startled, her eyes flew wide open – but it was just Pu-pele, breathing heavily below the triangular German-candle vigil Anna had placed above her head on the hospital floor.

Lying perfectly still underneath Mano's heavy arm, Manna looked around the dim hospital room at her three sleeping sisters – and recalled the covenant that started it all.

> *"From Moho shall come six – five mortals, one god.*
>
> > *One for Kane,*
> > *One for Pele,*
> > *One for Kanaloa,*
> > *One for Moho.*
> > *The Fifth to Keep the Sixth,*
> > *The Sixth, born for Ku."*

Squinting both eyes, Manna stared down at a teeth-gnashing Momi –

the responsible one ... born for Kane – but breathing a quick, "Humph! Humph!" a curled up Ailani caught Manna's eye.

The smart one (who listened to everything) was born for Kanaloa – Kanaloa, the one who tricked Kane with a cup of awa and a game of Test-A-Man – and suddenly, Manna realized.

Ailani was *always* the smartest person around, and she could trick anyone she chose – especially the ever-silly Pu-pele – the one born for the fire goddess herself.

With a hard body shudder, Manna remembered the goddess Pele in Volcano – and at that moment, Mano shook, too.

It had been easy to trick Pele ... but there was something eerie about what she said.

"Clever little girl, aren't you?" she had chortled to Manna. "But not clever enough to keep me ..." – and her eyes suddenly round with awe, Manna stared straight at a steaming Pu-pele.

Pu-pele would be Pele's Keeper – through the teachings of the Tahuna. And she, she alone, could keep Pele at bay while Manna obtained her Power Supreme ... that power coveted by each god involved.

Every one of the Akua paired with the children at the Covenant would try to steal Manna's power, and maybe even her life – and her four siblings were the only ones who could keep those Akua at bay!

That was insured by the wording of the Covenant ... and that was His plan.

To surround Manna with her much needed helpers – each one of which held a crucial role in Manna's success.

"Yes, Manna," whispered Ailani. "*Everything* happens for a reason."

Suddenly standing above Manna, Ailani smiled a kind, knowing smile – as her trickling rainbow-colored hair flowed over her shoulders and down her straightened, yellow-hued back. Grinning back at Ailani's angelic apparition, Manna knew Ailani wanted something – and this time, Manna was ready to give in order to receive.

"Which Fetcher worked?" asked Ailani, and Manna understood.

Ailani was the one who placed the two Fetchers on Mano's bed ... and as always, she craved the most intangible knowledge.

"I don't know," whispered Manna. "I used all three."

Ailani's eyes twinkled for a moment, as she deciphered Manna's words. Then she slipped her hand underneath Manna's hip and pulled out a crystally green piece of her personal awa – aka manu, planted by the birds.

"How did you transport without the awa?" asked Ailani, and remembering her struggle to fetch her brother, Manna repeated the words that she spoke.

"Hele ika hale o ..."

Cocking her head and squinching both of her delicate eyebrows together, Ailani translated.

"Go to the house of ..." – and Manna felt herself smile before she completed Tutu's chant ... with one of the names Moho growled.

"Pele!"

Her soft brown eyes suddenly wide with amazement, Ailani breathed, "What did you learn from her?" – and thoroughly stumped for a moment, Manna wondered what Ailani could not know ... and then it came to her.

"There is something special about human eyes," whispered Manna, and without humphing, Ailani pressed her delicate hands to her shimmering pink lips and whispered her understanding across Manna's cheek.

"Yes. In the corners ... they may enter and leave."

Unsure of what Ailani meant, Manna continued, knowing Ailani could grasp even that which appeared unseen.

"Your kino, your soul, can communicate words without sound, and the Akua hear them no matter what," whispered Manna, because Pele had read her mind. "And when your eyes meet the eyes of another soul, that soul hears your unspoken words, too," – for that is what Mano did, trapped in Pele's gourd where Manna couldn't hear his screams. Once Pele swung the gourd up to Manna's eye level and their eyes met, Manna heard all his thoughts and his screams.

Suddenly, something dark and chilly whizzed off Manna's back, and immediately, she remembered what Ku had done to her ... and Tutu's warning words.

"Never look the Akua in the eye," hissed Manna, "because if you do, they can hypnotize and control your mind!"

Ailani's bright eyes sparkled with surprise, and quivering softly, her pink lips curved up into a satisfied grin.

She had learned something vital from Manna, but there was one more thing Manna wanted her to know.

"The Akua," Manna grinned back, "are easily distracted and react without thinking first!" – because that's what both Pele and Ku did. Pele released Mano on the trade, without considering whether or not she could trust Manna; and Ku turned his head and steered his monkey-men away when he heard Pele speak – never considering His chances that Manna would get away.

A huge confident smile spread across Ailani's soft, glowing cheeks, and Manna could see it.

With her quick-thinking brain, Ailani could trick them all!

But suddenly, Ailani's face filled with pity ... for her little sister who lay before her.

"You know, he follows you," she whispered, and smiling reassuringly at Ailani, Manna whispered back, "Yes, I know," and for once, she felt glad to hear that familiar warning.

Her brother would protect her back.

Then suddenly, Manna remembered Mano's words at Volcano, and how they had saved them both from burning eternally in Pele's hell –

and she knew his words were the most important thing she had learned thus far.

"Good and Evil never prevail," she warned Ailani, using Mano's words. "Only power ... the power of Love ... conquers all."

Ailani's eyes lit up like never before, and what looked like a brilliant white halo shimmered right above her suddenly gushing, rainbow-colored hair. Then, smiling tenderly at Manna, she slowly disappeared.

Smiling back at her vanishing sister, Manna thought her the most beautiful guardian angel in the world – and her smile still intact, Manna slipped into a deep, tranquil sleep ... the most peaceful she had ever known.

"Yes, Manna ... Since the beginning of man – only love conquers all."

"My boy!" squealed Anna, her clear blue eyes sparkling with relief – and jolted awake, Manna sat straight up in bed next to Mano and saw her mother squeeze her stiff-legged brother tight – and at once, she heard herself giggle.

Wrapped in his white head-wound bandages, Mano looked more deflicted than ever before!

His sweaty black hair poked out between strips of pus-yellowed gauze and frayed up like spiky gorilla fur – and his pale, spindly arms flung open, stiff to his sides, as he wrinkled his flared, skin-flaking nose and endured Anna's motherly kisses and hugs. Strewn across his torn, blistered chest, fat plastic tubes pumped life-giving fluid into his popped-out, squiggly, blue veins – and sticking out of the bottom of his leg-hugging, white bed sheets, his long bony toes spread crooked and wide, like rough chimpanzee fingers.

Easily, Mano could pass for a prehistoric monkey boy raised by the mummies of the living dead!

"TITA!" hollered Aikoa, suddenly bursting through the hospital room door – with all the screaming cousins on her heels.

Scrambling to her feet, Pu-pele spun round to defend herself – but it was too late. With a rock-solid crack, Aikoa slugged Pu-pele in the face – and flying back eight feet, Pu-pele hit the wall and sunk.

The wind temporarily knocked out of her, a steaming Pu-pele glared up at a bandage-wrapped Aikoa with hate-filled, fiery green eyes – and glaring back at her, equally mad, Aikoa tossed her bushy brown hair off her blue-patterned hospital gown.

"Sorry I when poke fun at your moddah," muttered Aikoa, at the same time she scoffed at Pu-pele with fierce, undefeatable pride – and suddenly finding her breath, Pu-pele spat back, "Sorry I when miss your mouth!" and with a clamor of knee-slapping laughter, the room burst into relieved tummy-tickling mirth – and Manna thought it funny, too – that both girls could only *half* apologize.

Glancing around the room at the striking brown beauty of her proud, unwavering cousins, Manna knew she lived amongst the most inconquerable force of all – ohana ... and feeling a tingly wash of joy spread through her being, she realized an overwhelming sense of appreciation for the ones who would stand by her and guide her, and help her to succeed ... in defeating Ku.

Against the Kealohas – Ku would fail!

No matter how scared of Him and His slimy maggots Manna was, her ohana, with their leader, Cousin Ku-hai – the one who fears nothing at all – would overcome Him and all the evil He stood for.

And at once, Manna felt herself adore her oldest cousin – and his handsome, gleaming brown face, that seemed to be smiling right back at her ... and only her.

"What! Sucking up?" squawked Aikoa, her steely glare fixed on Manna – and biting her lip, Manna realized what Ku-hai and Moku meant in the Mo'o game when they said, "Put up with the rags!"

Aikoa was a jealous, big-time sore loser!

"Huh!" gasped Taro, the moment he swung open the hospital room door and found himself surrounded by his enemies.

"What you want, Buddah-head?" quipped Aikoa – and his yellow mole-rat cheeks flushed bright red, Taro glared at the ground and grunted, "I like see your cousin." Then stiffening his back and puffing out his lumpy, round chest, he shuffled over to Manna, pressed his hot, sweating face into her scrunched up nose, and blew his sushi-stink breath across her cheeks.

"My gangies stay cool – everybody's awake and okay. They going go tell big kine stories about sharks and killer fights at school – and everybody's gonna stay clear of you Kealohas!"

Looking deep into Taro's beady black eyes, Manna beamed happily at her newest best friend – but in response, Taro's ears burned a bright, splotchy red and his eyes shot to the ground.

"My moddah guys expect me to marry one Japan-ey," squeaked Taro, his hefty body suddenly shuffling from foot to foot. "But I like be friends ..." and that's when it hit Manna.

The prejudice that she and other kids endured, just for being different, was something created by *parents* – and handed down to their kids. But prejudice wasn't something a kid had keep or accept – he could just toss it right out the door ... and with a breathy, giggling, "Me, too!" Manna threw out Aikoa's hatred for this sweet Japanese boy.

"Puh! Those hapa-haoles stay attracting losers!" spit Aikoa, but Manna thought Taro brave – to say how he feels and walk into a room full of Kealohas. Confident with her choice, she knew that her friendship with this humble, portly boy was meant to be, because like Ailani said ... everything happens for a reason.

"I got you one Bento-Box," muttered Taro, still red in the face. Then he plopped a two-foot-long, rectangular, see-through plastic box onto Manna's lap – and instantly, her mouth filled with water.

The Japanese lunch box spilled over with Japanese treats, delicately decorated by a skilled artist's loving hand!

Fashioned into the leftmost corner of the tidy serving box, dark orange tangerine slices peeked out, behind daisy-shaped carrots and thinly sliced, pink ginger petals – and just below the fruits, fist-sized onigiri rice balls rolled close together, crisscrossed with black strips of clinging seaweed so that they appeared to be miniature soccer balls.

In the bottom left corner, bright orange chicken sprinkled with glistening, oiled sesame seeds puffed up – like deep-fried, orange-glazed doughnuts – next to tanned crunchy tempura-fried shrimp and glistening brown mini-hamburgers decorated with ketchup smily faces. Shiny pink spam, cut into thick, juicy wedges, piled up next to the other meats – and small, boiled quail eggs sporting yellow mustard bird faces chirped happily right next to them.

In the upper right corner of the stuffed, brimming box, long neat rows of rectangular, white rice cakes lined up, covered with pink and white-striped shrimp; plump, juicy, red ahi; and wedges of bright yellow, scrambled, fried eggs – and Manna noticed. The scrambled egg covered rice cakes had a thin strip of seaweed around their middle, like a dainty ribbon encircling a gift.

At the bottom right of the box, teriyaki-seaweed cones spilled over with pink Hawaiian crab, bright green avocado, and shiny pickled cucumber and carrot – and piled high next to them, sweet, vinegared, orange-flecked white rice crammed into scrambled-egg, crepe-like socks.

Lined in an intricate pattern through the box's wide center, a colorful array of round rolled-sushi slices sparkled – some wrapped in black seaweed with green avocado, white cucumber, and pink tuna arranged carefully through their middles – others wrapped in sweet white rice, dotted with bright orange, jellied balls, while all their brightly colored meats and dark green seaweed swirled thickly through their centers – but to Manna, the rolled sushi slices looked like the hand-decorated

German candies that Pu-pele used to steal on the way to the train stop – the ones with happy pictures baked into their centers – and at once, Manna felt impressed.

Taro's mother was an excellent cook.

Shaking with a sudden famished greed, Manna shoved a fist-sized, yellow-skinned sushi sock into her mouth, and with a sugary vinegar tinge, it filled her mouth with sweet, slippery joy ... and her mind with thoughts of inhaling the whole bento box. But now knowing she must *give* to receive, Manna clutched a sharp pang in her gut and squeaked the same offer to share that Moku spoke that first day, on their blue-painted porch.

"You like?"

Clunking heads, Taro and Mano grabbed first – and in under a second, the nine hungry cousins cleared off Manna's tray, with the scornful Aikoa snatching up two greedy handfuls for herself.

Scowling at her empty tray, Manna regretted having to share – until she saw Tutu's brimming lauhala basket swinging from Kokala's fat hand.

"Get grinds!" chortled Kokala, and at once, Manna thought it odd that someone of Kokala's volume and size could fear starvation the most – and as if trying to appease Aikoa, Moku grinned straight at her haggard, dried-blood-smeared face and offered, "Ladies first!"

~~~~~~

The dark blue ocean water crashed against the gleaming black rock and sprayed cool white foam across Manna's legs. She liked the way the coolness shocked the sun's heat off of her skin, and was glad that Mano had convinced her to come. It hadn't been easy, though.

First, he had to assure her that Ka'ahu-pahau would heed Moho's warning.

Then, he had to explain why Pele had to stay clear of the waves.

After that, he had to rip the half-disintegrated stitches from his forehead to prove that they wouldn't melt away in the saltwater and expose a gaping head wound.

And finally, he had to threaten her.

He'd go alone, without Moho's permission, and no one to watch out for him. If anything happened, it'd be all her fault because she *made* him go alone!

The threat had forced her decision – and she was glad for it now as she stood next to him on the rocky cliff.

They hadn't been surfing in three weeks, and the anticipation of the fun to come was intoxicating – for both of them!

Manna felt her brother's excitement meshing with her own. She glanced over at him, and he turned his head to look back at her.

His sweaty black hair stood practically on end, and a crazy white smile plastered across his wide-eyed face. Manna saw his stick-out tooth twinkle at her, and the scar on his forehead vibrate hard as he bounced up and down on his toes. The scar on his forehead, which had healed into a thick red groove, hooked up like a menacing shark fin.

Giggling, Manna thought her brother looked deranged – maybe even demonic.

"On the count of three, then go," he grinned, as usual. Except this time he grabbed her hand and added, "Together."

Their boards smacked the surface of the water in unison, and they punched through the first wave with ease – and as its cool waters washed over and away from Manna, so did all the pain of her first ten years ...

Dear Reader,

   As you may have noticed, many Hawaiian words have more than one meaning (for example, aloha means hello, goodbye and love). And perhaps, after reading this book's last chapter, you have guessed that any good Hawaiian story has more than one interpretation. However, what you may be interested in knowing, should you choose to once again peruse through this book, is that every chapter name holds more than one meaning - each of which embodies a significant twist in this tale.

   Enjoy ... and may love bless you and your family,

                                M. L. Kamahele